ALGORITHM·325

Erasmus Cromwell-Smith II

Books written by the author

In English,	En Español,
As Erasmus Cromwell-Smith II:	**Como Erasmus Cromwell-Smith II:**
- The Equilibrist series,	-La serie del Equilibrista,
(Inspirational/Philosophical)	(Inspiracional/Filosófico)
- The Happiness Triangle (Vol. 1)	- El triángulo de la felicidad (Vol. 1)
- Geniality (Vol. 2)	- Genialidad (Vol. 2)
- The Magic in Life (Vol. 3)	- La magia de la vida (Vol. 3)
- Poetry in Equilibrium	- Poesía en equilibrio
- The Equilibrist (Trilogy)	- El Equilibrista (La serie completa)
(Young Adults)	**(Jóvenes Adultos)**
-The Orloj of Prague (Vol. 1)	-El Orloj de Praga (Vol. 1)
-The Orloj of Venice (Vol. 2)	-El Orloj de Venecia (Vol. 2)
-The Orloj of Paris (Vol. 3)	-El Orloj de Paris (Vol. 3)
-The Orloj of London (Vol. 4)	-El Orloj de Londres (Vol. 4)
-The Orloj of Boston (Vol. 5)	-El Orloj de Boston (Vol. 5).
-Poetry in Balance	-Poesía en Balance
As Erasmus Cromwell-Smith II	**Como Erasmus Cromwell-Smith II**
The South Beach Conversational Method	**El Método Conversacional South Beach**
(Educational)	(Educacional)
-Spanish	-Inglés
-German	-Alemán
-French	-Francés
-Italian	-Italiano
-Portuguese	-Portugués
The Nicolas Tosh Series,	**La serie de Nicolás Tosh,**
(Sci-fi)	**(Ciencia ficción)**
- Algorithm-323	- Algoritmo -323
- Algorithm-325	- Algoritmo-325
- Algorithm-326	- Algoritmo-326
As Nelson Hamel (*)	**Como Nelsón Hamel (*)**
The Paradise Island Series,	**La serie de la isla paraíso**
(Action Thriller)	(Acción Suspenso)
-Miami Beach, Dangerous Liaisons	-Miami Beach, Relaciones peligrosas
The Rebel Hackers Series,	**La Serie de los Hackers Rebeldes,**
(Sci-fi)	(Ciencia Ficción)
-The Rebel Hackers of Point Breeze	-Los Hackers Rebeldes de Point Breeze
-The Rebel Hackers of the Glacial Dawn	-Los Hackers rebeldes del amanecer glacial
-Threshold of Embodiment	- Umbral de la encarnación

(*) in collaboration with Charles Sibley.
All titles are or will be available in audio book

TABLE OF CONTENTS

5

Author's Note	7
Preface	15
Chapter 1: Lingtao's New Dawn	31
Chapter 2: The Zermatt Data Center Under Siege	45
Chapter 3: Shifting Political Winds	59
Chapter 4: Alejandra's Counterpoint	77
Chapter 5: Emergence of a Rival Network	85
Chapter 6: Reunion in Zurich	115
Chapter 7: Lines in the Sand	133
Chapter 8: The Invasion of Zermatt	153
Chapter 9: A Moral Counteroffensive	179
Chapter 10: Showdown in Geneva	203
Chapter 11: Fallout and Reckoning	229
Epilogue: A Fragile Dawn	241
Prequel to Algorithm-326	265
Author's Parting Words	277

AUTHOR'S NOTE

When I first conceived *Algorithm-323,* the idea of a technology capable of deciphering and recording the entire breadth of a human mind felt almost too audacious—equal parts speculative fiction and near-future thriller. Yet in the few years since, companies like Neuralink have made remarkable strides in brain-computer interfaces, heightening the possibility that mental signals and ideas might soon be captured, interpreted, and even transmitted between individuals. As real-world science closes in on these once-fantastical frontiers, the challenge of crafting a worthy sequel has become even more pronounced: *Algorithm-325* must not only advance Nicolás Tosh's story but also mirror the accelerating pace of today's research.

A year has passed since the clandestine events at the Zermatt Data Center upended the balance of power, left corrupt conspirators subdued, and propelled a reserved mathematics professor into global prominence. In that short span, four key forces have taken shape:

1. **Tosh's Dual Role**
   Publicly, the towering figure of Artemis Wang still presides over Lingtao's empire—its social networks, marketplaces, and philanthropic spin-offs. Privately, however, Tosh wields genuine control via the Experta Foundation, guiding the direction of this vast global enterprise. This delicate arrangement forces him to reconcile philanthropic ideals with the profound weight of mind-reading technology.

2. **White House Ambitions**
   Meanwhile, the U.S. administration's waning term fuels a quiet scramble to formalize or even expand use of CDA technology for "national security." Rumors abound that any incoming president, eager to stamp a new mandate, will demand

unprecedented oversight—or exploitation—of these neural capabilities.

3. **Global Rumors**

Murmurs that "brain tech" is guiding prominent world figures continue to bubble in investigative journalism circles and online chatter. Though the Zermatt Data Center's exact role remains shrouded in secrecy, the mere hint of such power is enough to sow unease. Depending on one's perspective, Zermatt is either a hidden puppeteer or a vital bulwark against shadowy threats.

4. **Clash of Motives**

Just as real-world brain-computer interfaces promise revolutionary medical breakthroughs—or potential tools of surveillance—so *Algorithm-325* intensifies the dilemma. Lofty dreams of international security and social progress collide with the naked temptation to manipulate minds for profit, politics, or personal gain.

Continuing the narrative begun in *Algorithm-323* is a delicate balancing act: to broaden the scope—diving deeper into geopolitics, personal sacrifices, and ethical minefields—without losing sight of the raw human stakes. At its core, the series remains haunted by a fundamental question: If technology can penetrate the last frontier of personal privacy—the mind—can any good intention truly hold the line against eventual misuse? As *Algorithm-325* broadens its canvas to global scale, Tosh's conscience, and the uneasy alliances he's forged, will be tested as never before.

Real-world progress in neural interfaces—once deemed speculative—has now lent an urgent relevance to this fictional universe. As we journey again into Zermatt's covert corridors and the White House's guarded strategy sessions, I invite you to ponder: *How close are we, really, to translating the stuff of thrillers into everyday headlines?* And if such power emerges in our own lifetime, who will shoulder the burden of deciding its moral boundaries?

With those questions echoing, I welcome you back to join Nicolás Tosh, Artemis Wang, and their unlikely coalition of political and technological power players as they grapple with the aftermath—and next frontiers—of *Algorithm-323*.

GLOSSARY OF CHARACTERS

- **Nicolás Tosh**
  Mathematician and reluctant architect of the **CDA** (Cognitive Discrete Algorithms) technology, initially thrust into the limelight during the events of *Algorithm-323*. Now the de facto leader of both the **Zermatt Data Center** and a key figure in **Lingtao**'s philanthropic pivot under the **Experta Foundation.**

- **Alejandra Tosh**
  Nicolás's wife and moral anchor, who struggles with the widening chasm between their family life and the clandestine responsibilities her husband shoulders. Frequently questions the ethical boundaries of the technology and its impact on her family.

- **Rainer Sábato**
  Tosh's closest ally in the Zermatt Data Center. A logistics mastermind and technical operator, he oversees the day-to-day operations of **CDA** usage, encryption protocols, and infiltration defense. Torn between loyalty to Tosh and alarm at the expanding scope of mind-tech.

- **Artemis Wang**
  Formerly the flamboyant, uncontested head of **Lingtao** and global tech magnate. After surrendering most of his control to the Experta Foundation (and narrowly avoiding prison), he remains a public figurehead while quietly grappling with guilt and a diminished role.

- **President O'Sullivan**
  The U.S. President nearing the end of his term, previously allied with Tosh to contain conspiracies but increasingly pressed to expand CDA usage for national security. His departure sets the stage for Redwood's rise to power.

- **President Redwood** (or Senator Redwood pre-inauguration)
  The political rival and eventual successor to O'Sullivan, Redwood champions "total transparency" by pushing for maximum government control of mind-scanning technology. A central antagonist driving global adoption—and possible misuse—of the CDA suite.

- **Maggie Wu**
  An investigative tech reporter whose relentless curiosity repeatedly puts her on the cusp of exposing the real story behind **Zermatt, CDA** technology, and Lingtao's hush-hush crisis. A key foil to the secrecy binding the major players.
- **Dr. Miriam Faber**
  A quantum encryption specialist at the Zermatt Data Center. Integral to developing or refining the **CDA** algorithms, she frequently warns about the ethical implications and potential vulnerabilities of the system.
- **G-7 Liaisons** (e.g., Ambassador Celine Dubois, Minister Walter Lindholm)
  Representatives of the world's leading powers who jointly oversee the use of **CDA** technology, trying to maintain a precarious balance between privacy and security while suspecting the U.S. of overreach.
- **NeuraTech Extremists**
  A rogue ex-intelligence faction that emerges partway through *Algorithm-325*. Driven by the belief that they can forcibly "fix" corruption via Overwrite, they represent an amoral approach to mind-control technology.

GLOSSARY OF TERMS

- **CDA (Cognitive Discrete Algorithms)**
  A suite of advanced mathematical/quantum-driven tools originally designed to map and read human memory. Encompasses multiple versions (CDA-319, -320, -321, etc.) that communicate with or extract data from the human mind.
- **Overwrite**
  The ominous extension of **CDA** technology that goes beyond reading memories. Overwrite allows for forcibly altering or implanting thoughts and memories within a target's brain. A major ethical flashpoint in *Algorithm-325*.
- **CDA-325**
  The latest and most controversial iteration of **CDA**—capable of "vaccinating" or "inoculating" users against Overwrite attempts but also treading dangerously close to universal mind manipulation if misused.

- **Zermatt Data Center**
  A heavily fortified, subterranean complex in the Swiss Alps that houses the quantum servers powering CDA. Run initially in secret, it becomes the epicenter of global espionage, infiltration, and morally fraught decision-making.
- **Experta Foundation**
  Tosh's philanthropic umbrella organization that nominally manages Lingtao and channels resources into global humanitarian causes. Secretly serves as the legal and financial shield for Zermatt's hush-hush operations.
- **Lingtao**
  The global tech behemoth once controlled by Artemis Wang. Publicly pivoting to "ethical data solutions," it remains a front for philanthropic efforts while quietly interfacing with Zermatt's global data networks.
- **NeuraTech**
  A competing or rogue technology developed by extremist factions. Lacks ethical safeguards, allowing forced Overwrite of minds without limiting protocols.
- **White House Bunker / War Room**
  Refers to the secure underbelly of the U.S. government's decision-making apparatus, where Presidents O'Sullivan and later Redwood meet with top advisors. Central to shaping and extending CDA's reach in the name of national security.
- **G-7 / World Transparency Council**
  Initially the G-7 powers overseeing hush-hush usage of CDA technology, this grows into a broader council involving other global players. Tensions frequently arise over who truly controls or benefits from the technology.
- **Overwrite Vaccine**
  The clandestine deployment of **CDA-325** across vast swaths of the population as a means to protect individuals from external Overwrite. The moral ambiguity centers on the fact that it's often done without the individual's knowledge or consent.

PREFACE

They called it a quiet ending, but in truth, there was nothing quiet about it. There were no dramatic indictments, no blaring headlines, no spectacular courtroom dramas. Instead, the affair ended with whispered settlements, confidential court filings, and doors softly clicking shut—an anticlimactic conclusion to one of the most sensitive operations in recent memory. Yet for everyone who experienced the final hours of Algorithm-323, describing the conclusion as "quiet" felt deeply inadequate—like labeling the eerie calm after a devastating earthquake as mere silence, when beneath it, aftershocks still trembled.

Everything unraveled swiftly, in mere hours:

A once-disgraced mathematician, wrongfully imprisoned and nearly forgotten, became the pivotal figure in harnessing technology powerful enough to scan and preserve human consciousness.

A beleaguered president, previously trapped by powerful conspirators, managed last-minute secret negotiations that dismantled his opposition and buried the uncomfortable truths from public scrutiny.

A tech mogul of seemingly limitless influence quietly surrendered his empire, willingly exchanging his vast power to escape incarceration in the nation's harshest penitentiary.

The Final Day of Algorithm-323

On that last decisive day of Algorithm-323, Nicolás Tosh's meticulously concealed double life unraveled dramatically before the watchful eyes of the White House, the judiciary, and a world desperately craving normality. As the final conspirators were quietly apprehended—some overseas, others on American soil, still others within the highest echelons of power—it became indisputable that the formidable algorithms running within Tosh's Zermatt Data Center had fundamentally transformed the architecture of modern governance. In hushed, secretive negotiations behind tightly closed doors, these conspirators unanimously favored silence over public disgrace. Most capitulated willingly, bound by airtight non-disclosure agreements. Others, such as the influential corporate titan Leroy Sinclair and former President Thomas, quietly slipped into discreet exile. Their fates were reduced to cryptic, sealed court records referencing vaguely defined "high crimes against the state," documents destined never to be publicly scrutinized.

Where It Left Each Player

Nicolás Tosh's journey from wrongful imprisonment to redemption culminated not in relief but in an uneasy elevation to power. With his innocence restored, Tosh now found himself entrusted with oversight of an unprecedented, invasive technology capable of interpreting human thoughts. Simultaneously, he inherited control of Lingtao—the once preeminent global social marketplace—transferred from its disgraced founder, Artemis Wang. Now burdened by an extraordinary responsibility, Tosh navigates a precarious balance between his philanthropic image and the immense pressures from global governments, all wary of a technology they simultaneously covet and fear.

Artemis Wang having narrowly escaped prison, Artemis Wang exists now as a ceremonial figure, his outward freedom masking an internal captivity. In public, he remains the charismatic face of Lingtao, smiling and waving at carefully choreographed corporate events. Privately, however, he is reduced to a subordinate role within Tosh's Experta Foundation, subject to the oversight and judgment of others. For Wang, the bitter reality is clear: his vast commercial empire is no longer his to command, and the powerful figures who spared him incarceration wield the ability to revoke his carefully orchestrated freedom at will.

Zermatt Data Center hidden deep beneath the serene landscape of the Swiss Alps, the Zermatt Data Center evolved rapidly during Algorithm-323's final, chaotic hours. Once a secretive mathematical research lab, it is now a global nexus of advanced intelligence operations. Teams worked feverishly to secure extracted memories, deploy sophisticated "identifier" algorithms throughout key global regions, and fine-tune quantum servers to unprecedented levels. Today, Zermatt is under no single nation's jurisdiction; rather, it operates discreetly yet powerfully as part of Tosh's inner circle, quietly expanding its capability to reach into any human mind—growing steadily more potent with each passing month.

Experta Foundation originally designed as Tosh's charitable facade, the Experta Foundation swiftly transformed into an essential instrument of global stability. Amid the frenzied final hours of Algorithm-323, Experta's legal teams executed delicate negotiations, carefully maintaining plausible deniability for all involved parties. Today, the foundation projects an image of benevolence through worldwide charitable contributions, medical research funding, educational investments, and international relief efforts. Beneath this philanthropic surface, however, Experta serves as the vigilant guardian of a technology whose misuse could irreparably compromise the privacy and freedoms of every individual on the planet.

The U.S. Government considers the "Miami Conspiracy" and the "Thomas Affair" closed chapters. Informally, officials retain partial knowledge of the workings and immense potential of the CDA suites. An uneasy alliance exists with Tosh, marked by careful negotiation and cautious reliance. During Algorithm-323's final stages, the administration learned just enough to grasp the delicacy of their relationship with Tosh and his powerful technology. They can request, sometimes even insist upon, the CDA's capabilities when national security is at stake, yet they cannot entirely control Tosh. As the current administration nears the end of its term, political strategists urgently maneuver to solidify their influence before a new President step into power, potentially embracing full transparency regardless of the costs.

A Tense Calm—and the Threshold of Another Storm

For the moment, an uneasy calm prevails—a carefully maintained peace built on an implicit understanding: keep the groundbreaking technology concealed, utilize it sparingly, and nurture the comforting illusion that the resolution of the last conspiracy marked the end of all threats. Yet, deep within Zermatt's hidden supercomputers, the powerful device capable of unearthing humanity's deepest secrets continues its quiet, relentless operation. The crisis surrounding Algorithm-323 delivered an undeniable truth: the ability to access and manipulate the human mind cannot remain isolated or secret forever.

It is from this fragile equilibrium that Algorithm-325 emerges. With whispers and speculation about "brain tech" gaining momentum, a significant political shift on the horizon, and Lingtao's rising dominance in global markets, the next conflict between human ambition, ethical boundaries, and the elusive frontier of thought becomes inevitable. Those who believed the conclusion of Algorithm-323 represented the definitive end of invasive mental technologies will soon discover that its influence has permeated far deeper and wider than imagined, setting the stage for an unprecedented storm.

Introduction

3:11 A.M.

A vast, moonless darkness blanketed the Swiss Alps, turning their jagged peaks into ghostly silhouettes against an obsidian sky. The silent forests along the northern slope stood in stark, watchful rows, untouched by artificial illumination. Amid the dense shadows, four figures moved meticulously—phantoms dressed entirely in black tactical gear, their visors lowered and faces obscured. Each step deliberate, their boots pressed soundlessly into the thick carpet of damp pine needles.

Their breathing remained controlled but strained, punctuated by whispered commands barely audible to one another. "Three meters ahead. Watch your step," murmured the lead intruder—a figure whose confident bearing, and subtle gestures marked him clearly as the commander. Behind him trailed a wiry technician, eyes flickering nervously, a pair of broad-shouldered operatives whose movements betrayed military precision, and a slender individual who seemed perpetually on edge, glancing into the darkness as if expecting pursuit.

They moved steadily upward, weaving through twisted pines and ducking under thick branches, their pulses quickening against the heavy stillness. None noticed the slight, unnatural irregularity nestled high above—a sophisticated surveillance camera cleverly camouflaged within the gnarled knot of an ancient fir. Invisible infrared lenses tracked every careful movement, silently transmitting the intruders' progress miles away to a reinforced monitoring outpost.

A sudden burst of static crackled harshly through Zermatt's internal comms, drowning out urgent instructions. Rainer slammed his fist against the console. "Fix that channel now!" he barked sharply, watching the intruders edge dangerously closer to their goal.

Four miles distant, within the subterranean confines of Zermatt's central security facility, a red alert blinked ominously to life. A weary night-shift caretaker straightened in his chair, gaze sharpening on the alert icon. Movement detected—restricted perimeter, after hours.

Possibly wildlife, perhaps lost hikers... but the facility's recent history warranted immediate suspicion.

The caretaker's pulse quickened slightly as he triggered the protocol, forwarding the alert upward. The blinking red icon intensified, a silent acknowledgment that within moments, higher authorities would mobilize to confront whatever had breached Zermatt's carefully guarded silence.

Yet the intruders, singularly focused on their covert advance, remained oblivious that their presence had already rippled across the calm surface of a formidable technological stronghold—one prepared to defend its secrets at any cost.

Zermatt Command Suite

At the subterranean heart of the Zermatt Data Center, the dim glow of monitoring screens painted ghostly hues across the face of a solitary caretaker working the overnight shift. Suddenly, a single red icon began blinking quietly but insistently in the top corner of the largest screen. A proximity alert.

His brow furrowed slightly, a flicker of unease tightening his jaw. Leaning forward, he swiftly cross-referenced the alert with perimeter motion sensors, fingers dancing across the illuminated keyboard. The initial data was sparse yet troubling: movement detected in the highly restricted outer zone, well past midnight. He checked quickly—no maintenance scheduled, no authorized personnel on duty. It might be nothing more than wildlife wandering near sensors. Or perhaps lost hikers straying off-trail. But Zermatt's recent experience with Algorithm-323 had instilled an unyielding vigilance, a wariness of the fragile line between security and intrusion.

With practiced urgency, the caretaker initiated the escalation protocol, pressing a secure button that instantly transmitted the alert further up the operational chain. In less than a minute, the silent vibration of text notifications rippled discreetly across the personal devices of senior personnel—Rainer Sábato and two others responsible for crisis response.

The caretaker leaned back slightly, exhaling slowly in the quiet tension of the room. Unease prickled at the edges of his thoughts. He wished fervently for clearer intelligence, for anything that could resolve this uncertainty. Yet in the darkness beneath the Alps, clarity rarely arrived swiftly—and caution had become their strongest defense.

3:18 A.M.

The intruders reached the first tangible barrier to Zermatt's restricted perimeter—a formidable chain-link fence topped ominously with invisible alarm wires. The lead operative, a broad-shouldered figure with a disciplined, steely gaze, signaled for silence as he detached a compact, sophisticated device from his utility belt. With practiced precision, he pressed it gently against the lock mechanism. A faint, ghostly blue glow momentarily illuminated their masked faces, accompanied by a muted click as the lock yielded effortlessly.

The lookout, barely in his twenties, felt a surge of regret—memories flooding of the debts that had driven him to this desperate choice, leaving family behind with hollow promises of safety.

As they approached the fence line, a sudden flicker of red flashed from a concealed sensor. "Infrared perimeter trip," the lookout hissed urgently. Without hesitation, the leader signaled for the team to halt, swiftly adjusting a small handheld device to neutralize the sensor's signal. After a tense, breathless moment, the sensor's indicator dimmed once more. "We're clear—but double-check for more of those," the leader ordered quietly, acknowledging silently how close they'd come to early detection.

He paused, his gloved fingers lingering momentarily on the fence's cold metal, scanning methodically for surveillance cameras or hidden sensors. Satisfied, he gently eased the gate aside, a slow, silent motion that barely disturbed the stillness of the night. The other three operatives swiftly slipped through behind him, their movements coordinated, professional, and nearly soundless.

As the intruders moved stealthily up the wooded slope, the team leader's mind briefly flashed to their initial briefing—a dimly lit room in a nondescript office building far from Swiss soil. "This isn't just corporate espionage," their employer had emphasized, his voice edged with conviction. "This technology reshapes the global order—either we control it, or we become subjects to those who do." Those stark words echoed sharply in the leader's mind, reinforcing the weight and geopolitical stakes behind their risky mission.

Their mission was unambiguous: infiltrate Zermatt's remote facility, sabotage or extract key technology rumored to hold advanced mathematical codes—the neural interfaces once instrumental in exposing a high-level conspiracy within the White House. Yet despite meticulous planning, the team knew alarmingly little about Zermatt's true operational depth. They remained unaware of the silent watchers now mobilizing rapidly in response to their intrusion, or the subtle quantum threads already whispering unseen along neural pathways, gently probing the edges of their consciousness.

3:25 A.M.

In a small, secure substation adjacent to Zermatt's central command facility, Rainer Sábato stood bathed in the pale glow of multiple monitors, eyes sharp despite having been jolted awake less than ten minutes prior. The largest screen displayed phantom infrared silhouettes—four unidentified figures carefully advancing along the sloping terrain toward the heart of the restricted complex.

Inside Zermatt's security hub, Rainer's brows knitted in frustration as an unexpected error flashed across the CDA monitoring console. "Another calibration glitch?" he muttered sharply. "I thought we'd fixed this." He quickly tapped out diagnostic commands, fighting to regain stability even as the intruders moved steadily toward Warehouse C. Precious seconds drained away as he forced the system back online, each second deepening the urgency.

Rainer's fingers danced swiftly across the keyboard, prompting the facility's intelligence software to attempt a facial and gait recognition match. The system flickered briefly before returning zero matches— unknown entities, precise in their movements, disciplined and methodical.

With a tense exhale, Rainer toggled quickly to another screen, activating a direct video feed to the caretaker stationed within the main monitoring hub. The caretaker's anxious face appeared, shadows deepening the concern in his eyes.

"They're headed toward Warehouse C," the caretaker whispered urgently, his voice low but steady. "They breached the main fence without tripping any visible alarms. No visible weapons detected, but their coordination suggests military training."

Rainer's jaw tightened imperceptibly. "Are you certain there's no scheduled maintenance tonight or any covert operational tests authorized?"

The caretaker shook his head definitively. "Negative, sir. There's nothing authorized on our end."

A cold urgency gripped Rainer as he swiftly activated the facility's CDA-319 neural scanners, initiating a sophisticated sweep across the facility's perimeter. Within moments, delicate icons materialized over the facility's perimeter map—four clearly defined neural signatures. A chill traced its way down Rainer's spine; the intruders were dangerously close to the sensitive equipment in Warehouse C, home to Zermatt's cutting-edge quantum circuitry. The implications of sabotage or theft were catastrophic.

"We're getting scattered readings," Rainer reported tensely. The neural imagery flickered intermittently, revealing only fragmentary thoughts— brief images, indistinct fears. Tosh leaned forward, voice steady but edged with urgency. "Boost signal strength slowly; too fast, and they'll detect the intrusion." Rainer nodded sharply, gradually enhancing the neural scan resolution. "There… we have clearer mental signatures now. They're nervous. Starting to second-guess the mission."

With practiced composure, Rainer opened an encrypted communication line directly to Nicolás Tosh's personal device. Even in these early hours, Tosh's immediate involvement was non-negotiable during security breaches.

"Nicolás," Rainer's voice was calm yet firm, betraying none of his mounting anxiety. "We have intruders. I'm activating the full suite immediately."

3:31 A.M.

The interior of Warehouse C was cloaked in an eerie half-darkness, illuminated only by the pale, spectral glow of emergency lights. Towering stacks of metal crates loomed silently, forming narrow aisles through which the intruders moved cautiously, each breath carefully controlled, each step placed precisely to avoid making a sound.

The technician paused, his fingers trembling slightly over the delicate wires. "You ever wonder if we're on the right side of this?" he murmured softly, almost to himself. The demolition expert, eyes never leaving his task, replied tersely, "Right side? We're mercenaries—morality isn't part of the contract." The younger operative behind them bit his lip nervously, whispering barely audibly, "Then why does this feel so damned wrong?" The lead operative halted before a robust, heavily secured container. He withdrew a compact crowbar from his pack, placing its flattened edge against the crate's lid and applying steady, careful pressure. With a muted, metallic groan, the container's seal gave way, opening reluctantly to his insistent leverage.

One of the operatives glanced anxiously around, whispering sharply, "Keep your head down. We've got five minutes, maybe less, before they figure out something's wrong."

Ignoring the tense warning, the leader directed a slender beam of light from his flashlight into the crate's interior. Racks of intricate circuit boards, heavily encrypted storage drives, and neat bundles of fiber cables greeted their anxious gaze—each item labeled with innocuous yet indecipherable codes. The equipment could be mundane replacement parts, or it might represent the very core of Zermatt's clandestine neural network architecture.

The lead operative quickly extracted a polished, silver encryption module, carefully placing it on the concrete beside him. "Get everything you can copied—fast," he ordered, urgency threading through his composed tone.

Hands trembling slightly, he swiftly connected a compact portable drive to the exposed circuit board. The seconds ticked by agonizingly slow, filled only by the soft, anxious breaths of the intruders as they waited for the encrypted data to flow, acutely aware of the perilous thinness of their rapidly closing window of opportunity.

Zermatt Command

In the secured confines of Zermatt's central command suite, Nicolás Tosh stood in front of an array of monitors, his hair tousled from the abrupt awakening. He fixed an intense gaze on a side screen flickering with real-time mental telemetry—the intruders' neural signatures decoded by the advanced CDA-323 system. The data displayed was stark and unmistakable: panic had begun to set in, adrenal spikes translating their most immediate and unfiltered thoughts into clear text streams.
We should have brought more help... This job's too big... Keep it together...
Tosh exhaled slowly, maintaining his composure even as urgency surged beneath his calm exterior. Merely observing wasn't sufficient—they needed immediate intervention to disrupt the intruders' efforts.

"Rainer," he said firmly, his voice controlled yet carrying the undeniable weight of command, "can we bypass the local server access in Warehouse C?"

Across the room, Rainer's fingers moved rapidly over the console, deftly navigating security protocols. "On it," he responded crisply, eyes darting between screens. "Severing data ports to Warehouse C hardware… Now."

A separate monitor flashed live footage from a concealed camera high in the warehouse ceiling, offering an overhead view of the intruders' sudden confusion. They watched as download indicators abruptly stalled, transfer speeds collapsing to zero, and portable drives blinking defiantly with error codes.

Tosh carefully monitored the gradual clarity emerging from the CDA interface, watching thoughts crystallize from vague uncertainty to clear, panicked urgency. "Now we have them," he murmured, recognizing the precise moment their psychological defenses crumbled.

Tosh allowed himself a fleeting moment of grim satisfaction. The intruders now understood something was gravely wrong—their careful plans unraveling in real-time. Yet, the threat wasn't fully neutralized, and the next moves would be crucial.

3:35 A.M.

An oppressive silence gripped the intruders, anxiety mounting palpably. The operative wielding the crowbar cursed quietly, urgency straining his voice. "The circuit's locked us out—something's gone wrong!" he hissed through clenched teeth. "We're out of time. Shift immediately to Phase Two. Set the charges and prepare to detonate."

Another team member recoiled visibly, snapping back sharply in an anxious whisper, "We explicitly agreed—no major damage unless absolutely necessary!"

The leader's eyes flashed fiercely behind his visor, voice edged with desperation and cold logic. "The entire operation is compromised without the data. Our buyer explicitly authorized sabotage if extraction fails." With grim determination, he reached swiftly into a compact satchel strapped securely to his waist.

Under the ghostly, dim glow of the warehouse's emergency lights, the team watched as he withdrew a cluster of carefully arranged wires attached to a compact, old-fashioned detonator. Its metallic components gleamed ominously, a stark contrast against the shadows enveloping them. The operatives exchanged tense, uneasy glances, the gravity of their next move settling heavily over the group, each acutely aware of the dire consequences rapidly closing in.

Zermatt Urgent Command

Red warning lights flared urgently across the main control display, bathing the Zermatt command suite in an unsettling crimson hue. Rainer's voice was taut with urgency, barely above a whisper, yet clear and decisive. "They're preparing explosives—infrared sensors confirm they're rigging something inside Warehouse C."

Nicolás Tosh reacted immediately, his voice steady and authoritative. "Deploy the perimeter security team now. We can't afford any damage to our quantum infrastructure."

Without hesitation, Rainer activated a secured communication link to the Swiss emergency response teams on standby. "I'm authorizing immediate external intervention—" he began, before abruptly stopping, his eyes fixed on the neural readouts spiking vividly on his monitor. A volatile blend of fear and determination pulsed unmistakably from the intruders' neural signatures. They were counting down.

Tosh, his expression unyielding, issued a command laden with strategic intent. "Let them know we're inside their minds. It might disrupt their focus enough to buy us crucial seconds."

Rainer gave a quick, decisive nod and accessed a specialized console tab labeled CDA-320, the facility's powerful direct neural-link communication channel. Carefully, deliberately, he typed a brief, potent message into the interface and pressed transmit, watching as it flashed confirmation—each second stretching painfully as he awaited the intruders' reaction.

Warehouse Psych Confrontation

The intruders, moments away from arming their final explosive wire, abruptly froze as an unnatural, chilling presence flooded their minds. A voice, clear and disturbingly intimate, whispered directly into their consciousness:

"This is the Zermatt Data Center. We see you. We know your intentions, and we can hear your every thought. Put down the device and surrender immediately."

Panic surged through the group like an electric current, hearts hammering erratically as eyes darted around the dimly lit warehouse, desperately searching for hidden speakers or any evidence of technological deception. One operative, overwhelmed, sank to his knees, clutching his head as if to physically shield himself from the invasive force pressing relentlessly against his psyche.

Seconds dragged out painfully, silence gripping the warehouse as tightly as their escalating fear.

The voice returned, colder and more commanding than before, underscored by an unmistakable urgency:

"You have exactly one opportunity to exit alive. The Swiss authorities are inbound, and we possess the capacity to transmit your entire operation—including your deepest, most private confessions—to any global enforcement agency. Lay down your devices and surrender now."

As panic set in, the leader's thoughts flashed uncontrollably to the faceless brokers who'd hired them—their ruthless demands, their chilling warnings of failure. "They'll erase us if we're captured," he whispered, voice shaking, eyes darting wildly. The technician's breath hitched in terror, realizing abruptly the impossible bind: failure meant facing both their captors' wrath and their unseen employers' lethal retribution.

The intruders stood frozen, locked in internal battles of terror and disbelief as the stark reality of their vulnerability became brutally undeniable.

3:38 A.M.

The leader's eyes darted frantically around the dim warehouse, his breathing ragged as disbelief and dread overtook him. "This is impossible—some kind of advanced comm device," he muttered through clenched teeth, desperately trying to rationalize the intrusion into their minds. But even as he spoke, the final remnants of his determination fractured under the weight of undeniable reality.

Outside, the distant yet unmistakable wail of approaching sirens pierced the silence, a haunting confirmation that their escape route had been severed. The intruders' panicked thoughts ricocheted internally, each recognizing that their innermost fears and failures were now exposed, accessible at will by an invisible adversary.

With a defeated exhale, the leader let the detonator slip from his trembling grip, clattering loudly onto the cold concrete floor. "Stand down," he ordered, his voice hollow, barely audible over the ringing in their ears. "We're finished."

Abruptly, powerful headlights sliced through the gloom outside, throwing stark shadows across crates and machinery. Heavy footsteps echoed urgently on the asphalt as the swirling lights of red and blue flooded through every opening, illuminating the warehouse interior. The intruders, visibly trembling and resigned, slowly raised their hands above their heads, surrendering quietly to the overwhelming forces now converging upon them.

Zermatt Command

Rainer exhaled slowly, his pulse still hammering in his veins, the immediate danger subsiding into cautious relief. "Local authorities confirm the suspects are in custody," he reported, voice steady despite residual tension. "They're disarmed, and initial reports indicate no casualties."

Nicolás Tosh nodded deliberately; his relief tempered by an underlying sense of weary vigilance. "Good. We need full identification immediately. Initiate comprehensive memory scans—these intruders could be part of something much larger."

Suddenly, a fresh voice broke through the secure console—calm, authoritative, unmistakably one of the Swiss security officers on-site.

"Suspects secured, but they're remaining silent for now."

Rainer exchanged a meaningful glance with Tosh, the weight of their responsibility evident in their grim expressions. "They don't need to speak," Rainer said quietly, the implications of his words hanging heavy in the room. "We'll uncover everything we need directly from their minds soon enough."

Chapter 1

Lingtao's New Dawn

Lingtao Headquarters, San Francisco
10:00 A.M. PST

A symphony of camera shutters echoed through the luminous atrium, each rapid-fire click blending seamlessly into a tapestry of anticipation. Journalists subtly maneuvered, seeking vantage points from which to capture every nuance of the unfolding spectacle. Sunlight streamed through the towering glass façade, enveloping Lingtao's modernized headquarters in hues of vibrant blue and burnished gold, colors carefully chosen to evoke both innovation and stability—hallmarks of the global tech giant.

At the epicenter of this meticulously orchestrated event stood two commanding figures. Artemis Wang, Lingtao's legendary founder and an icon whose past charisma had inspired countless followers, now moved toward the podium with measured deliberation. His demeanor revealed hints of caution, evidence of recent trials etched subtly in his posture. At his side, Amara Leung exuded an air of assured tranquility and vibrant authority. Newly appointed as Lingtao's co-CEO, Amara carried the responsibility for steering the company's visionary "ethical data solutions" project, a landmark initiative conducted in partnership with the renowned Experta Foundation.

Wang paused briefly before speaking, allowing silence to accentuate the gravity of the moment. His tempered smile conveyed both humility and resilience, inviting the audience into this carefully crafted narrative. "Ladies and gentlemen," Wang's voice flowed effortlessly, amplified by discreetly positioned speakers, "we gather here today not merely to celebrate a corporate milestone but to affirm a profound recommitment. Guided by our partnership with the Experta Foundation, Lingtao now

"

dedicates itself unreservedly to the ideals of global philanthropy, transparency, and sustainable enterprise."

High above the public spectacle, Nicolás Tosh observed meticulously from a secluded executive suite. Hidden behind reflective glass walls designed to obscure his presence, he absorbed every gesture and every word through a secure CDA transmission that linked him intimately to the event. Though physically distant from the platform, Tosh's strategic influence permeated every aspect of Lingtao's carefully executed reinvention. His discrete earpiece buzzed softly with updates from trusted advisors scattered across strategic global points—Zurich's data centers, Miami's financial hubs, and local operatives embedded discreetly within San Francisco itself.

Despite Tosh's deliberate absence from the public eye, his invisible yet unmistakable hand shaped Lingtao's narrative with surgical precision. Each carefully chosen word Wang uttered resonated with Tosh's overarching vision, each strategic pause meticulously calculated. From behind his one-way mirror, Tosh quietly orchestrated the future, mindful of the delicate balance required to maintain appearances while protecting deeper, more fragile truths hidden beneath Lingtao's polished exterior.

A Whisper in the Ether

The discrete hum of Nicolás Tosh's earpiece was barely audible amidst the ambient quiet of his secluded executive suite. The familiar, composed voice of Rainer Sábato resonated softly from the heart of the Zermatt Data Center. "Nicolás," he began calmly, his tone reassuringly measured, "Artemis is adhering precisely to the script. No deviations detected thus far."

Tosh acknowledged Rainer's report with a subtle, almost imperceptible nod, his eyes unwaveringly fixed on the meticulously orchestrated event unfolding far below. "Good," he murmured softly. "Remain vigilant."

Surrounding Tosh, an intricate network of monitors illuminated the dim interior of the suite, each screen displaying streams of real-time intelligence that surged relentlessly from the Zermatt quantum servers. Patterns emerged and dissolved rapidly, revealing disquieting truths hidden far beyond the polished surface of the day's event: child trafficking operations silently navigating the shadows of Southeast Asia's remote regions; clandestine domestic abuse syndicates entrenched deeply within American communities; simmering conspiracies within an influential pilots' union, poised precariously on the brink of catastrophic negligence; and rampant corruption threatening to destabilize an Eastern European oil conglomerate.

Each revelation carried immense moral and operational weight, yet Tosh absorbed them quietly, his expression betraying neither fatigue nor dismay. The gravity of his covert responsibilities had long since become familiar, a necessary burden he carried with unwavering resolve. Utilizing the potent capabilities of CDA technology, he deftly navigated this hidden world of peril and secrecy, channeling intelligence discreetly through the philanthropic façade of the Experta Foundation. It was a delicate dance—shaping events without revealing the sophisticated mechanisms at his disposal.

Yet, despite the broader tumult of global crises demanding attention, Tosh's immediate focus remained locked firmly on Lingtao's strategic reinvention. The company's high-profile public pivot was not merely symbolic; it was foundational to his broader strategy. Legally securing control over Lingtao's expansive data networks under the banner of corporate philanthropy was crucial. This careful alignment ensured the continued, discreet infiltration of daily life by Zermatt's powerful analytics, safely cloaked beneath the veneer of corporate benevolence.

In the quiet isolation of his hidden vantage point, Tosh continued to watch carefully, keenly aware that the stability of countless future operations hinged delicately on today's success.

The Press Conference

Artemis Wang gracefully stepped aside, inviting Amara Leung forward with an open-handed gesture that conveyed deep respect. "It is my privilege," he said, his voice steady and genuine, "to introduce our new co-CEO, Ms. Leung, whose vision for Lingtao embodies our commitment to harmonizing corporate ambition with meaningful social impact. Today, we proudly announce two transformative initiatives: first, the creation of a global micro-loan fund designed to empower aspiring entrepreneurs in the world's most underserved communities; and second, significant breakthroughs in data encryption technology, reaffirming our unwavering dedication to protecting user privacy."

Warm applause erupted spontaneously throughout the expansive atrium as Amara stepped forward, her poise radiating confidence and heartfelt sincerity. "Thank you," she began with a gentle yet assured tone, her words effortlessly resonating throughout the hall. "It is an honor and a responsibility I do not take lightly. Lingtao pledges to channel a substantial portion of our net revenue this year into the Experta Foundation. Our focus will span urgent humanitarian needs—from rapid-response disaster relief to nurturing educational opportunities for vulnerable children, as well as setting robust ethical standards for global data management."

In the audience, Maggie Wu, a seasoned journalist from the International Digital Times, observed the unfolding events keenly. Sunlight glinted softly off her press badge as she raised her hand confidently, her expression carefully neutral yet unmistakably probing.

"May I direct a question to Mr. Wang?" she asked with practiced courtesy, her tone smooth yet pointedly precise.

Wang's carefully maintained smile tightened almost imperceptibly, betraying a flash of guarded apprehension beneath his composed façade. "Certainly," he replied, his voice calm yet carrying an undertone of tension.

"Lingtao faced substantial challenges over the past year," Maggie began thoughtfully, selecting her words with diplomatic care. "If the reports circulating in the tech community are accurate, the company underwent significant internal turbulence, including high-level dismissals and confidential settlements. Could you provide some clarity on what triggered these internal disruptions, and share with us how Lingtao has rebounded to emerge even stronger today?"

An expectant silence fell momentarily upon the room, charged with curiosity and anticipation. From his hidden vantage high above, Nicolás Tosh felt his pulse quicken, his attention immediately shifting to a smaller monitor discreetly positioned alongside his primary surveillance screens. It displayed a delicate neural readout courtesy of CDA-319—a real-time emotional and physiological analysis of Artemis Wang. The sudden spike in Wang's adrenaline levels told Tosh all he needed to know: beneath the carefully rehearsed composure, Lingtao's legendary leader felt a sharp pang of anxiety. The past, Tosh realized with sober clarity, was never fully buried.

Seeds of Intrigue

From the secluded vantage of the executive suite, Nicolás Tosh's intense focus was momentarily interrupted by a discreet but insistent ping emanating from his console—an alert reserved solely for urgent CDA intercepts. Almost instantly, Rainer Sábato's voice filtered through his earpiece, cautious yet unmistakably urgent.

"Nicolás, we've detected an unauthorized signal embedding itself into the press conference data stream. It's skillfully routed through a series of proxy servers, originating deep within Eastern Europe."

Tosh's expression darkened subtly, his mind rapidly evaluating the potential threats this intrusion implied. "Corporate espionage? Or perhaps another competitor probing our defenses?" he asked, his voice carefully even, betraying none of the tension he felt.

Rainer hesitated slightly, carefully measuring his response. "It's possible, but the sophistication and precision here indicate something more serious than mere corporate rivalry. Whoever is behind this knows exactly what they're looking for. They could be mining internal Lingtao communications or probing for vulnerabilities we haven't anticipated."

Tosh immediately understood the severity of such an incursion. Lingtao's public repositioning was critical—an intricate strategic maneuver designed to distance the company from past controversies publicly while privately securing its symbiotic relationship with the Zermatt Data Center. Should the delicate truth of Artemis Wang's quiet compliance or Lingtao's deeper connection to CDA technology be uncovered, it would unravel their careful construct of alliances, trigger dormant scandals, or ignite explosive new crises.

"Stay on this, Rainer," Tosh instructed calmly, the command firm yet quietly urgent. His thoughts already raced ahead, mapping potential breaches and countermeasures. "Identify who's behind it and ascertain their intentions as quickly as possible."

Below, the press conference was concluding precisely as choreographed. Artemis Wang and Amara Leung exchanged confident, carefully rehearsed smiles, thanking their audience warmly and hinting with practiced optimism at more groundbreaking developments ahead. The gathered crowd offered genuine, enthusiastic applause, seemingly unaware of the tenuous complexities underlying the polished corporate narrative.

Yet amid the polite applause, Tosh's attention locked onto Maggie Wu. Her gaze was penetrating, sharp, searching far deeper than the public relations veneer permitted. Tosh's instincts tightened with wary recognition. He saw more than mere journalistic curiosity—Maggie Wu was probing for a hidden truth.

And beyond her scrutiny, another unseen entity patiently awaited its moment. Hidden beneath sophisticated encryption and anonymity, this adversary quietly watched, ready to exploit even the smallest fracture in Lingtao's meticulously reconstructed image.

Parallel Threads: The Global Sweep

Reporters filed out, Tosh took a moment to scan the list of new intelligence leads rolling in through the Zermatt Data Center. As the lingering hum of conversation gradually faded with the departing journalists, Nicolás Tosh redirected his unwavering attention back to the intricate tapestry of intelligence displayed vividly across his screens, data streams pouring in relentlessly from the Zermatt Data Center. Each alert, each flicker of information, served as a stark reminder of the shadowed realities that CDA technology relentlessly unveiled.

Human Trafficking Cartel – CDA-322 cross-references geolocation pings in a notorious border region. Small but reliable leads emerge on a distribution ring that smuggles minors.

In one illuminated corner of Tosh's monitor, a cluster of precise alerts pinpointed a desolate stretch of borderland notorious for human trafficking operations. CDA-322's powerful analytics meticulously sifted through subtle, transient geolocation signals, assembling an intricate map of clandestine trafficking routes. Even the most cautious operatives left traceable imprints—delicate threads leading inexorably back to criminal hubs hidden deep within Southeast Asia. As these stark realities unfolded silently before him, Tosh felt an involuntary tightening in his chest, an emotional reflex he had not fully dulled, despite years entrenched in this covert battle.

Each child, each innocent victim recovered through these operations, signified a crucial triumph. Yet the victory was tempered by the stark awareness of the broader, seemingly relentless cycle of exploitation and human suffering. For every trafficker intercepted, countless others lurked unseen, constantly evolving their tactics. Despite CDA's formidable reach, Tosh felt the immense weight of the never-ending struggle against this darkness, acutely aware of the limits of even the most sophisticated surveillance technology.

He momentarily allowed his eyes to drift across the other alerts vying urgently for his attention—corruption at staggering scales, simmering cartel rivalries, and conspiracies brewing unnoticed by the broader world. Yet the plight of exploited innocents held his gaze the longest, crystallizing the immense responsibility he bore.

With quiet determination, Tosh authorized immediate action. Anonymous, detailed intelligence reports would soon reach international humanitarian agencies and carefully vetted law enforcement teams, setting in motion rescues and targeted interventions designed to dismantle trafficking rings systematically.

Still, beneath the quiet resolve with which Tosh operated, he grappled internally with the immense ethical complexity of his role. CDA's unrivaled analytical capabilities granted him unprecedented power—power to uncover hidden truths, prevent tragedies, and enact profound change. Yet the relentless exposure of these stark realities forced him to constantly confront an unsettling question: could one individual, one technology, ever fully balance the scales of justice?

State-Level Corruption – A chaotic chain of bribes funneled to a high-ranking government contractor in Western Asia threatens to defraud entire city infrastructures.

Nicolas' reflections were interrupted by another insistent alert, pulling him back into the complex web of simultaneous crises. The war he waged from his hidden vantage point was ceaseless, and each victory carried the sobering awareness of battles yet unwon.

In another illuminated section of Nicolás Tosh's expansive array of screens, a complex and disquieting scenario unfolded—this time deep within Western Asia, where rampant corruption had metastasized unchecked into the very heart of regional governance. Detailed intelligence, meticulously gathered by CDA's penetrating analytics, revealed a labyrinthine network of illicit transactions, expertly concealed bribes, and fraudulent contracts. At the heart of this insidious web lay powerful officials and shadowy intermediaries who manipulated vital public funds with brazen impunity.

Critical infrastructure—hospitals urgently needed by vulnerable communities, schools essential to the education of future generations, and vital utility projects—stood perilously close to failure, starved of resources siphoned off by the greed of corrupt actors. Tosh absorbed this grim data silently, his eyes tracing the intricate connections highlighted by the relentless probing of CDA technology.

Each piece of evidence carefully collated represented a delicate thread, meticulously designed to lead authorities subtly toward the core of the conspiracy without revealing the extraordinary means of its discovery. Disguised as anonymous tips and quietly disseminated through secure channels, these intelligence breadcrumbs served as precision-guided prompts—nudging local and international investigators toward the concealed truths.

Yet Tosh remained acutely aware of the inherent danger in such operations. The powerful individuals targeted by CDA's revelations would not yield their positions easily. The thin line he walked was precarious, laden with potential repercussions. His team's analytical might was immense, capable of dismantling even the most deeply entrenched corruption; however, should adversaries discern even a glimpse of their surveillance capabilities, the backlash could be swift, targeted, and devastating.

With a steady hand, Tosh confirmed the release of the carefully prepared intelligence report, masked meticulously to protect its source. He watched as encrypted communications quietly flowed toward strategic law enforcement agencies and non-governmental organizations poised to act.

Yet even as he orchestrated this unseen intervention, Tosh knew the delicate balance he maintained was perpetually at risk—each move carefully measured against potential retaliation. Justice was within reach, but achieving it safely required constant vigilance and subtlety, qualities Tosh had honed through relentless necessity.

Drug Syndicate Rivalry – Rival lords in South America planning a wave of violence near major shipping ports. Zermatt's early intercepts reveal potential sabotage of cargo fleets.

Urgent streams of intelligence flooded Nicolás Tosh's monitors, highlighting a rapidly escalating conflict between two formidable South American drug cartels. The simmering tension had reached a critical tipping point, poised precariously on the brink of explosive violence near strategic shipping ports crucial for international trade. CDA intercepts provided chilling clarity, revealing detailed preparations for sabotage— carefully rigged cargo shipments designed to unleash catastrophic consequences that would ripple far beyond the cartels' violent rivalry.

Tosh's eyes narrowed as he evaluated the unfolding threat. Every intercepted communication painted a darker picture of calculated ruthlessness and impending chaos. Understanding the grave potential for collateral damage and civilian casualties, he swiftly authorized the immediate dispatch of comprehensive intelligence dossiers to local law enforcement agencies and specialized NGOs equipped to respond decisively.

As the encrypted intelligence reports moved swiftly through secure channels, Tosh found himself momentarily grappling with a familiar moral disquiet. The remarkable effectiveness of CDA's analytics was undeniable—capable of intercepting and averting disasters with surgical precision. Yet this very effectiveness troubled him deeply, prompting unsettling reflections on the profound ethical implications of a single technological system wielding such enormous power over life-and-death outcomes.

He watched silently, the weight of responsibility heavy upon him, as his actions quietly shaped a safer, if uncertain, future.

Aviation Concern – Faulty plane part designs, flagged by a junior engineer's mental logs, show signs of hush-ups at a major aerospace firm—hundreds of passenger planes at risk.

A final urgent alert drew Nicolás Tosh's attention sharply toward a screen displaying troubling revelations from within the aviation industry. An extensive series of mental logs recorded by a junior aerospace engineer had surfaced through CDA analytics, each entry meticulously documenting critical design flaws that had been deliberately suppressed by senior corporate executives. These flaws posed imminent dangers to hundreds of commercial airplanes—endangering thousands of unsuspecting passengers with every flight.

As Tosh reviewed the chilling details, he felt a surge of quiet anger. Corporate negligence at this scale, driven by profit margins and internal politics, was intolerable. The CDA system, with its unparalleled ability to infiltrate the deepest layers of corporate secrecy, had provided unequivocal proof of intentional deceit and reckless disregard for human life.

Swiftly, Tosh authorized the secure transmission of an anonymous, rigorously compiled dossier directly to aviation safety authorities. Encoded to maintain absolute anonymity, the intelligence would trigger immediate regulatory scrutiny and rigorous investigations, compelling the aerospace giant to rectify the dangerous design flaws without ever revealing the covert methods behind the discovery.

Watching the encrypted reports leave his system, Tosh reflected briefly on the sheer enormity of the responsibility he wielded. CDA's silent yet powerful intervention could save thousands from unseen catastrophes, yet he remained continually aware of the fine ethical line he traversed daily, balancing secrecy with the necessity of decisive action.

The Weight of Responsibility

For Nicolás Tosh, each alert that streamed relentlessly across his monitors represented more than just intelligence data; it embodied a profound ethical burden. The ceaseless cascade of hidden tragedies illuminated by Zermatt's vigilant CDA technology carried with it an overwhelming sense of moral obligation. He often grappled silently with the unsettling questions that haunted him: Who drew the fine line between necessary secrecy and essential transparency? Where was the balance between delivering justice and risking intrusive overreach? Could any single technological entity, however powerful and advanced, responsibly shoulder the immense ethical weight of revealing humanity's darkest secrets?

A soft, persistent beep from his console gently disrupted Tosh's reflective moment, drawing him back into the pressing reality of his responsibilities. Ahead lay a critical debrief with Artemis Wang, Amara Leung, and Lingtao's influential board of directors. The carefully orchestrated unveiling had proceeded flawlessly, yet Tosh knew the true trials were only just beginning. Lingtao's ambitious philanthropic initiatives would inevitably draw heightened scrutiny from media and competitors alike.

Yet far more troubling was the sophisticated digital intrusion detected earlier by Rainer Sábato—an anonymous entity stealthily tracing Lingtao's intricate network. Despite the polished narrative of corporate rejuvenation presented to the world, Tosh felt an unsettling certainty growing within him: a potent and elusive threat lurked beneath the surface, patiently awaiting the perfect moment to strike.

Quiet Endings, No Such Thing

Nicolás Tosh stepped into the softly illuminated elevator, feeling a subtle shift beneath his feet as it began its descent toward the press floor. The muted hum was comforting, yet his mind remained sharply alert. Glancing back briefly at one of his surveillance monitors, he noticed Maggie Wu paused in a secluded corridor, engrossed in an urgent phone call. Though he couldn't discern her conversation, the intensity etched upon her brow spoke clearly enough. Determination gleamed unmistakably in her eyes.

She wouldn't easily let go of this thread, Tosh realized. Maggie Wu was a seasoned investigative journalist; a seeker whose instincts invariably steered her toward hidden truths. He felt a faint tightening in his chest—a mixture of respect for her persistence and anxiety over the complications her curiosity might soon unleash. The veil they had so carefully woven was delicate, easily frayed by determined scrutiny.

Half a world away, Tosh imagined an unknown presence monitoring quietly, invisible and patient. The subtle yet precise data incursion during the press conference was not coincidental; it awaited a slip, an opening— a vulnerability in Lingtao's meticulously crafted public persona. Tosh had little doubt that in the ensuing weeks, they would confront escalating challenges, rumors whispered in corporate corridors, calculated acts of sabotage, or even direct attempts at infiltration. Lingtao's façade of redemption was impressive but inherently fragile, susceptible to the precise strike of those who probed beneath the surface.

The calm that had cautiously settled after the upheaval caused by Algorithm-323 now showed signs of cracking, giving way to new dangers that threatened not only Lingtao but also the carefully guarded secrets linking Tosh, Zermatt, and certain high corridors of the White House.

Yet, for this fleeting moment, Lingtao's reinvented image shone brilliantly across global tech media. Stories of philanthropy, ethical responsibility, and transformative leadership created a narrative of redemption—glossy, compelling, and just vague enough to veil deeper complexities. Meanwhile, behind those luminous headlines, the Zermatt Data Center ceaselessly churned through oceans of unspoken truths— exposing global injustices, preempting tragedies, and swiftly constructing new layers of secrecy even as it dismantled others.

Stepping outside onto the bustling street, Tosh shielded his eyes against the bright, late-morning sunlight reflecting brilliantly off Lingtao's impressive steel-and-glass exterior. It seemed tranquil, inviting—a fresh start on a day that outwardly appeared ordinary.

But Nicolás Tosh understood the reality far too clearly. Beneath the polished surfaces, beneath the seamless public announcements and hopeful narratives, lay an intricate tangle of concealed conflicts and hidden dangers. Today marked not merely a beginning but the dawn of a complex new chapter—one fraught with risks and revelations the world had yet to imagine.

Chapter 2

The Zermatt Data Center Under Siege

Zermatt, Switzerland — The Data Center, 2017
Day 12, 8:00 A.M. CET)

A pale winter sun struggled to penetrate the thick alpine haze, its weak rays dissolving into shadows by the time they reached the hidden fortress beneath the snow-covered Swiss Alps. The subterranean corridors of the Zermatt Data Center buzzed softly, the rhythmic hum of quantum servers underscoring a rising tide of quiet anxiety. In the facility's central command room, tense murmurs threaded between technicians hunched over glowing screens, each flicker revealing glimpses of potential catastrophe.

Unauthorized "Pings" and New Threats

At the head of the polished mahogany table, Nicolás Tosh watched the unfolding data streams with practiced calmness, though a flutter of apprehension stirred imperceptibly with each flash of red on the main display. Beside him, Rainer Sábato furrowed his brow, swiftly navigating through complex digital readouts detailing unauthorized neural network intrusions.

"We have at least six distinct intrusion vectors, Nicolás," Rainer reported, his voice taut with strain. "These attacks are different—they're routed through compromised quantum nodes in Singapore, Amsterdam, maybe even Saint Petersburg. Every attempt we make to pinpoint a single origin only leads us deeper into a maze."

Tosh's unwavering gaze fixed on the spinning globe projection at the center of the expansive screen, watching red lines flicker in rapid succession-like veins of a troubled pulse. He leaned slightly forward, his fingers steepled beneath his chin, a subtle signal to the staff of escalating tension.

"Any recognizable patterns yet, Rainer?" Tosh asked quietly, trying to mask the apprehension tightening his chest.

"They're specifically targeting CDA's handshake protocols, attempting to mimic the encryption signature," Rainer explained, frustration creeping into his measured tone. "But these are rushed, experimental efforts. It's almost as if someone is desperately throwing advanced quantum techniques at us, hoping by sheer persistence they'll crack the inner workings."

Rainer hesitated momentarily, recalling the prototype tests he'd secretly reviewed. The thought sent a shiver down his spine. If these intruders knew about CDA-325, they wouldn't stop until they found it.

The room fell abruptly silent, the weight of his words settling like a tangible presence. Since the near-catastrophe the previous year, Zermatt had painstakingly enhanced its defenses—layers upon layers of cryptographic fortification, each intended to ensure absolute security. Yet, these new infiltrations hinted at unprecedented sophistication and dangerous determination, unlike anything they had faced before.

Tosh felt an icy knot tighten in his stomach. He recognized the telltale signs of an adversary driven by more than mere curiosity or financial gain. Whoever orchestrated these intrusions carried ambitions far darker, far more personal, and potentially catastrophic if left unchecked. The siege had begun, and Zermatt's carefully maintained illusion of invulnerability was now being tested in earnest.

Core Team Discussion

Around the polished mahogany table sat an elite assembly of the Experta Foundation's core team, each individual selected for their exceptional expertise: ethical scholars dedicated to responsible tech governance, renowned mathematicians with specialties in quantum algorithms, and cybersecurity strategists versed in anticipating threats before they surfaced.

Dr. Miriam Faber, the Foundation's newly recruited quantum encryption expert, rhythmically tapped her pen against the crisp file of code analysis in front of her. Her usually calm demeanor was tinged with an urgency that tightened her voice.

"This isn't trivial," she stated firmly, eyes scanning the tense faces.

"Whoever's behind this has formidable resources and no fear of using them. Privately, Miriam felt a shiver of apprehension ripple through her. She'd spent years theorizing these quantum vulnerabilities but seeing them weaponized so relentlessly was profoundly unsettling—making her question how prepared they truly were. "Whoever orchestrated these intrusions commands extraordinary computational resources and clearly isn't shy about deploying them."

Nicolás Tosh folded his arms across his chest, leaning back thoughtfully, the weight of potential consequences visibly etched into his expression. "We can't risk underestimating this threat. Even a partial compromise of our neural network would allow them to replicate or distort the CDA's core functionalities. Imagine the chaos if they gain that kind of leverage."

At Tosh's side, Rainer Sábato pivoted swiftly toward another console. Lines of code and digital maps cascaded down the screen as he examined a detailed list of system vulnerabilities. His brows knitted tightly.

"If we presume, they're nearing a successful breach of our handshake protocols," Rainer said gravely, "the safest course might be an immediate re-keying of our entire satellite network and node servers. But understand—doing so would effectively disable nearly half of Zermatt's global surveillance for several critical hours."

A heavy silence blanketed the room. Dr. Faber visibly winced at the implication, tension tightening her jawline. "That blackout window presents enormous operational risks. Real-time infiltrations—monitoring cartel activity, tracking corrupt officials, running covert anti-corruption stings—would immediately notice the sudden absence of our intelligence feed. We could lose months, maybe even years, of careful planning."

Privately, Dr. Faber wondered if their work had moved beyond ethical boundaries entirely—if the very innovations designed to protect humanity now posed its greatest threat.

A subtle yet unmistakable beep from Tosh's personal console interrupted the discussion, a stark reminder of the immediate human stakes involved. His screen flashed urgently, flagged with an alert labeled, "Child Trafficking Operation – Mainland Southeast Asia." The neural network had just pinpointed crucial figures assembling at a border checkpoint, poised at a decisive moment. Tosh's pulse quickened as he recognized the grave consequences: if Zermatt chose to shut down its network now, vital, potentially lifesaving intelligence could vanish into the shadows.

Moral Tensions: A Police-State Approach?

At the far end of the table, Marisol Alvarez quietly studied the internal memos that had just arrived from Washington, D.C. Her fingers traced the edges of her tablet, betraying a faint tremble. Clearing her throat gently, she finally spoke up.

"We've just received fresh requests from the U.S. administration," she said, her voice deliberately steady but edged with concern. "They're demanding another dramatic expansion of their 'compulsory checks'— the full-life memory scans for federal appointees."

Her announcement sent a ripple of tension through the assembled team. Dr. Miriam Faber placed her pen down carefully, her expression wary.

"Is that even permissible under international law—the G-7 protocols, for instance?" Dr. Faber asked, her gaze locking momentarily with Marisol's.

Marisol let out a measured sigh. "They're invoking national security again. This new mandate targets top-tier officials, but now also mid-level bureaucrats within defense, homeland security, and critical contracting firms. No oversight, no judicial warrants—just an unchecked authorization to employ CDA scans."

Marisol fought to suppress a wave of anger and unease. This creeping expansion of authority wasn't just bureaucratic overreach—it felt increasingly like complicity in something darker, something that blurred ethical lines she'd always sworn never to cross.

A chill spread through the room. Nicolás Tosh, usually composed and contemplative, felt a rising tide of frustration. His jaw tightened, betraying rare but controlled anger. "They're cornering us. If we keep ceding ground, the CDA technology becomes nothing more than a political weapon, an open-ended authorization for fishing expeditions. We're teetering dangerously close to endorsing a police-state apparatus."

Across from Tosh, Rainer Sábato exchanged a weighted glance with him. His voice was low, measured, yet carried an unmistakable gravity. "It's just a matter of time before someone demands we scan entire demographics—or entire populations."

Silence fell heavily across the room, charged with an unspoken dread. Each person present felt the ghost of Algorithm-323 looming in their minds—a potent reminder of how quickly unchecked authority could transform technology from protector into oppressor.

Foreshadowing: CDA-325 on the Horizon

Breaking the tense silence, Dr. Miriam Faber inclined her head toward a schematic quietly illuminating a secondary monitor. The lines and nodes were labeled ominously as "CDA-325."

Rainer cleared his throat, his voice edged with caution. "I've seen preliminary tests. Even in simulation, the implantation effects were... disturbingly effective. People couldn't distinguish between real and fabricated memories. Imagine the implications if that fell into hostile hands."

"We haven't openly addressed this yet," she began cautiously, her voice tinged with apprehension, "but everyone here has heard the whispers. We're no longer just discussing technology capable of reading the human mind. We're talking about an algorithm powerful enough to implant memories and data into it."

A shadow of unease briefly crossed Dr. Faber's normally controlled expression. Internally, doubts whispered persistently—had she underestimated the moral weight of the technology she'd once proudly pioneered?

Nicolás Tosh slowly exhaled, as though absorbing the weight of her words physically. His expression tightened, cautious yet firm. "We validated its theoretical feasibility," he said slowly, measuring each word. "But we placed strict controls on its use—even testing remains unauthorized. We've agreed the implications were too severe, the ethical lines far too blurred."

As the conversation lingered on CDA-325, Tosh's felt a sharp stab of anxiety, driven by a visceral understanding that they stood precariously at the brink. One wrong step now could redefine their entire legacy—transforming protectors into the very manipulators they opposed.

Marisol Alvarez shifted uneasily, her gaze darting toward the intricate strands of code displayed on-screen. Her voice dropped almost to a whisper, heavy with genuine dread. "If a hostile foreign power or rogue element within our own government discovered CDA-325, the fallout would be catastrophic. We'd be looking at a new and terrifying arms race—one fought entirely within the human psyche. This can never be allowed to surface."

Marisol felt a tightness coil around her chest, an instinctual protest against the rising tide of demands threatening to drown their careful ethical safeguards.

Unable to remain seated, Rainer Sábato stood abruptly and began pacing beside the curved glass wall that overlooked the vast quantum server room. Each server emitted a faint glow, their collective hum an unsettling backdrop. He stopped, turning sharply toward the group. "But the infiltration attempts we're facing now pose a direct risk. If intruders dig deep enough, they could stumble upon fragments of CDA-325's framework. Remember, it resides within the same repositories as CDA-323."

Rainer's jaw tightened imperceptibly; the surge of tension subtly mirrored in the quickening rhythm of his keystrokes as the infiltration attempts pressed ever closer.

Rainer glanced at Tosh, briefly considering how much their mission had changed since their idealistic beginnings. Were they still protectors, or had they unwittingly become gatekeepers of an even greater threat?

The full gravity of the scenario settled over the team. A tense silence filled the room as each contemplated the nightmare scenario: even a fragment of CDA-325 in unauthorized hands would not merely uncover hidden truths—it could rewrite realities entirely, embedding lies as deeply and convincingly as memory itself.

Parallel Threads: Continuing Global Operations
Human Trafficking & Child Exploitation

On the expansive monitor array, an urgent notification flashed vividly, demanding immediate attention. Nicolás Tosh leaned forward, his eyes narrowing as he read the intelligence summary:

"Significant increase detected in encrypted communications near a previously dormant clandestine harbor. A newly identified cartel contact, code-named 'Marlin,' may possess critical intelligence on a transnational child trafficking ring."

A hush descended over the command center as Marisol Alvarez quickly cross-checked details on her tablet. "Marlin is a new player, not someone we've encountered before. The sudden spike in messages indicates something big—potentially a major shipment of trafficked children. We have a limited window to intercept."

Dr. Miriam glanced at the live data streams, her voice tinged with urgency. "If we initiate a security shutdown for re-keying our systems now, we'll blind ourselves temporarily. The traffickers could relocate or disappear entirely before we regain visibility."

Tosh felt the weight of their predicament keenly. Every moment lost was a life potentially ruined. He scanned the faces around the table, sensing their collective tension. "Can we divert a satellite cluster specifically to this operation? Maintain minimal operational visibility without compromising the entire network?"

Rainer Sábato shook his head, frustration evident. "That might buy us a little bandwidth, but it's risky. If the infiltrators are as sophisticated as we suspect, they'll notice any irregularities immediately and exploit the vulnerabilities."

Marisol intervened quietly, her tone resolute. "Yet the cost of inaction is higher. Losing Marlin's trail now could set back months of investigative groundwork and allow hundreds more victims to slip through our fingers."

A moment of tense silence stretched out before Tosh finally spoke, his voice decisive. "Allocate whatever minimal bandwidth we can safely spare to keep eyes on Marlin's operation. Monitor communications passively—no active interference yet. If the traffickers attempt to move, we'll coordinate immediate action with local enforcement and humanitarian teams on standby."

As Tosh authorized the phased re-keying, a flicker of uncertainty touched the edges of his thoughts. The strategy was sound, yet even a momentary blind spot in their surveillance network filled him with quiet dread.

As the team sprang into motion, Tosh's eyes lingered on the flashing red alerts. The delicate balance they maintained was becoming increasingly precarious—every decision carried enormous stakes. The burden of leadership had never felt heavier, but the mission remained clear and uncompromising: protect the vulnerable at all costs.

Corruption at State Levels

In the heart of a modest European capital, nestled among historic buildings and cobblestone streets, an insidious crisis was unfolding behind the opulent facade of governmental authority. Detailed intelligence reports gathered by Zermatt's CDA analytics painted a bleak portrait of systemic corruption permeating every level of the government hierarchy.

Top officials—once respected public servants—had quietly embezzled staggering amounts from public coffers, jeopardizing critical social programs, infrastructure improvements, and essential services. Evidence meticulously compiled by CDA analytics showed shadowy transfers through offshore banks, encrypted communications with complicit corporate entities, and covert meetings in luxury hotels far from prying eyes.

Now, government insiders, recognizing the inevitability of exposure, had secretly reached out to Zermatt, seeking discreet channels similar to those employed by the United States to broker hush deals during the Algorithm-323 scandal. Each insider was driven by a tangled mix of guilt, fear, and desperation, aware that public outrage and prosecution loomed dangerously near.

Local informants—brave individuals risking personal safety—awaited instructions, poised to act on Zermatt's guidance. Their courage was a thin, fragile line separating rampant corruption from public justice. Yet, any disruption in Zermatt's surveillance or data transmission capabilities, such as the looming necessity to re-key neural network nodes, threatened to sever these critical intelligence pathways. Without immediate and continuous data support, carefully cultivated leads could quickly dissipate, allowing implicated officials to evade justice and bury the truth once again.

Nicolás Tosh, absorbing this sobering reality from his secure vantage point, felt the enormity of the decision resting heavily upon him. Exposing the scandal publicly would spark chaos but might restore integrity. Conversely, quiet negotiations could preserve temporary stability yet risk reinforcing cycles of corruption. Tosh knew each choice carried profound implications, testing the ethical foundation of Zermatt's global operations and his own resolve.

Tosh felt a surge of weary resignation. Corruption was an old enemy, familiar yet endlessly persistent. Each victory felt partial, each defeat personal.

Faulty Technology & Public Safety

At the heart of Zermatt's bustling command center, an urgent notification blinked insistently, drawing Nicolás Tosh's sharp attention. It detailed a rapidly escalating crisis involving a major European automotive plant. Recent CDA analytics had detected disturbing irregularities—a troubling breakdown in quality control standards around critical brake components.

Tosh absorbed the details swiftly, his pulse quickening slightly as the scale of the potential disaster became clear. Thousands of vehicles had already been shipped to dealerships across the continent, poised to enter the lives of countless families. Each one now represented a ticking time bomb, their compromised braking systems threatening catastrophic failure.

Dr. Miriam Faber, seated nearby, quickly skimmed the same report, her expression darkening with concern. "This is more than just corporate negligence," she said urgently, turning toward Tosh. "We're looking at a potential mass-casualty event if these cars hit the roads unchecked."

Tosh exhaled slowly, feeling the heavy weight of responsibility pressing firmly on his shoulders. "Do we have a secure communication channel established with regulatory authorities?"

Marisol Alvarez swiftly interjected, her fingers tapping rapidly on her tablet. "Yes, but they're typically slow-moving bureaucracies. Convincing them of the urgency without compromising our CDA capabilities will be challenging."

Rainer Sabato spoke up, his voice calm yet firm. "We could anonymously tip off trusted investigative journalists. A public exposé might trigger an immediate recall, bypassing bureaucratic delays."

Tosh nodded slowly, recognizing the precarious balance they needed to maintain—ensuring public safety without exposing the powerful tool that had revealed the danger. He felt a subtle tremor in his fingertips, an involuntary reaction he quickly suppressed, determined not to betray even a hint of the pressure mounting beneath his composed exterior.

For a brief, unsettling moment, Tosh visualized families unaware of the danger lurking in their everyday commute. The vivid image hardened his resolve—inaction was not an option.

"Initiate both actions," Tosh instructed decisively. "Quietly reach out to regulators and simultaneously leak a credible, carefully sanitized dossier to the media. We need to trigger immediate preventive measures without revealing the source."

Around the room, the team moved swiftly to enact his orders, the tense hum of activity masking deeper fears beneath. As they worked, Tosh stared briefly at the monitor, the blinking notification serving as a grim reminder of their immense power and the moral complexity that accompanied it.

Corporate Sabotage & Competitor Intrusions

Tosh's attention shifted to another alert blinking insistently on the Zermatt Data Center's central display, highlighting an escalating surge of covert cyber activities directed toward Lingtao. Rival tech giants had noticeably intensified their espionage campaigns, seemingly obsessed with uncovering the elusive formula behind Lingtao's remarkable revival and its rapidly expanding philanthropic endeavors.

Detailed intelligence analyses revealed that some of these corporate adversaries were not merely competitors but had concerning links to the sophisticated quantum infiltration attempts currently probing Zermatt's own secure networks. Tosh scrutinized the information carefully; these rivals were deploying an array of advanced intrusion methods, from subtle data phishing and insider threats to outright quantum breaches. Each attempt revealed a deeper layer of strategic coordination, suggesting that Lingtao's corporate resurgence was perceived as a substantial threat to established global technology players.

On his console, Rainer's face appeared, brows knitted in deep concern. "Nicolás, their methods are evolving. We've identified signatures consistent with state-level backing. It seems these tech giants aren't just competing—they may be fronting broader geopolitical ambitions. If they breach our philanthropic database, it won't just compromise Lingtao's market position; it could reveal the deeper operational secrets connecting Lingtao to Experta and Zermatt itself."

Tosh's jaw tightened imperceptibly. This was more than corporate rivalry—it was a deliberate, orchestrated campaign potentially designed to unravel the carefully constructed veil of secrecy around their global operations. He leaned forward, fingers hovering above his keyboard, carefully calculating the next move.

"We need to harden Lingtao's external interfaces immediately," Tosh directed calmly. "Double-check all personnel clearances, run deeper background checks on recent hires, and prepare contingency protocols for rapid isolation of our sensitive data. Whoever is behind this isn't just after trade secrets—they want leverage."

Rainer acknowledged the orders with a firm nod. As Tosh watched the intelligence streams shift to defensive actions, he pondered the broader implications. Lingtao's charitable façade and Zermatt's covert operations had always walked a delicate line. Now, it appeared their adversaries weren't merely testing corporate resilience; they were probing for vulnerabilities that could expose the foundation's hidden agendas. The stakes had never been higher, and Tosh knew every decision he made now would echo profoundly in the unseen battles yet to come.

Maggie Wu's Investigation

A discrete alert illuminated Nicolás Tosh's screen, drawing his immediate attention. Maggie Wu, the persistent and renowned tech journalist known for unearthing deeply buried industry secrets, had surfaced again. Intelligence flagged her recent booking—a flight bound for Zurich, Switzerland. Tosh felt an involuntary tightening in his chest. Her investigative skills were legendary; her tenacity unmatched.

On the monitor, a detailed dossier expanded, filled with meticulous records of her inquiries into Lingtao's data management policies and rumored links to a discreet facility hidden in the Swiss Alps. The hush-hush Swiss location could only refer to Zermatt, a connection that had to remain hidden at all costs.

Tosh exchanged a tense glance with Marisol Alvarez. "Wu isn't chasing random leads," he said gravely. "She's sensed the deeper story." Marisol scrolled through Wu's past articles, each headline a testament to her ability to piece together complex, concealed truths from seemingly innocuous clues. "If she ties Lingtao directly to Zermatt, we'll have global attention aimed right at us" she warned.

Marisol typed rapidly on her tablet. "This is a perfect storm—any re-keying or partial shutdown will hamper every one of these ops. But if we don't act, the infiltration could get worse."

Rainer, standing by the glass overlooking the data servers, turned sharply. "Monitor her discreetly. If she uncovers tangible evidence…" He didn't finish the thought, but everyone understood. Maggie Wu's discovery could unravel years of painstaking secrecy, exposing their covert surveillance operations to a public already wary of technology's pervasive reach.

Tosh's decision was immediate, underscored by urgency. "Deploy a specialized team," he instructed firmly. "Not to stop her—just to ensure we know exactly what she sees, who she meets, and what she uncovers."

A quiet ripple of guilt stirred within Tosh; surveillance, even in the name of protection, felt uncomfortably close to the intrusion they fought tirelessly to prevent. Yet the alternative—exposure—was unthinkable.

The room fell into a contemplative silence, each member recognizing the precarious nature of their position. Maggie Wu's investigation had elevated from a curiosity to a potential existential threat.

A Precarious Choice

Tosh remained silent for a brief moment, allowing the swirling array of threats converging upon the data center to settle in his mind. Then, decisively, he tapped the control panel, freezing the rolling infiltration map.

"Rainer, Dr. Faber—begin immediate re-coding of selected core nodes," Tosh directed calmly. "Do it in rolling phases—quantum nodes first, keep primary channels open. We can't afford downtime in the middle of these infiltrations. Our exposure must remain minimal."

He shifted his focus swiftly to Marisol. "Prepare an official response to the White House's latest requests. Firmly remind them that we adhere strictly to G-7 oversight protocols. I'll personally manage direct inquiries from the President or any emerging presidential candidates—but our formal stance needs to be unmistakably clear and on record."

Marisol acknowledged with a nod, her expression serious. "Should we reference CDA-325 explicitly?"

Tosh's jaw tightened noticeably. His voice carried a definitive edge. "Absolutely not. CDA-325 remains strictly off-limits in all communications. We cannot afford to fuel further demands—or curiosity."

Tosh felt a chill, recalling the hushed conversations he'd once overheard between the algorithm's creators—brilliant minds who later abandoned the project, shaken by their own creation. CDA-325 wasn't just dangerous; it bordered on playing god.

A tense silence settled over the room, underscoring the precarious balance of secrecy, ethics, and power they now navigated.

Under Siege, Yet Standing Firm

As the meeting dispersed, each team member returned to their station, burdened by the countless critical tasks entrusted to them. Outside the glass walls, the Zermatt Data Center hummed steadily—an engine of immense potential shadowed by impending danger. At the room's threshold, Tosh paused, his gaze drawn back to the flickering lights of the infiltration map, a stark reminder of the battles waged in unseen corners of the globe.

In the quiet left behind by fading footsteps, the low, steady whir of the servers resonated like distant thunder, underscoring Zermatt's tenuous situation: besieged by invisible adversaries, pressured by allies who sought dominance, and constantly tested by ethical boundaries that blurred with every new crisis.

Yet, despite the relentless pressure, the fortress hidden beneath the Swiss Alps remained steadfast, held firm by discreet alliances and the unwavering commitment of its dedicated core. Beyond these secure halls, the tendrils of injustice—from ruthless traffickers to corrupt governments—continued to tighten their grip, challenging the center's resolve daily.

Above all, lingering quietly in the encrypted silence of its quantum heart, lay the dormant but formidable CDA-325—an algorithm of unimaginable power, awaiting either reckless ambition or desperate necessity to bring it irrevocably to life.

Chapter 3

Shifting Political Winds

Washington, D.C. – The White House 2017
Day 15, 9:00 A.M. ET

In the corridors leading to the West Wing, the atmosphere crackled with barely contained tension. Junior staff rushed about, binders clutched tightly, their expressions carefully neutral. Press secretaries murmured cautiously into phones, managing the delicate dance of information. Beneath this outward efficiency lay a palpable sense of anxiety, thick as fog—one wrong step could unravel careers, alliances, even administrations. The approaching presidential transition amplified these fears, particularly surrounding the classified CDA technology known only to an elite few.

The Lame-Duck Administration

Inside a wood-paneled conference room adjoining the Oval Office, President O'Sullivan took his seat at the head of the table. His posture remained impeccable, but fatigue shadowed his eyes, marking him as a leader worn by endless crises and internal battles. To his left, Chief of Staff Daniel Harrington sat poised, his expression revealing the strain of managing delicate political maneuvers.

"We have six months left," the President started, his tone steady but heavy with gravity. "It's critical we solidify our security protocols. We must ensure that our approach to CDA technology isn't overturned the moment the keys to the White House change hands."

As President O'Sullivan spoke, Daniel Harrington glanced down at the polished table, recalling confidential briefings that hinted CDA's reach went beyond merely detecting corruption. He shivered inwardly at the thought—there were capabilities buried deeper, tools that had not yet been tested, much less disclosed.

President O'Sullivan's gaze briefly rested on a framed photo on the corner of his desk—his family smiling at him from better, simpler days. A fleeting pang of sorrow tightened his chest. Every decision he made now echoed beyond the White House, rippling into lives he'd never meet, shaping futures he couldn't predict. The weight felt heavier with every passing hour.

Harrington leaned back slightly, briefly closing his eyes. The quiet dread he'd felt over recent months seemed to crystallize now, settling heavily within him—a haunting awareness of responsibility, intertwined with the stark uncertainty of what lay ahead.

A hesitant quiet filled the room as advisors exchanged careful glances. Harrington cleared his throat, gently breaking the silence. "Mr. President, Senator Redwood—the leading candidate—has been vocal about his 'Truth at Any Cost' policy. He believes transparency outweighs our existing security measures."

President O'Sullivan exhaled slowly, a rare show of vulnerability slipping through his typically polished façade. "Transparency at any cost is compelling rhetoric," he admitted, "but dangerously naïve. Unchecked access to CDA means risking exploitation on an unprecedented scale."

Beside Harrington, security advisor Eleanor Drake leaned forward, her voice edged with quiet urgency. "Senator Redwood's team reached out again. They're pushing harder for pre-transition briefings, particularly around CDA's operational parameters. They seem to suspect we're hiding something significant."

Drake glanced nervously at her tablet, aware that Redwood's inquiries had grown more pointed over the past week—questions about CDA's ability to identify covert operatives abroad, to decode encrypted financial trails, even to penetrate the private communications of opposition parties. Each new question hinted ominously at the senator's broader ambitions.

Eleanor Drake adjusted her notes slowly, her expression shadowed with unease. She had joined the administration believing transparency would empower democracy. But hearing Redwood's relentless promise of "Truth at Any Cost," she wondered darkly if some truths were better kept carefully hidden—for the sake of stability, even safety.

"The problem," Harrington murmured, eyes briefly distant, "is we still don't fully understand the ultimate scope of CDA. Its architects hinted at layers beyond simple surveillance—capabilities none of us were ever meant to see."

The President glanced toward the table's far end, where political strategist Carl Bennett sat silently observing. "Carl, your read on Redwood's intentions?"

Carl Bennett's fingers intertwined, subtly betraying his internal turmoil. "Redwood isn't just posturing—he's committed. He genuinely believes that exposing corruption and misuse of power outweighs potential risks. If we deny his team access, we risk accusations of obstruction. If we comply fully, we lose control of CDA oversight entirely."

Carl Bennett hesitated, briefly allowing himself to imagine the consequences if Redwood's vision of transparency became reality. His gut tightened; transparency was laudable—but unchecked, it would empower populists who misunderstood the catastrophic potential of what lay beneath the Swiss Alps. "He's sincere," Carl quietly continued, more to himself than the room, "but sincerity doesn't erase risk."

Privately, Bennett wrestled with persistent doubts. He had glimpsed classified summaries that hinted at CDA's unspoken potential—subtle references to capabilities beyond memory scans, things labeled cryptically as "theoretical extensions." What if transparency spiraled out of control, he wondered—what deeper Pandora's box could they inadvertently open?

An uncomfortable quiet settled again, punctuated by soft shuffling of papers and stifled coughs. The President's jaw tightened almost imperceptibly. He knew the choice was stark: maintain a tightly guarded secrecy at the risk of political fallout, or open doors to CDA technology and unleash unpredictable consequences.

Harrington's voice cut through the tension, steady but laced with frustration. "We have allies on the Hill who understand the stakes. Maybe it's time we reinforce their influence—quietly, of course."

Daniel Harrington felt a twinge of guilt beneath his stern resolve. These covert manipulations went against his instinctive belief in democracy's openness, yet the alternative—allowing uncontrolled access to CDA—was far worse. He steeled himself; moral discomfort was a small price for stability.

The President nodded slowly. "Quietly. We must be subtle yet decisive. CDA isn't a tool for political agendas—it's the most powerful surveillance mechanism ever created. In the wrong hands, it could destroy more than it protects."

As Harrington nodded, he felt a troubling thought resurface—unclassified briefings had hinted CDA was still evolving, its true limits unknown even to senior administration officials. Was O'Sullivan aware of how deep this rabbit hole went, he wondered grimly, or was the President himself being kept partially in the dark?

Bennett leaned back slightly, allowing a small sigh to escape. "Then we prepare for a fight—one that may redefine transparency, privacy, and national security for generations."

President O'Sullivan's eyes met each of theirs in turn, the weight of impending decisions clearly visible. "Precisely," he concluded, rising deliberately from his chair. "But we must ensure it's a fight we can win."

As the meeting adjourned and advisors scattered quietly into hallways and offices, Harrington lingered briefly, catching the President's gaze.

"Sir," Harrington said, his voice low yet resolute, "no matter what happens, we must control the narrative. If Redwood gets even a hint of the full power beneath Zermatt, transparency won't be the result—chaos will."

President O'Sullivan paused at the doorway, his expression grimly reflective. "Agreed, Daniel. The line we're walking is thin and becoming thinner by the day."

With that quiet acknowledgment, he stepped back into the corridors of power, aware more than ever of the precarious balance he needed to maintain in these shifting political winds.

Parallel Threads Continued: Maintaining the Global Vigilance
Human Trafficking & Child Exploitation

At Zermatt's command center, Nicolás Tosh watched intently as Marisol Alvarez updated the tracking log for 'Marlin,' the elusive cartel figure whose activities hinted at a disturbing spike in child trafficking. On-screen, subtle shifts in geolocation data suggested imminent movement.

"Marlin's operational tempo is increasing," Marisol noted urgently.

"Encrypted messages indicate they're preparing to move the children. Possibly within the next 48 hours."

Tosh felt his stomach tighten. Each movement signaled a life potentially slipping from their grasp, vanishing into darkness. "Coordinate closely with local enforcement," he instructed firmly. "Let's activate humanitarian rescue teams on standby. If Marlin moves, we intercept immediately—minimal delay, maximum discretion."

Dr. Miriam Faber, quietly absorbing the exchange, felt a personal pang. The mathematical certainty she relied upon now intersected brutally with human vulnerability. Internally, she reaffirmed her resolve: technology must serve humanity, never overshadow it.

Rainer Sábato approached Tosh quietly. "We should reposition one of our surveillance drones to get real-time visual coverage on Marlin's exact location. Passive monitoring won't be enough when the action starts."

Tosh nodded. "Do it. And tell our contacts on the ground to stay alert but inconspicuous. Any hint of intervention too early, and these traffickers will vanish."

As Rainer began issuing instructions through the secure line, Tosh's gaze returned to the pulsing red dots tracking Marlin's network. The weight of their responsibility pressed heavily on him. Lives hung in precarious balance—every second counted, every decision pivotal.

In a quiet corner, Dr. Faber initiated an emergency protocol, diverting quantum processing power to reinforce tracking fidelity. The clarity of purpose steadied her trembling fingers. Every calculated move Zermatt made was designed to rescue innocence, each step a beacon pushing back against darkness.

Corruption at State Levels

On another feed, Dr. Faber's algorithms illuminated fresh intelligence streams flowing from the compromised European nation, each new detail amplifying the severity of systemic corruption entrenched within the government. Local informants, their courage precariously balanced against imminent danger, anxiously awaited Zermatt's decisive instructions. They stood ready to expose corrupt officials, yet every passing minute deepened their fears of discovery and brutal reprisals.

Marisol Alvarez reviewed the rapidly updating situation reports, her voice tightening with urgency. "Our window here is closing quickly," she warned. "The informants are getting jittery—it's understandable. If we delay much longer, they'll either flee or be permanently silenced."

Tosh, seated at the command table, exhaled slowly, feeling the heavy pressure of imminent consequence pressing down on him. Each choice represented lives either risked or saved, reputations shattered or salvaged. "Authorize carefully controlled leaks," he decided, voice resolute. "Use trusted international watchdog organizations to expose the financial trails first. Make sure our informants' identities remain shielded. We must control this exposure precisely—too sudden and we risk chaos, too slow and justice slips away."

Rainer Sábato hesitated momentarily, a rare shadow of doubt flickering across his normally composed features. Each revelation they facilitated had the potential to spark political upheaval and civil unrest—yet withholding the truth guaranteed the survival of a corrupt status quo. His internal conflict was brief but intense, reflecting the ethical complexity underlying their operations.

"I'll start coordination immediately," Rainer confirmed, his expression firming decisively as he began typing rapid instructions to his security team. He knew well the delicate balance required, mindful that each step forward tread carefully along the thin line between liberation and turmoil.

As the strategic measures unfolded, Tosh allowed himself a brief internal acknowledgment of the monumental stakes at play. Every move Zermatt made reverberated globally, yet for now, justice and integrity demanded swift, decisive action.

Faulty Technology & Public Safety

Simultaneously, in the softly lit command room at Zermatt, Nicolás Tosh observed as incoming reports from the communications team confirmed the successful dissemination of their covert dossier. Investigative journalists had acted swiftly, breaking headlines across Europe with a stark urgency that could not be ignored. Regulatory authorities, typically sluggish under bureaucratic inertia, were forced into immediate action.

Dr. Miriam Faber approached Tosh, relief mingled with lingering anxiety in her voice. "The recall has been officially mandated. They're pulling thousands of potentially faulty vehicles from dealerships as we speak."

Tosh briefly closed his eyes, allowing a wave of muted relief to settle over him. It was a rare victory amidst an ocean of continuous threats. His momentary solace was tempered by a familiar sense of caution; the fragile balance between leveraging CDA's power and maintaining absolute secrecy was one they could never afford to underestimate.

Marisol Alvarez stepped closer, quietly reflecting aloud, "We intervened in time—this could have ended tragically." Her words were steady, yet beneath the calm facade, she grappled with the weight of their responsibilities. Every life saved was a profound validation of their efforts, but each victory reminded her just how thinly they were stretched, how vulnerable they remained to the next crisis.

Rainer Sábato watched the unfolding updates on his console, the illuminated data streams reflecting off his glasses. "The press is crediting anonymous whistleblowers," he noted carefully, exchanging a meaningful glance with Tosh. "So far, our cover remains intact. But we need to stay vigilant—this won't go unnoticed by everyone."

Tosh nodded slowly, his expression hardening with renewed determination. "Then we continue carefully. Lives have been saved today, but tomorrow will bring new challenges. Our vigilance can never waver."

Corporate Sabotage & Competitor Intrusions

However, celebrations remained brief. An urgent red alert flashed vividly across the central screen, indicating yet another aggressive intrusion attempt targeting Lingtao's secure philanthropic accounts. Rainer Sábato leaned forward urgently, eyes narrowing as lines of rapidly scrolling data reflected in his glasses.

"The attacks are escalating," he said tensely. "They've shifted focus—now they're directly probing our philanthropic financial channels. This isn't mere corporate espionage; they're systematically hunting for vulnerabilities."

Nicolás Tosh immediately grasped the gravity of the situation. These incursions were calculated and precise, clearly driven by entities that viewed Lingtao not merely as business rivals but as strategic threats.

"Reinforce our cyber perimeter immediately," Tosh ordered decisively.

"Deploy advanced quantum firewalls across all sensitive channels and run exhaustive audits to pinpoint internal vulnerabilities. Prioritize isolating any compromised sectors. We cannot permit breaches that risk exposing our deeper operational connections to Zermatt and Experta."

Across the table, Marisol Alvarez met Tosh's gaze, an unspoken acknowledgment passing silently between them. Both understood these were not ordinary corporate competitors; these attackers were state-backed or strategically aligned actors intent on undermining the humanitarian facade protecting Zermatt's covert operations.

Marisol spoke quietly but firmly. "I'll initiate additional background checks on personnel with access to our philanthropic database. We must assume they're trying to exploit an insider—either knowingly or unknowingly."

Tosh nodded sharply. "Good. Stay vigilant—if these adversaries unearth even a fraction of the truth, everything we've worked to build could unravel overnight."

A new notification briefly diverted Nicolás Tosh's attention—a detailed report generated by CDA analytics illuminated fresh and disturbing developments within the aviation manufacturing industry. Internal whistleblowers, courageously defying corporate silence, had discreetly logged escalating concerns about dangerously substandard aircraft components. These defective parts, produced under compromised oversight, were at imminent risk of integration into commercial airplane fleets worldwide, potentially jeopardizing countless lives.

Tosh's eyes narrowed as he swiftly absorbed the magnitude of the crisis unfolding before him. He felt an immediate surge of urgency. "Activate immediate anonymous disclosures," he instructed decisively, his voice steady yet edged with intensity. "Ensure aviation safety authorities receive comprehensive, irrefutable proof. Absolutely no delays."

Around the room, the Zermatt team sprang into rapid, coordinated motion, each staff member deeply aware of the critical importance of their tasks. Marisol Alvarez quickly routed carefully sanitized evidence to regulatory officials, while Dr. Miriam Faber verified the precision and reliability of data integrity. Rainer Sábato simultaneously initiated secure communications channels, making certain the information reached its destinations without compromise or interception.

As the operations center hummed with focused efficiency, Tosh allowed himself a brief, internal reflection on the moral complexity of his role. The unparalleled analytical power of CDA continually exposed hidden threats and prevented disasters. Yet, every successful intervention reinforced the precarious nature of their global mandate. Ethical lines were increasingly blurred, moral dilemmas more frequent, and the stakes soared ever higher.

Tosh knew that vigilance was non-negotiable. Far too many lives depended on the delicate balance they tirelessly maintained between secrecy and action.

Tosh glanced around the bustling command room, momentarily seeing past screens and data streams to the invisible lives they touched. Every small victory reinforced the immense burden of responsibility they carried. Yet doubt lingered at the edges of his certainty—could any one group, no matter how skilled or ethical, sustain such control without eventually falling prey to their own good intentions?

Senators Demand "CDAs for All"

Before anyone could respond, an aide wearing a discreet earpiece entered the conference room, his expression tightly controlled but urgent.

"Mr. President, we have a situation concerning certain members of the Senate Oversight Committee," he said quietly, eyes darting quickly across the assembled aides before focusing solely on President O'Sullivan. "They've threatened to—" His hesitation was palpable, clearly wary of the gravity his next words carried.

The President exhaled deeply, rubbing his temples briefly before meeting the aide's troubled gaze. "Just say it, Randall."

Randall swallowed noticeably. "They're threatening to blow the whistle on the Zermatt Data Center," he said, his voice lowering further, barely above a whisper. "They're demanding full, unrestricted access to CDA technology. They claim it's the only solution capable of rooting out deep-seated corruption within their committees."

A suffocating silence descended upon the room, pressing heavily upon every occupant. The revelations of Algorithm-323, once narrowly averted from public scandal, had been painstakingly concealed through a web of meticulously negotiated hush agreements. Now, a small yet influential faction within the Senate was aggressively pushing the slogan "CDAs for All," publicly framing their demands as an urgent ethical necessity. But privately, President O'Sullivan and his team understood the deeper implication. Beneath the veneer of righteous transparency lay a starkly political ambition—control, leverage, and power.

Carl Bennett shifted uneasily in his chair, a nagging memory surfacing. During the crisis of Algorithm-323, he'd overheard whispers about a hidden protocol, something labeled CDA-325—an extension even senior leadership hesitated to fully discuss. If that was the Senators' real target, their demands posed an even greater threat than imagined.

In the hushed pause after Randall delivered the senators' ultimatum, the aides exchanged nervous glances. Each person present silently calculated the fallout—careers destroyed, alliances shattered, and above all, the perilous ethical boundary they were being asked to cross. The silence deepened, acknowledging the vast unknown ahead.

Carl Bennett allowed himself a brief inward shudder. He'd glimpsed the classified reports outlining CDA's capabilities—abilities hinted at, but never openly discussed. The sheer scale of potential intrusion chilled him deeply; the Senators were playing with something far more dangerous than they realized.

Chief of Staff Harrington leaned forward, his knuckles whitening as he gripped the edge of the polished conference table. "We're moving far beyond anything we agreed with Tosh or committed to under G-7 oversight," he said firmly, his voice edged with frustration. "Handing out open access to the CDA technology was never supposed to be on the table. This isn't transparency—it's a weaponization of truth."

The President's gaze drifted slowly around the room, seeing anxiety mirrored in every face. Finally, he turned back to Randall, voice calm yet heavy with resignation. "Arrange a private call with Nicolás Tosh," he ordered quietly. "Tell him it's urgent—we need to decide how we're going to hold the line on this before the entire system becomes compromised."

Randall nodded sharply and quickly withdrew from the room, leaving behind an oppressive silence. Each aide recognized the moment for what it was: a turning point, perhaps the last chance to maintain control over the unprecedented power that rested beneath the Swiss Alps.

A Quiet Call to Tosh

Less than an hour later, a secure line patched discreetly from the Oval Office directly to Nicolás Tosh.

As Tosh's secure line signaled the incoming call from the White House, he momentarily closed his eyes. Behind his calm facade, a familiar dread stirred. Each call from Washington felt increasingly like a blade edging closer to a moral artery—any misstep, and his carefully balanced world could bleed out, taking innocent lives down with it. He answered on the second ring, his voice composed yet cautious.

"Mr. President," Tosh said, instantly sensing the weight behind the silence. "I take it this isn't merely a courtesy check-in."

The President's voice tightened, barely audible, burdened with the strain of escalating tensions. "We've got a coalition of Senators backing us into a corner, Nicolás. They're threatening to publicly expose Zermatt—demanding full CDA access. They're framing it as a moral imperative—insisting that comprehensive scans are essential to uprooting entrenched corruption once and for all."

Tosh paused, the gravity of the situation settling heavily upon him. He chose his words deliberately. "They're playing a dangerous game. The CDA isn't something we can casually hand over. If word gets out about the full capabilities—or worse, if we permit unrestricted political use— the consequences would ripple far beyond any internal power struggle. Global trust would collapse; chaos would be inevitable."

Tosh paused, a silent hesitation underscoring the gravity of his next words. For a brief instant, his mind flashed to archived blueprints locked behind Zermatt's highest security clearance—proposals from CDA-325's preliminary stages. Those experimental notes haunted him: the ability not only to expose the truth but subtly alter it. If Senators gained even a whisper of that power, the consequences could prove catastrophic.

The President sighed deeply, glancing toward Chief of Staff Harrington, who stood nearby, his posture signaling grave agreement. "I'm fully aware of the risks, Nicolás, but we can't simply dismiss their demands outright. They're prepared to leak details at a Senate press briefing. Once they do, Senator Redwood and his allies will weaponize it politically, portraying my administration as complicit in secret power-brokering. They'll brand you as an invisible puppet master. With Redwood's obsession over 'total transparency,' there's no predicting how aggressively he'll exploit the CDA once he assumes power."

As Harrington nodded, he felt a troubling thought resurface— unclassified briefings had hinted CDA was still evolving, its true limits unknown even to senior administration officials. Was O'Sullivan aware of how deep this rabbit hole went, he wondered grimly, or was the President himself being kept partially in the dark?

Tosh absorbed the President's words, feeling a chill tighten around his chest. "We need to hold the line firmly," he finally responded. "Compromise carefully, yes—but make no mistake, if this technology slips into unrestricted hands, the consequences won't merely be political—they'll be catastrophic."

"I understand, Nicolás," the President said softly, his voice tinged with weary resignation. "But prepare yourself. The storm we've anticipated might already be here."

Tosh stared quietly at the darkened monitor, an image briefly flickering through his mind—streets filled with protesters, government halls echoing accusations of tyranny, global trust collapsing overnight. If CDA's capabilities were fully revealed, he feared, the chaos would dwarf every scandal they'd weathered thus far.

Balancing the Demands

That evening, Nicolás Tosh convened a rapid teleconference from the Zermatt Data Center, connecting with Rainer Sábato, key members of Experta Foundation's legal counsel, and policy advisor Marisol Alvarez. Screens flickered to life in the high-security briefing room, capturing the tense expressions of each participant, illuminated by the muted glow of operational monitors.

"We either stall them with partial compliance," Tosh began carefully, his voice controlled but weary, "or brace ourselves for a political disaster if they follow through with their threat. Full compliance is not even on the table—it would dismantle every safeguard we've painstakingly constructed."

Rainer, speaking from the bustling heart of Zermatt's command center, appeared visibly concerned. His brow knitted tightly as he leaned closer to the camera. "We absolutely cannot grant them unrestricted access," he warned sharply. "We're already fending off infiltration attempts that test our limits daily. The moment we allow Senators to casually sift through the private thoughts of their political rivals, the backlash will be immediate and severe—and we'll become the convenient scapegoats."

Marisol Alvarez listened intently, her thoughtful expression illuminated by the soft reflection of her tablet screen. She leaned forward, interjecting calmly but with urgency. "Perhaps we could propose a strategic compromise—carefully controlled scans limited strictly to high-priority federal roles, aligned precisely with existing G-7 oversight. We must firmly reject any expansion into mid-level positions. This could help pacify the Senators temporarily, at least until Senator Redwood clarifies his intentions more openly."

Tosh considered this carefully, tapping his fingers rhythmically against the console. He allowed the silence to linger for a moment, each participant acutely aware of the precarious stakes involved. Finally, he nodded slowly, his voice resolute. "A temporary measure. We can offer this limited compromise to maintain control and prevent total exposure. But make no mistake—this is a stopgap. We're merely buying time, hoping that the shifting political landscape might give us clearer ground to stand on."

Rainer hesitated slightly, glancing briefly at the encrypted layers cascading across his monitor. "If we craft a restricted access system," he explained carefully, "we risk exposing fragments of CDA's deeper logic. Even minor revelations could allow savvy users to reverse-engineer our protective layers. Any oversight here isn't just a technical breach—it's an existential threat."

As the conference concluded, each screen darkened one by one, leaving Tosh alone in quiet contemplation. The decision weighed heavily on him, an uneasy reminder of the thin, ever-fragile line they walked between maintaining security and safeguarding democracy itself.

Heightened Stakes

The tension swirling through Washington was palpable, underscoring a deeper and more unsettling truth: the discreet era of controlled CDA usage was teetering precariously toward its end. Senator Redwood's populist campaign promise—to use CDA technology to eradicate corruption throughout the entire government—had captured public imagination, igniting debates and energizing voters who had little understanding of the profound implications. Meanwhile, within the

Senate, influential hawks quietly maneuvered behind closed doors, wielding subtle threats about Zermatt's capabilities to secure personal and partisan leverage.

President O'Sullivan's voice carried a heavy note of forewarning in a follow-up call with Nicolás Tosh. "If Redwood harnesses this momentum and reaches the presidency, he'll demand complete transparency. He won't tolerate secrets—not from day one."

Tosh remained silent for a moment, his eyes flickering briefly toward the encrypted monitors arrayed before him. Each screen silently illuminated ongoing operations—real-time updates on the child trafficking ring, cryptic warnings about defective aircraft parts threatening thousands, and Maggie Wu's relentless pursuit of truth as she neared Zurich. These urgent crises unfolded relentlessly, each demanding CDA's unique, powerful intervention.

Yet the implications of a Redwood presidency loomed larger than all these pressing emergencies. If Redwood took office intent on implementing universal scans, the delicate ethical boundaries Tosh and Rainer had painstakingly upheld would disintegrate overnight. The moral lines separating security from invasive surveillance would vanish, replaced by unchecked power in the hands of political opportunists.

"I understand," Tosh finally responded, his voice firm yet tinged with the gravity of the moment. "We'll hold the line as long as we possibly can. But you should prepare contingencies for a scenario where we either pull the plug entirely or take Zermatt fully underground. If Redwood or these Senators push too aggressively, the entire operation may need to vanish, at least from public view."

A solemn pause settled over the conversation, the President's acknowledgment resonating with reluctant acceptance. "We'll do what we must—prepare quietly for every contingency. But Nicolás, keep me informed if you discover any technical alternatives or solutions. This country needs your operation—but not at the cost of turning it into an irreversible tyranny."

Tosh ended the call, exhaling deeply as he sat back, allowing the full weight of the situation to settle around him. The stakes had never been higher; each decision now carried implications capable of reshaping not just Zermatt, but the fundamental structure of freedom itself.

Consulting Rainer on Technical Solutions

Late into the night, Tosh reconnected with Rainer via an encrypted data link. The glowing screen cast a pale blue hue, emphasizing the deep fatigue etched into Rainer's features. Managing the complex re-keying process at Zermatt amidst relentless infiltration attempts was clearly wearing him down.

"Do we have any feasible options," Tosh asked cautiously, "for coding a limited-access version of CDA that satisfies the Senate demands without revealing its true depth?"

Rainer sighed, rubbing his temples as if to ease the mental strain. "Technically, we could construct a restricted interface—a stripped-down, read-only version that displays only surface-level indicators of corruption. It might satisfy them temporarily, offering transparency without full insight. But it's incredibly risky. If any senator realizes they're seeing a filtered view, it could inflame their suspicions that we're intentionally obscuring deeper capabilities. That alone could drive them to expose everything out of sheer resentment."

The two men fell silent, each acutely aware of how rapidly negotiated compromises had escalated into crises during the chaotic resolution of Algorithm-323. Illusions of transparency rarely ended well.

Rainer hesitated slightly, glancing briefly at the encrypted layers cascading across his monitor. "If we craft a restricted access system," he explained carefully, "we risk exposing fragments of CDA's deeper logic. Even minor revelations could allow savvy users to reverse-engineer our protective layers. Any oversight here isn't just a technical breach—it's an existential threat."

Rainer paused, eyes momentarily lost in troubled thought. "We've been close to catastrophe before," he admitted softly, recalling vividly how narrowly they'd averted disaster during the initial crisis. "Creating even a partial, deceptive access point doesn't just risk exposure—it risks our moral standing. We'd be willingly blurring ethical lines we've promised never to cross."

Tosh exhaled, considering carefully. "We'll propose limited access under stringent G-7 oversight. It might grant us a few critical months. If not...we'll have to confront that situation when it arises."

Rainer nodded solemnly, the unspoken reality hanging between them: this delicate balance was their only option to prevent immediate exposure. Yet both knew the equilibrium they sought was fragile—one misstep could unravel everything they'd worked to protect.

After the encrypted connection closed, Rainer rubbed his temples, exhausted. Each line of code they manipulated, every subtle deception they embedded, carried risks beyond mere exposure. His thoughts drifted involuntarily toward the countless people dependent on Zermatt's protection—children in dark harbors, families trusting their vehicles, informants whispering truths at deadly risk. One miscalculation could ripple catastrophically outward.

Chapter 4

Alejandra's Counterpoint

Miami, Florida — Tosh Family Home, 2017
Day 18, 6:00 P.M. ET)

Late-afternoon sunlight bathed the white walls of the Tosh residence, casting elongated shadows that seemed to stretch toward the encroaching dusk. The hum of distant traffic mingled gently with the breeze drifting off Biscayne Bay. Nicolás Tosh paused briefly in the foyer, suitcase resting at his side, an unfamiliar hesitancy holding him momentarily immobile. Once, stepping across this threshold had signaled relief, sanctuary from the relentless pressures outside. Now, it felt like venturing deeper into uncertainty.

From the kitchen drifted the soft, methodical clatter of dishes being arranged with precision—a sound Nicolás knew all too well. Alejandra had always found solace in routines, especially now, her movements deliberate, as if trying to impose order on a household subtly fracturing at the seams. Nicolás inhaled deeply, recognizing the subtle perfume of her favorite jasmine tea wafting through the hallway, a fragrance that tugged painfully at memories of simpler times.

When he finally stepped into the kitchen, Alejandra paused mid-motion, a glass suspended carefully in hand. Her eyes, usually warm and welcoming, were guarded, searching his face for hints of the invisible turmoil he brought home nightly.

"You're back early," she observed quietly, placing the glass down with measured precision.

"Meetings finished sooner than expected," Nicolás replied, his voice gentle but cautious. He sensed immediately the distance his answer had created, aware of how hollow his explanations had grown.

Alejandra turned her attention briefly toward the window, the golden glow outside highlighting the subtle tension lines around her eyes. When she spoke again, her voice was softer, tinged with a subtle fatigue that seemed deeper than mere physical exhaustion. "Do you even realize how quiet you've become lately, Nicolás? I watch you sometimes, and it feels as though you're somewhere else entirely."

Nicolás hesitated, choosing his next words carefully. "There's just a lot going on. Complex decisions, responsibilities… You know how it is."

She shook her head slowly, her fingers tightening around the kitchen counter, as though anchoring herself to something tangible amid their drifting worlds. "But I don't know. That's the issue. You've built walls around yourself, Nicolás. And lately, the kids have started to notice, too."

At her words, Nicolás felt an immediate pang, his stomach twisting into knots. He glanced toward the staircase, picturing Emilia and Sebastián secluded in their rooms, isolated in a house filled with half-truths and quiet evasions. Alejandra stepped closer, her expression shifting subtly from frustration to quiet pleading.

"Whatever you're facing, whatever secrets you're trying to protect—we're still your family. You don't have to do it alone. Can't you trust me?"

Nicolás reached out instinctively, briefly touching Alejandra's hand, the warmth of her skin jolting him into a painful awareness of the distance he'd inadvertently cultivated. "It's not about trust," he whispered, barely audible. "It's about protection. If I let you in too far, I risk dragging you and the kids into places I never want you to see."

Alejandra met his eyes directly, a quiet intensity resonating in her voice. "But can't you see it's already affecting us? Every silence, every whispered phone call… Nicolás, we feel it. The kids feel it." Her voice wavered slightly, a rare crack in her composed façade. "You're trying so hard to protect us that you're leaving us behind."

In the heavy silence that followed, Nicolás saw clearly the profound toll his dual life had taken—not just on himself, but on the family he cherished above everything. Alejandra's words lingered, an uncomfortable truth he could no longer deny. Behind every covert decision and clandestine operation lay human costs, subtle yet inescapable.

Alejandra stepped back slowly, turning once more to the dishes, her movements carefully composed, yet Nicolás could sense the raw emotions barely contained beneath. Watching her now, he knew Alejandra's patience was not limitless. She was his strongest ally, yet her strength was quietly eroding, battered daily by the shadowed complexities he brought home.

"I promise to find a way," Nicolás finally murmured, voice edged with a conviction he desperately hoped he could fulfill. Alejandra paused, considering his promise, her eyes briefly meeting his again. This time, the guarded caution in her gaze softened slightly into weary hope.

"For all our sakes," she replied gently, "I hope you can.

Personal Strain: Two Worlds Colliding

Alejandra greeted Tosh with a fleeting smile that faltered the moment she caught his gaze. In the quiet intensity of his eyes, she saw layers of hidden strain that had become all too familiar—shadows cast by obligations she could barely fathom. Just days before, she'd glimpsed him briefly on television, standing discreetly behind Artemis Wang at a Lingtao event. To the world, he had seemed calm, even impassive, but Alejandra recognized the subtle signs: the set of his jaw, the rigidity in his posture, and the flicker of exhaustion he quickly masked.

"You're barely here lately," she said, voice tight, betraying the hurt she'd vowed to suppress. She busied herself setting the table, her movements stiff, each action punctuated by tension. "I know you're juggling Lingtao's philanthropic programs, but it's more than that, isn't it?"

Tosh exhaled softly, a slow release of breath that carried weeks of accumulated fatigue and suppressed frustration. "It's… complicated." His gaze drifted to the window, where Biscayne Bay stretched calm and indifferent beneath a pastel sky, a stark contrast to the turmoil within him.

Alejandra paused, a dinner plate hanging in mid-air, and lifted an eyebrow, challenging his vagueness. Her voice hardened slightly, tinged with an edge of anxiety she could no longer disguise. "Complicated because of the technology," she pressed deliberately, placing the plate on the table with a muted thud that resonated between them. "Nicolás, how far are you willing to go? You've built a philanthropic façade that funnels money all over the globe, but behind the scenes, you're—what, scanning people's minds? Purging corruption in ways most can't even imagine?"

Tosh frowned deeply, feeling the weight of her accusation like a physical pressure against his chest. The tension tightened across his shoulders, a subtle but unmistakable sign of the burdens he'd been carrying silently. He took a step toward her, his tone softer, pleading for understanding. "We're trying to do good—there are child traffickers, violent criminals, entire rings we can dismantle if we can only get there first. The technology—"

"The technology," Alejandra interrupted gently, compassion suddenly breaking through her facade of frustration, "is also turning you into someone I barely recognize. You're consumed by a second life. And I'm afraid that second life is winning."

Her voice softened further, revealing the depth of her quiet despair. The room seemed suddenly small, suffused with the heaviness of her words. Tosh felt them deeply, recognizing the truth he'd refused to confront. He thought back to the countless nights he'd stood awake, staring blankly at digital streams from the Zermatt Data Center, each alert deepening his entanglement in moral complexities. Each crisis— each rescue operation and every infiltration attempt—demanded more of him, piece by piece, relentlessly pulling him further away from the life he'd once promised her.

Alejandra studied his face closely, seeing the inner struggle etched in lines he hadn't possessed just months ago. Reaching out hesitantly, she touched his arm. Her voice dropped almost to a whisper, barely audible yet piercingly sincere. "I need to know there's still room for us, Nicolás. I understand your mission. But I worry it's costing you everything else— everything that matters."

In the silence that followed, Tosh searched for words of reassurance but found none. Her fears echoed painfully in his own thoughts. He reached out slowly, his fingers brushing lightly against hers, the brief contact a fragile lifeline between two worlds increasingly at odds.

"I promise," he finally murmured, though even as he spoke, a shadow of doubt clouded his heart. Alejandra nodded softly, her gaze holding his, filled with quiet resignation. Both knew that promises had limits—and both feared just how close they had come to reaching them.

Family Subplot: A Child's Discovery

Before Tosh could respond, quick footsteps scuffed on the stairs, drawing their immediate attention. Emilia, their sixteen-year-old daughter, appeared in the doorway, her usually confident posture replaced by anxious uncertainty. Her eyes darted nervously between her parents, wide and questioning.

"Dad…" she hesitated, visibly struggling to find the right words. Her voice trembled slightly. "I—I found some files on your old laptop upstairs. It was like code… references to a data center in Switzerland? 'Zermatt'? And something called 'CDA'? I didn't open them all, I swear—just a couple lines."

Tosh felt his heartbeat quicken painfully, a surge of adrenaline sharpening his senses. He exchanged a brief, tense glance with Alejandra, whose face had drained of color. Alejandra's eyes locked onto Tosh's, silently demanding clarity—urgency mingling with a deeply rooted fear she'd long harbored.

He swallowed hard, attempting to keep his voice steady, calm yet authoritative. "That laptop's from the garage," he said carefully, aware of how thin his explanation sounded even to his own ears. "Emi, those files are private. They're… related to a foundation project that's not public."

Emilia's brow furrowed deeply, her expression a mixture of curiosity, hurt, and a dawning sense of betrayal. "I didn't get much, but it mentioned 'Neural Net'—like something out of science fiction. Is this… some big secret?" Her voice rose slightly at the end, edged with a childlike urgency, as though seeking reassurance from her father, someone she'd always viewed as solidly grounded in reality.

Alejandra stepped forward, gently placing a comforting hand on her daughter's shoulder. Her voice was soft, deliberately soothing. "Emilia," she interjected, locking eyes with her daughter, conveying the seriousness she felt deep inside. "It is. Something your dad's been working on. Please—don't share it. Not with friends, not on social media, nowhere."

A flicker of hurt passed across Emilia's face, tears now unmistakably forming in the corners of her eyes. She took a shaky breath, visibly battling emotions that threatened to overwhelm her teenage composure. "Mom, I—of course I won't. But this is huge, isn't it?" Her voice broke slightly as she looked from her mother to her father, eyes pleading for honesty. "I feel like you two are living a double life."

Tosh felt his chest tighten, guilt twisting like a knife in his heart. The weight of Emilia's accusation hung heavily between them, emphasizing how deeply his double life had fractured his family's foundation. For the first time, he fully comprehended the emotional damage his secrecy inflicted upon those he loved most.

He reached out gently, touching Emilia's hand, desperate to reassure her even as he knew complete honesty remained impossible. "I'm sorry, Emi," he said, his voice soft yet firm. "I promise when the time is right, I'll explain more. But for now..." He hesitated, acutely aware of how fragile trust had become, "Trust me, this is serious. You need to keep it to yourself for everyone's safety."

Emilia stood silent for a long moment, her youthful idealism visibly shaken. Finally, she nodded, swallowing back tears before fleeing up the stairs. The silence she left behind was oppressive, a tangible reminder of the growing distance between the lives they presented, and the truths hidden beneath.

Alejandra turned toward Tosh slowly, her gaze now heavy with resignation and quiet despair. In that shared, painful silence, Tosh felt the full emotional cost of his choices—a cost that might soon prove unbearable.

Emotional Undercurrent: Alejandra's Plea

Alejandra closed her eyes, visibly battling the storm of emotions roiling within her. "You see?" she whispered, her voice edged with a quiet desperation. "It's bleeding into our home. Into our children." She leaned back against the counter, arms folded protectively as if shielding herself from the invisible burdens that had seeped into their lives. "Emi's never going to look at us the same way. Neither will Sebastián, once he finds out."

A thick silence stretched between them, each moment deepening the fissure carved by unspoken regrets. Tosh hesitated, the air heavy around them, before gently approaching Alejandra. He placed a careful, reassuring hand on her arm, feeling the faint tremor beneath his touch.

"I never wanted our family in harm's way," he whispered softly, regret coloring each word. "But you know what's at stake. If we don't step up, others—more ruthless—"

"Stop," Alejandra interrupted gently, her eyes filling rapidly with unshed tears. "I can't keep hearing that argument. We can't shoulder the entire weight of the world's secrets, Nicolás. If this is destroying our family, how can it possibly be worth it?"

A wave of intense guilt swept through Tosh, sharp and immediate. His mind flashed back vividly to the dark days surrounding the Algorithm-323 fiasco—the frantic scramble, the near-collapse of everything they'd painstakingly built, and the shadowy deals that had ensnared them in an endless cycle of secrecy and moral compromise.

"I know it's not fair," Tosh said, his voice raw and exposed. "But this technology—if it ever fell into unscrupulous hands, the tyranny would be unimaginable. Redwood's push for universal scans, the relentless infiltration attempts on our network... Ale, we're already on the brink."

Alejandra took a trembling breath, her gaze searching his face with a heartbreaking blend of love and anguish. "Nicolás, then step away. We have enough money to vanish completely. We could find a place far from this madness, somewhere quiet, somewhere safe. Isn't there any path where we just... walk away?"

He hesitated, her plea slicing deeper into him than he had expected. Could they truly abandon everything? The intricacies binding them—Zermatt's secrets, the White House's ceaseless demands, the G-7's wary oversight, Redwood's looming presidency, and the relentless curiosity of Maggie Wu—these had become as entwined in their lives as the safety of their family. And beyond these pressures lay the vivid images that haunted his conscience daily: stolen children trafficked across invisible borders, entire communities teetering on the edge due to faulty infrastructure, and lives unwittingly endangered by hidden technological flaws. The crushing sense of responsibility clung to him relentlessly.

"If we leave now," he began slowly, each word heavy with gravity, "someone else will fill that void. Someone less moral, less scrupulous. Someone who wouldn't hesitate to abuse the technology. I can't ignore that, Ale." Tosh pressed his hand to his forehead, feeling a profound fatigue deep in his bones. "I can't promise you that we'll never leave. But right now, at this moment… the world still needs us."

Alejandra's eyes glimmered with tears, a mixture of sorrow and reluctant acceptance. She reached out, gently touching his cheek. "Then we'll stand by you, Nicolás. As long as we possibly can. But promise me—promise us—you'll be careful. I can't lose you to these secrets."

A surge of tenderness and gratitude washed over Tosh. He gently took her hand, holding it firmly in his own, anchoring himself in her warmth and strength. "I promise I'll try. And Emilia… I'll speak with her again. Just give me a day or two to figure out exactly how much I can safely share with her. Trust me on this."

Alejandra nodded, squeezing his hand gently, her eyes conveying both her lingering fears and enduring trust. In that quiet, fragile moment, they stood united—a family facing an uncertain horizon, bound by love and the quiet resilience that carried them forward through shadows they never asked to inherit.

Chapter 5

Emergence of a Rival Network

Eastern Europe — Underground Lab

A single fluorescent bulb flickered overhead, casting sickly shadows across the reinforced concrete walls. The air reeked of machine oil, stale sweat, and something metallic—fear, unmistakably human. Rows of advanced computer towers formed a crude semicircle around a steel table littered with tangled wires and blinking hardware. Six hackers, their faces hidden behind black masks and heavy hoods, hunched over consoles, typing furiously.

At the center stood their leader—a lean figure whose scarred knuckles flexed involuntarily, betraying barely restrained impatience. He scanned the monitor labeled in stark, ominous letters: "NeuraTech—ALPHA." Lines of glowing code scrolled continuously, casting an eerie blue hue onto his stern, shadowed face.

"We're through Phase One," reported a technician, her voice rasping softly beneath the mask. She hesitated momentarily, uncertainty creeping into her tone. "The infiltration subroutines are stable, but the mind capture protocols keep throwing exceptions. Each bypass attempt nearly fries the neural link."

The leader exhaled sharply, nostrils flaring. "No matter. Push forward. Our goal isn't merely to infiltrate; it's to outmaneuver Zermatt entirely. We need direct neural access, deeper than anything they've managed." His voice lowered to a harsh whisper, edged with ruthlessness. "We finish what we started, no matter the cost."

Across the room, in a shadowed corner beneath tangled cables and flickering monitors, a battered figure slumped, wrists and ankles loosely bound to a metal chair. The captive's eyelids flickered intermittently, eyes clouded by sedation yet twitching with involuntary terror. Wired electrodes extended from his temples, pulsating with electric currents.

This was no mere simulation.

Another technician, visibly tense despite the anonymity of his mask, glanced toward the captive nervously. "The cognitive pathways are eroding fast. His mind won't sustain much more without permanent damage."

The leader stared coldly at the trembling figure. "Collateral damage," he murmured dismissively. "This is about dominance. Zermatt and their precious ethical boundaries limit their power. But NeuraTech won't. Once we bypass their handshake protocol, not even Tosh can stop us."

His words hung chillingly in the stale air, underscored by the captive's soft, helpless moan as another wave of neural stimuli surged directly into his brain. Memories fractured under relentless, unfiltered pressure—no encryption, no safeguards, only brute force.

Suddenly, an alarm beeped insistently on a nearby console. The first technician's fingers flew across the keyboard, tension radiating visibly through her posture. "There's feedback from the subject's neural network. It's resisting the override. If we don't stabilize it now, he'll go brain-dead."

"Override the safeguards," snapped the leader. "If Zermatt can read minds, we'll rewrite them—no matter the cost. Proceed."

As the technician reluctantly obeyed, the leader's eyes narrowed, focusing on the glowing screen. Somewhere far away, Nicolás Tosh and Zermatt operated under their ethical constraints, their careful morals. But NeuraTech harbored no such illusions. Their technology wasn't built for protection—it was forged for conquest.

And conquest demanded sacrifice.

Hong Kong — Shadowed Apartment

Meanwhile, in a nondescript high-rise overlooking Victoria Harbor, a similarly clandestine scene unfolded. Through tinted floor-to-ceiling windows, the sparkling city lights below seemed oblivious to the sinister machinations occurring within. A sleek, polished table bore a state-of-the-art holographic projector cycling methodically through intricate data diagrams, each illuminating complex webs of encrypted communication channels and neural mappings.

Two impeccably dressed figures—a former diplomat with silver-streaked hair and calculating eyes, and a disgraced military officer whose rigid posture suggested lingering authority—stood in concentrated silence, poring over stolen files emblazoned ominously with the words "NeuraTech."

The officer leaned forward, tapping a slender finger decisively onto a topographic map of Switzerland projected in fine detail above the table. Her voice was a low murmur, edged with ruthless ambition. "Our contacts confirm these lines correspond precisely to Zermatt's satellite coverage," she explained. "If the lab's infiltration code can piggyback seamlessly onto those signals, we bypass half the globe's encryption in one move."

The ex-diplomat gave a short, affirming nod, his features composed yet eyes glinting with triumph. "This is the final puzzle piece," he said firmly. "We can intercept real-time brain signals—even manipulate them—once we integrate their satellite network mapping. By the time Tosh or the White House realize what's happening, we'll be entrenched."

The officer straightened, her gaze sharp with anticipation. "With Zermatt's defenses compromised, NeuraTech's reach will be absolute. Every government, every secret, every thought—we'll hold it all in our hands."

They shared a glance, a silent acknowledgment of the gravity of their ambitions—and the brutality required to achieve them. The city outside glittered innocently, unaware of the dark storm brewing above it, within the anonymous heights of a shadowed apartment.

1. Espionage Montage: Testing "NeuraTech"

The camera lens of this unfolding operation zoomed swiftly from the polished, sinister atmosphere of the Hong Kong hideout back to the stark, unforgiving reality of the Eastern European lab. Under harsh fluorescent lighting, a grim sequence of brutal experiments unfolded relentlessly.

Test subjects, their identities stripped away, were strapped to tilted examination cots, their limbs immobilized with heavy restraints, wired with a chaotic nest of electrodes. Many had been trafficked or coerced—

bodies and lives reduced to mere tools in the hackers' ruthless pursuit of technological dominance.

A battered woman, her skin pale and mottled with bruises, lay trembling, strapped tightly in place. Her eyelids fluttered, struggling against the invasive pulses fed directly into her neural pathways. A technician, impassive and masked, hovered near a console. His gloved finger pressed a key sequence labeled OVERWRITE-RUNTIME.

The woman's body arched violently, mouth open in a silent, agonized scream, as her mind was forcibly pulled between realities. Nearby, brainwave monitors lit up frantically, displaying jagged, lethal spikes of neural activity.

The technician glanced anxiously at his superior, his raspy voice tense beneath the unemotional mask. "She's rejecting the new memory sets," he muttered, frustration edging into fear. "Her mind keeps reverting to the original pattern."

The leader's eyes narrowed dangerously, his jaw tightening with cold determination. "Then we push harder," he snapped, his voice leaving no room for hesitation. "There's no going back. We have no room for failure now."

Around the room, other test subjects lay similarly bound and broken, eyes vacant or glazed with the confusion of minds tampered with repeatedly. No morality checks. No gating mechanisms or ethical constraints existed here. Unlike Tosh's carefully designed, multi-layered CDA algorithm, these hackers had engineered NeuraTech for sheer, unmitigated power.

It was a weapon capable not only of decoding thoughts but of forcefully rewriting them—breaking neural safeguards, embedding artificial memories, or erasing entire lifetimes at will. The brutal efficiency and ruthless ambition embodied in every keystroke, every overridden neural pulse, confirmed that the hackers would stop at nothing to achieve their objectives.

In this shadowed, secretive facility, humanity itself was reduced to raw data, expendable and modifiable. The ethical abyss widened with every experiment, every shriek silenced by soundproof walls. Here, power was absolute, and conscience was merely a weakness to be purged.

2. Threat: Forcible Overwrites & Lost Autonomy

The dim light in the Eastern European underground lab flickered irregularly, casting ghostly, shifting shadows over the silent, oppressive room. The scent of burned circuits mixed unsettlingly with the sharper tang of antiseptic, creating a sterile atmosphere of clinical horror. Around the chamber, half-conscious subjects lay bound on metal cots, their bodies slack, eyes rolled back and twitching beneath pale, perspiration-slicked eyelids.

At the center console, the leader stood unmoving, eyes locked onto a live feed. It displayed the deteriorating mental landscape of a kidnapped codebreaker, forcibly integrated into the NeuraTech pilot program. On screen, pulses of data raced by, occasionally broken by poignant images torn from the captive's memory: a child's carefree laughter at a sunny park, a gentle touch from an elderly hand, the radiant smile of a woman whose eyes promised safety and love.

But these tender memories flashed only briefly, instantly overwritten by ruthless streams of new instructions. Commands appeared with chilling efficiency: OBEY WITHOUT QUESTION, ELIMINATE TARGET ON SIGHT, REPORT TO HANDLER. Each line of code relentlessly drilled deeper, embedding itself into the neural fabric, systematically erasing the captive's sense of self.

"We can make them do anything," the ex-military officer had boasted confidently in their covert Hong Kong meeting. Her words, filled with unwavering conviction, echoed now in the leader's mind, underscoring the brutal potential of their invention. "We can rewrite them to kill or comply, whichever we choose."

A cold satisfaction curled the corners of the leader's lips. The ruthlessness, the absence of any moral constraint—this was their true innovation. Unlike Nicolás Tosh and Zermatt's carefully regulated CDA, NeuraTech operated without illusions, driven purely by raw, unchecked ambition. Messy, reckless, even bordering on madness, but powerful precisely because of its disregard for boundaries.

Behind the leader, a sudden groan broke through the tension, harsh and agonized, pulling attention momentarily from the screen. Turning slightly, the leader observed a subject convulsing violently against heavy restraints. Her limbs twisted at unnatural angles, teeth clenched, eyes staring blindly toward the ceiling as tears streamed down her face. It was a stark reminder of the human cost embedded in their quest for dominance.

"Vitals spiking—heart rate and cortical stress at critical levels," a technician reported nervously, his voice trembling beneath the mask.

"Maintain pressure," the leader instructed coolly. "NeuraTech thrives precisely at this edge. It's the breaking that makes room for reconstruction."

On the live feed, the codebreaker's mental resistance flickered, weakening under relentless assault. His desperate, fading internal voice briefly pierced through in jagged lines of script—Help… please… family… home…—only to vanish beneath a fresh cascade of enforced commands.

"No safeguards," the leader murmured quietly, almost to themselves. "No regulators looking over our shoulders. Just pure, unrestricted access."

In that sinister moment, the true extent of NeuraTech's ethical threat crystallized: absolute control, forcibly imposed, stripping individuals not only of their autonomy but their very identities. Every life was potentially expendable, every memory subject to violent overwrite. This technology wasn't just dangerous—it represented the complete negation of humanity.

The codebreaker on screen finally succumbed fully, the mental signature flattening into passive acceptance. A single command blinked softly on the monitor: INTEGRATION COMPLETE.

The leader exhaled slowly, savoring the raw power displayed before them. "Initiate the next phase," they ordered, voice steady and cold. "Show me what he can do."

3. Cliffhanger: Piggybacking Off Zermatt & Lingtao

In the dimly illuminated underground lab, the pained moans of test subjects reverberated softly, an unsettling backdrop to the frenzied activity at the main console. Suddenly, a triumphant beep sliced through the oppressive tension, causing every technician in the room to freeze simultaneously, eyes wide and breath held.

The leader moved forward swiftly, leaning over the technician's shoulder. The screen in front of them burst into life with rapidly scrolling data streams—strings of text interspersed with cryptic numeric sequences. The infiltration code had succeeded, latching onto an internal node buried deep within Lingtao's sprawling global data pipelines.

"We have a partial route," the raspy-voiced technician announced, his voice barely above a whisper yet resonant with excitement. His gloved finger tapped urgently at the highlighted section on the monitor. "They're re-keying some satellites, tightening security—but we still have access points. Old caches from their Hong Kong servers haven't been purged yet. It's our backdoor straight into Zermatt's orchard of signals."

A profound silence descended upon the group, punctuated only by the steady whirr of cooling fans and the soft beep of diagnostic machines. The leader straightened, eyes narrowed, scanning the room to ensure every team member grasped the gravity of this moment. It was more than just technological espionage—it marked the crossing of a threshold, an irreversible step into unchecked dominance.

The next moves were starkly clear: seize control of those signals, piggyback directly onto Zermatt's extensive satellite coverage, and covertly distribute NeuraTech's powerful Overwrite subroutine. Once deployed, it would embed itself into every connected device—phones, computers, vehicles, even harmless-seeming "identifiers" dispersed globally. Any device could become a tool, a hidden gateway to infiltrate and forcibly reshape minds at their whim.

The leader's hand hovered momentarily above the keyboard, a brief flicker of anticipation crossing their face before it hardened into resolute determination. A single line of stark text blinked insistently at the bottom of the console:

READY TO DEPLOY? [Y/N]

Taking a steadying breath, the leader pressed the key firmly:

Y.

Instantaneously, the screens erupted into a cascade of activity—lines of code racing, satellite feeds locking in, and global maps pinpointing Zermatt's compromised data nodes. The technicians exhaled sharply, some visibly trembling from adrenaline as their long hours and ruthless experimentation finally culminated in this chilling achievement.

A technician glanced hesitantly toward the leader, barely suppressing an anxious edge in his voice. "Once this integrates, there's no turning back. They'll know someone's inside."

"Let them know," the leader responded icily, eyes glittering with steely resolve. "By the time they react, our grip will already be unbreakable."

Across the screens, a network of lines expanded relentlessly, symbolizing NeuraTech's invasive reach extending rapidly across continents. Lingtao's and Zermatt's meticulously constructed defenses began unraveling, quietly breached through hidden digital crevices they had overlooked.

In a heartbeat, the room transformed from tense anticipation into the cold certainty of unstoppable momentum. The world stood oblivious on the precipice of a new era—an era dominated by an entity with no ethical constraints, no respect for autonomy, and no hesitation to rewrite reality itself.

The leader allowed a thin smile, barely noticeable but filled with chilling satisfaction. "Now," they whispered into the electrified silence, "we shape the future."

Parallel Threads: Resolutions and New Crusades

Meanwhile, in the broader landscape of crises and intrigues, fresh tensions mounted:

Human Trafficking & Child Exploitation (Precision-Guided Takedown)

In a discreet operation near a bustling seaport, Marisol Alvarez watched intently from a dimly lit command van, screens flickering with infrared drone footage of the docks below. Every detail of the carefully planned raid had been meticulously rehearsed, yet adrenaline coursed sharply through her veins, heightening each sense to razor-sharp acuity.

"Alpha Team, you're green for entry," Marisol confirmed calmly into her headset, eyes locked on the grainy image of a warehouse nestled amidst rusted shipping containers. The warehouse, nondescript and shadowed, hid unimaginable horrors—a critical node in Marlin's extensive trafficking network.

As if choreographed by instinct and relentless training, tactical teams moved swiftly, their movements synchronized to perfection. They advanced silently, cutting through the dark like ghosts, their presence unknown to the oblivious guards standing watch.

Inside, chaos erupted as doors splintered under precision charges. Flashlights pierced the darkness, illuminating frightened, hopeful eyes peering from makeshift cages and hidden compartments—dozens of children, their innocence battered but spirits fiercely resilient.

Marisol held her breath, gripping the console edge tightly as each child was swiftly secured, extracted carefully by operatives speaking softly, reassuringly. "You're safe now," the rescuers murmured gently, their voices echoing with quiet compassion amid the stark brutality of their surroundings.

Yet even as triumph sparked briefly within her heart, Marisol's eyes narrowed at another screen—surveillance footage from the warehouse perimeter. A shadowy figure, identifiable instantly by his calculated gait, slipped deftly into the maze of stacked containers. It was Marlin himself, elusive as ever, vanishing swiftly into shadows the moment chaos unfolded.

Nicolás Tosh stood silently behind her, watching the same feed, his expression tightening in grim determination. He understood the victory's fragility, the cruel irony that even amidst salvation, darkness retained its elusive power.

"Our battle is won today, but the war continues," Tosh murmured quietly, his voice heavy with the burden of relentless responsibility. Each word was measured, carrying the full weight of a lifelong commitment. He turned his gaze to Marisol, resolve burning fiercely within his eyes. "This network doesn't collapse with one raid. Vigilance can never cease until every child is safe."

Marisol nodded solemnly, her determination mirroring his. She knew, deep within, that each rescued child represented hope and healing—a testament to their fight's critical importance. Yet the shadow of Marlin's escape loomed large, reinforcing the harsh truth they both understood clearly: until predators like him were permanently stopped, their crusade would remain unending.

As the teams quietly extracted into the protective anonymity of the night, Marisol reaffirmed her unwavering dedication. The war against human trafficking demanded tireless resolve and unyielding courage. Each life saved fueled their commitment anew, propelling them forward into battles yet to come.

Corruption at State Levels

In the heart of Zermatt's control room, Nicolás Tosh watched international news feeds cascade across the central screens, illuminating the profound impact of their carefully orchestrated leaks. Footage depicted masses rallying passionately in the compromised European nation, their collective voice demanding justice and transparency. High-ranking officials, faces etched with shock and anger, publicly resigned amidst mounting evidence of their corrupt dealings.

Rainer Sábato, standing near Tosh, monitored incoming reports with intense focus. His careful coordination had triggered precisely the kind of global outrage and local upheaval they had intended. Yet, even as the public outcry grew louder and demands for reform resonated worldwide, disturbing intelligence filtered quietly into Zermatt's secure communications channels.

"Multiple targets have disappeared," Marisol Alvarez reported grimly, her eyes narrowing as fresh intelligence scrolled rapidly across her monitor. "They moved quickly—bank accounts emptied, private jets chartered at the last moment. Our key power players escaped with illicit funds, securing safe havens before authorities could intercept."

Tosh sighed deeply, an internal struggle briefly visible in the lines etched on his face. He had hoped for a complete victory, yet the reality remained stubbornly complex and incomplete. He slowly turned toward his dedicated team, capturing their attention with quiet authority.

"We've exposed the wound, but infection runs deep," he addressed them solemnly, each word resonating with quiet, powerful intensity. "Our crusade against corruption can't rest until accountability becomes the rule, not the exception."

His statement lingered heavily in the charged silence, echoing profoundly within each team member. Dr. Miriam Faber moved decisively, initiating fresh analytics to track the fleeing officials' digital footprints and financial trails.

"We will follow every lead," she asserted, her voice firm and resolute. "No refuge should remain secure enough to shield these perpetrators indefinitely."

Rainer, acknowledging Tosh's solemn determination, immediately coordinated with global intelligence assets, aiming to infiltrate and dismantle the safe havens harboring the corrupt officials.

Marisol glanced thoughtfully at Tosh, her resolve visibly hardening. "The public stands with us now," she reminded quietly but forcefully. "The fight has expanded beyond Zermatt—this momentum could become a catalyst for permanent change."

Tosh nodded thoughtfully, inspired by his team's unwavering dedication. "Then we harness that momentum fully. Corruption thrives in shadows; our relentless vigilance must expose it continually. Justice delayed cannot become justice denied."

With renewed focus, the Zermatt team moved swiftly, actions underlined by a solemn recognition that their fight had just begun. The battle against state-level corruption was arduous, intricate, and prolonged—yet their resolve was unyielding. Every incremental victory represented progress toward a world where integrity triumphed, and accountability ruled supreme.

Across Europe, thousands of potentially catastrophic automotive malfunctions had been narrowly averted, thanks to Zermatt's timely warnings and coordinated regulatory actions. In the softly lit operations center, Marisol Alvarez allowed herself a rare, brief exhalation of genuine relief as data streams confirmed the successful recall and stringent new safety measures being enforced continent-wide.

"All compromised vehicles have been secured," Marisol announced, a note of guarded optimism coloring her voice. "Regulatory oversight has tightened significantly—at least for now."

Yet, Dr. Miriam Faber's reaction tempered the momentary reprieve. Her expression, stern and unyielding, drew attention instantly. She stepped forward purposefully, presenting fresh analytics projected sharply across the primary screen. The data, vivid and alarming, outlined troubling patterns from corporations worldwide, each chart illustrating calculated negligence rooted firmly in financial gain.

"Complacency is dangerous," Dr. Faber cautioned gravely, her voice measured but resolute. "Our interventions must not lull us into false security. New intelligence clearly indicates numerous other corporations are also cutting corners—jeopardizing public safety to maximize profit margins."

Nicolás Tosh absorbed this stark revelation quietly, his jaw set in grim acknowledgment. He understood Dr. Faber's concern profoundly. Their victories, though substantial, represented battles won—not the greater war against reckless greed.

Tosh stepped forward decisively, addressing his team with succinct intensity. "Every recall is merely a symptom," he stated, voice resonating with unwavering conviction. "The underlying disease—profit over human life—remains deeply entrenched. Our surveillance and interventions must intensify, not lessen."

His words settled heavily, igniting fresh determination within the assembled analysts and operatives. Marisol nodded solemnly, immediately initiating further investigations and surveillance sweeps to preempt the next potential crisis. Dr. Faber began meticulously coordinating predictive algorithms, seeking to expose hidden risks lurking beneath polished corporate facades.

Rainer Sábato, reviewing the rapidly updating information, acknowledged Tosh's directive thoughtfully. "We will double our vigilance," he affirmed strongly. "No life should ever be a casualty of corporate negligence."

As his dedicated team returned urgently to their tasks, Tosh reflected on the relentless nature of their mission. Public safety, he knew intimately, demanded constant vigilance. Each crisis averted was meaningful but transient; the systemic challenge required persistent, unwavering commitment.

The quiet resolve filling the command center confirmed their shared understanding clearly: their crusade against corporate irresponsibility and technological malpractice would continue unabated, driven by the certainty that human life must always triumph over profit.

Corporate Sabotage & Competitor Intrusions

In Lingtao's advanced cybersecurity command center, the soft hum of powerful quantum servers underscored a controlled yet tense atmosphere. Analysts monitored screens glowing with streams of real-time cyber threat intelligence, their faces intense with focused determination. A recent wave of attacks had just been decisively thwarted, the cyber perimeter reinforced effectively to protect Lingtao's crucial philanthropic initiatives.

Yet Nicolás Tosh stood silently near the main data screen, a deeper worry furrowing his brow. The immediate threat was neutralized, but intelligence continued to stream in, signaling troubling developments. Reports revealed unsettling signs of systemic espionage, extending far beyond Lingtao alone. Other global organizations committed to humanitarian missions faced similar threats—carefully masked infiltrations designed to compromise their integrity and operations from within.

Rainer Sábato approached Tosh, his voice grave and filled with urgency. "Our foes aren't discouraged—they're adapting," he cautioned seriously, eyes fixed on Tosh with resolute intensity. "Corporate sabotage now wears humanitarian masks. Our efforts must constantly evolve, outpacing their deceit."

Tosh nodded, fully comprehending the implications. He knew this new tactic presented a unique danger, exploiting trust and goodwill—turning altruism into vulnerability. He surveyed the room, taking in the dedication of his assembled team, each individual tirelessly defending their systems against a shadowy enemy.

"Expand our intelligence sharing with trusted humanitarian allies immediately," Tosh instructed decisively, his voice firm and unyielding. "Establish a joint, encrypted task force—global vigilance is essential. Any infiltration of these critical humanitarian operations must be identified and neutralized before irreversible damage occurs."

Dr. Miriam Faber swiftly initiated analytical protocols, running advanced pattern recognition algorithms aimed at unmasking the subtle signs of sabotage cloaked as benevolent cooperation. Her focused expression was mirrored across the room, a collective understanding emerging: their adversaries had chosen deception as their new battlefield.

Marisol Alvarez, overseeing direct communications, immediately transmitted secure alerts to allied organizations worldwide. Her voice carried calm yet unwavering authority, warning each recipient to heighten their cybersecurity awareness and tighten internal controls.

"Ensure every ally knows the gravity of this situation," Marisol advised firmly, her eyes meeting Tosh's with determined conviction. "Unity and vigilance are our strongest defenses."

Tosh's acknowledgment was resolute and immediate. "Agreed. Our adversaries underestimate our commitment. Their deceit strengthens our resolve. Together, we must ensure humanitarian missions remain secure, uncompromised, and authentic. Our constant vigilance is our greatest asset—one we will never surrender."

As the command center surged into action, reinforcing alliances and defenses, Tosh felt renewed determination. In the face of calculated deceit, their mission to safeguard integrity and humanity had never been more vital. He knew they must remain perpetually ahead, confronting sabotage head-on with unwavering vigilance and absolute resolve.

Aviation Safety

In Zermatt's operational heart, a hushed but vibrant energy filled the room. Analysts swiftly moved through a complex web of real-time data feeds, confirming the rapid grounding of potentially lethal aircraft worldwide. The swift dissemination of detailed dossiers, meticulously compiled by Zermatt's investigative teams, had undeniably prevented immediate aviation disasters.

Yet Nicolás Tosh stood apart from the subtle hum of triumph, his thoughts somberly introspective. His eyes scanned the wall of monitors displaying grounded fleets, regulatory warnings, and urgent inspections now mandated globally. Each successful intervention was a stark reminder of a deeper, more insidious danger that still lurked within corporate cultures—the prioritization of profit over human safety.

"We prevented tragedies today," Marisol Alvarez reported cautiously, acknowledging Tosh's subdued demeanor. "The coordinated effort was flawless. Regulators acted immediately."

"Agreed," Tosh responded softly, meeting Marisol's gaze briefly before turning toward the assembled team. He felt the weight of their expectant attention, recognizing the importance of addressing the underlying issue clearly and directly.

"Yet we remain uneasy," Dr. Miriam Faber interjected, her expression solemn as she highlighted disturbing new patterns emerging from predictive analyses. "The underlying culture driving such negligence is entrenched. Financial incentives consistently overshadow safety considerations. Our intervention was timely, but only a temporary measure."

Tosh stepped forward, his presence commanding immediate attention. He addressed his dedicated team with unwavering seriousness. "Until corporate cultures change fundamentally, vigilance alone is insufficient," he declared firmly. His voice carried through the operations center with calm authority, ensuring every operative understood the profound truth behind his words. "Our work protecting public safety continues, relentless and unyielding."

Rainer Sábato nodded deeply, quickly organizing heightened monitoring protocols. "We'll implement broader surveillance and analysis, targeting corporate decisions and financial flows," he stated decisively. "This will enable preemptive interventions to safeguard lives proactively."

Dr. Faber moved swiftly, initiating further quantum computational analyses to detect subtle indicators of systemic neglect across aviation corporations. She reinforced their approach, ensuring every potential risk was identified long before it could threaten public safety.

Marisol Alvarez set additional communications measures in motion, ensuring global regulatory bodies maintained constant awareness of ongoing threats. Her voice remained calm yet resolute as she instructed teams to maintain absolute transparency in their reporting.

Watching his team mobilize with reinforced determination, Nicolás Tosh allowed himself a brief moment of cautious optimism. Each life protected through their actions was profoundly significant, yet he knew well that their broader battle was far from over.

"We will not rest until accountability and safety become universal standards," he reminded them gravely, affirming Zermatt's unwavering dedication. Together, united in purpose, their relentless vigilance would continue, steadfast in confronting every hidden danger lurking beneath corporate greed.

New Crusades Begin

Child Abuse & Exploitation Imagery

Within Zermatt's high-security intelligence center, Nicolás Tosh studied new intelligence reports flooding in from global law enforcement agencies. Each line of text, each digital image referenced, portrayed a stark and distressing reality: despite intensified international policing and relentless enforcement efforts, disturbing imagery of child exploitation continued to proliferate across the internet's darkest corners.

Tosh's expression darkened, visibly moved and deeply unsettled by the graphic details. His typically calm demeanor betrayed a profound emotional struggle, a reaction he rarely allowed himself to reveal openly. The distressing truth—children victimized, innocence shattered—resonated deeply within him, reinforcing his resolve.

Marisol Alvarez observed his reaction quietly, sensing the depth of his silent outrage. "These criminal networks are more sophisticated than ever," she acknowledged grimly. "Their methods evolve rapidly to evade detection."

Dr. Miriam Faber immediately began adjusting analytical algorithms, heightening the sophistication of Zermatt's digital surveillance to trace even the faintest clues leading to these hidden networks. Her voice remained steady yet compassionate. "We'll refine our predictive analytics to target the precise digital behaviors characteristic of these operations. They cannot remain hidden indefinitely."

Tosh's response was immediate and definitive, carrying a fierce determination. "These networks thrive on anonymity," he vowed firmly, his voice resonating through the room, galvanizing the entire team's focus. "We will shine an unrelenting light until darkness has nowhere left to hide."

Rainer Sábato promptly mobilized their global network of operatives, enhancing collaboration with international cyber-crime units to dismantle these illicit platforms systematically. His instructions were clear and decisive. "Expand our partnerships and information-sharing. The predators must understand—there is no sanctuary safe enough for their activities."

Marisol coordinated swiftly with global advocacy groups and law enforcement, preparing detailed dossiers designed for rapid dissemination to relevant international bodies. "Transparency and swift action," she emphasized resolutely. "Every child rescued, every predator apprehended, weakens their hold and sends a message of zero tolerance."

Tosh's gaze hardened, his commitment to the fight against child abuse solidifying further with every passing second. He turned decisively to his team, his voice filled with a profound sense of mission. "Our vigilance must be absolute. Each step forward is a step closer to justice and safety for every child threatened by these horrors. Our efforts will not cease, not waver, until we have eradicated this evil entirely."

United by shared resolve, the Zermatt team intensified their efforts, determined that no dark corner of the internet would remain beyond their reach. Driven by unyielding compassion and unwavering commitment, their fight against child abuse and exploitation imagery would continue relentlessly until every shadow was eradicated.

Domestic & Spousal Abuse

Inside Zermatt's analytical hub, an unsettling quiet pervaded as Dr. Miriam Faber shared her recent findings. On the screen behind her, disturbing statistics illuminated the grim reality: a sharp rise in domestic violence cases worldwide, exacerbated significantly by ongoing socioeconomic instability and the inadequate responses from overwhelmed local authorities.

Dr. Faber's voice, steady yet filled with heartfelt urgency, carried clearly through the room as she outlined the data. "These victims are trapped, isolated by circumstances, and neglected by strained response systems. Traditional interventions come too late—often after irreparable harm has already occurred."

The profound silence that followed her words reflected shared concern and deep compassion among the gathered analysts and operatives. Nicolás Tosh's expression tightened visibly, absorbing the human toll behind each statistic. He understood deeply that behind every number was an individual, a family—lives irreversibly impacted by violence.

Seeing the effect on her team, Dr. Faber stepped forward passionately, determined to shift from despair toward proactive solutions. "We have an unprecedented opportunity," she explained earnestly, referencing Zermatt's advanced CDA predictive algorithms. "Our technology can identify early behavioral indicators, patterns of escalation before violence erupts. We have the capacity to intervene decisively, offering protection and support precisely when it's most needed."

She paused momentarily, her voice trembling slightly with emotional intensity as she continued, "We must give silent victims a voice and safety—a promise, not merely an aspiration."

Tosh immediately stepped forward, fully endorsing Dr. Faber's proposal. His gaze swept the room decisively, galvanizing the team's commitment. "We must act swiftly. Begin collaboration with frontline domestic abuse organizations immediately. Establish secure channels for predictive intelligence to flow directly to those capable of intervening."

Marisol Alvarez initiated swift communications with global support networks and local intervention agencies. Her calm, determined voice reinforced the critical importance of coordinated, timely responses. "We'll ensure this intelligence translates directly into tangible protections—safe houses, proactive outreach, real-time intervention."

Rainer Sábato, committed and resolute, began overseeing operational protocols to ensure that predictive alerts triggered immediate, secure responses, effectively bridging the gap between technological foresight and human intervention. "This isn't just about anticipating violence," Rainer emphasized clearly. "It's about actively reshaping outcomes, safeguarding vulnerable lives proactively."

Dr. Faber watched her colleagues spring into action, her initial urgency transforming into determined resolve. She knew this moment marked a pivotal shift—Zermatt's commitment to combat domestic and spousal abuse now extended beyond passive monitoring into proactive, life-saving intervention.

In the charged atmosphere of purpose and compassion, Nicolás Tosh summarized their shared resolve succinctly: "We have a moral imperative to protect those who cannot protect themselves. Our promise of safety must become reality—uncompromising and enduring."

Fugitives of Serious Crimes

In Zermatt's secure operations room, Rainer Sábato stood before an array of global intelligence feeds, his sharp gaze meticulously tracking the paths of fugitives who had long evaded justice. Screens displayed the faces and histories of individuals wanted internationally for violent crimes—each a stark reminder of justice denied and the threat posed to communities worldwide.

With quiet intensity, Rainer initiated new tracking protocols leveraging Zermatt's cutting-edge surveillance technology, enhanced with sophisticated predictive analytics. These tools promised to significantly improve the chances of locating and apprehending criminals whose prolonged freedom posed serious risks.

His actions drew the attention of Nicolás Tosh, who approached with thoughtful concern, studying the dynamic digital maps highlighting probable locations of the fugitives.

"Do you think these new measures will finally turn the tide?" Tosh asked carefully, aware of the delicate balance between hope and realism.

Rainer nodded confidently, eyes never leaving the constantly updating screens. "They'll make a difference," he asserted decisively. "We're using behavioral analytics, deep network pattern recognition, and predictive movements based on past behaviors. This isn't merely surveillance—it's active anticipation."

Marisol Alvarez stepped closer, intrigued and cautiously optimistic. "How quickly can we expect results?" she queried, considering the implications for global safety.

"We're already identifying patterns," Rainer explained with measured determination. "These criminals rely on anonymity and instability in enforcement coordination. We're stripping away those advantages systematically, piece by piece."

Pausing briefly, Rainer faced the gathered team, his expression earnest, communicating deep conviction. "Justice delayed erodes faith in law itself," he emphasized passionately, reinforcing the moral urgency underlying their operations. "We owe society assurance that escape is never permanent."

Tosh immediately backed this sentiment, addressing the room with calm, compelling authority. "Every criminal brought to justice restores trust and reinforces security. Our duty goes beyond mere capture—it's about restoring societal faith in justice itself."

Dr. Miriam Faber swiftly adjusted quantum computational resources, enhancing predictive precision and increasing their capacity to process vast amounts of surveillance data. "I've directed additional quantum processing power to ensure real-time adaptability," she informed them, her voice steady and resolute.

Marisol swiftly mobilized international communications, collaborating closely with Interpol and national law enforcement agencies to ensure immediate responses when targets were identified.

Rainer observed the activity around him, feeling a profound responsibility yet inspired by the collective dedication. Each team member shared an unwavering commitment to upholding justice, reaffirming his determination.

"Together," he concluded with solemn resolution, "we will deliver a clear message to fugitives worldwide: justice is inevitable. Every victim, every community affected, deserves nothing less than our relentless pursuit until the scales are balanced once again."

Unknown Subjects of Violent Crimes

Inside a high-security digital forensics center, analysts stared in disbelief and then awe at the rapidly updating monitors. Databases that had previously been filled with thousands of unidentified DNA samples—cold cases lingering in unresolved silence—began to illuminate with precision and startling clarity.

Suddenly, thousands upon thousands of DNA samples of unknown subjects were matched with names and addresses in the state police and FBI computer files. Analysts swiftly verified the results, their shock swiftly turning into focused, energized determination. The implications were staggering, as decades-old cases of murder, rape, terrorism, and violent assaults suddenly came sharply into focus.

Word quickly reached Zermatt, prompting Nicolás Tosh to convene an immediate briefing with his core team. Marisol Alvarez presented the results vividly, highlighting key breakthroughs. "We're looking at a seismic shift," she stated emphatically, her eyes filled with the gravity of this momentous occasion. "Families who've waited years, sometimes decades, for answers finally have a real chance at justice."

Dr. Miriam Faber, examining the technical details closely, nodded in approval. "Quantum-driven matching algorithms increased precision exponentially," she explained to the attentive team. "Cold cases, previously deemed unsolvable due to lack of actionable leads, are now being reopened and solved in real-time."

Tosh absorbed this information deeply, fully recognizing the magnitude of the event unfolding before them. He addressed his team with solemn authority, underscoring their shared responsibility. "Every match isn't just data," Tosh reminded them firmly. "It represents closure for victims and accountability for perpetrators who thought their crimes had been forgotten."

Rainer Sábato quickly coordinated with international law enforcement, ensuring swift operational follow-through to apprehend newly identified suspects. "Rapid response teams are already mobilizing," Rainer reported decisively. "We'll maintain continuous tracking until every subject is securely in custody."

Marisol, understanding the profound emotional impact of these revelations, quickly initiated compassionate outreach programs designed to inform affected families sensitively and respectfully. "We'll support these families with dignity and empathy as they confront new realities," she emphasized clearly.

Tosh summarized their mission succinctly, reinforcing their dedication and the ethical imperative guiding their work. "Justice, no matter how long delayed, must always be pursued relentlessly. Our duty extends beyond technical identification—it's about restoring faith, offering solace, and reaffirming society's commitment to accountability and justice."

With purposeful resolve, Zermatt's team continued their critical work, driven by renewed energy and profound responsibility. This unprecedented breakthrough heralded a new era in criminal justice—one defined not by anonymity and escape, but by certainty, closure, and relentless pursuit of truth.

Financial Market Manipulation

Within Zermatt's advanced financial intelligence center, screens flashed vividly, highlighting a troubling surge of irregular transactions across global stock markets. Analysts observed with growing concern as sophisticated financial firms leveraged complex algorithms and discreet trade networks to manipulate markets on an unprecedented scale, posing severe threats to economic stability worldwide.

Nicolás Tosh studied the data meticulously, recognizing immediately the broader implications. The hidden trades, subtly executed and deliberately obscured, were eroding public trust and market integrity, exacerbating wealth disparities, and destabilizing national economies.

Tosh turned decisively toward his assembled team, articulating clear directives with unwavering determination. "Expose their hidden trades," he ordered unequivocally, his voice firm with ethical conviction. "Corruption thrives when invisible. Visibility brings accountability."

Marisol Alvarez swiftly coordinated the deployment of comprehensive intelligence reports, channeling detailed evidence to financial regulators and investigative journalists globally. "Every illicit transaction will be meticulously documented and transparently shared," she confirmed resolutely, her efforts aimed at restoring fairness and trust.

Dr. Miriam Faber employed advanced analytical tools powered by quantum computing, dissecting trade data at astonishing speeds to reveal intricate patterns of deceitful financial behavior. "We're uncovering deeply embedded manipulation techniques," she reported confidently. "These analyses provide irrefutable evidence necessary to prompt immediate regulatory action."

Rainer Sábato, cognizant of the international stakes, swiftly enhanced security protocols to protect whistleblowers and insiders willing to expose corruption from within. "Safeguarding those who courageously reveal truth is paramount," he affirmed with grave seriousness. "Their testimonies are indispensable to dismantling these fraudulent schemes."

Tosh acknowledged his team's rapid mobilization with quiet approval, emphasizing the significance of their mission. "Financial manipulation isn't victimless—it devastates communities, economies, and livelihoods. Our actions today signify a critical stance against greed and corruption."

Unified by purpose and dedication, Zermatt's operatives worked diligently to disrupt systemic market abuses, driven by the knowledge that their vigilance was crucial in securing financial transparency and economic fairness worldwide. Each exposed transaction represented more than a mere data point—it symbolized a decisive step toward accountability, stability, and economic justice.

Maggie Wu's Investigation

Zurich lay under a silvery drizzle, its streets slick with rain that shimmered like liquid mercury under the streetlights. Maggie Wu moved briskly along a narrow alleyway, her footsteps muted by the wet pavement, senses sharpened by the familiar thrill of imminent discovery. Her heart quickened as she approached the inconspicuous doorway—her source had insisted on absolute discretion, fearful eyes darting beneath a heavy hood, voice barely audible above the bustling café noise when they had arranged this meeting.

She tapped three times, a deliberate rhythm, and waited. After a tense pause, the door creaked open just wide enough for Maggie to slip inside. The room beyond was sparsely furnished, lit dimly by a solitary lamp that cast eerie shadows across peeling wallpaper. A figure stood nervously by a small wooden table, fingers twisting anxiously.

"Ms. Wu?" the voice whispered uncertainly.

"Yes," Maggie responded firmly, stepping into the lamplight to reassure her jittery contact. "You said you have information about Experta's satellite mind scans?"

The contact lowered her hood, revealing a face etched with fear and exhaustion. "Yes, I was there," she began, voice shaking slightly but gaining strength with each word. "I worked inside Experta's covert projects division. We were assured the research was benign—neural mapping, mental health diagnostics, that sort of thing. But then I saw something else. Something terrifying."

Maggie's pulse quickened, the reporter's instinct sharpening her attention. "Go on," she urged gently, pulling out a small encrypted recorder, nodding encouragement. "I'm listening."

"They call it a 'rogue system,'" the former Experta employee continued, eyes wide with suppressed panic. "It bypasses ethical controls, hijacking satellite data streams to scan brains remotely—without consent or awareness. Experta claims it never left prototype stage, but I know otherwise. It's active, hidden deep beneath layers of standard communications. Anyone can be targeted—corporate executives, politicians, activists, journalists—without leaving a single digital footprint."

The implications struck Maggie with stark clarity, sending chills down her spine. This could explain reports she'd received of sudden changes in decision-making among influential figures, erratic behavior among previously steadfast individuals.

"You can prove this?" Maggie pressed carefully.

The woman nodded sharply, handing over a tiny encrypted data stick with trembling fingers. "Everything is here—access logs, code fragments, internal communications. It's enough to prove Experta's complicity. But Maggie," her voice dropped to a fearful whisper, eyes darting nervously toward the door, "once you publish this, they'll come for you. For both of us."

Maggie's hand closed protectively around the data stick, her resolve steeling with renewed purpose. She understood the risks. Exposing Experta—and potentially unraveling a global conspiracy—was exactly why she became a journalist.

"Let them come," Maggie responded firmly, eyes flashing with fierce determination. "The world deserves the truth, whatever the cost."

Stepping back into the rainy Zurich night, Maggie Wu knew her investigation had reached a tipping point. With the rogue system now exposed, her next exposé wouldn't merely shake Experta—it could tear through the veil of secrecy, exposing every dark secret they had hoped to hide.

CDA-325's Dormant Power

In the quiet solitude of his Miami residence, Nicolás Tosh stared contemplatively at the ocean's gentle waves rolling endlessly toward the shore. Yet his mind offered no peace; it churned restlessly, echoing with ethical quandaries and escalating fears. The unprecedented rise of NeuraTech—a rogue entity wielding unchecked neural manipulation technology—haunted him, representing precisely the nightmare scenario he'd fought tirelessly to prevent.

Across the globe, NeuraTech's emergence had ignited an unseen yet fiercely contested arms race. Tosh knew the CDA-325 algorithm, secured in Zermatt's most guarded quantum vault, remained far more powerful than the version actively deployed in the field. It had been deliberately limited, restrained by rigorous ethical barriers—safeguards personally championed by Tosh himself.

But now, as intelligence reports detailed NeuraTech's ruthless brute-force tactics, Tosh faced an excruciating dilemma. NeuraTech's brute-force approach threatened to bypass all caution—a living, horrifying demonstration of how destructive mind-tech could become once unleashed from moral oversight. Every principle Tosh held dear, every careful ethical boundary he'd established, was now openly mocked by NeuraTech's reckless ambition.

Tosh paced slowly, the weight of responsibility pressing heavily upon him. He knew exactly what CDA-325 could become if those carefully programmed constraints were ever lifted. Its dormant power, terrifying in potential, could surpass NeuraTech's crude aggression with surgical precision and devastating efficiency. It had the capacity not only to counteract, but potentially dismantle NeuraTech's destructive reach— but at what moral cost?

"Every power unleashed carries consequences," he whispered solemnly to the empty room, voicing the internal struggle that tormented him. He envisioned CDA-325 in its unbridled form—capable of rewriting consciousness, reshaping entire populations' perceptions, emotions, even memories. The potential for abuse, for slipping irreversibly down a path from protector to tyrant, felt all too plausible.

Yet, if he did nothing, he risked allowing NeuraTech's brutal ideology to dominate unopposed, plunging humanity into a dystopian era devoid of autonomy, dignity, or freedom. His ethical hesitation was precisely the weakness NeuraTech sought to exploit.

Standing by the expansive window, Tosh felt trapped between equally perilous choices: unleash a controlled form of power he'd sworn never to deploy or watch as unrestrained aggression destroyed the world he had vowed to protect.

With the sun setting, casting long shadows across his somber features, Nicolás Tosh reached for his secure communicator. His fingers trembled slightly as he keyed in a command, activating an encrypted link to Zermatt's command center.

"We need to discuss the dormant algorithms in CDA-325," he stated quietly, his voice resolute yet tinged with profound sadness. "Prepare the ethical oversight committee. We may need to consider activating measures I hoped would forever remain unnecessary."

As the connection closed, silence enveloped him once again, thick with dread and determination. The dormant power of CDA-325 was waking—and with it, the very future of humanity hung precariously in the balance.

Each new endeavor reflected Zermatt's unwavering commitment to leveraging CDA technology responsibly, ethically confronting threats that persisted stubbornly beneath society's surface. Tosh surveyed his dedicated team, his voice strong and clear: "Our crusades endure—not only to expose darkness but to empower humanity toward lasting solutions. The path is arduous, the stakes immense—but our resolve remains unbreakable."

Eastern Europe — Lab Interior, Final Moments

The stark glow of a half-dozen screens bathed the dim, oppressive room in cold blue light, each monitor humming with tense, focused energy. Set atop a battered metal table, open communication links displayed critical feeds. One screen mapped out satellite orbits circling quietly above Earth, another streamed a live feed from the clandestine

Hong Kong hideout, revealing operatives in hushed, strategic conversations.

In the center of this charged atmosphere stood the leader, who slowly, deliberately removed their mask. Beneath it was a face harshly etched by old scars, bearing unmistakable signs of battles fought and ruthless decisions made. Their eyes gleamed coldly, reflecting a boundless ambition, completely untethered from moral constraints.

"Soon," the leader murmured softly, voice laced with chilling resolve, "we will show the world what real power is—no half measures, no illusions of virtue."

Behind them, strapped securely to a chair, a test subject emitted a broken, final cry—raw, filled with anguish—before abruptly falling silent, eyes clouding over into a lifeless glaze. The invasive Overwrite protocol had taken hold, a ruthless demonstration of NeuraTech's chilling capabilities. The experiment had crossed a definitive line from theoretical to terrifyingly practical.

Nearby, a console pulsated with frenzied activity, lines of code racing furiously across the screen, creating an unstoppable digital bridge. Data surged rapidly outward from this hidden facility, leaping silently to the concealed servers in Hong Kong. From there, connections edged menacingly closer to penetrating the secure digital pathways controlled by Lingtao and Zermatt.

The technicians surrounding the leader held their collective breath, their attention riveted to the scrolling data, anticipation building palpably within the oppressive silence of the lab.

Then, with startling clarity, a single line of text flashed urgently across the central console:

RELAY ESTABLISHED — STANDBY FOR MIND-FEED

A potent, expectant hush enveloped the room, even the low hum of equipment momentarily muted by the gravity of this digital breakthrough. NeuraTech had irrevocably stepped onto the global stage, revealing a lethal, uncompromising potential capable of reshaping minds, altering truths, and subjugating wills.

Unbeknownst to Zermatt, oblivious in their distant headquarters, a formidable new storm had risen quietly but rapidly. This emerging threat operated entirely without the ethical restraints Tosh's CDA technology had rigorously upheld. NeuraTech promised absolute control, wielding power devoid of morality, restraint, or human empathy—a true weaponization of the mind.

In this isolated Eastern European lab, illuminated only by cold screens and ruthless ambition, the balance of global power teetered dangerously. Humanity stood unknowingly at the brink, facing a perilous future dictated not by ethics or accountability, but by sheer, unbridled dominance.

Chapter 6

Reunion in Zurich

Zurich, Switzerland — Experta Foundation Headquarters, 2017
Day 20, 9:00 A.M. CET

The morning sun glinted brilliantly off the mirrored facade of the Experta Foundation's headquarters, a shimmering beacon in Zurich's bustling downtown. Yet within its secure, high-tech interior, an atmosphere of tense anticipation permeated a heavily fortified boardroom, accessible only via rigorous biometric clearance protocols.

At the center of the meticulously arranged circular table stood Nicolás Tosh, his posture reflecting the gravity of the moment. Around him were gathered a tight-knit group whose collective experience was formidable: Rainer Sábato, several serious-faced G-7 liaisons, and key staff from Experta Foundation. The room resonated with palpable silence, an unspoken acknowledgment of the stakes that rested upon their shoulders.

Suspended above the table, a sweeping holographic projection illuminated the faces in stark shades of light and shadow, drawing all attention toward its intricate display. A single red pulse blinked insistently across Eastern Europe, capturing immediate focus. Below it, stark text offered a grim, digital prognosis: "NeuraTech infiltration potential: 68%."

Adjacent to this ominous statistic, a dense cluster of illuminated trajectories branched outward, tracing probable infiltration routes meticulously calculated through Hong Kong. With each passing moment, the display updated in real-time, refining and adjusting its assessment with alarming precision. It was painfully clear to every observer in the room—NeuraTech's sinister advancement was neither hypothetical nor distant; it was unfolding right before their eyes, minute by minute, inexorably.

Tosh studied the data intently, his face hardened with resolve yet betraying subtle traces of anxiety. "This isn't merely an infiltration," he stated gravely, addressing the room with controlled urgency. "This is an aggressive expansion designed to outpace our containment strategies. NeuraTech is no longer a shadowy threat—they're poised to strike openly, challenging us directly on the global stage."

Rainer Sábato nodded solemnly, quickly absorbing the escalating threat level. His voice held a tone of somber authority. "We must anticipate their next moves. Immediate coordination with all affected regions is critical—particularly Eastern Europe and Hong Kong. Our response must be swift, decisive, and completely synchronized."

A senior G-7 liaison interjected, concern evident in his strained voice. "Do we have the resources to counteract their reach, Nicolás? Our capabilities are formidable, but this scenario demands extraordinary precision."

Tosh's gaze moved purposefully around the table, making deliberate eye contact with each team member, reinforcing the urgency of collective action. "We have no alternative. We must marshal every tool at our disposal—diplomatic, technological, and operational—to neutralize their expansion. If NeuraTech establishes an unimpeded global foothold, the consequences will be catastrophic."

Dr. Miriam Faber, observing remotely through secure communications, swiftly mobilized Experta's quantum computing assets. "We're enhancing predictive algorithms to preempt their infiltration pathways," she informed the assembly, her voice steady with assurance. "Our goal must be to outmaneuver their every tactic."

Marisol Alvarez spoke up decisively, clearly determined and resolute. "Immediate outreach to global intelligence networks and cybersecurity units is underway. We will leverage every partnership, every resource available. The international community must recognize the magnitude of this threat."

Tosh concluded the briefing with unwavering resolve, encapsulating their collective duty succinctly. "Today defines our legacy—our commitment to safeguarding humanity from unrestrained technological power. We act now, united and uncompromising, or we risk surrendering the very foundations of freedom and autonomy."

As the team dispersed swiftly into focused action, the tension within Experta Foundation's Zurich headquarters transformed into purposeful energy. The battle against NeuraTech had reached a crucial juncture, one demanding exceptional unity, unparalleled vigilance, and absolute determination.

Strategic Summit: Containing the New Threat

In the Experta Foundation's secure boardroom, tension was palpable. The holographic display cast an eerie blue light over the assembled leaders, amplifying the gravity of the situation at hand. Rainer Sábato cleared his throat softly, meticulously cycling through multiple digital vantage points projected before the group.

"We've confirmed partial evidence that NeuraTech is piggybacking on old Lingtao data nodes," Rainer announced, his voice steady yet underscored by urgency. "If they crack our re-keying protocols, they could siphon portions of Zermatt's satellite coverage."

An immediate ripple of unease flickered visibly across the table. Ambassador Celine Dubois, one of the G-7 liaisons, exhaled sharply, her brow creasing with deep concern. "We can't allow that," she interjected firmly, her voice edged with intensity. "Our intelligence suggests NeuraTech has no ethical gating—no limit to how far they'll push mind-control or forced overwrites. The moment they get a foothold in your network, all bets are off."

The assembled leaders exchanged uneasy glances, absorbing the grim implications of her statement. Nicolás Tosh maintained a steady gaze, addressing the concerns with measured clarity. "We're working on new encryption layers. But if we leave holes unpatched to keep the White House requests afloat—like scanning additional government officials— NeuraTech might slip through. We need a unified approach."

Minister Walter Lindholm, another seasoned G-7 liaison, adjusted his reading glasses thoughtfully before speaking. His tone was diplomatic yet carried undeniable authority. "Unified approach or not, your technology is at risk, Mr. Tosh. The G-7 is prepared to assist… but only if you let us do so transparently."

A brief silence settled around the table as Tosh weighed the minister's words. He understood clearly the delicate balance between collaboration and operational autonomy. "Transparency is non-negotiable," Tosh affirmed calmly, decisively addressing the entire group. "But we must maintain operational integrity and confidentiality. Trust must flow both ways."

Ambassador Dubois leaned forward, acknowledging Tosh's concerns. "Then let's establish clear boundaries and robust oversight frameworks," she proposed resolutely. "Our collective strength lies in transparency, cooperation, and vigilance. Zermatt's resources paired with international oversight could offer the strongest barrier against NeuraTech's infiltration."

Rainer interjected carefully, "We have preliminary protocols drafted for just such collaboration—enhanced encryption paired with multi-layered verification procedures. Combined efforts from Zermatt, Lingtao, and Experta could solidify our defensive measures significantly."

Minister Lindholm nodded approvingly. "Then let's formalize this arrangement swiftly. Our adversaries won't pause while we debate procedural details. Speed and decisiveness are our greatest assets now."

Tosh straightened, resolutely accepting the challenge ahead. "Agreed. Our unified approach must be swift, transparent, and uncompromising. This partnership isn't merely strategic—it's a necessity."

With newfound resolve, the leaders around the table swiftly transitioned from discussion to action. In this moment of strategic clarity, the Experta Foundation boardroom became the nerve center of an unprecedented global alliance, determined to counteract a threat that transcended borders, challenging the very essence of human autonomy.

The CDA-325 Debate: Preemptive "Inoculation"

A tense hush filled the Experta Foundation's secure boardroom as Dr. Miriam Faber, renowned quantum encryption specialist, activated a new slide titled: "CDA-325 Deployment Scenarios." Beneath the ominous heading, five bullet points glowed, each representing complex, unprecedented possibilities.

Dr. Faber took a steadying breath, fully aware of the volatile implications her next words held. "We've speculated on using Algorithm-325 as a defensive measure," she began carefully, her voice firm yet reflective of the ethical gravity. "A 'vaccine,' if you will, that could block outside infiltration by layering protective code inside a target's neural pathways. In theory, it renders them immune to Overwrite attempts."

A palpable spike of tension coursed through the assembled leaders. The very mention of CDA-325 sent ripples of unease, for everyone understood its capabilities far surpassed mere surveillance; it was an invasive technology capable of rewriting human thought. The notion of deploying it widely carried profound ethical weight.

Ambassador Celine Dubois was the first to break the stunned silence, arching an elegant brow skeptically. "You propose we roll out CDA-325 across entire populations? Like vaccinating them against forced mind invasion?" she queried pointedly, her tone clearly illustrating her reservations.

Rainer Sábato intervened swiftly, sensing Nicolás Tosh's ambivalence and aiming to provide a measured response. "We'd limit it to high-risk targets first—world leaders, key officials, maybe corporate CEOs most vulnerable to blackmail. Essentially, the people NeuraTech would target."

From across the expansive table, Artemis Wang stepped forward abruptly. He had arrived only moments earlier, but his urgent demeanor commanded immediate attention. Clad in a formal suit, his voice carried the weight of ethical urgency. "Everyone, wait. If we start injecting entire groups with CDA-325, we cross a line we once swore never to approach. The normalizing effect alone… it's exactly what these rogue operators want."

His words resonated heavily within the room, provoking thoughtful silence as each attendee grappled internally with the moral complexities.

Nicolás Tosh's gaze fell, his thoughts momentarily consumed by echoes of Alejandra's fervent appeals for caution and ethical restraint.

Tosh finally spoke, his voice quiet yet profoundly resolute. "It's the same fundamental question we've faced since Algorithm-323: do we sacrifice privacy for security? Because once we expand the usage, we're no better than the ones we're fighting."

Dr. Faber nodded gravely, her expression pensive yet understanding. "We must carefully balance urgency with ethics. CDA-325 has the potential to protect, but its misuse—or even its perceived misuse—could irreparably erode the very freedoms we aim to safeguard."

Minister Walter Lindholm leaned forward earnestly, voicing a perspective rooted in practicality. "Perhaps a controlled pilot program with stringent oversight might offer a responsible path forward. Absolute transparency, restricted scope, and rigorous ethical standards."

The debate lingered unresolved, a profound silence enveloping the room. The collective understanding remained starkly clear: the path ahead was fraught with perilous choices, each decision capable of shaping humanity's future profoundly. The ethical boundaries they now approached were indistinct and perilously thin, demanding vigilance, integrity, and above all, humility.

Character Reversals: Wang Takes a Cautious Stance

An uneasy silence settled briefly over the secure Experta Foundation boardroom. Artemis Wang, previously the assertive face of Lingtao, now wore a rare expression of cautious deliberation as he assessed the tense atmosphere surrounding him. His gaze moved slowly, thoughtfully, across each face, registering their anxiety and concern.

Wang's voice emerged calm yet resolute. "We risk playing into their hands. If the public discovers we've used an implanting algorithm—albeit for 'defensive' reasons—imagine the outcry. We become the story, not NeuraTech."

Ambassador Celine Dubois reacted visibly, momentarily caught off guard by this unexpected caution from a man known for decisive, assertive actions. Her eyebrows lifted slightly, betraying a flicker of surprise. "I'm... impressed by your caution, Mr. Wang," she admitted carefully, clearly weighing her words. "But the threat is real. NeuraTech's inhuman testing suggests they're weeks, maybe days, from an operational system that can enslave entire corporate boards or government agencies."

Minister Walter Lindholm, a seasoned statesman, inclined his head slightly, reinforcing the Ambassador's concerns. His voice was measured yet carried an edge of urgency. "If you hesitate too long, entire sectors of Western security could be compromised."

Wang listened intently, understanding deeply the stakes involved, his own stance shifting under the gravity of the potential consequences. "I'm not advocating for paralysis," he clarified deliberately. "But we must ensure our actions don't inadvertently validate NeuraTech's approach. Public trust, once lost, is nearly impossible to regain. We must operate transparently, with clear boundaries and accountability, or we risk eroding the ethical high ground that sets us apart."

Nicolás Tosh glanced briefly at the swirling data on the projection— trafficking rings, infiltration logs, the ceaseless flood of global crises— and his expression firmed decisively. "We can't let them run unchecked," he stated firmly, determination clearly shaping his tone. "But if we deploy CDA-325, even in limited form, we must do so under strict controls. And once we open that door… it may never close."

Rainer Sábato nodded in thoughtful agreement. "Then we must establish immediate, rigorous oversight," he proposed calmly. "Every deployment must be scrutinized, recorded, and justified transparently. It's the only way to safeguard our integrity."

Ambassador Dubois exhaled softly, recognizing the delicate balance they must maintain. "Our objective is clear—protect the world without sacrificing the ethical core that defines us. We proceed carefully, cautiously, but decisively."

Wang's cautious stance had clearly resonated deeply, shifting the room's dynamic toward a thoughtful unity. As the leaders moved forward with deliberate care, each was acutely aware that their next decisions would not merely respond to NeuraTech's immediate threat but also shape humanity's ethical landscape for generations to come.

A curt, insistent beep sharply punctuated the tense silence in the Experta Foundation boardroom, signaling an urgent encrypted communication. Rainer Sábato swiftly tapped the console, his eyes rapidly scanning the incoming text. His expression grew increasingly somber with each passing moment.

"It's from the G-7 Security Secretariat," he summarized quietly yet urgently. "They want immediate decisive action against NeuraTech. They say we either neutralize them or risk losing G-7 support altogether."

A distinct flicker of alarm crossed Dr. Miriam Faber's usually composed features. The implications were immediately clear. "Without G-7 cover," she stated anxiously, "Redwood and the rogue Senators in the U.S. might isolate us. If we don't produce results, they'll claim we're incompetent at safeguarding the technology."

Ambassador Celine Dubois nodded grimly, her posture rigid with the gravity of the situation. "Exactly. The G-7 needs a show of force. The infiltration attempts spike every day. If you don't strike back—forcefully—they'll consider the Zermatt Data Center compromised."

Artemis Wang reacted sharply, his expression hardening, clearly disturbed by the escalating demands. "Their demands might push us to weaponize CDA-325. We do that, we hand them a golden chance to manipulate the technology behind closed doors. That's a short step to universal scanning."

A taut, oppressive silence enveloped the room, amplifying the moral complexities they all now faced. Nicolás Tosh slowly surveyed each face around the table, carefully noting the mixture of determination, caution, and unease reflected back at him. Internally, he grappled deeply with the conflicting pressures, vividly recalling Alejandra's urgent and poignant question echoing relentlessly in his mind: How far are you willing to go?

Breaking the silence with deliberate care, Tosh spoke quietly yet with unmistakable firmness. "We must demonstrate decisive action without compromising our core principles. Surrendering ethical boundaries under pressure is exactly the trap NeuraTech hopes we'll fall into."

Minister Walter Lindholm interjected with diplomatic caution, sensing the thin line they were treading. "Perhaps there is a middle ground. A targeted strike, carefully executed and transparently documented, might reassure the G-7 without opening the door to unchecked usage of CDA-325."

Ambassador Dubois leaned forward, supportive yet clearly anxious about the potential fallout. "Transparency and restraint must define our response. Any action taken must withstand global scrutiny."

Dr. Faber recalibrated quickly, her analytical mind rapidly processing potential scenarios. "We can deploy focused quantum encryption attacks on NeuraTech's infrastructure, publicly demonstrating our defensive capabilities without resorting to invasive technology. It could satisfy the immediate demands while preserving ethical standards."

Tosh met her eyes appreciatively, recognizing the wisdom in her proposal. "Agreed. We act swiftly, decisively, and transparently—but above all, ethically. We must reaffirm our position not just technologically, but morally."

Unified by Tosh's resolution, the room transformed its apprehension into purposeful momentum. Each leader understood clearly that the decisions made now would resonate deeply, shaping both immediate and future global security landscapes. This was more than a confrontation— it was a definitive test of their shared humanity and collective responsibility.

Parallel Threads and Mounting Pressures

Even as the summit in Zurich wrestled with existential decisions, the world outside advanced relentlessly:

Human Trafficking & Child Exploitation

Simultaneously, even as critical decisions unfolded within the Zurich summit, global crises persisted with relentless urgency. Within the bustling operations center at Zermatt, analysts and field operatives struggled beneath an atmosphere heavy with tension. A sudden alert flashed urgently on the central monitoring screen, drawing immediate attention.

Zermatt's advanced intelligence had achieved a partial breakthrough: they flagged a cross-border convoy in Southeast Asia possibly linked to a major trafficking ring. The convoy, meticulously camouflaged within ordinary logistical traffic, moved covertly along obscure routes. Initial assessments indicated this network was responsible for substantial human trafficking activities, exploiting innocent lives with cold efficiency.

"If we don't intercept them soon, the ringleaders might vanish indefinitely," Marisol Alvarez reported urgently, her voice edged with anxiety. The immense gravity of the moment was evident in her tightly clenched jaw.

Yet, a frustrating technical hurdle loomed ominously over their efforts. The ongoing re-keying of satellites slowed real-time tracking, risking lost opportunities. Each passing moment amplified the tension, as operators watched helplessly while vital tracking data lagged dangerously behind the swiftly moving convoy.

Dr. Miriam Faber, her expression deeply concerned, rapidly coordinated with technicians to enhance data transmission efficiency. "We're attempting to accelerate signal processing, but our window is closing rapidly," she warned gravely. "Any delay could cost innocent lives."

Across the room, Rainer Sábato urgently relayed commands to field operatives. "Deploy all local assets for immediate interception readiness," he ordered decisively. "We must not let them slip through our fingers."

Amidst this controlled chaos, Nicolás Tosh monitored the unfolding crisis closely from Zurich, remotely connecting with the operations room. "Every available resource must be activated. Coordinate closely with local enforcement; make sure humanitarian rescue teams are primed and ready."

Rainer acknowledged swiftly, already enacting the directives. "Teams are on standby, Nicolás. But we must resolve the tracking delays quickly or risk losing the convoy."

Tosh exhaled sharply, his thoughts momentarily drawn away from the strategic summit to the painful human cost represented by this convoy. He spoke firmly, voice layered with urgency and resolve. "No matter what happens, stay on them. We owe these victims swift justice and decisive action. We cannot fail."

As the Zermatt team galvanized its efforts, every operative understood the stark reality clearly: each delay, each small failure, translated directly into prolonged suffering for victims. Their collective determination solidified anew, driven by an unwavering commitment to safeguard vulnerable lives against exploitation and brutality. The fight against human trafficking was relentless, each partial breakthrough a fragile victory on a difficult road toward complete eradication.

Corruption at State Levels

As the Zurich summit grappled intensely with global strategic threats, another urgent alert flashed silently across Zermatt's secure communications channels, escalating tensions further.

Analysts exchanged wary glances as the message unfolded: Another small nation threatened to hush up an entire scandal if Zermatt wouldn't help scan certain officials. The implications were immediate and deeply troubling, striking directly at Zermatt's foundational principles of integrity and impartiality.

Marisol Alvarez swiftly relayed the developing situation to Nicolás Tosh, her voice strained by the precarious ethical line now drawn clearly before them. "If we refuse, we risk enabling an entire corrupt regime to escape accountability. Yet if we agree, we compromise our core principles," she explained urgently.

Tosh's jaw tightened perceptibly, his internal struggle vividly apparent to everyone listening. "We cannot become a tool for blackmail," he responded firmly. "Our mandate demands transparency and accountability, not clandestine coercion."

From across the room, Rainer Sábato spoke quietly but insistently, highlighting the dangerous secondary implications. "It's not just about this small nation, Nicolás. Could they trust the data center if G-7 turned against them? Any perceived weakness or compliance with unethical demands might provide G-7 the justification they need to withdraw support completely."

Ambassador Dubois, tuned in remotely from the summit, interjected forcefully, her voice resonating clearly despite the distance. "We must maintain our credibility. If the international community sees us yield to threats, our effectiveness diminishes drastically. Transparency and ethical clarity are our strongest weapons against corruption."

Dr. Miriam Faber carefully analyzed the technical implications. "We could publicly offer impartial scanning as part of a broader anti-corruption initiative, open to international oversight. This might pressure them into accepting accountability without us appearing complicit."

Tosh considered her proposal carefully, recognizing its potential value. "Make it clear to this nation—and publicly—that our scanning operations are independent, transparent, and never selectively deployed under coercion."

Rainer nodded approvingly. "We'll emphasize our ethical commitment openly. This positions us firmly against corruption without compromising trust or yielding to blackmail."

As directives rapidly disseminated, each Zermatt team member understood the precarious balance they now navigated. The fight against state-level corruption was unending and fraught with complex moral dilemmas, demanding continuous vigilance and absolute adherence to ethical principles. They stood unwavering, resolved to uphold integrity even under relentless pressure.

Faulty Technology & Public Safety

In the heart of Zermatt's high-stakes operational headquarters, analysts worked under heightened stress, juggling multiple critical threats simultaneously. Their recent swift intervention had narrowly prevented catastrophe—a potentially devastating meltdown near a hydroelectric plant had been averted thanks to timely identification and rapid response.

Yet relief proved fleeting, quickly overshadowed by emerging crises. Fresh alerts flashed urgently across monitoring screens, capturing immediate attention: new red flags popped up in a major transatlantic airline's maintenance logs. The implications were stark and chillingly immediate.

Marisol Alvarez rapidly assessed the new threat data, her fingers moving swiftly across her console, tension tightening her expression. "These reports indicate systemic negligence," she reported, voice strained by the gravity of her findings. "Critical maintenance procedures bypassed to meet aggressive turnaround schedules. Lives could be lost if this isn't urgently addressed."

Dr. Miriam Faber, deeply engrossed in technical analysis, concurred grimly. "This airline has neglected vital safety checks. We're looking at potential catastrophic failures—engine malfunctions, compromised flight systems. We must alert aviation authorities immediately."

The room grew quieter as the severity of the moment sank in. Nicolás Tosh connected remotely, his voice firm yet weary from the cumulative pressure. "Coordinate closely with international aviation regulators and investigative journalists. Ensure immediate grounding of any aircraft identified as compromised. Lives depend on swift and transparent action."

Rainer Sábato glanced worriedly at Tosh through the screen, his usually composed demeanor clearly strained. "Nicolás, resources are stretched thin. If the data center turns fully inward to fight NeuraTech, we risk missing these crucial warnings."

Tosh nodded soberly, deeply conscious of the monumental balancing act required. "We can't afford tunnel vision," he emphasized firmly. "Public safety remains paramount. Allocate dedicated teams specifically for infrastructure and transportation monitoring. We must not let vigilance slip, even briefly."

Ambassador Dubois interjected supportively, her voice resonating with diplomatic resolve. "The international community expects decisive intervention in these safety matters. This could reinforce global confidence in Zermatt's impartiality and reliability."

Resolutely, the operations team recalibrated swiftly, acknowledging the critical dual challenge they faced: countering NeuraTech's aggressive infiltration attempts without compromising public safety vigilance. Their renewed determination echoed clearly across their faces—a silent, unwavering commitment to protect lives at all costs.

Corporate Sabotage & Competitor Intrusions

As the Experta Foundation grappled internally with escalating threats, external pressures intensified dangerously. Rival giants hovered like vultures, itching to exploit any vacuum if the G-7 forced Tosh to shut down major parts of the network. Global tech conglomerates, sensing potential weaknesses, discreetly intensified their espionage operations, each ready to fill the void and gain strategic advantage.

At the periphery, a troubling new dynamic emerged—Redwood's advisors courted them, promising regulatory freedom in exchange for financial backing. These clandestine negotiations suggested an alarming alliance of convenience, threatening to undermine Zermatt's carefully maintained ethical standards.

Inside Zermatt's data monitoring center, Marisol Alvarez rapidly processed incoming threat assessments, her expression increasingly tense. "Espionage activities are escalating sharply," she informed Nicolás Tosh via secure link. "Rivals sense opportunity. They're aggressively probing our defenses, seeking vulnerabilities."

Rainer Sábato, standing nearby, added soberly, "These aren't ordinary corporate rivals—they're powerful entities, politically connected, ready to seize on any perceived weakness. Redwood's team has positioned itself as an intermediary, actively facilitating these dangerous overtures."

Tosh absorbed this quietly, understanding immediately the delicate strategic maneuvering at play. His voice, when he spoke, resonated with controlled determination. "We cannot afford even the appearance of instability. Reinforce our cybersecurity infrastructure immediately. Alert all partners—trust and transparency must remain our highest priority."

Dr. Miriam Faber swiftly coordinated security upgrades, her analytical calm contrasting sharply with the underlying urgency of the situation. "Enhanced quantum encryption protocols are going live now," she reported decisively. "Our defenses must hold, especially against adversaries emboldened by Redwood's assurances."

Ambassador Celine Dubois joined the discussion, her diplomatic experience sharply clarifying the political stakes. "If rivals secure footholds during this vulnerable period, global trust in our integrity could erode quickly. We must publicly reaffirm our commitment to ethical oversight to reassure international stakeholders."

Wang, typically assertive but now measured and cautious, interjected firmly, "Transparency and ethical governance are our strongest defenses. Any perceived compromise could invite disaster. We must remain unwavering, clearly signaling to both Redwood and rival corporations that we are neither for sale nor open to coercion."

Tosh nodded resolutely, reinforcing the collective resolve. "Agreed. We maintain our position clearly, unequivocally. Corporate sabotage thrives on uncertainty—let's ensure there is none."

With a renewed sense of purpose and urgency, Zermatt's teams moved swiftly, reinforcing cybersecurity measures and communicating clearly to global stakeholders. The message was explicit: integrity and transparency remained non-negotiable, their vigilance steadfast in face of rising corporate threats.

Maggie Wu's Investigation

In the midst of Zurich's meticulous calm, investigative journalist Maggie Wu had quietly arrived, bringing with her an undercurrent of tension. Her reputation preceded her—relentless, meticulous, and fearless in uncovering hidden truths. Word rapidly circulated among Experta Foundation personnel: Maggie had arrived in Zurich. Rumor had it she was already sniffing around Experta's offices, seeking interviews or "misplaced memos."

Maggie moved deliberately, eyes sharp and observant, quickly noting any subtle shift in expression or hesitant response as she spoke informally with employees outside the Experta Foundation's gleaming facade. Her keen instincts guided her directly toward gaps in official statements and areas of suppressed unease. With each conversation, she drew closer to piecing together fragments of a story potentially explosive enough to ripple through international channels.

Inside Experta's secure boardroom, Rainer Sábato relayed the journalist's presence to Nicolás Tosh with undisguised urgency. "She's probing carefully," he warned quietly. "Asking precise, strategic questions—any hesitation or minor slip-up, and she'll find something to leverage."

Ambassador Celine Dubois immediately recognized the perilous timing. "If Maggie's exposé breaks now, it could directly intersect with the ongoing G-7 crisis," she remarked grimly. "Any appearance of impropriety or secrecy on our part might severely undermine international trust at the worst possible moment."

Tosh felt the weight of these compounded pressures acutely. Maggie Wu's investigation represented a dangerous wildcard—unpredictable and uncontrollable. His expression remained steady, though his thoughts churned deeply beneath a composed exterior. "Ensure full transparency internally," he instructed firmly. "Verify all protocols and procedures meticulously. We must anticipate her moves without obstructing her legitimate inquiries."

Wang listened closely, clearly unsettled by this development yet aware of its inevitability. "Perhaps we engage directly," he suggested cautiously. "Offer Maggie controlled access—show our commitment to openness, but manage carefully to prevent any misinterpretation."

Rainer nodded thoughtfully. "Controlled transparency might be our best defense. She's less likely to find cracks if we openly acknowledge difficult questions and respond directly."

Dr. Miriam Faber added supportively, her analytical perspective valuable. "Preparedness is crucial. Review all internal documents. Eliminate ambiguity that Maggie might exploit."

Unified by a strategy of transparency and proactive engagement, Experta's leadership mobilized quickly. They understood clearly that Maggie Wu's presence symbolized more than just a journalistic threat—it was a test of their ethical resolve and their commitment to transparency amidst mounting external pressures. Each member prepared for the looming confrontation, determined to preserve integrity and public trust at a critical juncture.

Conclusion of the Summit

Under the cold overhead lights, the debate wound down without a firm resolution—only an uneasy plan for a "stopgap" approach. Nicolás Tosh would coordinate closely with Rainer Sábato to finalize a limited version of CDA-325—robust enough to protect critical nodes and selected high-profile leaders from NeuraTech infiltration, but carefully constrained to avoid initiating mass deployment.

The G-7 liaisons expressed their impatience clearly: time was running short. If Zermatt didn't demonstrate a credible means of containing NeuraTech soon, an international coalition might intervene. Each diplomat emphasized the high stakes, subtly signaling that Zermatt's autonomy and global credibility teetered precariously on the effectiveness of their next move.

To everyone's mild surprise, Artemis Wang supported Tosh's cautious, more ethically constrained route, his voice quietly firm as he reminded those assembled, "A rushed solution could spawn unstoppable tyranny." The statement resonated deeply, temporarily quieting even the most vocal proponents of aggressive intervention.

As the group disbanded, a tense hush settled over the corridor outside the secure meeting chamber. Each participant seemed momentarily lost in private contemplation, grappling individually with the profound ethical implications that lingered unresolved. Nicolás Tosh paused beside a wide, floor-to-ceiling window, his gaze drifting thoughtfully across Zurich's bustling skyline, momentarily detached from the urgent realities he faced.

Somewhere, half a world away, he knew an unhinged faction relentlessly forged NeuraTech into a ruthless tool of mind subjugation. The specter of their unchecked ambition loomed dangerously large. Here in Zurich, within the walls of Experta, the custodians of CDA technology stood at a pivotal crossroads. Deploying Algorithm-325 might effectively curb the looming threat—but it also risked opening a Pandora's box with consequences darker than any had imagined.

Quietly, Tosh exhaled, a breath carrying the weight of decisions not yet fully made. The countdown had already begun, ticking steadily toward a moment when their choices would irreversibly shape the future—not just of Zermatt, but of global conscience itself.

Chapter 7

Lines in the Sand

Washington, D.C. — The White House Bunker, 2017
Day 21, 4:00 P.M. ET

The lights in the old "War Room" were harsh and clinical, a strategic nerve center hidden beneath marble corridors and layers of reinforced security. President O'Sullivan stood at the head of a long metal table, flanked by top security advisors, each face tense with urgency. The subdued hum of air filtration underscored the seriousness of the moment.

Nicolás Tosh glanced around the bunker's walls, draped with large screens cycling satellite feeds and infiltration logs. In bold letters on one screen: "NEURATECH – PRIORITY THREAT." The hush in the room was broken only by the President's calm yet steeled voice.

President O'Sullivan's gaze moved steadily around the room, making eye contact with each advisor as she spoke clearly and deliberately. "We find ourselves at a pivotal juncture. Our response to NeuraTech will define our ethical boundaries for decades."

General Maxwell Peterson, a seasoned military strategist with piercing grey eyes, leaned forward urgently. "Madam President, intelligence confirms NeuraTech's aggressive capability. Their technology can penetrate and rewrite minds without constraints or moral oversight. We must take immediate, decisive action."

Tosh met Peterson's intensity with composed resolve. "Madam President, General Peterson is correct about the threat. However, rushing into full-scale action without meticulous precautions might precipitate exactly the global chaos we aim to avoid. Our response must be measured, calculated."

The tension heightened palpably. Secretary of State Elizabeth Roark spoke decisively, her voice steady. "Nicolás, your caution is admirable, but global stability hangs by a thread. Allies are demanding a tangible

133

demonstration of our control over this technology. Without swift containment, international trust may fracture irreparably."

Tosh nodded in understanding but stood firm. "I propose targeted interventions focused on strategic nodes. Deploy CDA-325 selectively to secure critical infrastructure and protect key political and corporate leaders. This balances immediate safety needs with long-term ethical considerations."

The President's thoughtful silence lasted several seconds. Finally, she addressed the room with authoritative clarity. "Agreed. We draw our line clearly. Deploy Algorithm-325 in the most restrained, controlled manner possible. Every step will be transparent to the G-7 and monitored independently."

Peterson's posture stiffened slightly, dissatisfaction evident, but he acknowledged the President's command. "Understood, Madam President. My team will coordinate closely with Zermatt to identify and secure priority targets immediately."

President O'Sullivan turned deliberately toward Tosh. "Nicolás, maintaining ethical clarity amidst this crisis is paramount. Your team must operate with the utmost transparency—no exceptions."

"Yes, Madam President," Tosh replied evenly, aware of the enormous responsibility now explicitly placed on Zermatt's shoulders. "Transparency and ethical oversight remain our highest priorities."

As the meeting concluded, the participants dispersed swiftly, each acutely aware that the decisions made here would reverberate globally. Tosh lingered momentarily, eyes lingering on the stark warning on the screen: "NEURATECH – PRIORITY THREAT." The path forward was defined clearly—yet each step forward was fraught with profound moral risk.

Presidential Ultimatum

"Tosh," the President began, hands clasped behind his back, "we're out of time. My advisors are unanimous: NeuraTech's infiltration attempts have escalated. We suspect they've gained partial access to nodes in Eastern Europe and Asia. We need you to do whatever is necessary to neutralize them. That includes deploying any… weaponized aspects of the CDA if you need to.”

The finality in his tone sent a ripple of discomfort through Tosh. While O'Sullivan had quietly condoned the discreet usage of CDA to quash conspiracies before, never had he invoked it so openly as a blunt instrument.

“Mr. President,” Tosh said carefully, “we have protocols for defensive measures. But unleashing the full capabilities of the CDA suite—like… advanced Overwrite or forced mental captures—”

“Is on the table,” O'Sullivan finished, his gaze unwavering. “I've signed a classified directive, authorizing it under the same war powers used for existential threats. And make no mistake, NeuraTech qualifies.”

General Collins, seated beside the President, nodded in grim agreement. “We're at a crossroads. We have intelligence that these rogue players are forcibly overwriting minds. They aren't holding back. If we do, we risk letting them get the upper hand.”

Tosh's chest tightened. He thought of Alejandra's plea, of Rainer's caution, of the G-7's stance. Weaponizing the CDA? It was precisely the slippery slope they had pledged to avoid. Yet the President's eyes were resolute, a reflection of the swirling crisis.

Secretary Roark interjected gently yet firmly, sensing Tosh's internal struggle. “Nicolás, none of us embrace this lightly. But the world we vowed to protect is on the brink. Limited and strategic deployment might be our only option left.”

The weight of silence pressed in as Tosh processed their words. He knew this moment was inevitable, yet it shook him profoundly now that it had arrived. “Understood,” he finally conceded, his voice a careful mixture of resolve and regret. “We'll move with precision. Every action carefully documented, every decision scrutinized.”

President O'Sullivan nodded solemnly, visibly relieved yet acutely aware of the moral weight just transferred onto Tosh's shoulders. “Thank you, Nicolás. We trust your judgment. History will judge us by these decisions—but first, we must ensure history continues at all.”

As Tosh exited the bunker, his mind raced with tactical scenarios, ethical boundaries, and the heavy realization of actions he never wanted to authorize. Outside, the fading daylight felt unusually cold, mirroring the chill of the decisions now resting firmly upon him. Each step forward into this uncertain terrain felt irrevocable—one more step along the perilous edge between preserving humanity's freedom and inadvertently becoming its oppressor.

Backroom Conflicts: Redwood's Competing Demand

Only moments after O'Sullivan's meeting concluded, Tosh was ushered into a smaller, windowless side chamber used for secure communications. There, a communications officer quietly informed him: "Senator Redwood wants to speak. He insisted."

Tosh braced himself. Redwood was the current front-runner in the upcoming presidential election—his slogan of "Total Transparency for All" had already rattled Tosh's alliance with the White House. Sure enough, Redwood's voice crackled over the secure line:

"Mr. Tosh," Redwood drawled, "I trust you've had quite a discussion with the current administration about these infiltration threats. I have a different request. Let me be clear: if I win the presidency, I want full transparency into the technology you wield. No more secrets. No more private foundation controlling what's essentially national security property."

Tosh's stomach churned. Redwood's stance was hardly a surprise, but hearing it stated so bluntly drove the point home.

"Senator Redwood," Tosh replied evenly, "we're dealing with a global threat. We need to maintain certain checks and balances—"

"Checks and balances?" Redwood's laugh was humorless. "Since when does an unelected mathematician decide how far we go to protect our nation from mind infiltration? If I take office, your foundation's illusions will end. The CDA belongs to the people, and I'll see to it that we harness it fully."

Harness it fully—the phrase hammered Tosh's nerves. Redwood didn't bother with nuance or moral disclaimers; he might turn the entire population into scanning subjects overnight. At least O'Sullivan tries to be discreet, Tosh reflected.

"Senator," he said, "I hear your position. For now, my team is focused on stopping NeuraTech. That's enough on our plate."

Redwood's voice chilled. "Yes. And if you succeed, know that you'll owe me an explanation of every method you used—once I'm in power. We're done letting you run the show from behind the curtain."

A click, and the line went dead. Tosh exhaled, the bunker's low hum resonating in his ears like an oncoming storm.

Alone now, Tosh stood in the cramped chamber, a surge of frustration mixing with anxiety. Redwood's open hostility promised not only a political challenge but a profound ideological confrontation. Tosh had always understood the gravity of wielding CDA technology, and the ethical boundaries he'd fought hard to maintain. Yet Redwood's uncompromising push for total transparency threatened to dismantle years of carefully established ethical guardrails overnight.

He felt a deepening dread at the thought of a presidency willing to exploit fears and technology for political leverage. Tosh knew he was caught between two opposing forces—the current administration pressing for immediate action to counter NeuraTech, and a prospective administration bent on dismantling every safeguard that kept CDA from becoming a tool of invasive control.

Stepping out of the claustrophobic confines of the secure communications room, Tosh's mind raced through potential moves. He recognized the imminent clash of ideals now looming before him. Ensuring global security had become only half the battle; protecting the world from the very solutions they employed was rapidly becoming an equally urgent priority.

Doubt and Dissent: Moral Compass Falters

Re-emerging into the corridor, Tosh nearly collided with Chief of Staff Harrington, who had Re-emerging into the corridor, Tosh nearly collided with Chief of Staff Harrington, who had presumably overheard the Redwood exchange through official channels.

"Tosh," Harrington said in a low voice, "this is the reality now. Two factions—O'Sullivan's team wants you to use everything you've got to crush NeuraTech, Redwood wants the technology in his hands. Either path leads to a level of exploitation none of us wanted."

Tosh pinched the bridge of his nose, feeling the weight of a second world pressing in. "It's as if both sides are pulling me in directions I can't ethically go. If Redwood wins, the scale of forced scanning might dwarf anything we've done."

Harrington shook his head, crossing his arms. "If you do nothing, though, NeuraTech could overthrow half the Western world, rewriting officials at will. No matter who's in power, the technology is in danger."

Silence stretched, thick with unspoken anxieties. Tosh thought of the sub-plots he was juggling: Human trafficking rings operating in plain sight yet always slipping just beyond reach; corrupt officials manipulating entire nations from shadowy backrooms; aviation disasters narrowly averted yet always lurking one step away due to corporate negligence; ruthless corporate espionage masking itself behind charitable fronts; and the growing web of exploitation imagery on hidden corners of the internet.

Each subplot, each crisis, represented lives hanging precariously between salvation and oblivion. The tension built like a storm inside Tosh, an intense pressure that was becoming impossible to navigate. The technology designed to save humanity was becoming a tool that could irrevocably corrupt it.

Harrington studied Tosh, sensing the storm within. "I wish I could tell you there's a clear path here, Nicolás, but there isn't. We have to choose between imperfect options."

"Imperfect?" Tosh's voice was strained, nearly breaking under the moral weight. "Imperfect doesn't begin to describe it. We're dancing on the razor's edge between guardian and tyrant. Every move we make now has consequences we can't even fathom."

"Agreed," Harrington responded quietly. "But consider this—inaction guarantees chaos. Action, despite its moral cost, at least gives us a chance to steer the outcome."

Tosh stared past Harrington, his gaze distant, burdened. "But at what cost, Harrington? If we become as ruthless as our enemies, we've already lost. The technology we hold wasn't meant to subjugate—it was supposed to liberate, to protect. If it turns oppressive, we've betrayed everything we stood for."

Harrington rested a comforting hand on Tosh's shoulder, voice firm yet compassionate. "Then hold the line. Protect those principles fiercely. We have no easy answers, only difficult choices. But remember—if we abandon our moral compass now, there's no going back."

Tosh closed his eyes briefly, acknowledging Harrington's wisdom even as the suffocating weight of responsibility grew heavier. Opening them again, he nodded slowly. "You're right. The cost of losing ourselves is too high. We'll hold the line, no matter how hard it gets. But the margin for error has never been thinner."

Silence stretched, thick with unspoken anxieties. Tosh thought of the sub-plots he was juggling:

Drug Trafficking – Comprehensive Global Crackdown

Within Zermatt's high-security command center, Nicolás Tosh meticulously scrutinized multiple screens filled with streaming intelligence data, surveillance imagery, and encrypted communications. The team had worked tirelessly for months, collecting and analyzing intelligence across continents. Now, it was time to strike.

"Initiate simultaneous operations," Tosh instructed decisively, eyes firmly set on the primary tactical screen. "Coordinate with local authorities—South America and Asia first."

In the dense jungles of Colombia and Peru, precise coordinates provided by Zermatt guided swift military raids on clandestine coca plantations. Surveillance drones relayed real-time footage, capturing fields ablaze and apprehensions in progress. Simultaneously, across Southeast Asia's remote valleys and mountain villages, heroin processing labs hidden from international view fell rapidly under assault from coordinated local police actions. Authorities seized huge caches of illicit substances, dismantling months of production in mere hours.

"Routes and logistics chains next," Tosh commanded, signaling Marisol Alvarez. She swiftly relayed encrypted coordinates and detailed intelligence packages to authorities across multiple jurisdictions. The meticulously mapped trafficking routes—hidden trails, rivers, clandestine airstrips—were simultaneously disrupted. Transportation vehicles carrying large caches of narcotics were intercepted at key choke points, their smugglers detained swiftly and silently.

Within hours, Zermatt's detailed intelligence reached international ports and border crossings, spotlighting corrupt officials who had facilitated these dangerous commodities' entry into markets. Secure documents and transaction records were handed anonymously to international regulatory and law enforcement agencies, immediately prompting investigations, arrests, and rapid closures of compromised entry points.

The deepest impact came next, targeting the king-makers and masterminds who controlled global narcotics distribution networks. Zermatt exposed extensive criminal hierarchies previously invisible, unveiling powerful figures who had long operated with impunity. Bank accounts, front companies, luxury real estate, and secret vaults containing vast amounts of cash were systematically pinpointed and reported to financial authorities worldwide.

"Freeze every asset," Tosh commanded firmly, his voice edged with the resolve of a relentless crusade. "Sever their cash flow and ensure complete paralysis of their financial infrastructure."

Global banks, now alerted, swiftly complied, freezing hundreds of accounts identified through irrefutable evidence as proceeds from drug trafficking. Luxury assets—mansions, yachts, private jets—purchased with dirty money were seized across continents, their owners suddenly stripped of resources, influence, and power.

Concurrently, Rainer Sábato spearheaded an intensive assault specifically targeting fentanyl networks, identifying labs hidden deep within industrial facilities in China and clandestine production centers scattered across North America. Highly coordinated raids executed simultaneously by local authorities led to extensive seizures of precursor chemicals, finished fentanyl, and specialized equipment.

"Every route, every courier, every financier—shut them down," Rainer directed, voice resolute as encrypted operational details flooded law enforcement agencies. Within hours, international drug enforcement units apprehended countless couriers at airports, border checkpoints, and distribution hubs. The meticulously mapped financial networks supporting fentanyl trafficking were immediately dismantled, and vast sums of laundered money were frozen or seized.

As the operation progressed, Tosh felt a somber yet profound sense of fulfillment. This wasn't merely law enforcement—it was a systematic dismantling of global criminal infrastructures, an uncompromising stand against an epidemic destroying countless lives.

Yet even amid initial triumph, Tosh remained vigilant. He understood clearly the adaptability and resilience of criminal networks. Leaning against the console, he met Marisol's sober gaze. "Today we've struck deeply," he acknowledged, voice low yet powerful. "But this battle won't end overnight. Our vigilance must remain unyielding until this scourge is entirely eradicated."

Marisol nodded solemnly, returning her attention to the ongoing data streams. The global war on drug trafficking had reached a historic turning point, but Zermatt's fight was far from over.

Human Trafficking & Child Exploitation

The operations room at Zermatt buzzed with a grim intensity. Marisol Alvarez stood at the central console, frustration tightening her jaw as she reviewed the latest intelligence feed from Southeast Asia. The brightly glowing screens projected geolocation maps and encrypted chatter, each line of data painting an increasingly bleak picture.

"The trail's gone lukewarm," she reported tersely, glancing toward Nicolás Tosh. "Our on-the-ground sources confirm the traffickers have grown suspicious. They're altering routes multiple times daily—now mostly ad hoc, unpredictable."

Tosh felt his gut twist, the familiar, harrowing disappointment of leads evaporating right when they needed action most. "Are our surveillance drones still in position?"

"Limited coverage," Marisol admitted reluctantly. "The re-keying for satellite security against NeuraTech is slowing down real-time access. Every gap in coverage gives them another chance to slip away."

Nearby, Rainer Sábato leaned forward, his typically composed demeanor shadowed by urgency. "What about the local authorities? Are they still collaborating?"

Marisol hesitated, choosing her words carefully. "Yes, but they're cautious. Every raid that doesn't yield results puts their officers and our informants at risk. Trust is wearing thin."

Tosh exhaled slowly, his eyes distant as he processed the implications. Every passing minute reduced the likelihood of rescue, every diverted route threatened more innocent lives slipping beyond their reach.

Dr. Miriam Faber approached quietly, her voice steady yet edged with resolve. "We can't afford to lose this cell entirely. It's crucial we maintain surveillance pressure—even reduced capacity might force them into a mistake. We need patience, Nicolás. Any premature move and they'll scatter completely."

Rainer nodded in somber agreement. "Miriam's right. We recalibrate, increase our clandestine monitoring, and await their slip-up. But we must accept the bitter truth that each day we wait, the odds grow dimmer."

The operations room fell momentarily quiet, the hum of equipment underscoring the heavy, unspoken anxiety. Tosh finally broke the silence, voice firm despite the deep emotional strain. "Then we wait, watching relentlessly. But the second they slip, no hesitation—we strike with everything we've got."

He turned back toward the screens, staring at the flickering dots representing human lives caught in darkness. The painful realization weighed heavily upon him: their efforts, though tireless and earnest, might still fall short. Yet the resolve remained unwavering. Tosh knew they would continue their pursuit, no matter how faint the trail became, because every lost lead was not merely a setback—it was a call to press harder, to hold tighter, and to never abandon hope.

Corruption at State Levels – Looming Deadlines

Inside the dimly lit intelligence briefing room at Zermatt, the tension was palpable. Nicolás Tosh watched a cascade of reports roll in from diplomatic backchannels, each marked by urgency and a growing sense of desperation. Pressure from small European and African nations had intensified overnight, their leaders sending thinly veiled threats wrapped as diplomatic pleas.

Marisol Alvarez projected a detailed map onto the main screen, pinpointing each country requesting discreet scans of certain influential figures. "They're terrified of losing G-7 financial backing if any corruption scandals erupt publicly. We're getting hush requests almost hourly now—each one couched in vague promises of cooperation but clearly driven by panic."

Tosh paced slowly, deep in thought, weighing the heavy implications. "Each request is essentially asking us to compromise our transparency, our integrity. But turning them down risks destabilizing entire regions."

Rainer Sábato leaned forward, folding his hands tightly on the table, eyes narrowed in contemplation. "This isn't mere corruption—it's systemic. Entire administrations could collapse if exposed, plunging millions into chaos. Yet if we shield them, we're complicit."

Dr. Miriam Faber stood off to the side, her voice soft yet firm, laced with ethical determination. "The G-7's deadlines are tightening. If we give into these demands, we undermine the very foundation we built. The CDA technology was never intended to be a political bargaining chip."

Tosh nodded gravely. "Agreed. But neither can we allow entire populations to suffer due to the actions of corrupt elites. It's a moral paradox."

Marisol interjected cautiously. "Perhaps a middle ground exists— limited disclosure to G-7 oversight without publicly exposing the weakest nations. We control the release of information carefully to ensure stability."

Rainer's expression hardened. "Even limited compromise sets a dangerous precedent. Once that door opens, there's no closing it. The G-7 will keep pushing further."

The room fell into a heavy silence, each individual grappling internally with the weight of the decision looming before them. Tosh finally broke the quiet, voice resolute but weary from the persistent ethical strain.

"We'll grant no hush agreements. Instead, offer conditional assistance: anti-corruption support in exchange for transparent governance commitments. If they refuse, they accept the consequences. Our stance remains clear—Zermatt protects human dignity, not corrupt systems."

His words hung in the air, underscored by the ongoing tension of the rapidly ticking clock, each passing second narrowing their room for maneuvering. The storm of international diplomacy and ethical dilemmas was far from over, yet Tosh stood firm, determined to uphold the delicate balance between justice and stability.

Faulty Technology & Public Safety – Another defective airline part flagged. Tosh had staff scrambling, but resources were stretched, overshadowed by the NeuraTech crisis.

Inside Zermatt's bustling command center, screens flashed urgent alerts in rapid succession. One monitor, highlighted ominously in red, displayed critical warnings about yet another airline part failing to meet safety specifications. Nicolás Tosh stood rigidly, arms folded tightly across his chest, eyes rapidly absorbing each line of scrolling data.

"How widespread is this issue?" Tosh demanded sharply, turning swiftly to face Marisol Alvarez.

She pressed a finger to her earpiece, relaying information even as it reached her. "At least forty commercial jets across three international carriers," Marisol reported, her voice taut with restrained alarm. "Initial tests indicate compromised landing gear hydraulics. It could lead to catastrophic failures on landing."

Tosh exhaled heavily, briefly closing his eyes in frustration. They'd narrowly prevented similar disasters before, yet every victory felt temporary, a bandage covering an ever-widening wound.

"We need immediate grounding protocols activated," he ordered decisively, voice cutting clearly through the murmurs of tension. "Push regulatory agencies aggressively. No plane fitted with these parts leaves the runway until we've fully verified replacement."

Marisol nodded briskly, already transmitting emergency directives through secure channels. Beside her, Dr. Miriam Faber monitored predictive analytics, anxiety marking subtle lines across her forehead. "The real issue isn't just these parts," Miriam interjected softly, her eyes focused intensely on the shifting statistical models on-screen. "It's systemic negligence driven by greed. This isn't isolated; it's symptomatic of deeper rot."

Tosh felt the truth of her words keenly, a heavy acknowledgment pressing on his conscience. Their resources, finite and increasingly diverted by the looming threat of NeuraTech, were nearing exhaustion. Each crisis pulled them thinner, each failure to anticipate or intercept had potentially lethal consequences.

Across the command room, Rainer Sábato leaned in urgently from his workstation. "Regulators are responding slower than usual. They're overwhelmed with verifying compliance while juggling ongoing investigations into the last recall," he cautioned. "They're stretched thin too."

Tosh paced briefly, the weight of simultaneous crises nearly overwhelming him. "We cannot relent. Lean on our whistleblower networks. Ensure the press has the necessary details to push public pressure. Lives depend on immediate, unequivocal action."

His words hung in the air, a potent reminder of the gravity surrounding each decision. Despite the enormity of the NeuraTech crisis, Tosh was determined that no risk to human safety, however overshadowed, would be overlooked or dismissed. Yet the grim reality pressed harshly: How long could they continue scrambling to contain disasters while resources dwindled, overshadowed by an even darker threat rising unchecked?

Corporate Sabotage & Competitor Intrusions – Redwood's campaign advisers quietly courted big tech players, feeding the rumor that once Redwood was elected, the CDA might be "open for business."

In a sleek, dimly-lit lounge hidden on the upper floors of a luxury Washington hotel, Senator Redwood's senior campaign advisers discreetly mingled among executives from the nation's largest technology firms. Crystal glasses clinked quietly, subdued laughter punctuated earnest conversations, and hushed voices navigated carefully around sensitive topics. Each attendee had been vetted meticulously, ensuring discretion while delivering a clear, unspoken message: the potential for unprecedented access was on the horizon.

Jonathan Mercer, Redwood's chief adviser, leaned in closely to the CEO of a prominent artificial intelligence firm, his voice pitched low yet clear enough to convey absolute confidence. "Senator Redwood is very clear on this," Mercer emphasized softly, his words precisely measured. "Under his administration, transparency won't just be a promise—it will be the operational reality. CDA will no longer be hidden behind private foundations or backroom agreements. Instead, think of it as an open field—regulated, of course, but with ample room for innovative partnerships."

The CEO raised an eyebrow, intrigued yet cautious. "You're suggesting direct corporate access to the CDA? Even partial integration would transform entire industries. The potential profitability is immense, but ethically... it's unprecedented."

Mercer flashed a calculated, reassuring smile, his tone becoming even smoother. "We're merely talking about responsible democratization of technology. Imagine predictive analytics applied to market forecasts, mental health diagnostics, even consumer insights—with strict oversight, naturally."

At the far corner, another adviser, Elena Brooks, spoke softly with representatives of a global conglomerate known for pushing regulatory boundaries. She chose her words deliberately, threading the needle between plausibility and deniability. "Of course, any cooperation would strictly adhere to ethical guidelines," Elena affirmed diplomatically, "but under Redwood, the CDA won't be locked behind closed doors. Business could thrive under sensible but streamlined oversight. Transparency and profit aren't mutually exclusive."

The subtle overtures resonated deeply. Executives exchanged cautious glances, the implications thrilling yet unsettling. If Redwood succeeded, the competitive landscape could shift overnight, redefining global market dynamics.

Meanwhile, away from the glittering cityscape, Nicolás Tosh sat tensely inside his office, oblivious yet intuitively aware of the strategic whispers undermining the careful ethical boundaries he had fought to uphold. Reports trickled in, vague yet persistent rumors of Redwood's ambitious promises unsettling his thoughts.

Rainer Sábato, visibly concerned, entered the office swiftly. "Nicolás, our contacts confirm Redwood's team is quietly signaling big tech," he announced urgently. "They're floating the idea that the CDA could become widely accessible. If this narrative takes hold, corporate espionage will surge."

Tosh leaned back slowly, feeling a deep foreboding settle in his chest. "Redwood's playing with fire. He sees transparency as political currency, ignoring how quickly it could spiral into rampant exploitation."

Rainer nodded gravely. "The corporate world senses opportunity. They'll position themselves aggressively. If Redwood wins, the floodgates open."

Tosh stood, staring out across the quiet city skyline, his resolve firming despite rising anxiety. "Then we have two fronts to fight," he said quietly but resolutely. "Neutralize NeuraTech and ensure Redwood never gains unfettered access. Our vigilance must double—too much depends on it."

As evening shadows lengthened, the tension between responsible oversight and reckless transparency grew clearer. Redwood's quiet promises to big tech whispered of an uncertain future, one in which profit might swiftly eclipse principle.

Maggie Wu's Investigation – Already in Zurich, rumored to be swirling near the heart of Experta. If she uncovered Redwood's private demands, or the White House directive, the scandal could erupt prematurely.

The cobbled streets of Zurich glittered under a drizzle as Maggie Wu navigated swiftly through the morning crowd, her figure a fleeting shadow amid umbrellas and trench coats. She moved purposefully toward the Experta Foundation headquarters, her steps guided by the pulse of a relentless instinct for truth. Her sharp eyes scanned the modern glass façade, reflective yet impenetrable—a fitting metaphor for the secrets housed within.

Inside her hotel room hours earlier, Wu had meticulously pieced together threads from scattered sources. Her informants, former employees quietly disgruntled and cautiously fearful, had whispered tantalizing hints about private demands from Senator Redwood—demands that threatened the integrity of the very technology Tosh guarded so jealously. A separate, even more explosive tip suggested that the White House had issued a secret directive, explicitly authorizing Zermatt to use CDA as a weapon.

Now, mere blocks away from Experta, Wu's pulse quickened. This story was more than another exposé; it was seismic, capable of reshaping geopolitical realities overnight. But evidence remained elusive, intangible. She needed concrete proof—emails, memos, a misplaced document—anything that could solidify whispers into irrefutable fact.

At a small café opposite Experta, Maggie took a seat by the window, pretending to thumb casually through her phone as she discreetly observed the stream of foundation employees entering the building. Each face, each interaction, became a potential avenue into the hidden truth.

Her phone buzzed softly—a message from a secure number. Wu glanced at the screen:

"Mid-level analyst willing to talk. Details on CDA-325 'weaponization.' Meet at 19:00, west dock."

She exhaled slowly, her mind racing. The stakes were enormous. Redwood's campaign rhetoric of "Total Transparency" masked ambitions that threatened to unravel the delicate ethical balance Tosh had maintained. Meanwhile, the White House directive hinted at a covert desperation.

Hours later, beneath the muted glow of dockside lamps, Wu stood silently. The faint slap of waves against pilings marked time until a figure approached—young, nervous, glancing frequently over his shoulder.

"I can't stay long," he whispered urgently, eyes darting fearfully. "They've been tracking internal leaks."

"What do you have?" Wu asked sharply, her recorder discreetly capturing every breath.

"Internal memos," the analyst murmured, handing over a slim data drive. "Redwood's demands are detailed. He wants Experta's entire control surrendered upon his election—nothing withheld. And there's more. O'Sullivan's directive explicitly authorized Tosh to deploy CDA aggressively against NeuraTech. Weaponizing minds is now officially sanctioned."

Maggie's fingers closed tightly around the drive, heart pounding fiercely in her chest. She understood clearly: publication meant igniting chaos. But silence would betray every journalistic principle she cherished.

Returning to her hotel, Wu opened her laptop, loading the drive's explosive contents onto her encrypted server. Her fingers hovered over the keyboard, momentarily frozen by the weight of impending global impact. The decision was hers alone—to publish immediately, exposing secrets that could halt clandestine misuse, or wait, risking further unchecked escalation.

As Zurich's city lights reflected softly off the wet pavement below, Maggie Wu drew a deep, steadying breath, steeling herself against doubt. Truth, she reminded herself firmly, was a burden—but silence, far heavier.

The War Room's Final Word

In the stark illumination of the White House bunker, Nicolás Tosh absorbed the heavy silence following President O'Sullivan's definitive statements. Around the metallic conference table, faces were etched with tension, reflecting the gravity of the moment.

Immediate Reinforcement

Zermatt's cybersecurity teams would intensify their pace, accelerating advanced quantum encryption methods specifically designed to thwart NeuraTech's relentless infiltration attempts. Coordinating discreetly with allied intelligence services, Tosh authorized minimal expansions of targeted neural scanning protocols, strictly limited to critical high-level government officials. However, to Tosh's quiet relief, the President had made no open mention of employing the dangerous Overwrite function or authorizing a sweeping deployment of Algorithm-325.

Watchful Eye on Redwood

As the official briefing concluded, a senior White House advisor discreetly approached Tosh, leaning in with guarded urgency. "The President requires an additional step," he murmured quietly. "Redwood and his inner circle—we must know their intentions. Your scans should extend, carefully, just enough to alert us of any move Redwood might make against the presidency itself."

The request sent a cold ripple through Tosh. It was exactly the kind of unchecked surveillance he had always warned against. Yet, seeing the determination in the advisor's eyes, he recognized the underlying fear— a fear that Redwood's transparent threats might culminate in a catastrophic misuse of CDA. With a reluctant nod, Tosh accepted the distasteful reality, aware that his careful limits were now bending toward practices disturbingly close to those of a surveillance state.

Targeting the Rogue Faction

Before Tosh could depart, President O'Sullivan spoke again, his voice lowered yet unyielding. "If clear evidence emerges that NeuraTech has successfully infiltrated significant operational nodes, I'm authorizing immediate covert counterstrikes. You have my full sanction to execute raids or cyber-attacks as necessary. Neutralize their capabilities— however it must be done."

Tosh felt the words weigh heavily upon him. The President had just granted explicit license to employ lethal mental weaponry—a step Tosh had vehemently resisted for years. Yet the severity of the threat was undeniable. Each scenario running through his mind highlighted the grim possibilities: inaction equaled catastrophic compromise; action meant moral peril.

Conclusion of the Meeting

Finally, the bunker doors slid open with a soft hiss. Tosh stepped into the hushed corridor, heart heavy with the complex calculus of morality and necessity. The carefully maintained veneer of democracy had become thin, translucent, and dangerously brittle. Lines had been irrevocably drawn—by Redwood's ambition, by President O'Sullivan's desperate pragmatism, and he acknowledged quietly, by his own reluctant acquiescence.

Standing silently amid the subdued quietness of the White House, Tosh felt an overwhelming sense of vulnerability. The choices made in that sterile room beneath the capital's revered halls held ramifications that would ripple far beyond his control, potentially reshaping the fabric of global governance and the essence of human autonomy itself. The lines were clear now—but Tosh understood bitterly that with each passing crisis, each decisive act, they threatened to blur further until the moral high ground he had so fervently protected could vanish entirely.

Chapter 8

The Invasion of Zermatt

Zermatt, Switzerland — The Data Center, 2017
Day 22, 2:00 A.M. CET)

Faint starlight blanketed the Swiss Alps, the jagged peaks etched against a midnight sky. Beneath tons of rock and ice, the Zermatt Data Center glowed with artificial illumination, humming with quantum processing power. The hush of the mountain night belied the looming storm—one that would arrive in both cyberspace and the physical world.

Inside the vast, cavernous facility, technicians monitored banks of quantum servers that pulsed with a quiet intensity, oblivious to the chaos their meticulous precision would soon face. Nicolás Tosh, standing near the central operations console, stared intently at streams of encrypted data cascading down a dozen screens. Something wasn't right—the patterns shifting subtly, like shadows behind frosted glass.

"What's happening?" Tosh asked, his voice tight with suspicion.

Dr. Miriam Faber, swiftly analyzing anomalous quantum signals, shook her head in disbelief. "Our encryption layers—they're being penetrated. Someone's already inside."

A sudden chill coursed through Tosh as he absorbed the implication. "NeuraTech?"

Miriam's expression was grim. "It appears they've piggybacked off a dormant Lingtao cache. Their system is… aggressive."

The monitors suddenly flashed red warnings as alarms began to blare. Zermatt's quantum firewalls trembled under an unprecedented assault. Data streams fractured into violent flurries of activity. "Emergency lockdown!" Tosh commanded, struggling to steady his voice amidst the burgeoning chaos.

Doors sealed instantly with mechanical finality, locking the command team inside the central node. Outside, faint tremors of detonations—small, strategic explosions—echoed through the walls. Tosh's heart raced, realizing that NeuraTech wasn't just launching a digital siege; they'd brought their fight to the real world.

"External security breach," Rainer Sábato's voice crackled urgently over the intercom. "Multiple intruders, armed and moving fast."

"Lock down the server clusters!" Tosh ordered, eyes darting frantically between screens. He glanced at Marisol Alvarez, who was coordinating defense efforts.

Marisol nodded sharply. "Deploying active countermeasures now."

A moment later, remote-controlled security drones buzzed from concealed panels, their compact forms scanning corridors with infrared precision. Elsewhere, automated sentry guns emerged from camouflaged housings, their targeting systems primed.

"How did they get past our perimeter defenses?" Tosh muttered, disbelief and anger warring in his voice.

Miriam pointed urgently to her screen, her fingers trembling slightly. "They've cracked segments of our re-keyed encryption through the Hong Kong nodes. They're overriding our internal defenses remotely—bypassing physical barriers entirely."

Tosh felt an intense wave of dread. "Sever those connections now!"

"We can't," Miriam's voice was tinged with panic. "They've embedded recursive feedback loops. If we cut off abruptly, we risk cascading failures across our entire network."

A deep, thunderous boom resonated above them, shaking dust loose from the ceiling panels. Tosh exchanged a grim look with Marisol. "They're attempting to breach physically. Rainer, status?"

"They're sophisticated and fast—likely ex-military contractors," Rainer replied sharply, strain evident in his voice. "They're using tactical shaped charges. It'll take time, but they'll breach eventually."

Tosh's fists clenched, his mind racing for solutions. "Backup data—start remote transfer to Experta immediately. If this facility falls, the technology cannot."

Marisol swiftly keyed in commands, initiating the data evacuation protocols. Quantum packets raced through emergency channels toward Zurich, their precious information fleeing ahead of the advancing intruders.

Miriam turned to Tosh, anxiety etched deep into her features. "If they gain control of the primary quantum nodes, they'll have access to CDA-325."

"That won't happen," Tosh vowed darkly. "Activate Algorithm-325's fail-safe."

Miriam hesitated, knowing the magnitude of what Tosh asked. "You understand the consequences—permanent data loss, years of development gone in seconds."

"Better destroyed than weaponized," Tosh replied with grim finality.

Miriam nodded slowly, her finger hovering over the red-illuminated key on her console. Tosh looked one last time at the monitors, at the desperate fight unfolding digitally and physically.

"Do it."

The fail-safe activated with a soft chime, a deceptively gentle sound marking the brutal self-destruction of Algorithm-325's core structures. Around them, quantum servers hummed louder, an elegy for sacrificed brilliance.

Moments later, Rainer's voice again, urgent and strained: "They're almost inside. Tosh, you need to evacuate."

Tosh hesitated for just a heartbeat, then gave the command. "Begin full personnel evacuation. Protect lives first."

"Understood," Rainer's acknowledgment was clipped but determined.

As Tosh and his core team moved swiftly toward the hidden emergency exit, explosions reverberated behind them, their echoes filled with fury and intent. They had taken the hardest possible decision—one that safeguarded humanity but forfeited years of progress.

Emerging into the icy alpine night, Tosh felt the freezing air bite sharply into his lungs. Behind him, the facility burned, hidden beneath rock and snow but fully visible in his mind's eye. The heart of Zermatt, their sanctuary and strength, had been invaded and ravaged.

Yet, amid his grief and rage, resolve surged through Tosh like cold fire. NeuraTech had struck at the core of what he'd vowed to protect, and now it was personal. The storm had come—and Tosh knew it was only just beginning.

Coordinated Digital Attack

Inside a subterranean command hub beneath Zermatt, Rainer Sábato stood rigid before a wall of screens, each flickering frantically with lines of invasive code. The normally serene data streams were chaotic, weaving aggressively through the defenses as alarms wailed in urgent, repetitive pulses. A secure video feed from London's G-7 headquarters crackled sharply through speakers mounted overhead.

"Sustained infiltration attempts detected, originating from multiple global nodes—NeuraTech signature confirmed. Threat level critical."

"Understood," Rainer responded sharply, his voice steady despite the tension that rippled visibly through his frame. His hands darted expertly across a glowing console, instantly broadcasting an emergency site-wide alert.

"All security teams, this is not a drill. We have a live digital breach. Assume highest combat readiness—activate emergency protocols now."

As his command echoed through hidden corridors and fortified security rooms, doors sealed with a decisive clang, locking down every access route automatically. Security drones emerged swiftly from concealed bays, their silent, ominous forms scanning corridors methodically.

Adjacent to Rainer's post, Dr. Miriam Faber's fingers blurred over her keyboard, unleashing countermeasures in real time. Her heart pounded against her ribs as she watched the invasive code attempt to dismantle Zermatt's encryption layer by meticulous layer.

"This is unprecedented," she muttered, alarmed eyes reflecting rapidly scrolling threats. "They're using adaptive algorithms—they're learning our defensive patterns and responding faster than we can counteract."

"They're going for the core neural protocols," Rainer confirmed grimly, pointing to lines of malicious code attacking the handshake nodes. "If they seize control of those, they can overwrite our entire quantum infrastructure—satellites, secure data clusters—everything."

The screens suddenly flashed crimson in unison. "Critical defense sector breach detected," an automated voice warned coldly, amplifying the pressure.

Miriam tapped furiously, rerouting counter-intrusion algorithms, desperate to anticipate NeuraTech's next moves. "They're embedding deep recursive loops into our system, interwoven with legitimate access credentials. If we forcibly sever the connections now, it might trigger cascading system failures across our global network."

Rainer exhaled tensely. "Then isolate their nodes incrementally, trap them in segmented loops—buy us time."

Before Miriam could initiate the command, another warning chimed ominously. The facility trembled with a low, resonating boom from above, sending fine particles of concrete dust showering down.

"They're physically breaching us," Rainer breathed out sharply, tapping his communication device. "Tosh, we have incoming physical threats. Tactical explosive breaches confirmed. Prepare for immediate evac."

He quickly pivoted back to Miriam, urgency searing his voice. "Initiate data evacuation protocols—get everything critical backed up to Experta, now."

Miriam's fingers flew across the console, initializing emergency quantum packet transfers. Data surged through secure underground lines, racing at light speed toward Zurich.

"We need Algorithm-325's fail-safe primed," Rainer said, his voice heavy with foreboding.

Miriam paused briefly, fingers trembling slightly. She nodded once, steeling herself. "Understood. Preparing fail-safe for immediate activation. If we engage, we lose all our recent advancements permanently."

"Better erased than weaponized," Rainer said with grim certainty. He watched her finger hover momentarily before she keyed the activation.

A gentle, haunting chime rang out—a disturbingly tranquil sound signaling irreversible data destruction. Rainer's stomach twisted sharply as he witnessed years of profound work vanish instantly into oblivion, sacrificed to safeguard humanity from unchecked mind control.

The facility shook violently again, walls rattling as another shaped charge detonated, closer and fiercer. Rainer reached instinctively to steady Miriam as the lights momentarily flickered.

"Tosh," he spoke urgently into his comm link, "NeuraTech forces are minutes from breaching central command. You have to get out now."

Another explosion echoed through the cavernous tunnels, stronger, more immediate. Rainer quickly activated an emergency evacuation beacon, sending alerts throughout the facility. "All teams, fall back to extraction points immediately. Defend only to secure safe withdrawal."

As security drones engaged intruders with precision bursts of fire, corridors filled with thick smoke and crackling sparks. Gunfire echoed, resonating in brutal, measured exchanges between automated defenses and highly trained human operatives pushing relentlessly inward.

At the command hub's doorway, Rainer and Miriam made a final, painful sweep of their consoles. They locked eyes briefly, each recognizing the gravity of what had transpired—Zermatt had been irrevocably breached, its secrets either destroyed or on the brink of capture.

"We need to move," Rainer urged, guiding Miriam swiftly toward the concealed evacuation tunnels.

Outside, as cold alpine air sliced across their faces, Rainer looked back, breath misting heavily in the icy darkness. Beneath snow and granite, their fortress burned silently, its digital heart ruptured.

Yet in the crisp night, Rainer felt resolve harden sharply. This attack had set clear lines—humanity versus technological tyranny. Tonight,

NeuraTech had struck a brutal blow, but the fight, Rainer knew instinctively, had only just begun.

Physical Incursion: A Raid on the Outskirts

High above Zermatt, a rugged mountain road stretched along the ridgeline, its surface a thin ribbon under starlit skies. Silence dominated the alpine surroundings, broken only by the distant whispers of wind through evergreen branches. Suddenly, the quiet was shattered by the low rumble of engines, tires crunching gravel as two blacked-out SUVs coasted to a precise stop, their headlights extinguished.

Doors swung open simultaneously; lean figures clad entirely in dark tactical gear emerged silently. Their movements precise, disciplined. The leader raised a gloved hand, and his team dispersed immediately into prearranged positions. Equipment was quickly unloaded: compact drilling apparatuses, small breaching charges, and sophisticated electronic sensors that blinked muted green signals in the darkness.

"Two minutes," the team leader whispered into his throat mic, the words crisp with urgency. "Locate the hidden entrance silently. Charges are last resort only."

A second vehicle stopped further down the mountain road, team members deploying swiftly into observation points. Through high-powered night-vision goggles, they scanned the slopes meticulously, their breaths controlled and even despite the altitude and tension.

Nearby, partially obscured by dense underbrush, two Swiss border guards patrolled casually, unaware of the impending assault. One guard noticed shadows shifting oddly against the moonlit terrain. Squinting suspiciously, he reached slowly for his radio, thumb pressing to transmit. "Central, we may have something—"

The transmission ended abruptly as a shadow lunged from the darkness, knocking the radio from his grip. The guard staggered, instinctively grappling with the attacker. A rapid, brutal struggle ensued, muffled gasps and grunts mingling as the attacker twisted expertly, pinning the guard securely against the icy ground. The second guard, startled, tried to draw his weapon, but another operative swiftly closed in, neutralizing him with ruthless efficiency. Both guards lay immobilized, restrained swiftly and silently.

Back at the entry point, operatives pressed their equipment against a seemingly innocuous rock formation, sensors pulsing softly as they searched for structural anomalies. A faint vibration hummed beneath gloved fingertips.

"Here," whispered one operative confidently, pointing out an irregular seam barely visible in the shadows. "Cutting the lock."

A laser cutter ignited, its beam slicing quietly through metal bolts concealed by rock façade. The team leader's radio crackled softly. "Perimeter secured. Two sentries down."

"Confirmed," he replied tersely, eyes fixed on his team as they pried open the newly revealed door. The metal portal swung inward, revealing a dimly lit service tunnel descending sharply underground. The air within smelled sterile, tinged faintly with ozone.

As the team stepped forward, their motion triggered a nearly invisible infrared sensor embedded in the corridor wall. Miles away, deep within Zermatt's control center, a security guard frowned as a motion sensor pinged quietly. He toggled through camera feeds—one by one, each screen went black.

The security guard surged upright, panic tightening his chest. "We're blind on perimeter three," he barked urgently into his comm. "Possible breach—"

A thunderous explosion ripped through the mountain silence, sending shockwaves reverberating into the facility's core. Concrete dust and splinters showered down, clouding corridors and security cameras. The infiltrators had abandoned stealth, knowing their silent approach was compromised.

"Move fast!" shouted their leader over the commotion, his voice ringing clearly amid the chaos. "Neutralize all defenses!"

The operatives surged forward, weapons drawn. Automated defense drones emerged swiftly from concealed compartments, humming aggressively. The corridor erupted into fierce exchanges of gunfire;

sharp, methodical bursts rang out, punctuated by the high-pitched whines of drones spiraling into metal wreckage against the corridor floor.

Deeper within Zermatt's subterranean labyrinth, Rainer Sábato stood rigid, eyes locked on flashing alarms cascading across his screens. "Physical security compromised," he warned urgently through his radio. "Initiate immediate defensive response. Evacuate non-essential personnel now!"

Security doors slammed shut with resonating clangs, sealing sections of the facility into isolated pockets. Intruders advanced methodically, explosive charges rupturing sealed barriers, sending echoes of destruction roaring through the tunnels. Smoke thickened, and the acrid stench of burnt wiring filled every breath.

Rainer quickly grabbed a pistol from beneath his console, signaling Dr. Miriam Faber to follow him to the concealed evacuation tunnel. Their hurried footsteps echoed in time with distant bursts of gunfire. As they reached the exit, another explosion thundered closer, shattering lights overhead.

Bursting into the frigid mountain air, Rainer turned back briefly, watching smoke curl upward into the alpine night. Below, the heart of Zermatt smoldered silently beneath layers of granite, under relentless assault.

His gaze hardened, knowing fully the implications of this incursion. Tonight marked a turning point—NeuraTech had shown its hand clearly, leaving no doubts. Zermatt had fallen under siege, but the battle for humanity's freedom was just beginning.

Heroic Stand: Emergency Defense and Lockdown

Deep in the subterranean corridors, Rainer and a small security detail sprinted to a makeshift command post, their hurried footsteps echoing loudly off the reinforced walls. Overhead, emergency lights cast shifting crimson shadows across tense faces, bathing the labyrinth in an unsettling glow.

"They're hitting us digitally and physically," Rainer barked tersely into his comm. "All staff, secure your stations. Prepare for topside incursion immediately!"

Multiple acknowledgments crackled through the channel as personnel scrambled to implement protocols drilled countless times but never truly anticipated. Screens flashed critical warnings, indicating the breaches at multiple surface points.

Suddenly, Nicolás Tosh's stern visage appeared on the main screen via a direct, encrypted link from Zurich. His jaw set tightly, eyes burning with intensity.

"Rainer," Tosh said, voice steady but brimming with urgency, "you must hold the line. Protect the quantum servers at all costs. Lock down every access route from the surface. I'm en route now—but it's two hours at best."

Above ground, piercing sirens wailed, splitting the alpine tranquility as Swiss emergency units swiftly mobilized. Patrol helicopters rose rapidly from the nearby airfield, their powerful searchlights slicing across the snow-capped peaks and ridgelines in stark, sweeping arcs. Below them, shadowy figures moved with deliberate speed, precision evident in their disciplined movements.

At the ventilation shafts, the attackers quickly placed shaped charges along steel shutters, timers blinking ominously. Each operative moved with cold efficiency, ignoring the roar of incoming helicopters as they primed their explosives.

Inside Zermatt's facility, automated defense systems sprang into immediate action. Steel blast doors slammed shut sequentially, sealing off critical server wings one by one with reverberating clangs that echoed deep into the mountain. Rainer directed security teams, eyes flicking rapidly between monitors as he coordinated their defensive posture.

"Security partitions fully activated," shouted an engineer from a nearby terminal, fingers flying over the keyboard, eyes wide with adrenaline. "No one gets through without setting off every alarm we've got!"

Rainer's eyes narrowed in determination. "Redirect drones topside. Give them air cover until the Swiss units arrive!"

Above ground, defense drones burst from concealed compartments in a blur, quickly ascending to engage the attackers, their rotors slicing the frigid air sharply. The infiltrators scattered, swiftly raising compact rifles fitted with EMP emitters. Pulsing electromagnetic waves rippled through the air, dropping drones from the sky as sparks trailed like fiery rain.

Back in the corridors, explosions shook the foundations, dust cascading from the ceilings. An intercom crackled: "Intruders breached upper-level ventilation access—Section 12 compromised!"

Without hesitation, Rainer bolted from the command post, his security team following closely, weapons drawn. Their tactical boots pounded across grated flooring, breaths quick and measured despite the escalating chaos around them.

A blast erupted nearby, and debris showered the corridor ahead. Through the smoke, black-clad figures charged forward, opening fire immediately. Muzzle flashes illuminated the dim passageways, bullets ricocheting wildly against reinforced concrete and steel. Rainer and his team took defensive positions, returning fire with rapid, precise bursts, momentarily halting the intruders' advance.

"Fallback position Bravo!" Rainer shouted; voice barely audible over the cacophony of gunfire. His team pivoted smoothly, engaging strategically while withdrawing to maintain cover.

Simultaneously, in the main data hub, Dr. Miriam Faber scrambled desperately to reinforce firewall protocols as the digital assault surged. Screens scrolled rapidly with malicious code, each line a potential gateway for the attackers to penetrate Zermatt's neural handshake protocols.

"We're losing layers!" Miriam called out frantically. "They're adapting faster than we can counter!"

Rainer heard her through his earpiece, jaw clenched tight with resolve. "Hold them off as long as you can! Reinforcements are inbound!"

A fresh explosion obliterated the corridor behind Rainer's team, forcing them deeper into the labyrinth. Smoke filled the air, stinging their lungs, vision blurred. Yet they pressed on, disciplined and unyielding, navigating swiftly to the emergency tunnel system.

Finally reaching the reinforced evacuation tunnel, Rainer keyed a rapid series of codes into the security pad. Heavy bolts released with a hydraulic hiss, and the thick metal doors parted grudgingly. As they moved into the tunnel, another concussive blast rocked the structure, the shockwave knocking several of his team off balance.

Regrouping quickly, they surged into the night air, emerging onto a hidden mountain path above Zermatt. Below, fires flickered amid the scattered debris, the facility partially compromised yet still resisting fiercely.

Gazing down, Rainer's expression hardened into cold fury. Zermatt was wounded, but far from broken. This battle had merely begun, and the fight for humanity's future was now more personal than ever.

Partial Breach: Access to CDA-325

Amidst the chaos engulfing Zermatt's subterranean command center, Dr. Miriam Faber stared at her console, eyes wide with disbelief. Lines of malignant code cascaded down her screen like digital rainfall, each character glowing menacingly red against the black background. Her fingers trembled slightly as she typed frantically, attempting to intercept the threat.

"They've spun up something new—a multi-vector Trojan," she called out urgently, her voice cutting through the rising alarm klaxons. "It's attached itself to one of our offline servers, a rack we were re-keying."

Rainer Sábato sprinted across the control room, urgency written in every line of his face. He peered over her shoulder, eyes narrowing as the implications became clear. "What exactly are they accessing?"

Dr. Faber's voice was tight with suppressed panic. "The old repository... including partial references to CDA-325. They're mining our data."

A tense silence fell, broken only by the distant echoes of explosions and gunfire from deeper within the complex. CDA-325's code was the cornerstone of Zermatt's most sensitive protocols—Overwrite technology capable of reshaping memories and perceptions. Even limited fragments in NeuraTech's hands could spell disaster.

Rainer lunged toward the central control terminal, fingers flying over the keyboard in rapid succession. "Initiate an emergency shutdown," he barked sharply to the stunned technicians nearby. "Kill power to that entire rack immediately!"

A technician complied swiftly, slamming his palm onto a series of emergency cut-off switches beneath a glass panel. Instantly, rows of server lights began to blink out systematically, plunging portions of the control room into unsettling darkness. The overhead lights flickered and dimmed, as though the data center itself was wounded.

All eyes fixed on the main screen where the invasive code writhed like a dying serpent, the infiltration progress bar stalling mid-transfer. For a heartbeat, hope surged through the command room.

Then, abruptly, one final burst of inbound data flashed onto the screen—a final, defiant packet of malicious code spiked the infiltration readout to a chilling 100 percent. A collective gasp filled the room as the screen dissolved into a swirl of digital static, then vanished completely, leaving an ominous blankness.

Rainer slammed his fist onto the console, his jaw clenched tight. "Damn it," he muttered bitterly, breathing heavily through the tension. "They extracted something. We just can't confirm what or how much."

Dr. Faber exhaled shakily, her mind racing as she assessed the potential damage. The ramifications were catastrophic; even fragments of CDA-325 could enable NeuraTech to drastically refine and enhance their invasive technology, escalating their capability to overwrite memories and identities to terrifying new levels.

Around them, security personnel rushed about in controlled panic, checking defensive protocols and reinforcing internal barriers. But Rainer and Miriam stood frozen, confronting the stark truth illuminated by that blinking cursor on a darkened screen.

NeuraTech had broken through their digital fortress, leaving Zermatt's most guarded secret dangerously vulnerable. The war for control over humanity's mind had just entered its most perilous phase yet.

Above Ground

A deep rumble shook the Alpine slope, sending cascades of loose gravel skittering downhill as the paramilitary team detonated a precisely positioned charge at a ventilation hatch. Dust billowed into the chilly mountain air, obscuring visibility for precious seconds. Operatives surged forward through the haze, weapons raised, boots crunching urgently over shards of shattered concrete.

The lead operative halted abruptly, a beam of his flashlight cutting through the dust, illuminating a blank, reinforced concrete wall where they had anticipated an open entryway. A growl of frustration escaped him, amplified harshly through his throat mic. "It's a dead end! We're trapped!"

From a ridge below, powerful floodlights abruptly flared to life, casting the invaders' shadows starkly against the rock face. The sudden roar of engines signaled trouble. Three Swiss border patrol vehicles barreled aggressively up the narrow gravel track, gravel spewing from beneath churning tires.

"Fallback to Rally Point A! Swiss forces incoming!" barked the team leader, urgency tightening his voice. The operatives pivoted immediately, their tactical precision devolving into frantic urgency. Their silent approach dissolved into chaos as bursts of gunfire tore through the night. Muzzle flashes blossomed violently, illuminating the rocky terrain in brief, staccato bursts.

Bullets sparked off stone and ricocheted unpredictably, forcing the operatives to dive for scant cover behind boulders and shrubs. The Swiss patrols leaped from their vehicles, taking disciplined positions behind armored doors, returning fire in precise volleys. The staccato crack of automatic weapons echoed harshly off the mountainsides, each shot reverberating ominously across the valley.

Pinned down, the intruders responded desperately, volleying suppressive fire in rapid bursts as they scrambled toward their extraction point. Shouts of pain pierced the firefight as an operative was struck, tumbling forward to the ground, clutching a wounded leg. A comrade grabbed his vest, dragging him swiftly behind the shelter of a rocky outcrop.

Above, a rhythmic pounding filled the air as a sleek, matte-black helicopter thundered into position, descending aggressively, rotor wash whipping loose snow and debris into a vortex. Its side doors slid open, revealing masked figures reaching urgently outward, beckoning to their embattled teammates.

The paramilitary operatives abandoned scattered equipment and sprinted toward their hovering salvation, hurling themselves aboard even as rounds ricocheted dangerously close. The helicopter lifted swiftly, banking sharply away from the valley, leaving behind Swiss patrols shouting into radios, spotlights tracking futilely through the darkness.

In mere moments, the mountain returned to eerie silence, disturbed only by drifting clouds of smoke and the lingering scent of cordite. The failed assault had left behind unanswered questions, abandoned gear, and a lingering threat in the crisp Alpine air.

In the Command Hub

The air in the command hub felt electrically charged, punctuated by the piercing wail of alarms that echoed off reinforced walls. Emergency lights bathed the control room in a stark crimson glow, casting urgent shadows across technicians' tense faces as they raced between consoles, fingers dancing rapidly across keyboards. Digital readouts flashed ominously, a chaotic symphony of warning signals that underscored the fragility of their defenses.

Rainer Sábato leaned heavily against a central console, his breath ragged, heart pounding in sync with the alarms. Sweat glistened at his temples, and a slight tremble in his hands betrayed the adrenaline surging through his veins. Around him, technicians scrambled, voices sharp yet controlled, trying to restore power and seal compromised digital pathways.

"Get that secondary firewall back up!" Rainer barked, urgency clipping his words. "We can't afford another breach!"

To his left, a wall of screens flickered with security feeds from the surface, their grainy images painting a grim picture: Swiss medics in reflective gear crouched over wounded guards, emergency lights pulsating rhythmically. Despite the chaos, no lifeless forms lay sprawled in the snow—no fatalities yet, but the toll on those defending Zermatt was visible and severe.

A sudden chime brought his attention sharply forward. Nicolás Tosh's weary but determined face filled the primary command screen, backlit by the faint glow of the vehicle's interior lights as it raced down winding Alpine roads, urgency etched deeply into his features.

"Update, Rainer!" Tosh's voice was tense, strained by the gravity of the situation.

Rainer straightened, drawing a deep breath to steady his voice. "They retreated," he reported, exhaustion and relief mixed with lingering dread. "We contained the physical breach, but…" He hesitated, swallowing against a wave of apprehension. "Not before they got partial data from the old server. It's possible they have a fraction of the CDA-325 Overwrite structure—just enough to refine their own. We can't be sure yet."

The effect of Rainer's words on Tosh was immediate and profound. Tosh's jaw tightened, his eyes narrowing slightly in restrained fury. Rainer saw clearly the wave of dread pass across Tosh's face, the realization of the enormity of what had just transpired hitting him like a physical blow.

For Zermatt, the CDA-325 had always been a guarded technological marvel, strictly controlled by intricate, ethical gating systems. It was the only thing keeping its immense capabilities from spiraling into catastrophic misuse. The idea that NeuraTech could now possess even a fragment of that technology, stripped of those ethical restraints, was terrifying. It meant the difference between manageable threat and unstoppable menace.

"Rainer," Tosh spoke carefully, each word dripping with restrained intensity, "I'm twenty minutes out. Secure every trace you can, isolate any suspicious code. We'll regroup immediately and initiate a thorough damage assessment. Expect a full digital audit—every line of code, every file. Brace your team for the worst."

Rainer nodded curtly, gripping the edge of the console tightly as if to anchor himself. "Understood. We're already locking everything down, reviewing every byte. But Tosh… if they have even a sliver—"

Tosh cut him off gently but firmly, voice heavy with responsibility and resolve. "Then we have no choice but to adapt and counteract. We've faced setbacks before, and we've always responded. We'll find a way to neutralize this new advantage of theirs. Hold strong, Rainer. Keep the team focused and vigilant. Everything depends on it now."

The connection flickered briefly, Tosh's image freezing momentarily before resolving itself again. His final words echoed chillingly through the command hub. "This changes everything."

As the screen went dark, Rainer turned, rallying his shaken team with newfound determination. The alarms still blared, technicians still worked feverishly, but a renewed clarity had settled over him. They were bruised, but not yet beaten. This was far from over.

Fallout from the Invasion

A suffocating silence enveloped the Zermatt Data Center in the immediate wake of the incursion, punctuated only by the fading echoes of sirens and the distant hum of helicopters. Technicians moved swiftly yet methodically, weaving through darkened corridors, their expressions drawn tight with exhaustion and tension.

Outside, under the sweeping glow of high-powered floodlights, Swiss authorities had transformed the tranquil Alpine slopes into a scene of intense scrutiny. Officers scoured the rocky terrain inch by inch, illuminating every crevice and shadow. Yet frustration grew palpable as the search yielded nothing concrete—only enigmatic remnants of the attackers' sophisticated assault. On a makeshift table beneath a hastily erected command tent, forensic specialists sorted through discarded equipment, lifting small, advanced weaponry and cryptic gear into evidence bags, shaking their heads in grim confusion.

Inside the Data Center, Rainer Sábato moved from station to station, his face pale but resolute, assessing damage alongside his top engineers. Entire sections of servers lay dormant, their indicator lights extinguished, networks strangled into temporary silence. Every shutdown system added to the mounting delays: operations against global threats such as entrenched human trafficking rings, revelations of governmental corruption, and critical safety breaches—including urgent aviation threats—slowed or halted entirely.

In the heart of the compromised server room, Dr. Miriam Faber knelt before a partially dismantled server rack, her hands steady despite the turmoil in her eyes. Behind her, on multiple screens, lines of code streamed rapidly as analysts traced infiltration vectors.

"Did they get CDA-325?" asked Rainer softly, trying and failing to mask his anxiety.

Faber's voice trembled slightly, betraying her calm exterior. "We can't yet confirm how much, but they definitely accessed fragments of the Overwrite framework. Even partial code in their hands could be catastrophic."

Across the room, a monitor flickered to life, casting a stark glow onto Rainer's strained features. Nicolás Tosh appeared on-screen, his expression grim, framed by the blurred outlines of Swiss mountain roads speeding past his vehicle's windows.

"Tell me how bad it is," Tosh demanded, urgency sharpening his tone.

Rainer's jaw tightened. "Physical damage is contained, but digital intrusion is confirmed. Partial CDA-325 code exposure. They might have enough to stabilize their own Overwrite process."

Tosh exhaled slowly, visibly absorbing the gravity of the revelation. The subtle vulnerability that shadowed his eyes sent a chill through Rainer—never had he seen his mentor look so shaken.

"Start immediate containment protocols," Tosh ordered decisively. "Change every encryption layer, every gate protocol. Shut down and isolate anything touched by that Trojan until we know exactly what was taken. I'll be there soon."

Throughout the long night, Zermatt's remaining staff worked tirelessly, fingers flying over keyboards, eyes scanning endless lines of data, hearts pounding with the dreadful understanding of their new reality. They had weathered bullets, explosions, and direct assault, yet the insidious, invisible theft of their most guarded technology haunted them all far worse than any physical damage.

A quiet, oppressive fear took root, deeper and darker than any external threat: What if the attackers had exactly what they needed? What if, in those few stolen lines of code, they'd unlocked the potential for unprecedented devastation?

As dawn approached, an uneasy stillness settled over the facility—a brief respite before inevitable escalation. Zermatt's defenses had been penetrated, their secrets exposed. The smallest breach, seemingly insignificant amidst the chaos, might now set the stage for a nightmare scenario that Tosh and his team had long feared.

They had defended valiantly, yet in their hearts, each knew the harsh truth: the war for control of CDA-325 had just taken its most dangerous turn.

Where We Stand

The frigid dawn air whispered sharply over the peaks surrounding Zermatt, the serenity of early morning deceptively masking the devastation below. Smoke still curled faintly from hidden fissures in the mountainside, weaving ghostly patterns against the pale blue sky. At ground level, emergency crews hustled urgently, their reflective gear catching the first tentative rays of sunlight. The once-secret facility had transformed into an active crime scene, alive with anxious, controlled urgency.

Rainer Sábato stood at the facility's upper entrance, his fingers curled tightly around a steaming cup of bitter coffee, its warmth barely noticed against the cold dread tightening his chest. His eyes moved methodically over the chaotic ballet unfolding beneath him—technicians wrestling cables and repair equipment into position, security officers pacing the perimeter, eyes hard with lingering tension, scanning every shadow as if another attack could erupt any second.

On the opposite side, near a hastily erected command tent, Nicolás Tosh stepped out of an armored vehicle, his presence immediately shifting the air. Despite exhaustion carved deeply into his face, Tosh moved with relentless focus, radiating a quiet authority that cut through the lingering confusion. He approached Rainer directly, their gazes locking in silent acknowledgment of the gravity weighing upon them both.

"We have to assume NeuraTech is already mobilizing," Tosh began, skipping pleasantries, his voice quiet yet filled with razor-sharp intensity. "Whatever fragments of CDA-325 they secured—they won't waste time refining it."

Rainer nodded solemnly, sipping the bitter coffee reflexively. The taste anchored him, kept him steady amid the turbulence swirling inside. "The physical damage can be repaired in weeks, but the digital breach… That wound runs deeper. We don't even know the full extent of what they took yet."

A forensic technician hurriedly approached them, visibly breathless from the altitude and pressure. She held a data pad clutched tightly to her chest, her voice shaking slightly as she spoke. "Initial analysis shows they targeted neural handshake protocols. Even a small segment of CDA-325 might let them bridge critical gaps in their own Overwrite technology."

Tosh exhaled slowly, absorbing the implications carefully. "So their weapon evolves—from blunt trauma to precision strikes. Instead of simply erasing memories, they could soon rewrite entire personalities seamlessly."

The silence following Tosh's words pressed down heavily upon them, a weight amplified by distant echoes of drilling and clanging metal. Rainer glanced toward the horizon, squinting as the sun broke decisively over a jagged ridgeline, casting stark shadows across the damaged ground. It felt symbolic—a harsh illumination of the brutal reality they now faced.

Suddenly, the tense quiet shattered as a technician shouted, panic edging his voice: "We've got secondary anomalies on perimeter sensors!"

Instantly, security forces mobilized, weapons snapping upward in instinctive readiness. Technicians scrambled back toward the facility's partially compromised inner sanctum, eyes wide, movements sharp and frantic. Tosh and Rainer both bolted toward the command tent, their feet crunching urgently over frozen gravel.

Inside, screens flickered rapidly through sensor data, depicting multiple movements in the shadows of distant ridges—vague shapes, blurry and indistinct, but undeniably real.

"Recon drones, now!" Tosh barked sharply, leaning forward to study the screens intensely, his fingers tapping impatiently against the console.

The drone feeds streamed in quickly, crystal-clear images snapping sharply into view, revealing stark landscapes that seconds ago had appeared quiet and undisturbed. Now, the screens showed multiple human figures moving swiftly, precisely—clad in advanced camouflage gear, unmistakably professional, their movements efficient and deadly.

"They're still here," Rainer murmured, his voice barely above a whisper, disbelief creeping into his tone.

"Not retreating—regrouping," Tosh finished grimly, voice cold with realization. "They're planning a second strike, forcing our hand."

Rainer grabbed the radio, his voice urgent, controlled. "All teams, prepare for immediate defensive maneuvers. Hostiles confirmed, approaching rapidly from the north and east ridgelines."

The command echoed instantly through every earpiece, security personnel snapping into disciplined, trained response patterns. Below ground, the facility hummed urgently, reinforced doors slamming shut decisively, sealing off vulnerable sectors, technicians racing against the clock to secure digital defenses.

On the ridgeline, the attackers moved silently but swiftly, each operative carrying specialized gear—explosive charges, precision rifles, advanced jamming devices designed specifically to disrupt defensive drones. They dispersed methodically, shadows blending seamlessly into the rocky landscape, becoming one with the terrain as they readied for another assault.

Inside the facility, a tense, silent determination spread rapidly among the defenders. They had weathered the first storm, but knew now that their adversaries were relentless, ruthlessly efficient, and dangerously close to victory. Rainer and Tosh exchanged a final look, a shared resolve crystalizing in their eyes.

"They won't get another piece," Tosh vowed softly, his voice steel-edged and unyielding.

"No," Rainer agreed, heart pounding sharply in his chest as adrenaline surged anew. "This ends now."

Outside, dawn fully illuminated the frozen slopes, bringing everything into stark relief. The defenders steadied their weapons, breathing shallowly, awaiting the next move from their unseen enemies.

In less than an hour, Zermatt had withstood a two-pronged onslaught—digital infiltration that siphoned crucial lines of code, and a paramilitary incursion that rattled the facility's secure outer perimeter. Now, the attackers retreated to the shadows, armed with the partial building blocks of CDA-325. Their next move might see NeuraTech ascending from a half-formed, brutal mind-tool to a refined, devastating weapon.

The question looming before every defender was clear and chilling:

Could they halt NeuraTech before it was too late, or was humanity already lost in the shadows gathering on the mountainside?

The Final Push

Zermatt, Switzerland — The Alpine Facility, 2017
Day 22, 4:35 A.M. CET)

The high-altitude cold cut sharply through Major Elliot Ramsey's thermal combat suit, but his focus remained unbroken. His U.S. Joint Special Operations Command (JSOC) alongside elite Swiss forces, had been tracking NeuraTech's paramilitary operatives for weeks, carefully gathering intelligence, coordinating closely with Swiss intelligence, and awaiting official authorization to intervene on foreign soil. Bureaucratic red tape and delicate diplomatic negotiations had delayed the response—until Zermatt's desperate emergency broadcast shattered the stalemate, triggering immediate joint Swiss-American intervention.

Ramsey's breath came slow and steady, frosting lightly in the predawn air, his sense razor-sharp. The rugged terrain stretched ominously before him, moonlight painting jagged silhouettes onto snow and granite. He signaled to his unit, elite soldiers silently dispersing into precise positions along the ridgeline. Below them, the facility flickered with sporadic gunfire and dimming security lights—a site of fierce battle, and now distressingly quiet.

"We're moving in now," Ramsey whispered sharply into his mic, eyes locked on the target facility nestled deep within the mountain face.

"Command, we have visual confirmation," Ramsey reported quietly into his comm. "Engaging hostile forces now."

Below him, precision floodlights flickered erratically around Zermatt, the facility under siege for hours now struggling desperately against a relentless assault by the paramilitary operatives from NeuraTech. Intelligence chatter had revealed NeuraTech's brutal efficiency—their theft of crucial data, their physical incursion, and their ruthless resolve to extract even more.

Ramsey raised a gloved hand, signaling silently. His team spread expertly across the ridge, blending into the rocks and snow, their movements fluid and ghostlike. He felt the adrenaline surge, sharpening his senses. Every detail mattered now, every moment pivotal.

Ramsey's team surged down the slopes, movements swift and disciplined, rifles raised and sighted with clinical precision. Gunfire erupted instantly as NeuraTech operatives responded desperately. Bullets whistled past Ramsey's position, smashing violently into the frozen rocks around him.

Far below, security drones suddenly spiraled upward, their infrared sensors flashing urgently. NeuraTech's attackers, their camouflage disrupted by JSOC's aggressive electronic warfare tactics, scrambled to respond, caught off guard by the sudden new front.

"Strike teams Alpha and Bravo, breach and clear!" Ramsey's command sliced through the cold air, crisp and unequivocal.

Two Swiss assault helicopters emerged from behind a ridgeline, their rotors slicing through frigid air with deafening roars. Bright beams pierced downward, casting pools of illumination over fleeing NeuraTech operatives. They had launched simultaneously from an advanced forward-operating base in the nearby Swiss valleys, carefully hidden and prepared for such contingencies. The sudden illumination threw NeuraTech's operatives into momentary disarray, their camouflage compromised, their cohesion shattered

On the ground, Ramsey and his teams surged forward, descending swiftly, weapons raised and ready, surging down the slopes, movements swift and disciplined, rifles raised and sighted with clinical precision. Gunfire erupted instantly as NeuraTech operatives responded desperately. Bullets whistled past Ramsey's position, smashing violently into the frozen rocks around him.

Gunfire quickly intensified violently from both sides. The night became a battlefield of precise, lethal exchanges, muzzle flashes illuminating stark expressions of determination. Ramsey sprinted forward, his pulse thundering, ducking behind a boulder as bullets whizzed overhead.

"Sniper, rooftop, northwest corner!" someone barked urgently over the comm.

A suppressed rifle barked softly beside Ramsey, and he saw the distant figure crumple, neutralized instantly. Swiftly, methodically, Ramsey and his squad closed the gap, their coordination flawless.

Ramsey pushed forward, moving fluidly through the hail of gunfire. Explosions echoed sharply off the surrounding peaks as tactical grenades disrupted entrenched positions, sending operatives sprawling. The precision and shock of the joint assault rapidly overwhelmed the attackers' defenses, fracturing their formation.

"Frag out!" A grenade spun through the air, landing amidst the entrenched attackers. An explosion reverberated across the mountainside, momentarily illuminating the terrain in stark relief. Shouts of pain and urgency rose from the blast area.

The defensive perimeter was breaking. The attackers were losing cohesion, forced backward by the relentless joint assault. Ramsey pushed onward, rallying his forces to press the advantage.

"Hold formation, keep pushing!" Ramsey commanded, hearing his own heart pounding against his ribs.

A firefight flared to life near Zermatt's main ventilation shafts. Swiss units rapidly deployed, coordinated bursts of gunfire punctuating the chaos. Ramsey pivoted sharply toward the sound, radio crackling fiercely in his ear.

"Hostiles retreating to extraction zone," a voice reported tersely.

Ramsey's jaw tightened. "Cut them off! Do not let them escape!"

From above, a second wave of Swiss helicopters swept in low, deploying special forces directly onto the escape route. Caught between Ramsey's advancing teams and aerial reinforcement, NeuraTech operatives found themselves cornered, their precise, disciplined ranks fracturing into disarray.

Ramsey raised his voice powerfully, echoing across the frozen landscape: "Stand down! Drop your weapons! You're surrounded!"

Slowly, reluctantly, the operatives complied. Weapons clattered to the ground, hands rose cautiously into the chill air. Ramsey's team moved forward methodically, securing each captive with swift efficiency.

"Confirm the security of all prisoners and immediately search for data devices or stolen materials," Ramsey commanded sharply, eyes narrowing. They found encrypted drives, gear, and weapons—but nothing clearly identifying CDA-325 fragments.

"Facility secured, Command," Ramsey reported over comms, his voice calm yet weighted with unresolved tension. "All hostiles in custody. Material recovered, but unable to confirm possession of CDA-325 fragments."

Acknowledgment crackled back, cautious relief tempered by uncertainty.

In the facility's interior, Nicolás Tosh and Rainer Sábato listened silently to Ramsey's transmission. Relief momentarily softened their faces, but a shared glance communicated a lingering dread. Despite capturing NeuraTech's operatives, they knew this might be only a partial victory. If even a fragment of CDA-325 had already been relayed to NeuraTech's senior leadership, the real battle had only just begun.

As dawn broke fully, illuminating the damaged but resilient facility, Ramsey watched technicians and medics hurry across the landscape. He exhaled sharply, aware that while today's immediate threat was contained, tomorrow's uncertainty loomed dangerously. Zermatt had survived, wounded but resolute, prepared for the coming storm.

Chapter 9

A Moral Counteroffensive

Zurich, Switzerland — Experta Foundation Crisis Room 2017
Day 23, 11:00 A.M. CET

The sterile hush of the conference suite was oppressive, amplifying every muted beep and subtle murmur, underscoring the strain within its polished walls. Nicolás Tosh sat rigidly at the head of the long oval table, his eyes intense beneath furrowed brows, fingers steepled tightly in front of him. Beside him, Rainer Sábato sat tensely, jaw clenched, eyes fixed on the continuous scroll of live data across multiple screens lining the room.

At Tosh's other side, Artemis Wang's posture was sharp, focused, her gaze scanning faces on the international video feeds—faces projected from Washington, Geneva, and London, each set in grim determination. A subtle electronic beep announced another incoming feed, echoing like a warning bell. Technicians hurried discreetly in the background, whispering urgently among themselves, fingers dancing swiftly over keyboards, ensuring the integrity of secure connections.

Tosh took a deep breath, the measured exhale betraying none of the turbulent anxiety he felt inside. "As you're all aware, NeuraTech successfully infiltrated Zermatt. While the facility itself is secure now, thanks to swift U.S. and Swiss Special Forces intervention, the uncertainty regarding the fragments of CDA-325 remains our foremost concern."

A tense silence settled momentarily before General Harrison, the gruff, seasoned U.S. liaison from the Pentagon, leaned forward into his screen, his face hard and eyes probing. "Any updates on whether NeuraTech managed to transfer those fragments to their higher command?"

Rainer responded, his voice carefully measured, a slight tremor betraying underlying stress. "We've analyzed every captured device. Encrypted drives, equipment, field communications—all meticulously examined. Yet, nothing explicitly indicates whether they transmitted CDA-325 fragments before their capture."

"So, we must assume they succeeded," Artemis interjected sharply, her tone carrying unmistakable urgency. "We can't afford optimism. If NeuraTech's higher-ups have access to even a partial structure of CDA-325, their capacity for catastrophic damage multiplies exponentially."

The room remained uncomfortably quiet as those words hung heavily in the air, a shadow of dread spreading across the assembled faces.

"Agreed," Tosh said firmly, breaking the silence. "We must respond preemptively. It's not enough to defend anymore. We need to launch a targeted counteroffensive—morally and strategically."

A rapid exchange of looks passed between the screens. Ambassador Dupont from Geneva, typically calm and diplomatic, now wore a somber expression. "Nicolás, are you suggesting a direct engagement? That could escalate matters substantially."

"We're past the point of diplomatic caution," Tosh replied, his voice low, edged with steel. "NeuraTech's assault on Zermatt crossed every imaginable line. If we delay, their advantage solidifies. A coordinated response targeting their infrastructure—disabling their servers, disrupting their communications—is now imperative."

General Harrison nodded gravely. "We have actionable intelligence on several key NeuraTech operational hubs—London, Shanghai, New York. We can execute synchronized cyber and tactical operations within twenty-four hours."

Rainer shifted slightly in his chair, leaning forward with urgency. "This must be executed flawlessly. Any misstep could provoke immediate retaliation, potentially global in scale."

Tosh nodded solemnly, his eyes narrowed with conviction. "Then our response must not only be precise but also demonstrate restraint—incapacitate their operational capabilities without loss of civilian lives. It must be a moral counteroffensive, clearly delineating our ethical stance compared to their ruthlessness."

"Understood," Artemis said, determination evident in her voice. "We have teams standing by. Once we give the green light, simultaneous cyberattacks will incapacitate their communications and defense systems."

"We have global support," Tosh added, meeting eyes through the digital screens with each ally in turn. "The world is watching. Let's ensure they see clearly who we are—and what we stand for."

Silence returned briefly, deep and thoughtful, broken only by the soft murmur of technicians and the electronic pulse of data. Finally, Ambassador Dupont exhaled slowly, nodding agreement. "Then we stand united."

Tosh straightened, resolve radiating from every fiber of his being. "Prepare your teams. We strike tomorrow at dawn."

The room's tension shifted perceptibly, determination replacing anxiety as leaders around the world exchanged nods of solidarity. Though the uncertainty about CDA-325's fate lingered darkly, there was clarity in their purpose: they would fight, not just for survival, but for humanity itself.

As the screens faded to standby, Tosh leaned back momentarily, allowing himself a brief pause. The quiet hum of machinery filled the silence, a reminder of the technological warfare ahead. Yet, despite the daunting uncertainty, he felt something stronger stirring—hope.

Revelation: NeuraTech's Agenda

General Collins, appearing live from the Pentagon's secure communication suite, shifted uneasily in his seat. His broad shoulders, usually firm and steady, sagged slightly under the weight of the revelation he was about to deliver. His image was projected sharply, every crease of his concerned expression clearly visible to those gathered in the Experta Foundation crisis room.

He cleared his throat, a heavy, reluctant sound that quieted the anxious murmur immediately. "Before we begin, I want to acknowledge the successful intervention by our U.S. and Swiss Special Forces in Zermatt.

I deeply regret the operational delay. Bureaucratic red tape slowed down authorization significantly more than anticipated. This won't happen again."

Tosh gave a slight nod, his expression somber but understanding, aware of the complexities the General faced in mobilizing international action swiftly.

General Collins continued, urgency coloring his every word. "Intel from our Eastern European channels confirms our worst fears: the extremist network behind NeuraTech has openly stated their intention to 'fix global corruption.'" He paused, the strain evident as he searched for words. "But their method involves forcibly rewriting the minds of politicians, CEOs, and entire military commands. They aim to create a 'post-human democracy'—free, as they put it, from the 'flaws of human conscience.'"

An incredulous gasp echoed around the table, blending with uneasy whispers and tense exchanges. Faces on multiple screens—Washington, Geneva, London—twisted with horror and disbelief, each reaction visible in perfect clarity. Nicolás Tosh pressed his palms firmly onto the polished table, his knuckles whitening as anger mixed with dread.

"They truly believe the ends justify the means," Tosh spoke, his voice hollow yet razor-sharp, echoing like steel in the quiet room. Memories flashed before him—leaked images from a compromised lab, faces distorted in agony, their humanity violently overwritten. "They think virtues can be programmed into society, forcibly overriding free will, stripping away everything fundamentally human."

Alejandra, seated to Tosh's left, visibly recoiled, her breath catching sharply. She had arrived just hours earlier, exhausted and tense from a turbulent, anxious flight out of Miami, refusing to be absent when decisions of such magnitude were being made. Her voice trembled slightly but carried defiant strength. "So, their idea of saving the world involves taking away our ability to choose? That's monstrous. It's an abomination."

A moment of stark silence gripped the room, broken by Ambassador Celine Dubois from the G-7 liaison, her brow furrowed deeply, her image clear despite the thousands of miles separating her. "Monstrous or not, we can't underestimate their capability. Even limited access to the CDA-325 fragments gives them enough to destabilize governments. If NeuraTech successfully reprograms even a handful of key global leaders, the domino effect could spiral catastrophically out of control."

Around the table and across screens, expressions tightened further. The palpable realization of this unprecedented threat seeped into the room's tense atmosphere. Tosh lifted his gaze deliberately, making eye contact with each participant in turn, conveying both gravity and resolve.

"We must act decisively and immediately," Tosh said, his voice quiet yet resonant with authority. "Our moral stance must counter theirs clearly and unequivocally. This is not just a fight for political or strategic advantage. This is a fight for the very fabric of human dignity and freedom."

General Collins straightened, resolve steadying his previously uncertain posture. "Agreed. Strategic and moral alignment across all allied forces is critical. We must demonstrate our commitment not only to counter their immediate threat but also to uphold the ethical standards that define us."

Silence again filled the room briefly as the weight of their task settled over the assembled leaders. They knew clearly now—this was more than a conflict. It was a battle for humanity's soul. Tosh's eyes narrowed with determination, the powerful resolve mirrored clearly in the faces of his colleagues and allies around the globe. They had uncovered the depth of NeuraTech's ambition. Now, united, they would confront it.

The Only Hope: Launching CDA-325 as a "Counter-Vaccine"

With a tense silence cloaking the Experta Foundation crisis room, Rainer Sábato keyed a sequence into his console, bringing up a stark, precisely detailed schematic of CDA-325 onto the central display. Every eye in the room fixed anxiously on the intricate diagram—lines of code interwoven intricately, complex yet frighteningly clear in their purpose.

"We've known for months that Algorithm-325 can do far more than simply read neural patterns," Rainer began steadily, his voice calm but charged with underlying intensity. "Its architecture allows us to implant protective triggers, essentially creating a neural inoculation. We could immunize minds against unauthorized Overwrite attempts."

A profound hush settled, the implications hanging heavy in the air. The blueprint scrolled slowly, almost hypnotically, detailing how a small data packet, seamlessly integrated into a subject's memory framework, could instantly detect and neutralize any external attempt at mental intrusion.

Artemis Wang broke the silence first, leaning forward intently, her face illuminated by the scrolling data. "Mass deployment of this technology means registering the neural signatures of entire populations. There is no feasible way to conceal such an initiative indefinitely. Once discovered, public backlash would be swift and severe."

Nicolás Tosh sat motionless, hands steepled, memories of prior public outrage over selective neural scans vivid in his mind. The sheer magnitude of what they were considering pressed down upon him heavily, yet he knew hesitation meant risking catastrophic consequences.

"I'm fully aware of the cost," Tosh replied quietly, each word weighed deliberately. His gaze moved from face to face, ensuring they understood his resolve. "But if NeuraTech acts first, thousands—perhaps millions—will become helpless victims. We must not allow their enslavement of humanity to happen."

The weight of Tosh's words resonated deeply. Everyone present felt the gravity of this choice—a decision with profound moral implications. The very core of human freedom was at stake, balanced precariously against their desperate circumstances.

Suddenly, an insistent beep shattered the solemn quiet. Technicians swiftly adjusted their consoles, the screens filling rapidly with incoming encrypted data streams. Tosh and Rainer exchanged tense glances as the intercepted message crystallized into stark clarity on the main screen:

"Deploy primary Overwrite on Eastern Europe cluster. Target: heads of state, finance ministers, key military brass."

Alejandra gasped audibly, eyes widening in alarm and disbelief. She had fought fatigue and fear to travel here from Miami, determined not to remain passive as their fate unfolded. Her voice was taut with urgency. "They've transitioned from isolated tests to a full-scale operation?"

Rainer, his eyes never leaving the damning message, nodded slowly, gravely. "Yes. Their timeline has accelerated dramatically. We may have only days—or less—before they begin widespread forced reprogramming."

Faces around the table paled visibly, the immediacy of the threat piercing through their earlier reservations.

Tosh rose deliberately from his chair, the quiet strength of his resolve evident as he surveyed the room. "Then our choice is clear. If we delay, NeuraTech will erase freedom itself from the consciousness of entire populations. We must act now, swiftly and decisively. CDA-325 must be deployed immediately as our last line of defense."

General Collins' image flickered slightly as he leaned forward urgently from his Pentagon feed, his voice carrying an unmistakable note of solemn agreement. "Nicolás is right. The ethical cost is immense, but the alternative is unthinkable. We must defend free will, even if that means preemptively safeguarding minds on an unprecedented scale."

One by one, around the physical and virtual table, solemn nods of assent spread, united by an ironclad determination.

"We will mobilize immediately," Tosh declared firmly, his voice imbued with renewed strength. "We have one chance to get this right. Let's ensure history remembers us as protectors of humanity, not passive observers of its demise."

The room filled swiftly with activity, voices sharply coordinating immediate actions. Technicians and strategists surged into focused preparation. Tosh met Rainer's gaze one final time, exchanging silent affirmation. They had passed the point of doubt—this was humanity's only hope, and failure was no longer an option.

Decision: Limited Deployment to "Key Targets"

The conference room erupted into fierce debate, tension cascading through heated exchanges that sliced through the air. Voices overlapped, concerns sharp as blades—worries about diplomatic blowback from the G-7, anxiety over Redwood's likely maneuvers within the United States, and visceral fears about the devastating potential if CDA-325 were ever misused or fell into the wrong hands. The weight of decision loomed heavily, visible on every strained expression.

Finally, Nicolás Tosh rose deliberately, pushing his chair back with controlled determination, hands placed firmly on the gleaming surface of the polished conference table. The room quieted instantly, every eye turning toward him, drawn by the force of his calm resolve.

"We'll move forward—but cautiously," Tosh declared, his voice steady and measured, the authority unmistakable. "I propose we implement CDA-325 selectively, strictly limited to strategic individuals—heads of state, influential innovators, and key figures NeuraTech will inevitably target first. The operation must remain covert, concealed as routine, standard security assessments."

Ambassador Celine Dubois adjusted her glasses, glancing down thoughtfully at the meticulous notes before her. "The G-7 alliance will only support such a delicate strategy if we're fully transparent with operational logs. They require undeniable proof that deployment remains strictly confined to essential targets."

Artemis Wang visibly relaxed, tension briefly leaving his shoulders as he nodded cautiously. Anxiety still shimmered faintly behind his composed demeanor. "If we maintain complete secrecy, operating quietly and systematically, perhaps we can navigate this minefield without triggering mass panic or uncontrollable escalation. However," his voice darkened ominously, "if Redwood even suspects a limited deployment, he may insist we extend immunization broadly—or worse, seize control entirely."

Alejandra's expression tightened instantly, the memory of Redwood's ruthless pragmatism sharp in her mind. Her voice was firm, tinged with stark caution. "Under no circumstances trust Redwood. If he learns of our capability to grant mass neural immunity, he'll push relentlessly to expand coverage, no matter the ethical consequences. He'll use it to secure absolute control, masking his intentions under national security."

Tosh met her gaze directly, acknowledging the validity of her warning with a firm nod. "Agreed. Redwood remains a critical threat. But our immediate priority is countering NeuraTech's imminent assault. Rainer,"

Tosh turned decisively toward Sábato, whose expression was fiercely resolute, "Begin crafting a stealth operational plan immediately. Identify a highly selective list of essential individuals—three to four hundred at most. Integrate deployment into existing routine procedures, such as annual security clearances for nuclear launch codes or high-profile corporate transactions. Ensure the program remains invisible, leaving minimal digital and operational footprints."

Rainer's jaw tightened, resolve blazing vividly in his eyes as he nodded sharply. "Understood, Nicolás. We'll discreetly embed CDA-325 within pre-existing neural security assessments. Deployment carriers will activate in strategic 'brain wave hotspots': major international summits like the G-7 and UN meetings, and elite corporate and economic conferences. It will be quick, silent, and efficient."

The room's tension shifted slightly, palpable urgency reshaped into focused determination. Tosh's posture straightened, projecting calm strength, every word delivered clearly to ensure absolute comprehension.

"Remember," Tosh cautioned gravely, his gaze scanning each attentive face around the table, "absolute discretion is paramount. Our margin for error is nonexistent. This targeted immunization isn't merely defensive—it's our only viable line of defense. One mistake, one leak, and we could trigger exactly the scenario we're desperately trying to avoid."

An electric intensity filled the room as the magnitude of the task crystalized. Strategic teams began immediate discussions, voices lowered yet charged with purposeful resolve. Technicians and analysts quietly initiated secure communications, their swift actions methodically precise.

Rainer met Tosh's eyes once more, the silent exchange reaffirming their shared commitment. They had chosen their path—limited but potent, cautious yet decisive. Now, they would walk it with unyielding precision, fully aware that the world's future hung precariously in the balance.

Foreshadowing: A Grave Moral Compromise

The silence in the Experta Foundation crisis room thickened into something oppressive, suffocating the occupants beneath the weight of their looming decision. Miriam Faber stood by the central screen, its illuminated surface casting harsh, artificial light across her drawn features. Her slender finger pointed toward the digital projection's ominous final sequence:

$$\text{overwrite} \rightarrow \text{embed} \rightarrow \text{immunize}$$

She visibly swallowed, the action audible in the stifling quiet. Her voice trembled slightly, a stark contrast to her usual precise, clinical tone. "Once we cross this line, there's no going back. This isn't just defensive code—this is direct, intentional intrusion into human minds. Even if our intentions are benevolent, we cannot overlook what we're about to commit to."

Every gaze in the room shifted anxiously toward Nicolás Tosh, whose expression had become a careful mask, shielding deeper turmoil beneath. His eyes briefly met Alejandra's—her intense, searching gaze silently posed the question that resonated unspoken: Are we truly prepared for this?

Tosh drew in a measured breath, memories flashing vividly through his mind—the brutal infiltration attempts at Zermatt, paramilitary assaults, tortured faces from the leaked NeuraTech lab footage. He saw clearly the stark reality facing humanity: global mind enslavement or strategic, controlled intrusion to protect what remained free. Was there truly a choice?

He forced steadiness into his voice, each word deliberate and carefully chosen. "We move forward with extreme caution, implementing the absolute minimum intervention required. But understand clearly— failure here means a future where NeuraTech forcibly rewrites entire governments and militaries, creating a nightmare we cannot undo. Yes, this is a compromise none of us ever wished to make. But it's a compromise we can't avoid."

Rainer stepped forward quietly, laying a firm, supportive hand on Tosh's shoulder. His usually calm eyes carried a fierce determination tempered by compassion, fully comprehending the heavy burden resting on Tosh's conscience. "We must believe we're choosing the lesser of two evils. If we hesitate now, NeuraTech's Overwrite will spread uncontested, annihilating every shred of human autonomy. Our careful, minimal intrusion is the only remaining safeguard."

The room fell back into a tense quiet, each occupant silently wrestling with the enormity of what had been decided. Artemis Wang stood off to the side, arms tightly crossed, his eyes darkened by internal conflict. Once a billionaire driven by unstoppable ambition, even Wang now recoiled visibly at the ethical precipice before them.

Tosh straightened, his back rigid with renewed purpose despite the crushing moral weight. His gaze swept slowly across the assembled group, locking briefly with each individual to share a silent pledge, binding them all together in this shared resolve and inevitable guilt.

"We'll proceed with clarity and restraint," he said finally, his voice low yet resolute. "We'll document meticulously, ensure transparency to our allies, and accept responsibility for every step we take from here forward. We can't allow ourselves to become what we're fighting against."

A heavy collective nod rippled slowly through the room, acceptance mingling bitterly with resolve. The path forward was fraught with moral ambiguity, yet there was undeniable unity in the quiet determination that settled upon them all. The haunting echoes of this crisis meeting lingered, underscoring the irreversible step they were about to take into humanity's uncertain future.

Human Trafficking & Child Exploitation Time was relentlessly slipping away, each second amplifying the stakes as the largest human trafficking and child exploitation ring in Southeast Asia inched closer to vanishing into the shadows once again. In the bustling command center of the Experta Foundation, screens flickered frantically, each displaying real-time data streams and urgent intercept communications. Analysts moved rapidly, tension etched into every urgent movement, their voices clipped and strained.

"We're losing critical intel from the Southeast Asia nodes!" cried out Ava Nguyen, the head analyst, her fingers flying across her keyboard in desperate rhythm. Her usually steady voice cracked under mounting pressure. "The partial re-keying meltdown at Zermatt is throttling our entire data flow."

Rainer Sábato rushed over, his eyes narrowing sharply as he scanned the fragmented streams of data cascading across Ava's screens. The usually precise digital code was now erratic, jittering wildly—a direct casualty of the recent breaches and urgent re-encryption protocols.

"Can we route through another data hub temporarily?" Rainer demanded, urgency coloring every word. "We can't afford delays."

Ava shook her head, frustration visible in every tense muscle of her posture. "The 'vaccination' effort is monopolizing all our available carriers. The covert transmissions for CDA-325 deployments are saturating every secure channel we've got. We're hitting bandwidth ceilings everywhere."

Rainer slammed his palm against the workstation, the harsh sound echoing through the busy room. "Find me even a sliver of bandwidth, Ava. This trafficking ring is about to disappear underground for another year—maybe longer. We lose them now, hundreds more innocents will vanish forever."

Across the room, Nicolás Tosh was locked in fierce, whispered debate with Artemis Wang, their expressions grim and eyes shadowed by ethical turmoil. Alejandra watched them closely, the tension around her palpable, aware that the delicate balance between urgent strategic deployments and immediate humanitarian crises was fraying at the seams.

Suddenly, a new alert flashed urgently across Ava's screen—a burst of intercepted communication, chaotic and incomplete but devastatingly clear.

"Cargo transfer accelerating—children relocated tonight. Final auction imminent."

Ava's eyes widened, horror momentarily freezing her in place. Her voice trembled with barely contained emotion. "They're moving the kids now—tonight. If we don't act immediately, it's too late."

Rainer straightened sharply, turning toward Tosh with fierce determination blazing in his gaze. "Nicolás, I need immediate authorization to reroute bandwidth from CDA-325 deployments. Southeast Asia ops must become priority number one, right now."

Tosh, visibly torn, quickly exchanged a strained glance with Artemis, whose expression darkened in quiet resignation. Tosh nodded briskly, his voice commanding and decisive. "Authorize immediate bandwidth reallocation. Carve out what you need, Rainer, and do it fast. Save those children."

Instantly, the command center erupted into rapid, disciplined action. Ava's team shifted swiftly, their fingers flying over keyboards, rapidly reassigning data streams, fighting the encroaching chaos. New pathways opened, data feeds stabilizing, and intelligence began flowing clearly once more.

"Southeast Asia channel stabilizing," Ava announced breathlessly, relief flooding her features. "We're regaining visual and audio intel."

Rainer leaned forward intently, watching screens as satellite imagery zoomed sharply onto a remote coastal dock hidden beneath thick jungle canopy. Shadowy figures moved hurriedly, unaware of the surveillance cameras now locked onto their every action.

"Deploy rescue teams immediately," Rainer ordered decisively, his voice echoing with powerful resolve. "Coordinate with local special forces. We have one chance—no room for mistakes."

As operational orders flashed rapidly across the screens, Rainer exchanged a grim but determined look with Tosh. The room pulsed with renewed energy, each analyst and technician driven by singular purpose, fully aware of the devastating human cost of failure.

This wasn't just a crisis—it was humanity's darkest cruelty laid bare. For every person in the command room, stopping this exploitation ring was no longer merely operational—it had become deeply personal.

They had mere hours, perhaps less. Every moment counted. And no one would rest until those innocent lives were freed from the nightmare threatening to consume them.

Corruption at State Levels

The sleek and ultra-modern briefing room at Zermatt felt uncomfortably small under the heavy atmosphere. Multiple screens flickered with incoming messages, their insistent beeps signaling another wave of desperate appeals from officials of smaller nations. Each encrypted message carried the same sordid undertone: hush deals, secret payoffs, hidden agreements. The incessant flow was overwhelming, persistent in its blatant disregard for ethical governance.

Standing rigid at the head of the control panel, Tosh's expression grew darker with every successive alert. His eyes flashed rapidly across incoming communications, their relentless barrage etching deep lines of strain across his face.

"Another one from Southeast Africa," announced Ava Nguyen, clearly frustrated as she swept a hand through her short-cropped hair. Her voice carried a bitter edge of anger, barely contained. "They're willing to offer undisclosed funds in exchange for silence on illegal mining operations."

Tosh's jaw tightened, muscles flexing visibly beneath his skin. His knuckles whitened as he gripped the edge of the console, wrestling internally with the impossible calculus of priority—each demand pulling at his attention, fragmenting their critical resources.

"This keeps coming," Artemis Wang interjected sharply, his voice tight with barely restrained fury, eyes narrowed with profound disgust. "These corrupt officials know the global Overwrite crisis overshadows their petty schemes. They're betting on our distraction."

Alejandra moved forward silently, studying the relentless incoming messages with undisguised disdain. Her voice, when she spoke, was quiet yet powerful, cutting clearly through the tension-filled air. "If we ignore these cases now, we risk reinforcing the belief that Zermatt can be manipulated—that justice can be circumvented."

"Yet, can we truly afford to divert critical attention away from stopping NeuraTech's Overwrite threat?" Tosh asked quietly, frustration and anguish clearly battling within his words. His eyes met Alejandra's, searching deeply. "Each moment we spend on this corruption pulls us away from a crisis that threatens free will itself."

From the corner, Rainer Sábato observed silently, arms crossed tightly across his chest. His gaze flickered between the screens, reading the clear desperation in each message, recognizing the urgency, yet keenly aware of the broader danger they faced.

"These nations are small but vital," he finally said, stepping decisively forward. "If their leaders succumb completely to corruption, they become easy targets for NeuraTech's Overwrite. We can't dismiss them entirely."

Tosh sighed deeply, visibly grappling with internal turmoil. "Then we intervene selectively," he declared finally, authority solidifying in his voice. "Pick the most critical, blatant cases—where corruption directly threatens regional stability or human life. Quietly relay warnings and gather intelligence."

Ava nodded sharply, fingers already flying rapidly across her keyboard. "I'll reroute some lower-priority intel streams. We can at least start tracking financial movements, keep watch quietly."

Artemis clenched his fists, a fierce determination igniting his eyes. "We must make it clear to these corrupt players—no matter how small or seemingly inconsequential their nation—that exploiting chaos for personal gain will no longer remain hidden."

"Exactly," Tosh affirmed, strength returning to his voice. "Send discreet but firm warnings to each identified official. Make it explicit that Zermatt is watching. We'll act decisively if necessary."

Immediately, the room sprang into organized action, analysts and operatives quickly implementing instructions. Satellite links flickered, secure channels hummed to life, and messages began to flow outward— calm yet unequivocally firm.

Despite this focused efficiency, an underlying current of unease remained palpable. Each team member knew well the precarious tightrope they now walked—balancing limited resources between urgent global threats and corrosive local corruption.

As messages streamed out, Tosh stood motionless, his eyes narrowed in determined contemplation. He understood fully that while their decision was fraught with potential risk, silence would cost far more than mere credibility. It might inadvertently open another, more insidious front in the global war for humanity's freedom.

Faulty Technology & Public Safety

Rainer Sábato stood rigidly, eyes locked on the flashing screens in front of him, anxiety etched deeply across his features. The bustling crisis management hub at Zermatt hummed with tension, every technician and analyst swept up in their own urgent crises. Yet, amidst the storm of overlapping emergencies, a single alert glared starkly from his monitor—a relentless reminder that the world's dangers extended far beyond NeuraTech's insidious reach.

"Urgent—Lingtao's aviation defects detected," the alert blinked insistently, each pulse fueling Rainer's growing dread.

Lingtao, a global technology conglomerate famed for its philanthropic ventures, had quietly been funding advanced avionics for commercial aircraft worldwide. Now, buried beneath its benevolent facade, a glaring defect had surfaced—a software glitch embedded deeply in critical flight navigation systems, potentially catastrophic in scale.

Rainer's hand hovered tensely over his comm, heart racing as he digested each new line of incoming data. Lingtao's systems failure risked the safety of thousands, perhaps millions of passengers. Yet, around him, attention was almost entirely consumed by the looming global Overwrite crisis.

"We have confirmed reports from Europe and Asia," Ava Nguyen called sharply across the crowded room, her voice tense with suppressed urgency. "Initial system faults linked directly to Lingtao's navigation software."

Rainer moved swiftly to her station, his eyes swiftly scanning the incoming technical reports. Code fragments streamed across Ava's screen, errors highlighted in red, flashing ominously—each line detailing escalating hazards.

"This isn't just an isolated glitch," Ava continued grimly, eyes meeting Rainer's with steely resolve. "Multiple commercial flights have reported erratic altitude shifts and inaccurate coordinates. If these failures cascade, we're facing potential midair collisions or catastrophic failures."

Rainer's throat tightened, recognizing the unbearable stakes. His gaze darted across the command center, landing on Nicolás Tosh, who stood absorbed in heated dialogue about the Overwrite infiltration. For a fraction of a second, Rainer hesitated, conflicted by the knowledge that diverting resources from the primary threat could leave vulnerabilities elsewhere.

"Nicolás," Rainer's voice cut sharply through the overlapping conversations, carrying an urgency that drew immediate attention. "Lingtao's navigation software is compromised. If we don't intervene now, we'll see catastrophic aviation incidents within hours."

Tosh's expression darkened immediately, swiftly absorbing the magnitude of Rainer's words. His response was immediate, decisive. "Prioritize it. Coordinate with Lingtao's philanthropic team—patch the defects, ground the affected aircraft if necessary. Public safety cannot wait."

Rainer nodded curtly, his relief momentary but profound. Ava was already relaying directives, coordinating rapid communications with aviation authorities worldwide, pushing for immediate grounding of vulnerable fleets.

"Issue emergency advisories," Rainer commanded firmly, adrenaline sharpening his tone. "Coordinate with international aviation bodies— every affected plane lands immediately. No exceptions."

The room burst into intensified action. Analysts scrambled, satellite communications surged to life, transmitting emergency orders at lightning speed. Rainer monitored the situation intensely, every nerve taut with awareness of the narrow margin separating safety from catastrophe.

Suddenly, an alarm blared, harsh and insistent, signaling a critical alert. A commercial airliner over the Atlantic Ocean was rapidly losing altitude, Lingtao's faulty software sending it spiraling dangerously.

"Intercept protocol, now!" Rainer barked, fingers clenched white-knuckled at the edges of Ava's workstation. "Feed corrected navigation data immediately. Override Lingtao's system remotely!"

Technicians and analysts moved frantically, fingers flying over keyboards, code streams colliding and correcting in frantic, precise bursts. Rainer watched, his heart hammering painfully as altitude readings plummeted alarmingly.

"Altitude stabilizing!" Ava cried out, relief flooding her voice. "Pilot confirms manual override successful. Aircraft regaining control."

A collective sigh surged through the room, brief yet profound. Rainer exhaled deeply, hands shaking imperceptibly as the immediate crisis eased, though his mind remained sharply alert.

"Continue monitoring," he instructed firmly, eyes never leaving the screens. "Coordinate directly with Lingtao—ensure every patch is permanent. Not a single aircraft takes flight until safety is guaranteed."

Around him, activity persisted urgently, analysts reinforcing defenses, ensuring every potential threat was systematically neutralized. Rainer, muscles aching from sustained tension, allowed himself only a fleeting second of relief before steeling once more for the next crisis.

Public safety remained precariously balanced—each decision vital, each second invaluable. He knew intimately the relentless stakes of this struggle—one misstep, one overlooked threat, could cost countless innocent lives.

Corporate Sabotage & Competitor Intrusions

In a discreet, dimly lit meeting room high above the bustling heart of Silicon Valley, Redwood's top corporate allies had gathered. The sleek mahogany table gleamed under strategically placed recessed lighting, reflecting the tension etched deeply into the faces of powerful executives. Redwood himself stood at the head of the table, his formidable presence casting an imposing shadow.

Screens embedded into the walls displayed confidential intelligence streams, data on potential rival moves, and cryptic messages exchanged with allied corporate entities. Each flicker of information reflected strategic shifts across the global technological landscape.

"Zermatt's silence is telling," Redwood mused aloud, his deep voice carefully controlled yet resonating with latent impatience. "We know they're up to something. Their focus has shifted—intensely. If they have a new technological play, we must know exactly what it is."

Sophia Blake, the formidable CEO of a leading tech firm and Redwood's closest corporate ally, leaned forward intently, fingers steepled thoughtfully. Her piercing gaze betrayed intense calculation beneath a carefully neutral exterior. "Our channels suggest Zermatt is considering a defensive deployment—a neural 'vaccine,' possibly leveraging CDA-325."

An immediate ripple of tension surged through the gathered executives, glances exchanged swiftly around the table. Redwood's eyes sharpened visibly, the implications clear and profound.

"A limited deployment?" Redwood's voice sharpened, demanding clarity.

"Highly targeted, strategic," Blake confirmed, her tone precise, clipped. "Heads of state, top innovators. Minimal footprint. They're concerned about backlash, moral implications."

"Concerned about morals?" Redwood's voice dripped contempt. "Morality won't save humanity from chaos. If they have an effective inoculation against NeuraTech's Overwrite, why limit it? They must expand immediately."

"Precisely," Blake concurred, her expression unreadable yet her voice firm with strategic resolve. "If we allow Zermatt to proceed covertly, our interests remain vulnerable. We must insist on a rapid, comprehensive rollout."

Redwood paced deliberately, each step radiating calculated dominance. "Then we must press our leverage—immediately. Make it clear to Zermatt that selective deployment is insufficient. The world needs universal inoculation. Public demand will back us."

Blake nodded swiftly, signaling an aide to transmit prepared messages instantly. Redwood watched closely, acutely aware of the delicate balance of power at play. A single misstep, a hint of hesitation, could weaken their corporate advantage irreparably.

Meanwhile, hidden from view in a secure data-analysis hub at Zermatt, Rainer Sábato monitored signals with escalating apprehension. Ava Nguyen's screens flashed urgently, incoming alerts pulsating red.

"Redwood's allies are mobilizing aggressively," Ava reported sharply, her voice taut with tension. "They're pushing for immediate global deployment of CDA-325."

Rainer's stomach twisted painfully. His eyes narrowed, scanning rapidly through intercepted communiques. "They've guessed our strategy. If Redwood demands an expansive rollout, we'll lose control. Mass deployment now would trigger widespread panic—exactly what we aimed to avoid."

He moved decisively to the communications relay, swiftly keying in an encrypted message to Tosh, urgency sharpening his every movement. "Redwood's onto us. They're preparing public pressure. We must reinforce covert channels and maintain our original, limited strategy."

Back in Silicon Valley, Redwood studied the encrypted confirmations streaming in, satisfaction briefly flickering in his eyes. "They'll have no choice," he announced confidently, turning back to his assembled allies. "We've positioned ourselves strategically—public opinion, corporate influence, governmental backing. If Zermatt hesitates, we'll force their hand."

Sophia Blake's expression hardened, eyes glittering with quiet anticipation. "We'll control the narrative. Frame universal deployment as essential for global security. Public sentiment will demand compliance."

Redwood allowed himself a brief, cold smile. "Exactly. Zermatt believes they can control the pace. We'll ensure they understand their mistake—rapidly and unequivocally."

Across the globe, Rainer and Ava watched anxiously as Redwood's allies began their orchestrated maneuver, their screens filling with meticulously coordinated statements. Rainer felt an intense rush of dread.

"Brace for impact," he whispered grimly, steeling himself against the inevitable confrontation ahead. "This isn't just sabotage—it's a strategic siege."

As tensions spiraled, both sides understood clearly: this corporate battle would shape the very fabric of global control and autonomy. Every action, every reaction, would ripple far beyond boardrooms, defining humanity's fragile future.

Maggie Wu's Investigation

In the dimly lit corner of an upscale Washington, D.C. café, investigative journalist Maggie Wu sat poised like a predator on the brink of the chase. Her dark eyes, sharp and probing, barely blinked as she studied the young man across from her. Sweat beaded visibly on his forehead despite the café's cool climate-controlled air, his fingers nervously tapping on the polished oak tabletop.

"So," Maggie leaned in slightly, voice low yet unyielding, "let's revisit your role at Experta."

The mid-level Experta staffer swallowed hard, eyes darting toward the exit, visibly calculating the cost of running versus cooperating. Maggie allowed a momentary smile, faint but coldly reassuring.

"I already know more than you think," she pressed quietly, sliding a tablet forward. It displayed a series of financial transactions and encrypted messages—enough to confirm the depth of her sources. "I'm giving you a chance to clarify, to set the record straight before this goes public. Tell me about Zermatt's expansions."

The staffer inhaled sharply, voice a whisper now, weighed by the gravity of betrayal. "They've been scrutinizing financial flows—government contracts, defense, disaster relief—any entity leveraging political contributions to secure undeserved bids. It's systematic. Zermatt's mapping the corruption, exposing officials who are complicit. They're close to unraveling some major players."

Maggie's pulse quickened, a predatory gleam illuminating her eyes. "Names?"

He hesitated, fear flickering visibly. "I… I don't know specifics. They compartmentalize data. But they've traced gross overcharges, suspiciously awarded contracts, kickbacks camouflaged as campaign contributions. They've compiled evidence—detailed, damning evidence."

Maggie leaned back thoughtfully, absorbing the revelation, piecing together the implications with practiced precision. Her fingers twitched subtly, the thrill of imminent disclosure surging through her veins.

Across the city, in Zermatt's Washington satellite office, Ava Nguyen's computer flashed an urgent alert. She scanned the details swiftly, eyes widening in alarm. Turning abruptly to Rainer Sábato, her voice tightened sharply. "We have a leak. Maggie Wu has cornered one of our staff. She's about to go public—days at most."

Rainer's face hardened instantly, every muscle tensed. "Identify the leak. Contain this immediately. We need to know exactly what she has."

Technicians scrambled, monitoring communication lines, tracing the compromised staffer's last known location. Data analysts frantically pieced together any potential information exposure, screens alive with rapid-fire intelligence streams.

Back in the café, Maggie stood, slipping her tablet decisively into her bag. "You've been very helpful. If I were you, I'd lay low. Things will get turbulent soon."

Stepping outside into the bustling D.C. Street, Maggie swiftly dialed her editor, heart racing with excitement, voice firm with professional authority. "We have it. Zermatt's tracking government contractor corruption—defense, federal, disaster relief—all of it. High-level exposure, possibly implicating major officials."

Across the network, Zermatt's rapid-response unit sprang into immediate action. Notifications flew urgently—to federal authorities, impacted government agencies, and selected congressional oversight committees. Detailed dossiers flooded through secure channels, outlining evidence of rigged bids, inflated charges, and political paybacks. Each document meticulously verified, compelling and irrefutable.

Yet, despite their swift defensive measures, Rainer and Ava knew the danger Maggie Wu posed. Her ability to thread scattered details into coherent, explosive revelations was legendary. If Wu broke the story prematurely, Zermatt's delicate investigation could collapse under public scrutiny, their covert tracking exposed and undermined.

Rainer's jaw tightened grimly, addressing Ava with urgent intensity. "We must move faster. Contain Maggie Wu's source, confirm precisely what information she holds. Our entire operation depends on controlling this narrative."

Ava nodded sharply, fingers flying across her console, initiating contingency protocols. She knew, just as Rainer did, the clock was ticking inexorably toward a decisive reckoning—Zermatt racing to safeguard justice, Maggie Wu racing to unveil the truth, both sides hurtling inevitably toward a volatile confrontation that would reshape the landscape of power and corruption.

The meeting concluded under a heavy pall of silence, each participant slowly rising from their chairs as though burdened by unseen weights. The sterile brightness of the conference room now felt oppressive, harshly illuminating the somber faces around the table. Nicolás Tosh stood at the head of the oval table, his usual aura of steadfast determination overshadowed by a weary resignation that lined his features deeply.

As Artemis Wang quietly gathered his documents, his movements slow and deliberate, the tension in his shoulders betrayed his inner turmoil. Rainer Sábato lingered, his gaze distant, fixed on the stark lines of data frozen on the now-darkened screen before him. Alejandra hesitated by the doorway, eyes glancing toward Tosh in silent empathy, yet she offered no comforting words—there were none sufficient for what they now faced.

One by one, the delegates filed out, their footsteps echoing softly against the polished marble floors, the sound carrying a grim finality. Ambassador Dubois departed last, her stern gaze meeting Tosh's with a nod of grave understanding—a quiet acknowledgment of the moral precipice they all stood upon.

Left alone, Tosh sank back into his chair, fingers trembling subtly as he pressed them against his temple, a vain attempt to steady the storm within. His mind raced relentlessly over their decision—the once forbidden option, a line they swore they'd never cross, now seemed the only path forward. The tool they had crafted to defend humanity had become their reluctant weapon, a blade they prayed would not cut too deeply into the fabric of freedom.

Outside, dusk settled silently over Zurich, the evening's quiet hues casting long shadows through the vast windows. Tosh watched as darkness slowly swallowed the daylight, symbolic of their own descent into uncertain territory. Each shadow seemed to whisper the quiet truth he had barely dared to admit—that heroism and tyranny stood perilously close, separated by only the finest thread of intention.

A gentle knock at the door pulled Tosh from his contemplation. Ava Nguyen stood quietly in the entrance, her usually sharp expression softened by concern.

"They've all left," she said gently, stepping carefully into the room, sensing the fragile quiet. "Is there anything more you need?"

Tosh raised his eyes slowly, holding her gaze. In that brief silence, volumes passed between them—an understanding of shared dread, an unspoken resolve to bear the coming storm.

"Just ensure the protocols are strictly enforced, Ava. Every step monitored, every action recorded. No deviations."

She nodded solemnly, understanding the gravity underpinning his instructions. "Of course. I'll personally oversee it."

"Good," Tosh whispered, turning his gaze once more toward the darkening horizon. "Because from here, there are no second chances."

Ava quietly exited, leaving Tosh once again enveloped by silence, haunted by the knowledge that each choice now carried a cost far greater than they ever imagined. The quiet stillness in the room lingered heavily, a silent testament to the profound moral compromise they had embraced, marking the thin and perilous boundary between salvation and ruin.

Chapter 10

Showdown in Geneva

Geneva, Switzerland — International Conference Center, 2017
Day 25, 2:00 P.M. CET)

A crisp autumn wind rustled the flags lining the wide boulevard outside Geneva's stately conference center, each flag snapping sharply as though in anticipation of the imminent confrontation within. The vibrant colors of the G-7 nations fluttered alongside smaller states, their representatives stepping from sleek vehicles with guarded expressions and hurried, whispered conversations. Nicolás Tosh exited a discreet black sedan, his jaw set with an unspoken resolve, closely followed by Rainer Sábato and Artemis Wang, both carrying the weight of what awaited inside.

The entrance hall was a hive of controlled chaos, murmured conversations underscored by a palpable tension. Security personnel moved swiftly and discreetly, their vigilance heightened, scanning faces with penetrating glances. Inside the grand assembly hall, world leaders and ambassadors took their seats cautiously, exchanging wary nods. Above them, massive chandeliers cast a cool, crystalline glow, doing nothing to soften the stark gravity that blanketed the room.

Tosh stepped forward, flanked by his companions, his presence immediately drawing sharp glances and a renewed hush through the assembly. He could feel the weight of countless eyes—some supportive, others wary, a few outright hostile—each set measuring him silently.

At the front of the hall, Ambassador Dubois was deep in a tense conversation with the U.S. Secretary of State, their voices low but edged with unmistakable urgency. She acknowledged Tosh with a curt, serious nod, a subtle reassurance in her otherwise stern expression.

Artemis Wang moved swiftly toward a secure comm station at the side of the hall, double-checking encryption layers, his fingers deftly working across the console. His movements were calm but urgent, each keystroke reflecting the monumental stakes.

Rainer leaned close to Tosh, speaking quietly yet firmly. "Everyone here suspects why we've gathered. If NeuraTech makes good on their threat, the fallout will be unimaginable. We need to control the narrative."

Tosh gave a tight nod, eyes narrowing slightly in calculated thought. "NeuraTech has played its hand openly. They count on our fear to paralyze us. But fear can't dictate our response. We're here to confront, expose, and neutralize."

A sudden, piercing feedback echoed through the speakers, signaling the commencement of proceedings. Conversations halted abruptly as a tall, severe-looking moderator stepped to the podium, his voice resonant with practiced neutrality.

"Esteemed delegates, we convene today under extraordinary circumstances," the moderator began gravely. "Rumors and threats concerning a new technology capable of unprecedented mental manipulation have forced this urgent assembly. We invite representatives to address these allegations directly."

An uneasy quiet settled over the hall, disrupted only by the tense rustling of papers and soft shifting in seats. Tosh stood deliberately, the creak of his chair audible in the vast room. He approached the podium with measured steps, every movement exuding a quiet authority.

"Ladies and gentlemen," Tosh began, his voice strong yet carefully controlled, echoing slightly from the marble walls, "the threat we face today is not merely technological—it's existential. A rogue element within NeuraTech seeks to subvert human autonomy by exploiting groundbreaking technology to manipulate and control the human mind."

Murmurs of disbelief rippled through the audience. Tosh raised a hand gently, quieting them. "The threats they've issued aren't idle. Their intentions are starkly clear—coercion, exposure, and domination. But we stand prepared. We have evidence, and we have means to counteract this menace."

A sharp interruption came from the British delegate, voice bristling with suspicion. "And your solution—is it not just another form of manipulation?"

Tosh met the delegate's gaze unflinchingly. "Our measure is protective, not coercive. It immunizes against unwanted intrusion, safeguarding autonomy rather than eroding it. We stand firmly on the side of free will."

Tension crackled through the hall, the implications sinking deeply into every delegate's awareness. Artemis subtly signaled Tosh, indicating readiness. Rainer shifted slightly, alert and watchful, as the moment of reckoning approached rapidly.

"Make no mistake," Tosh concluded firmly, eyes sweeping across the gathered assembly, "we face a decisive crossroads. We can choose courage over fear, action over paralysis. Together, we must dismantle this threat decisively and swiftly. The survival of freedom itself depends upon it."

As Tosh stepped back, the hall erupted in a cacophony of urgent debate. The lines were now clearly drawn, decisions inevitable, the moment charged with the electricity of imminent confrontation—a showdown whose outcome would irrevocably shape the future.

Diplomatic Chess: G-7 vs. Rogue Negotiators

Ambassador Celine Dubois ascended the podium with deliberate composure, her gaze unwavering, voice firm and authoritative. "We face an unprecedented threat of mass infiltration," she declared, each word resonating powerfully throughout the expansive conference hall. "We stand united in condemning any technology aimed at forcibly overriding human will."

A crisp, restrained applause rose briefly from the G-7 block, an affirmation carefully measured to convey unity without celebration. The tension, thick and oppressive, lingered palpably, settling heavily upon every attendee. Eyes shifted discreetly, gauging reactions, noting every subtlety in body language, every nuanced shift in expressions.

Across the hall, a tightly clustered group dressed in impeccably tailored dark suits observed silently, faces void of expression. Rumors had already circulated about their true allegiance—representatives or associates of NeuraTech's paramilitary faction. They exuded a quiet, menacing confidence, their mere presence a tangible statement of intent. Behind them, representatives of several smaller nations exchanged wary glances, whispers swift and anxious, their suspicion toward the G-7's hidden motivations clearly evident.

When the session momentarily adjourned for a scheduled break, Nicolás Tosh swiftly led Artemis Wang and Rainer Sábato into a secluded side lounge guarded closely by Swiss security forces. Waiting inside were Ambassador Dubois, the Swiss security chief, and several senior European ministers. The room, dimly lit and enclosed in secure silence, became a refuge of anxious, strategic whispers.

"They're playing hardball," Tosh began immediately, his tone grim but steady. "The paramilitary operatives in the hall have delivered a clear ultimatum—either we fully disclose the clandestine capabilities of Zermatt, or they'll auction off the Overwrite technology to the highest bidders. It's blatant, aggressive blackmail on a global scale."

Minister Lindholm of Sweden visibly paled, exhaling sharply. Her usually composed voice trembled slightly as she spoke, "And if we yield to their demands, we confirm the existence of Zermatt's advanced capabilities, inevitably igniting the exact arms race we have struggled to avoid."

Dubois nodded gravely, eyes narrowing in steely resolve. "We cannot afford to blink first. This isn't mere diplomacy—it's a high-stakes chess match. Any misstep will destabilize global order irrevocably."

Rainer stepped forward, tension etched deeply into his features. "They're counting on our fear. Our response needs to be precise and unequivocal. If they sense any hesitation, they'll exploit it."

Artemis tapped thoughtfully on his tablet, scrolling swiftly through recent communications. "Their threat is credible—intelligence confirms potential buyers already in negotiations. States, rogue actors, corporations—they're lining up. If NeuraTech successfully auctions the technology, we'll face unchecked proliferation."

Dubois's expression tightened, a cold clarity entering her voice. "Then we must act decisively. Our counterproposal must discredit NeuraTech publicly while simultaneously offering transparent safeguards. We demonstrate unified strength and moral clarity."

Tosh met her gaze firmly, agreement flickering in his eyes. "Precisely. We expose their agenda openly. The world must see them as blackmailers, not visionaries. Our only path is to force NeuraTech onto the defensive."

As the group nodded, each member recognizing the gravity of their collective responsibility, Tosh's voice hardened with resolve. "This isn't just about neutralizing NeuraTech's threat today—it's about protecting humanity's right to autonomy tomorrow. We hold the line here."

They rose together, unified in determination, each step back toward the conference hall resonating with renewed resolve. The intricate game of diplomatic chess had reached a critical juncture, and each participant knew that their next move would echo through history.

Simultaneous Cyber-Battle: CDA-325 "Vaccine" Deployed

Inside the confined interior of the high-tech operations van parked discreetly beside Geneva's international conference center, Rainer Sábato stood rigidly, eyes darting between rapidly updating screens. The mobile command center hummed softly, bathed in the eerie glow of dozens of monitors, each pulsating with encrypted data streams. Beside him, a tightly coordinated team of elite engineers and analysts worked feverishly, headsets in place, fingers flying across keyboards, voices clipped with controlled urgency.

"Initiating injection protocols," an engineer murmured tersely, her eyes fixed on scrolling lines of complex code. "We've achieved entry into critical infrastructure—airports, city grids, intelligence satellites—all systems verified as accessible."

Rainer nodded once, his heartbeat audible to his own ears, each beat echoing the enormity of their clandestine action. "Proceed carefully. Stealth is crucial."

"Injecting CDA-325 now," another technician confirmed, hands trembling imperceptibly over the keyboard. His screen blinked rapidly, signaling the silent deployment of Zermatt's most closely guarded secret—the neural 'vaccine' designed to shield minds from forcible overwrite.

"Status report?" Rainer demanded softly, sweat trickling slowly down his temple, betraying the stress he fought to hide.

"We're live across nine major satellite networks," the lead engineer announced quietly, her tone unwavering despite the unprecedented stakes. "Coverage confirmed—civil aviation channels throughout Europe and North America, partial feeds in critical sectors of Asia."

Rainer exhaled deeply, tension coiling within him like a tightened spring. Each passing second meant another layer of protection deployed invisibly, passively safeguarding billions from forced mental infiltration. Yet the morality of their act weighed heavily upon him—a secret breach designed paradoxically to safeguard autonomy.

"Billions of neural signatures are now passively receiving CDA-325," the technician continued softly, voice barely audible yet heavy with understanding. "Subjects remain completely unaware."

Rainer paused, eyes briefly closing as the full ethical weight of their actions settled upon his conscience. "This is a Rubicon we've crossed," he whispered to himself, an internal admission of the profound moral compromise they had committed. Opening his eyes again, he steadied his voice, addressing his team with renewed resolve. "Maintain absolute stealth. Redwood and the paramilitaries cannot detect our activities until it's too late. If they realize what we're doing—"

"We know," the technician interrupted quietly, her eyes locking briefly with Rainer's. "The political fallout would be catastrophic. We'll keep it under the radar as long as humanly possible."

Suddenly, an alarm chirped softly but urgently from the console nearest the door. The engineer spun toward it, rapidly assessing the alert. "We have incoming network probes—someone's sensed unusual activity."

Rainer's jaw tightened sharply. "Diversion protocols, immediately. Redirect their attention. Create noise on decoy networks."

The team leaped into action, fingers dancing across the consoles, crafting complex distractions. Data flowed swiftly, a digital smoke screen designed to confuse and misdirect their adversaries' cyber scouts. Rainer watched intently, his breath shallow as he tracked each defensive maneuver.

"Diversion successful," the lead engineer confirmed after tense, endless seconds, her shoulders visibly relaxing. "Probes have disengaged, for now."

"Good," Rainer said curtly, eyes narrowing with cautious relief. "Keep monitoring closely. No room for error—everything depends on maintaining secrecy."

Inside the van, silence briefly settled, punctuated only by the steady hum of electronics. Each technician understood implicitly that they were operating on the razor's edge, balancing profound risk against critical necessity.

Rainer turned back to the monitors, his reflection ghostly against the digital glare. "Every moment we hold this line is a moment closer to neutralizing NeuraTech's threat permanently," he murmured, rallying himself as much as his team. "Stay vigilant. The battle isn't over yet."

The Climax: NeuraTech Attempts Mind-Hijack

Back inside the grand auditorium of Geneva's international conference center, an eerie quiet fell over the assembly as delegates rose for the scheduled afternoon recess. Nicolás Tosh felt a vibration in his pocket and discreetly pulled out his phone, his pulse quickening at the sight of an urgent alert flashing onscreen. Rainer's voice came through the discreet earpiece, tense and low.

"They're flipping the switch—NeuraTech is initiating remote Overwrite signals targeting key delegates right now."

Tosh's heart thundered in his chest. Instantly, his eyes sought Artemis Wang, who caught his glance with an equally grim understanding and gave a terse nod. Swiftly, Tosh's gaze swept the hall, spotting several key figures—heads of state and influential ambassadors—casually adjusting earpieces or glancing down at their phones. They remained entirely unaware that invisible tendrils of malicious code were streaming toward their neural signatures, seeking to rewrite their consciousness in real-time.

The extremist operatives stood quietly at the back of the hall, their faces rigidly composed but eyes glittering with predatory anticipation. They awaited the imminent public display of their terrifying capability—expecting these high-ranking individuals to suddenly seize up, their minds forcibly commandeered.

But nothing happened.

The targeted delegates blinked uncertainly, several pressing fingers to their temples in mild confusion, exchanging puzzled looks. The expected mental hijacking—visible panic, loss of control, or immediate compliance—simply did not materialize.

Tosh released a breath he hadn't realized he'd been holding, whispering softly, almost incredulously, "CDA-325 is blocking them. It's working."

Rainer's quiet voice confirmed, "Every attack is bouncing harmlessly. They're neutralized."

Across the auditorium, the extremist operatives shifted visibly from anticipation to stunned disbelief. One, his expression twisting into a scowl, rapidly withdrew a phone and began typing furiously, urgently seeking confirmation. Their covert plan was unraveling in real-time, the leverage they had counted upon evaporating before their eyes.

In a surge of desperation and rage, one operative moved decisively toward the central aisle, voice loud and cutting sharply through the uncertain murmurs. "Listen carefully!" he declared forcefully, instantly commanding silence and attention. "We know you have an advanced neural technology at your disposal. Surrender your data center's secrets immediately, or we'll sabotage the entire power grid across half of Europe!"

Instantly, chaos erupted. A ripple of alarm surged through the crowd. Journalists leaped to their feet, cameras flashing urgently, capturing every moment. Security teams surged forward, swiftly positioning themselves protectively around delegates as leaders urgently called for calm. Voices rose in a panicked cacophony, echoing off the auditorium's vaulted ceiling.

Amidst the tumult, Tosh remained steadfastly composed, eyes narrowing with intense determination. The gamble had paid off—the protection was holding firm, but the situation remained volatile.

"Tosh," Artemis murmured urgently, "we need to respond, now. Public confidence hangs by a thread."

Tosh gave a resolute nod. Stepping forward, voice ringing clearly, he addressed the assembly. "These extremists attempted a covert assault on your minds, intending to prove their capability to subjugate human autonomy. But they have failed. Our defensive protocols have prevailed. Now, it is imperative we stand together against their blackmail."

The room gradually quieted, eyes turning toward Tosh, drawn by his unshakeable conviction. "They threaten us because they fear exposure. They threaten because they have lost control," he declared fiercely. "Let us send a clear message today—human freedom cannot and will not be compromised."

As his words settled heavily across the auditorium, the extremist agents slowly backed toward exits, expressions dark with defeat. Tosh felt a surge of cautious triumph, yet he knew the true battle was far from over. Their enemies were cornered but desperate, and the confrontation had only just begun.

Betrayal or Noble Sacrifice: Wang's Public Reveal

Suddenly, amidst the commotion and lingering tension, Artemis Wang strode purposefully to the dais, brushing aside startled aides who reached out in confusion. His face, illuminated sharply by the auditorium lights, was solemn yet resolute, revealing no trace of hesitation. With a swift, authoritative gesture, he raised his hand, demanding immediate silence. Cameras swiveled rapidly toward him, their lenses capturing every nuanced expression of the man once globally revered as the visionary behind Lingtao Technologies.

"I'm Artemis Wang," he began firmly, voice resonating through the hall with quiet authority. "Many of you recognize me as a tech entrepreneur. Some among you speculate about my involvement in secrets far deeper and darker than publicly admitted. You are correct."

An immediate, profound hush enveloped the room, delegates frozen in mid-motion, the weight of his confession pressing down like a physical presence. Wang took a steadying breath, his gaze scanning the captivated assembly, their faces a tapestry of confusion, fear, and intrigue.

"The talk of forcibly rewriting human minds—whether from NeuraTech or any other source—is an unspeakable atrocity. The rumors you've heard are true," he admitted, each word measured yet raw with sincerity. "Yes, there is a hidden data center. Yes, this facility can access and potentially manipulate neural patterns. Misused, it could dominate free will. But I am standing here today not to perpetuate this horror, but to offer a solution—if, and only if, those threatening us stand down immediately."

Nicolás Tosh stiffened, his pulse quickening sharply. His breath caught in his chest as uncertainty and dread surged through him. Artemis Wang had not consulted him about making a public revelation. Tosh glanced rapidly around, noting the wide-eyed stares and muted whispers that rippled through the stunned crowd. Had Wang decided unilaterally to unveil Zermatt's closely guarded secrets?

Yet Wang pressed on, voice calm and decisive. "I have partial control over the very technology that you crave. If your genuine goal is transparency and accountability, then I am willing to talk. But mark my words clearly—attempting to blackmail continents, unleashing sabotage or chaos, will gain you nothing but ruin."

At the far end of the auditorium, the paramilitary operatives exchanged rapid, anxious glances. Wang's unexpected proposition dangled enticingly before them. Could this be a genuine offer, a chance to negotiate for actual access to the code they desperately sought? Their indecision was visible, their tight-knit group momentarily fracturing under the pressure of Wang's bold maneuver.

Meanwhile, unnoticed by most in the hall, Swiss security forces were quietly closing ranks around the building's perimeter. Forewarned by Rainer's covert infiltration, they tightened their net methodically, preparing to seal off any escape routes. Radios crackled softly, issuing discreet tactical orders, agents positioning themselves strategically, eyes trained carefully on every entrance and exit.

Wang, seemingly oblivious to the external maneuverings, stood tall and unwavering at the dais. He was a solitary figure at the epicenter of a storm, choosing an unprecedented path that skirted the line between betrayal and noble sacrifice. His eyes, clear and piercing, silently challenged those arrayed against him, daring them to reveal their true intentions.

Tosh watched him carefully, heart hammering in his chest, uncertainty gnawing at his resolve. He understood implicitly that Wang's daring gambit had set in motion forces neither fully predictable nor easily controllable. Yet, amidst his anxiety, Tosh recognized the courage it required to stand alone, vulnerable yet unyielding, confronting both friend and foe with nothing but integrity and a steadfast commitment to truth.

The auditorium remained suspended in tense silence, each second stretching unbearably, every individual present acutely aware that Artemis Wang had irrevocably changed the stakes. In the profound stillness, everyone waited breathlessly for the next move—a collective heartbeat suspended between hope and catastrophe.

The Final Standoff

Amid the swirling tension inside the grand auditorium, one of the paramilitary negotiators stepped boldly forward, his presence immediately menacing, his dark eyes narrowed dangerously. "Mr. Wang," he growled, voice resonating with thinly veiled hostility, "if you genuinely want to avoid a catastrophic meltdown, you'll hand over every line of code. Now."

Artemis Wang's expression tightened, his features sharpening with cold resolve, a glimmer of defiance flickering briefly in his eyes. He took a measured breath, then calmly replied, "Let's discuss it backstage." His voice carried a hint of controlled strength, seemingly untroubled by the brazen threat. The negotiator hesitated, eyes darting suspiciously toward Wang, uncertainty flickering momentarily across his hardened face. But curiosity and greed ultimately overrode caution, and with a curt nod, he indicated agreement.

Every camera lens pivoted urgently toward the unfolding drama, capturing the scene with electrifying intensity. Security personnel swiftly parted the crowd, some hoping desperately for a peaceful resolution, others bracing instinctively for the eruption of violence. Wang led the way confidently, his stride purposeful, betraying no hint of vulnerability. The negotiator followed closely, eyes scanning sharply for any sign of deception or ambush.

Unknown to the paramilitary operatives, Wang's calm demeanor concealed a strategic trap carefully laid beneath the façade of negotiation. As they stepped through the stage door into the dimly lit corridor behind the auditorium, Swiss special forces—alerted by Rainer's meticulous preparation—quietly flooded the side passages, moving with coordinated precision. Their movements were silent, disciplined, each agent poised with practiced calm, awaiting the signal to strike.

The negotiator paused suddenly, sensing something amiss. His eyes darted nervously around the narrow passageway, fingers twitching instinctively toward his concealed weapon. But before he could react fully, the shadows exploded into rapid, controlled motion. Armed operatives surged forward, closing in from every side with ruthless efficiency.

A brief but violent scuffle erupted. The negotiator fought fiercely, attempting to break through the tightening circle of special forces, his desperation evident. His fists struck wildly, movements panicked yet determined. The operatives countered expertly, their swift, precise actions minimizing any potential harm, rapidly restraining and disarming him. One by one, additional paramilitary agents entering the hallway were similarly subdued, their shouts of surprise cut short by swift, calculated takedowns.

Realizing their defeat, the paramilitary team, now fully cornered and overwhelmed, reluctantly raised their hands, signaling their surrender. The narrow corridor fell silent, tension dissipating slowly as Swiss agents methodically secured each individual, efficiently removing any lingering threats.

Wang stood slightly apart, observing quietly, his features still composed yet carrying an unspoken weight. He had risked everything on a bold maneuver, strategically luring their adversaries into a trap. Now, as he watched the final agents being led away, relief mingled briefly with solemn acknowledgment of the moral and ethical complexities he had navigated to reach this moment.

From inside the auditorium, muffled sounds of confusion and anxiety continued, delegates and spectators still unaware of the precise resolution occurring just beyond their sight. Artemis Wang exchanged a brief, intense glance with Nicolás Tosh, who had appeared silently at the corridor's entrance, both men understanding implicitly the narrow margin by which catastrophe had been averted.

As the subdued paramilitary negotiators were quietly escorted out, Wang drew a deep, steadying breath, his heartbeat gradually slowing. The final standoff had ended decisively, yet the broader struggle remained far from over. This victory, though significant, was merely one crucial battle in a war whose outcome remained perilously uncertain.

Resolution: The Extremist Ring Subdued

Over the next hour, the bustling corridors and tense chambers of the Geneva conference center were intermittently pierced by urgent bulletins. Reporters crowded around screens, relaying the unfolding updates with voices edged by nervous excitement: the extremist group responsible for the looming catastrophe had been decisively taken into custody. Swiss authorities, their movements swift and coordinated, had meticulously defused hidden sabotage devices planted dangerously close to major power relay stations across Europe. The threatened public meltdown, once hanging ominously over the continent, evaporated quietly into an unrealized nightmare.

Delegates and spectators, previously gripped by fear and uncertainty, breathed cautious sighs of relief, exchanging hesitant glances of disbelief and gratitude. Yet, beneath the fragile surface of their relief lay a deep, unsettling awareness of averted disaster—a fleeting reprieve that did little to dispel lingering anxieties about the technological menace still lurking in the shadows.

At that moment, Artemis Wang emerged from the backstage corridor, stepping back into the public eye. Cameras snapped hurriedly, zooming in on his composed yet visibly weary expression. A faint bruise marked his temple, evidence of the brief but intense struggle behind the scenes—a stark, silent testament to the physical confrontation that had briefly erupted before his adversaries had surrendered.

Across the bustling hall, Nicolás Tosh stood frozen, eyes locked intently on Wang as he moved deliberately forward. Their gazes met, a complex exchange of unspoken sentiments passing swiftly between them—profound relief intertwined with a quiet, aching sorrow. The cost of victory weighed heavily upon both men, the moral burden unmistakable in their solemn expressions. They had successfully navigated the crisis, but the ethical price of their secretive actions lingered palpably.

Around them, delegates murmured softly, suspicion and curiosity flickering openly across their faces. Half the room wore expressions reflecting newfound apprehension, sensing intuitively that today's dramatic events barely concealed a far deeper, more potent technological threat. Speculation and whispered theories quickly circulated, fueled by the alarming certainty that hidden powers, capable of infiltrating and manipulating the very foundations of human cognition, remained dangerously close.

As Wang finally reached Tosh, both men stood silently amidst the swirl of uncertain voices, the muted hum of unanswered questions surrounding them. The extremist ring had been subdued, but the confrontation had illuminated unsettling truths—about themselves, their adversaries, and the precarious balance they sought to maintain. With every lens still pointed their way, both Wang and Tosh felt the immense gravity of their actions—the delicate line between safeguarding humanity and wielding a power that could, at any moment, become monstrous.

Their fleeting victory, hard-won and precarious, had left a lasting mark. In the eyes of those watching closely, the boundaries between savior and oppressor had blurred dangerously, a silent reminder that the battle for control of the human mind was far from over.

Aftermath & Lingering Concerns

Federal Contractors Unmasked: Zermatt's Covert Offensive Late at night, deep within Zermatt's subterranean data center, screens flickered ceaselessly, their glow casting stark shadows across the focused faces of the investigative analysts. Each workstation pulsed with lines of encrypted data, cascading rapidly as the digital warriors delved deeper into the murky labyrinth of U.S. government financial records. Their task was clear, yet daunting: uncovering systemic corruption buried beneath layers of government bureaucracy, hidden in plain sight within multimillion-dollar contracts.

A seasoned analyst, his fingers a blur over the keyboard, murmured through the headset to the adjacent team, "I've traced a discrepancy—defense contractor, massive overcharge embedded in their supply contracts. It's recurring, too clean to be an error." His voice, low and intense, drew immediate attention from supervisors hovering close by.

Across the room, another specialist swiftly joined the investigation, pulling up intersecting cash-flow charts and transaction histories. They meticulously pieced together a web of deceit—contractors repeatedly securing bids at inflated rates. Defense, disaster relief, infrastructure, cybersecurity—every major sector seemed infiltrated by companies subtly siphoning taxpayer dollars.

Hours passed unnoticed. The team unearthed shocking patterns: prominent defense contractors billing millions for nonexistent equipment; disaster relief companies exploiting natural calamities by inflating emergency response costs; infrastructure contractors consistently winning bids despite submitting significantly higher costs. Each lucrative deal aligned suspiciously with corresponding spikes in political campaign contributions.

"Here's another one," whispered a younger analyst, her eyes widening as she highlighted irregularities in disaster-relief contracts—companies funneling a portion of exorbitant charges directly back into political coffers. "This can't be coincidence."

Supervisor Helena Navarro leaned in closely, absorbing the magnitude of the discovery. "Connect all financial records directly to the political donations. Highlight every official involved." Her voice was steady, firm—she knew the explosive implications of their findings.

A flurry of activity erupted across the data center. Each analyst meticulously linked the financial footprints, tracing payments through offshore accounts, shadow corporations, and meticulously masked donations. The evidence painted a damning portrait: politicians and bureaucrats openly receiving kickbacks disguised as legitimate contributions, enabling contractors to reap enormous profits at the public's expense.

Within hours, Zermatt had compiled an ironclad dossier, meticulously detailing gross overcharges, undeserved bids, and covert paybacks. The air in the room grew thick with adrenaline and anticipation as the report took shape, each line another hammer strike against institutionalized corruption.

Navarro reviewed the final document, heart pounding with the weight of impending accountability. "Send it out," she finally ordered, her voice clear, determined. "Authorities, the implicated government agencies, and directly to Congress. Make sure every single detail is irrefutable."

The analyst tapped a key decisively. In seconds, digital transmissions raced through encrypted channels, instantly appearing in secure inboxes across Washington, D.C. Within moments, phones lit up across the capital—late-night calls piercing the stillness of political households, government offices, and newsrooms.

By dawn, a storm erupted. News alerts flooded screens nationwide, unleashing waves of outrage and disbelief. Headlines blared accusations, naming names and detailing damning evidence. Senators, representatives, and agency officials scrambled frantically, confronted by incontrovertible proof of corruption. Investigations were launched overnight, federal agents dispatched with warrants at first light, offices sealed, and executives detained.

At Zermatt, exhaustion mixed with somber satisfaction. They had peeled back layers of corruption, exposing the raw nerve of greed infecting governance. But as the analysts finally stepped away from their consoles, each knew this was merely one battle—one powerful victory in a relentless war against entrenched corruption. The fight for transparency had entered a fierce new chapter, illuminated now by the bright, unforgiving glare of truth.

Human Trafficking & Child Exploitation

The Geneva crisis had barely settled when Nicolás Tosh's phone buzzed urgently, its screen pulsing insistently amidst the echoing whispers and tension still hanging thick in the conference hall. Tosh stepped swiftly away, heart tightening as he absorbed the terse message glowing ominously on his phone: the Southeast Asian human trafficking ring had shifted locations yet again, deftly eluding detection once more. Zermatt's limited, damaged data streams were fraying under pressure, leaving their coverage fragmented and unreliable.

In the remote control room at Zermatt, operators frantically pieced together digital fragments and satellite imagery, their screens alive with snippets of intercepted chatter, blurred surveillance photos, and data pings from uncertain coordinates. Analyst Mei Lin leaned forward sharply, her voice taut with urgency. "They've moved again—new hideout confirmed near the Myanmar-Thailand border. At least thirty new victims, children and teenagers, identified." Her fingers shook slightly as she enlarged grainy images on the screen, revealing frightened, blurred faces hidden in the shadows.

Supervisor Marcus Davies paced restlessly behind her, eyes locked grimly on the screens. He rubbed a weary hand across his face, knowing their window of opportunity was shrinking rapidly. "Patch it all through to Tosh immediately," he instructed sharply. "We have to mobilize local enforcement now."

Back in Geneva, Tosh felt a visceral surge of frustration and anger, his jaw tightening fiercely as he absorbed the chilling updates. His fingers flew across the phone screen, rapidly coordinating with the nearest operatives stationed in Thailand. "Deploy immediate rescue," he typed urgently, pulse racing with adrenaline. "We can't risk losing them again."

Within minutes, a covert operations team—comprised of elite local agents briefed and supported by Zermatt—mobilized swiftly through dense jungle terrain under the cover of darkness. Silence enveloped their movements, broken only by hushed commands whispered through encrypted radios, their approach disciplined, swift, relentless.

At the traffickers' hidden encampment, the darkness was pierced by sporadic lights from makeshift lamps, the captors oblivious to the encroaching danger. Inside, frightened victims huddled tightly, murmurs of fear drifting softly through the night air. Suddenly, chaos erupted. Zermatt's team breached the perimeter with coordinated precision, agents moving fluidly through shadows, neutralizing guards silently and swiftly, ensuring minimal harm to the terrified captives.

As the traffickers' panicked shouts and footsteps echoed chaotically, the operatives surged forward decisively, locating and securing the children and teens, their movements swift yet gentle, reassuring the terrified victims with quiet, calming words. Within minutes, the compound fell silent again, the brief, violent confrontation resolved decisively.

Back in Zermatt's control room, Davies and Mei Lin exhaled shakily as confirmations streamed in—each message marking another victim safely rescued. Relief mixed starkly with sorrow on their faces as they registered the grim reality of those saved and those still lost. Mei Lin closed her eyes briefly, fighting tears borne from a mixture of exhaustion and muted victory.

Across continents, Tosh received final confirmation of the successful rescue. He steadied himself against the cool corridor wall, momentary relief washing over him. Yet beneath his fleeting solace lay a dark, persistent awareness—this victory, though critical, underscored how thinly stretched their operations had become. Each success seemed shadowed by an endless tide of new threats, a haunting reminder that their battle was far from over.

As Tosh stepped back into the bustling conference hall, he felt deeply the dual weight of triumph and relentless urgency. The fight against human exploitation never paused, never relented, demanding constant vigilance. They had won this skirmish, but the war stretched on endlessly, each rescued life reinforcing their unyielding resolve to fight onward.

Corruption at State Levels

The auditorium was nearly empty now, the lingering tension of the Geneva crisis dissipating slowly into the sterile conference air. Nicolás Tosh had barely caught his breath from the Southeast Asian rescue when Ambassador Celine Dubois from the G-7 approached him, eyes sharp and determined. Her voice was low yet carried a steely urgency. "Tosh, the situation with the extremist group is handled for now, but the corruption agenda can't wait. We need your commitment, now more than ever."

Tosh felt the immediate pressure, his pulse quickening with frustration. The weight of responsibilities pulled at him relentlessly: Redwood's aggressive campaign looming closer in the United States, the endless battle against human exploitation, and now the insistent demands of the G-7 to pivot instantly toward systemic corruption. He met Dubois's gaze, silently acknowledging the challenge with a grim nod.

Back at Zermatt's control center, screens flickered vividly as data analysts rapidly shifted focus, adjusting algorithms to track down covert financial networks. The operations room buzzed with tense, focused energy as the team shifted seamlessly from crisis management to methodical scrutiny of international finance trails.

Senior analyst Aaron Gray moved swiftly through layers of digital data, his fingers dancing urgently across his keyboard. Streams of encrypted financial transactions scrolled past, each highlighting suspect transfers. "There it is," Gray announced sharply, pointing to clusters of suspicious transactions—hidden payments cloaked as "consulting fees" or "international investments," repeatedly funneling back to accounts linked directly to state officials.

Supervisor Olivia Martinez stepped in closer, eyes narrowing as she absorbed the intricate web of deceit displayed on the screen. "Map them out explicitly. We need indisputable proof," she instructed decisively.

Within moments, a vivid chart of corruption appeared, revealing entrenched networks of government officials from various states receiving bribes disguised as legitimate transactions. Smaller nations, often overshadowed by the louder scandals of powerful countries, revealed shocking vulnerabilities. Officials from these governments, demanding discreet hush payments to approve projects or ignore regulatory infractions, formed a deeply troubling pattern.

Gray leaned forward intently, highlighting key transfers. "Each of these is tied to state-approved contracts, resource exploitation, infrastructure deals—every transaction benefiting companies and officials directly," he explained urgently. Martinez exhaled deeply, her gaze darkening with anger.

Back in Geneva, Tosh received a rapid update on his secured device, his heart sinking at the scale of corruption detailed. The moral imperative pressed sharply against him, despite his exhaustion. Swiftly, he relayed a brief, encrypted message back: "Proceed immediately—distribute findings to all relevant G-7 officials, local authorities, and international oversight bodies. No exceptions."

Within hours, dossiers filled with undeniable evidence of corruption flooded diplomatic channels. Scandals erupted simultaneously in several nations, officials scrambling desperately to deny or deflect accusations, but the evidence meticulously compiled by Zermatt left little room for doubt. Public outrage ignited swiftly, citizens taking to the streets demanding justice, transparency, and immediate accountability.

In the G-7 assembly room, Ambassador Dubois met Tosh again, her expression solemn yet satisfied. "You did the right thing," she affirmed quietly. Tosh, exhaustion evident in his features, nodded slowly. "It's never enough," he replied, voice tinged with quiet resignation. "But at least it's a start."

As Tosh walked away, he felt the relentless pull of multiple crises—a constant reminder of the thin line between justice and exhaustion. The fight against corruption, relentless and critical, now joined the myriad battles he faced daily, each victory both essential and fleeting, each challenge deeper and more complex than the last.

Dr. Miriam Faber's heart pounded as she hurried into Zermatt's secondary control room, the hurried clicks of her heels echoing sharply against polished floors. Screens glowed urgently, illuminating a skeleton crew scrambling to respond to an escalating crisis—a new airline scare unfolding in real-time. Zermatt's primary focus had been siphoned off by the catastrophic NeuraTech confrontation, but public safety waited for no one.

As Faber took her position, technicians quickly briefed her: a commercial airliner was experiencing a critical navigation systems failure over the densely populated skies of Central Europe. Flight data streamed frantically across the main screen, altitude and velocity indicators fluctuating dangerously.

"Which airline?" Faber asked urgently, her voice clipped with tension as she swiftly adjusted her headset.

"European Skyways, Flight ES-379," a technician responded immediately, eyes glued to his monitor. "They're reporting severe navigation inconsistencies, possible sabotage or malfunction—unclear yet."

Faber's jaw tightened. She knew immediately the stakes: hundreds of lives hanging by a thread, reliant on their swift intervention. She leaned over the control panel, fingers flying expertly across the keyboard, initiating an emergency diagnostic through remote channels. "Pull logs from the aircraft's recent maintenance and all Lingtao technology integrations," she instructed sharply, her eyes scanning the data flooding her screen.

Within seconds, another analyst, gripping the armrests of her chair with white-knuckled urgency, pinpointed an anomaly. "Navigation firmware updated just hours before departure. It matches the pattern of the Lingtao defects we've tracked."

Faber nodded briskly, mind racing. "Confirm backup manual control availability onboard," she ordered urgently. Simultaneously, she began crafting a quick override patch, her fingers precise despite mounting pressure.

Tension crackled through the control room, each second feeling stretched and fragile as technicians communicated rapidly with airline authorities, air traffic control, and onboard pilots. Pilot communications crackled through the speakers, voices tense yet controlled, relaying altitude adjustments and escalating alarm.

"I've got the override patch ready," Faber announced tersely. "Deploy it immediately—route it through Zurich's emergency navigation uplink." She hit the send key decisively, watching anxiously as the data packet shot toward the distressed airliner.

Every breath felt heavy with anxiety. The room's silence deepened as they watched the navigation readouts flicker—waiting, hoping. Then suddenly, stabilization. Altitude and velocity indicators steadied, and pilot communications flooded the channel again, relieved but cautious.

"System stabilized!" The pilot's voice came clearly through the audio, thick with palpable relief. "Flight control restored. Initiating immediate landing at nearest airport."

Faber exhaled, releasing the breath she hadn't realized she'd been holding, her pulse beginning to steady. She leaned back, running a shaky hand across her forehead, her eyes briefly closing in relief. Around her, the tension dissipated into subdued murmurs of cautious celebration.

But relief was fleeting. Faber opened her eyes, scanning the team quickly as she reminded herself of the harsh reality: they'd barely averted disaster, and the underlying technological faults remained unresolved. She glanced anxiously toward her screens, acutely aware of the next inevitable crisis waiting just beyond the horizon.

"We secured this one, but stay vigilant," Faber warned quietly. "It's only a matter of time until the next one emerges."

Corporate Sabotage & Competitor Intrusions

From a dimly lit conference room overlooking Capitol Hill, Redwood's allies watched the Geneva fallout unfold, eyes gleaming with anticipation. Monitors flickered with live coverage and muted commentary, casting long, ominous shadows across the faces of influential lobbyists and corporate executives. At the room's head stood Dominic Redwood himself, poised, confident, and calculating. His narrowed eyes tracked each news report, measuring every syllable spoken by exhausted reporters detailing Zermatt's harrowing near-miss.

As murmurs filled the room, Redwood's chief strategist, Elaine Carter, stepped forward with calculated coolness. "We can spin this beautifully," she suggested, her voice smooth and steady. "The narrative writes itself: Zermatt's incompetence allowed NeuraTech's infiltration. A massive security breach nearly plunged Europe into darkness. The public will demand answers."

Redwood smiled faintly, his fingers tapping thoughtfully against polished mahogany. "And naturally, we'll provide them," he mused, voice dripping with satisfaction. "It's clear that private control of such powerful technology is reckless. It's time the CDA falls under strict federal oversight."

Carter nodded eagerly, recognizing the strategic brilliance. "We emphasize accountability, public safety, and national security. If we frame this correctly, the voters will practically beg us to take control."

Nearby, a tech magnate from one of Silicon Valley's most influential corporations leaned in, lowering his voice conspiratorially. "My contacts confirm lingering vulnerabilities inside Zermatt. They're stretched too thin, too reactive. Another minor breach could tip public sentiment irreversibly."

Redwood's eyes sharpened instantly. "Then we apply pressure," he declared firmly. "Discreetly. Leak to the press that Zermatt's resources are compromised, that they're hiding the true scale of the risk. Heighten public anxiety. Make the CDA a key election issue."

At the far end of the table, a defense contractor executive shifted uneasily, glancing toward Redwood. "But we tread carefully. If we're caught manipulating security threats…"

Redwood silenced him with a dismissive wave. "We tread boldly. We present ourselves as protectors—ensuring technology safeguards democracy, rather than undermines it."

An intense silence hung momentarily before Redwood stood decisively, straightening his jacket. His voice resonated with quiet authority, a final directive. "Activate the PR teams, seed the narratives.

By election day, the public must demand federal control of the CDA—
our control."

As Redwood's allies dispersed, Carter lingered, turning to him with
subtle admiration. "This could redefine our power for decades," she
murmured.

Redwood fixed his gaze sharply out the window, watching lights blink
across Washington's skyline. "It will redefine everything."

Maggie Wu's Investigation

Maggie Wu stood rigid at the edge of the press pool, camera gripped
tightly in her steady hands. Her sharp eyes scanned the conference room,
capturing subtle movements, whispered exchanges, and hesitant glances
that others missed. Her pulse quickened as Artemis Wang strode
purposefully toward the podium, brushing past aides whose faces
registered shock and confusion.

Wu raised her camera swiftly, focusing the lens to capture every detail
of Wang's troubled expression as he began his statement. "I'm Artemis
Wang," his voice echoed, resolute and controlled, yet layered with
tension. "Many of you know me as a tech entrepreneur. Some suspect
I'm involved in deeper secrets. You're right."

Murmurs erupted across the room, but Maggie tuned them out, laser-
focused on Wang's next words. Her camera clicked rapidly, preserving
every nuance of his partial confession. Her investigative instincts roared
alive, sensing a deeper story beneath Wang's carefully chosen words.

She lowered her camera momentarily, her mind racing. Wang's
revelation was partial—deliberately vague, but undeniably significant. A
puzzle piece in the elaborate mosaic of rumors about Zermatt, mind-
altering technology, and clandestine government involvement. She felt
the exhilarating tension of an imminent breakthrough—one powerful
enough to topple the delicate balance of secrecy surrounding these
shadowy deals.

After Wang stepped away, Wu swiftly exited the press pool, navigating
corridors until she reached a quiet corner. Her hands trembled slightly,
adrenaline surging as she scrolled through captured images and hastily
typed notes into her encrypted device. Wang's cautious admission was a

thread; if she pulled at it carefully, it might unravel the entire hidden tapestry.

Maggie Wu took a deep, steadying breath, steeling herself for the chaos and danger she knew would follow once her story hit the news cycle. But there was no hesitation—her job, her passion, was to illuminate truths that others wanted buried. With renewed resolve, she slipped her device back into her pocket and strode confidently toward the exit. The world needed to know—and she was going to tell them.

As the delegates filed out and the day's adrenaline settled, Tosh, Wang, and Rainer exchanged weary glances in a cordoned-off corner of the now quieting auditorium. Tosh ran his hand through disheveled hair, exhaustion etched deeply into his features. Wang leaned against the wall, arms crossed, eyes distant and thoughtful, still processing the weight of his public revelation. Rainer, ever vigilant, scanned the thinning crowd, suspicion still lingering in his sharp gaze.

"We've subdued them—for now," Tosh said softly, his voice carrying the weight of barely contained tension. The echoes of the day's chaos lingered in his tone. "But we can't rest easy. Fragments of our code are still out there, scattered and hidden."

Rainer nodded grimly, eyes narrowing with unease. "We eliminated the immediate threat, but those hackers we couldn't trace, those who slipped through our fingers—they could resurface at any moment." His fingers twitched slightly, a subtle sign of anxiety from a man who rarely showed vulnerability.

Wang exhaled slowly, the heavy burden of their recent confrontation visible in the slump of his shoulders. "And Redwood's closer to the presidency every day. He won't hesitate to leverage any vulnerability to rip apart everything we've protected."

Silence enveloped the trio, each lost momentarily in personal dread and collective responsibility. The grandeur of the auditorium felt stifling now, the banners and insignias meaningless symbols in the aftermath of narrowly avoided catastrophe. Tosh glanced up at the large digital clock above the dais, its bright numbers stark against the dimming lights, a silent reminder that their reprieve was temporary.

"We've only seen the tip of this iceberg," Tosh murmured finally, meeting Wang's and Rainer's determined gazes with renewed resolve. "The real battle lies ahead. We can't afford complacency."

They exchanged solemn nods, silently reaffirming their bond forged through shared trials and unspoken agreements. As the trio stepped away from their hidden corner, each knew the delicate balance they'd maintained was precarious, threatened by every revelation, every whispered rumor, every political maneuver. Their steps echoed quietly, carrying them into an uncertain future shadowed by truths still lurking in darkness.

Chapter 11

Fallout and Reckoning

The Quiet Aftermath

In the hushed, subdued atmosphere backstage of the Geneva International Conference Center, Nicolás Tosh, Rainer Sábato, and Artemis Wang stood in heavy silence. The echoes of their recent confrontation reverberated in their minds, each man privately absorbing the enormity of what had just transpired. The vibrant urgency of the hall had given way to a stark quiet, broken only by the faint hum of distant conversations beyond the heavy curtains.

Artemis Wang was the first to speak, his voice steady but tinged with a reflective resignation. "I can't continue this," he began quietly, eyes fixed on some distant point beyond the confines of the room. "This constant balancing act—ethical dilemmas, political battles—it's drained whatever strength I had left."

Nicolás watched him closely, understanding but quietly dismayed. "What are you saying, Artemis?"

Wang turned slowly, meeting Tosh's eyes directly, the weight of his decision clear and unshakeable. "I'm stepping away. Completely. Lingtao, public life, all of it. I've given everything I could, and now it's time to let go."

Rainer moved forward slightly, his expression somber yet understanding. "You're sure about this? Once you walk away, there's no turning back."

Artemis nodded slowly, conviction unmistakable in the firm set of his jaw. "I've already signed the necessary documents. Lingtao will carry on without me. Perhaps it's better this way—someone less burdened can lead them now."

A quiet tension settled between them, each man reflecting on the profound personal toll exacted by their recent actions. Nicolás exhaled softly, his shoulders heavy with the weight of unresolved ethical questions. "We did what we had to do," he said quietly, almost to himself. "But the cost..."

"Is enormous," Artemis finished for him, voice softer now. "Each of us knows what we've sacrificed. We carry it with us, forever."

Rainer cleared his throat quietly, drawing their attention. "There's more," he said, tone cautious yet urgent. "Dominic Redwood isn't wasting any time. I've received reports—he's already initiating subtle but strategic political moves, using what happened here as leverage. He'll frame our actions as instability, pushing harder for immediate universal deployment."

Tosh's eyes darkened, reflecting the anger and frustration bubbling just beneath the surface. "Then our fight isn't over," he murmured, almost resigned. "We've won a critical battle today, but the real war—the war for the soul of humanity—is still ahead of us."

The trio stood quietly once more, a fragile solidarity binding them together in the quiet aftermath. As they each contemplated the uncertain path forward, the solemn weight of their choices hung palpably in the stillness, a silent acknowledgment of the reckoning yet to come.

Redwood's Executive Expansion

In the discreet confines of his private office in Washington D.C., Dominic Redwood sat poised at his polished mahogany desk, the muted light reflecting off its glossy surface. His expression, carefully composed yet faintly triumphant, revealed little of the ambitious calculations churning beneath.

Across from Redwood, Elaine Carter, his astute chief advisor, swiftly navigated a series of digital reports projected onto a sleek tablet, her sharp eyes dissecting intricate layers of polling data. "Public sentiment is shifting exactly as anticipated," she noted coolly, a satisfied glint in her gaze. "The Geneva incident has thoroughly unsettled the populace. Your stance on universal CDA-325 deployment is gaining momentum."

Redwood leaned back slightly, fingers steepled thoughtfully. "Excellent," he responded, voice smooth, authoritative. "It's crucial we maintain pressure. Highlight Zermatt's hesitation, frame their caution as incompetence—paint their ethical reservations as dangerous indecision."

Elaine nodded, her fingers deftly maneuvering across the tablet. "The strategic leaks to the press have already set the narrative. Zermatt's credibility is steadily eroding, and public fear is proving invaluable for our agenda."

"Perfect," Redwood affirmed quietly. "Now, let's accelerate the timeline. Draft an executive order immediately—expand the mandatory CDA-325 scans. Target all high-level government positions. We'll emphasize national security, transparency, and accountability."

Elaine hesitated briefly, meeting Redwood's gaze directly. "And if there's resistance? Particularly from those who understand the implications?"

A thin smile played briefly across Redwood's lips, cold and confident. "Then remind them—privately—of Geneva. Fear is powerful, Elaine. They'll fall into line when they recognize the risk of opposing us."

She smiled knowingly, a shared understanding evident in her steady gaze. "I'll have the executive order ready within the hour."

Redwood nodded approvingly, turning slightly to gaze out the expansive window overlooking the bustling cityscape. "Soon, Elaine," he murmured quietly, conviction steeling his voice, "the world will finally understand the value of controlled transparency. Our transparency."

As Elaine silently withdrew to execute their strategy, Redwood's contemplative gaze remained fixed on the distant horizon, a calculating assurance settling over him. He understood clearly: the path was set, momentum irreversible. Geneva had provided him exactly what he needed—a crisis, an opportunity, and the perfect catalyst for the sweeping change he envisioned.

Moral Confrontation

Soft moonlight filtered gently through sheer curtains, casting a silvery glow across the quiet living room of Nicolás and Alejandra Tosh's Miami home. Nicolás stood silently by the large glass doors, gazing absently at the tranquil waters beyond, his posture tense, burdened with unspoken thoughts.

The quiet was shattered gently by Alejandra's footsteps. She paused at the threshold, studying Nicolás thoughtfully, compassion and anxiety mixing subtly on her face.

"Nicolás," she began softly, her voice steady yet laden with quiet urgency. He turned slowly, drawn reluctantly from his contemplation, meeting her intense, searching gaze.

"I can't pretend everything is fine," Alejandra continued, her voice firming with gentle resolve. "What you've done—what we've justified—is deeply troubling. Forced mind infiltrations, Nicolás? How can we rationalize such a profound violation?"

Nicolás exhaled sharply, tension evident in his taut shoulders. "Alejandra, you know the stakes we faced. It was never easy; none of this was done lightly."

"I know your intentions," she replied quickly, stepping forward, eyes bright with determination. "But intentions don't erase consequences. You saved lives, yes—but at what moral cost? Do we discard ethics so readily when the world frightens us?"

He sighed deeply, frustration and anguish flickering across his face. "You think this doesn't haunt me? Every night, every quiet moment, I'm reminded of the lines we've crossed. But the alternative was worse— uncontrolled, rampant manipulation. We stopped a catastrophe, Alejandra."

Her gaze softened slightly but remained resolute. "And in doing so, we became part of the problem. We chose who to save and who to sacrifice. That's a terrifying power, Nicolás—a power no one should hold."

A painful silence stretched between them, thick with unresolved emotions and moral ambiguity. Nicolás looked away, eyes shadowed by internal struggle, his voice lowering almost to a whisper. "I don't know how else we could have acted. Every path was dangerous. Every choice carried consequences."

Alejandra reached out gently, her fingers brushing softly against his arm, urging him to face her again. "Then we must face the truth clearly now. We must never accept this as normal. Promise me, Nicolás, we'll never let fear justify these actions again. Promise me you'll fight just as fiercely to restore what we've compromised."

Nicolás met her gaze, pain and resolve mingling deeply within him. "I promise," he finally murmured, the weight of that vow settling heavily on both their hearts.

Yet even as he spoke, both understood the precariousness of his promise—the harsh realities of their world had already shown how easily good intentions could blur into ethical shadows, leaving a haunting question lingering between them in the quiet stillness of their home.

Wang's Final Departure

The corporate boardroom atop Lingtao's headquarters in Shanghai was unusually silent, its pristine glass walls overlooking the city's bustling skyline, shimmering softly in the late afternoon sun. Artemis Wang sat at the head of the polished table, documents meticulously arranged before him. A small group of executives and attorneys, respectful yet impassive, observed quietly, fully aware of the gravity of the moment.

Without hesitation, Wang took a pen from the ornate holder beside him and signed the final document, his hand steady despite the finality of the act. The soft scratch of the pen on paper was the only sound in the room, a quiet, poignant echo underscoring his decision.

"It's done," he said simply, placing the pen gently down. His voice was calm yet tinged with profound weariness.

The executives rose silently, exchanging muted nods, offering Wang discreet, respectful gestures before quietly filing out of the room. Alone now, Wang allowed himself a brief moment of reflection, turning slowly toward the expansive windows.

He gazed thoughtfully at the sprawling metropolis below, lights beginning to sparkle softly in the waning daylight. His reflection in the glass was contemplative, tinged with melancholy and quiet resignation. He had once believed firmly in his ability to steer technology toward genuine progress and human betterment. Yet, the unstoppable tide of power and manipulation had eroded his idealism, leaving behind only a heavy sense of disillusionment.

"How quickly power fades," he whispered to his reflection, the words soft yet resonant with bitter truth. "How fleeting our influence truly is in the face of unstoppable change."

Gathering himself, Wang rose steadily, taking one final look around the room that had witnessed countless pivotal decisions, victories, and moral compromises. His departure felt less like a defeat and more like a solemn acknowledgment—a quiet acceptance that some battles, once joined, can only be exited through surrender.

With a composed resolve, he exited the boardroom, the door closing softly behind him. His departure was quiet, unobtrusive, yet deeply symbolic—an ending that marked not just a personal retreat but a broader reckoning with ethics, technology, and the profound responsibilities that come with wielding immense power.

Lingering Threats and Maggie Wu's Investigation

In the secluded back corner of Café Luce, Maggie Wu sat hunched over her sleek laptop, fingers flying across the keyboard with practiced precision. Her posture was tense, eyes sharply focused on the encrypted files rapidly opening before her, their glow casting stark shadows across her determined features.

Her breath quickened slightly as the full scope of the documents unfolded on the screen—detailed evidence of Redwood's covert activities, the aggressive push for universal CDA-325 implementation, and secret neural-mapping operations conducted without public knowledge. The implications were chilling, stark proof of the growing threats she'd risked everything to uncover.

She paused briefly, glancing cautiously around the dimly lit café, reassuring herself that she remained unnoticed. Her fingers trembled slightly as she opened a secure messaging window, carefully typing a brief but urgent message.

"Jason, files confirmed. Redwood's agenda is worse than we thought. Immediate publication is critical."

Moments later, her phone vibrated softly. Maggie glanced quickly at the message, heart pounding in relief and tension.

"We're ready," came Jason Laird's terse reply. "Zermatt fully supports your disclosure. Proceed with caution."

She exhaled slowly, nerves steeling into quiet determination. The weight of responsibility was immense, the risks enormous. Yet, beneath her anxiety, a fierce resolve burned brightly—a commitment to truth, transparency, and justice.

Carefully closing her laptop, Maggie took a steadying breath, feeling the heavy, electric anticipation of the moment. She rose swiftly, slipping quietly through the café's back exit, clutching her bag protectively against her side, fully aware that from this point forward, every step would ripple outward, shaping the future irrevocably.

Zermatt's Strategic Reorientation

In the secure depths of the Zermatt Data Center, Nicolás Tosh and Rainer Sábato stood before a gathered group of analysts, engineers, and strategic advisors. The subterranean control room was dimly illuminated by arrays of monitors displaying intricate data streams and global surveillance maps, a quiet hum underscoring the room's tense anticipation.

Tosh, eyes dark with intensity, stepped forward to address the team, his voice steady and resolute. "Redwood has escalated his executive orders. The push for universal CDA-325 implementation is intensifying by the hour. Our window to counteract this narrative is narrowing rapidly."

Rainer nodded, stepping beside Nicolás. "Our ethical stance has always set us apart, but we must clearly define and communicate this distinction now more than ever. We cannot allow fear to dictate policy."

At that moment, Alejandra Tosh entered the room, her presence immediately commanding attention. She carried a small tablet, the glow of its screen illuminating her composed, focused expression. "We've developed something critical," she began calmly yet firmly. "Working closely with Experta, we've crafted a new set of ethical protocols designed specifically to counterbalance security demands with unwavering respect for individual autonomy and human rights."

The gathered team leaned in attentively, interest piqued by Alejandra's clear conviction.

She continued, her voice strong with resolve, "These protocols mandate complete transparency in neural monitoring practices, enforce stringent oversight on the deployment of CDA technology, and strictly prohibit forced neural interventions without explicit consent."

Nicolás met Alejandra's eyes, silent pride and deep gratitude reflected clearly in his gaze. "This is our path forward," he affirmed to the room. "We must embrace these protocols fully. They represent not just our operational guidelines but our moral compass."

Murmurs of approval and cautious optimism rippled among the assembled staff. Rainer quickly stepped forward to formalize the moment. "All in favor of immediately adopting these ethical protocols as official Zermatt policy?"

The room erupted into unanimous agreement, a moment of genuine solidarity filling the air. Alejandra, Nicolás, and Rainer exchanged brief, meaningful glances, understanding the significance of their decision—one that represented not just a strategic reorientation but a profound reaffirmation of their core values.

As the group dispersed purposefully to implement these new guidelines, Tosh felt a renewed sense of determination. Challenges remained immense, but for the first time in weeks, the path ahead felt clear, guided unmistakably by integrity and conviction.

International Tension at the World Transparency Council

The grand assembly hall at the Geneva International Conference Center buzzed with charged, tense anticipation. Delegates from across the globe sat rigidly, eyes sharp with apprehension and expectation. At the center table, Nicolás Tosh, Ambassador Celine Dubois, and Rainer Sábato exchanged subtle, knowing glances, recognizing clearly the stakes of the impending discussion.

Ambassador Dubois called the council to order, her authoritative voice slicing through the hushed murmurs. "Delegates, we are at an unprecedented crossroads. The universal deployment of CDA-325 technology has sparked urgent ethical and practical questions we must address decisively today."

Immediately, heated debate ignited. Advocates argued fervently, emphasizing security imperatives and the necessity of broad neural safeguards. Opponents countered passionately, warning against unchecked surveillance, potential abuses of power, and the erosion of essential human rights.

As the debate grew increasingly contentious, Nicolás Tosh stood, his composed presence commanding immediate attention. Guided resolutely by Alejandra's carefully crafted ethical framework, he spoke deliberately, his voice measured yet imbued with profound urgency.

"We cannot allow fear and panic to drive us toward unchecked surveillance," Tosh declared firmly, gaze sweeping across the delegates. "Transparency must always balance respect for individual autonomy and dignity. We need rigorous oversight, stringent ethical standards, and absolute accountability if CDA-325 is to serve humanity rather than control it."

His words resonated clearly, sparking quieter, more introspective discussion among delegates. Ambassador Dubois nodded appreciatively, reinforcing Tosh's points decisively.

Rainer quickly stepped forward, underscoring the gravity of their choice. "This decision defines our collective moral identity. We must choose wisely, ensuring we protect freedoms rather than inadvertently dismantling them."

After tense deliberation, Ambassador Dubois called for a formal vote. Silence settled thickly over the room as delegates cast their decisions, the weight of their collective choice palpable in every quiet breath and subtle shift.

When the results appeared on the large screens above, the hall stirred briefly with collective relief and cautious resolve: a narrow majority had passed the resolution mandating deployment—but critically, it stipulated stringent oversight conditions and rigorous transparency requirements.

Nicolás met Rainer and Ambassador Dubois's gazes, silently acknowledging the delicate compromise reached. It was not a perfect solution—but it offered a fragile hope, a cautious step forward amidst profound uncertainty, clearly marking the intricate balance between guardianship and potential tyranny they now carried together.

Quiet Reckoning

In the subdued atmosphere of Zermatt's subterranean command center, Nicolás Tosh, Rainer Sábato, and Alejandra Tosh gathered quietly, the soft illumination of monitors and terminals casting gentle shadows around them. The facility hummed softly, a steady, reassuring pulse beneath their feet, mirroring the reflective quiet of the trio.

Nicolás glanced toward the immense digital screens displaying the finalized World Transparency Council guidelines. The intricate web of protocols shimmered softly, an ethereal glow symbolic of their fragile balance between ethical guardianship and potential overreach.

Alejandra stepped closer, her voice gentle but resolute, breaking the contemplative silence. "We've achieved something significant. These protocols offer genuine transparency, genuine oversight. But the true test lies ahead—maintaining integrity amidst inevitable pressures."

Rainer nodded thoughtfully, eyes distant yet sharp with awareness of their ongoing challenges. "Human trafficking, state-level corruption, technological vulnerabilities—these issues remain dauntingly real. We can respond more effectively now, but each response must align with our renewed ethical commitments."

Nicolás exhaled slowly, the depth of his responsibilities reflected clearly in his steady gaze. "The lines we've drawn are clear, but the temptations of power and control will never fade. We must remain vigilant, unwavering in our principles."

They stood quietly once more, united in silent acknowledgment of the immense challenges ahead. Yet, amidst uncertainty, a fragile optimism took root—a cautious belief in their capacity to safeguard humanity without compromising its fundamental freedoms.

In the gentle hum of the data center, a quiet reckoning settled over them—a recognition of their profound responsibility and the delicate, perpetual balance they now held. Together, they faced the uncertain dawn, resolved to guard carefully against the ever-present shadows of tyranny, vigilant stewards of humanity's future.

Epilogue

A Fragile Dawn

Zermatt, Switzerland — Data Center Subterranean Wing
(Months Later)

A hush lingered in the glass-walled observation deck deep beneath the Swiss Alps, where Nicolás Tosh and Rainer Sábato stood side by side in quiet contemplation. Below them, endless rows of quantum servers stretched into the dim distance, bathed in the faint, surreal glow of blue and green indicator lights. Each aisle hummed with the subtle vibration of immeasurable data flow, resonating with a pulse that mirrored the heartbeat of a global network.

On the immense curved screens overhead, a digital map of the globe glowed in luminous detail, displaying countless swirling markers that tracked satellite nodes, almost fully blanketing the Earth. The scale was staggering, a visual testament to how far their surveillance—and protection—had expanded.

Tosh's eyes traced the pulsing data points silently, the weight of their responsibility reflected in his solemn gaze. The glow from the screens cast deep, shifting shadows across his features, highlighting lines of strain that had deepened considerably in recent months.

"Hard to believe," Tosh finally whispered, breaking the heavy silence, "that beneath this calm surface, we're juggling a thousand crises simultaneously. The world sees nothing but quiet efficiency."

Rainer exhaled softly, a tight smile flickering briefly across his lips. "Efficiency at the brink of chaos," he remarked quietly, eyes narrowing slightly as he surveyed the vast labyrinth of servers below. "But at least, for now, we hold the line."

A low chime interrupted their quiet reflection, signaling the arrival of Alejandra as she stepped onto the observation deck. Her expression was a careful blend of optimism and caution, eyes bright with determination but guarded by experience.

"I've got the latest update from Experta," Alejandra said, her voice gentle but resolute. "The new protocols are holding. No fresh breaches have been reported since we implemented the final safeguards."

Tosh nodded slowly, absorbing the cautious good news. "Yet every victory feels temporary," he murmured. "Every barrier we build, someone else tries to tear down. Redwood's people, NeuraTech loyalists... they'll keep testing us."

Alejandra stepped closer, glancing thoughtfully toward the endless rows of servers stretching into shadows. "But we're stronger now. Wiser. We've learned to anticipate, to adapt. We might not prevent every attempt, but we're quicker to respond, quicker to rebuild."

Rainer turned fully toward the screens again, shoulders straightening as a newfound resilience entered his voice. "Then let them come. Each attack makes us sharper. And every scar reminds us why we're here."

Tosh allowed himself a small smile, moved by Rainer's steadfast resolve. "Yes," he agreed softly, his voice strengthening with quiet conviction. "Let them come. We'll be ready."

The trio stood silently once more, watching the ceaseless dance of data and connections, feeling the quiet hum of Zermatt's heart beneath their feet. The fragile dawn of peace they now shared was precious—and perilous. For now, the storm had receded, but all three knew their calm was fleeting. The battles they'd faced had prepared them, but the true war lay ahead, lurking in the unseen depths of a future they had vowed to protect at all costs.

A Meeting with the "World Transparency Council"

At a polished ebony table in a newly constructed wing, top members of the World Transparency Council—an outgrowth of the G-7, joined by select additional powers—quietly gathered. The conference room's sleek, modern design seemed almost clinical, amplifying the tension that filled the air. Each participant sat rigidly, their expressions ranging from stern and resolute to deeply uncertain. These were men and women accustomed to wielding immense power, now tasked with decisions that blurred the lines between guardianship and intrusion.

Ambassador Celine Dubois, positioned at the head of the table, glanced around the room before leaning forward slightly, her tone measured and clear, cutting through the anticipatory silence.

"We recognize that the crisis was narrowly averted, but now we must address the next phase." Her gaze was piercing, making eye contact with each delegate. "The question at hand: Do we move forward with universal deployment of CDA-325 as a global safeguard?"

Her words hung heavily in the air, prompting a burst of whispered conversations. The murmurs quickly rose, filling the room with an indistinct hum of debate. Representatives from the U.S., Germany, and Japan swiftly voiced strong support, their arguments based on fear—fear of another NeuraTech-style incident, fear of losing control, fear of being blindsided again by unseen threats.

Across from them, a more cautious coalition—including delegates from Canada, Sweden, and several corporate liaisons—fought back with equally intense emotion. They warned about the irreversible slide into oppressive surveillance, about the chilling precedent this universal deployment could set. The thin veneer of civility began to fracture, revealing deep ideological divides.

Seated quietly near the table's end, Nicolás Tosh watched the heated exchanges with a sense of weary familiarity. His mind drifted briefly back to the events in Geneva, remembering vividly the suffocating weight of the near catastrophe they'd barely prevented. The extremism of NeuraTech and the narrowly avoided public meltdown were vivid reminders of the potential consequences of failure.

Yet Tosh also recognized the seductive danger in expanding control. Each new security measure, each additional layer of surveillance, always rationalized in the name of safety and global security, tightened the invisible chains that bound the very freedom they sought to protect.

Ambassador Dubois finally raised her hand again, silencing the growing discord. Her voice steadied, edged with quiet determination. "We must not forget that this discussion is fundamentally about trust.

Trust among ourselves, trust from our citizens. Whatever we decide, transparency and accountability must guide us."

Rainer Sábato, seated directly across from Tosh, cleared his throat softly, drawing attention with his careful, deliberate tone. "And trust requires restraint," he said, his voice steady. "We have the technology. We've seen its effectiveness. But we must ask ourselves—just because we can, does it mean we should?"

His words quieted the room again, a wave of introspection passing visibly across the gathered delegates. For a long, tense moment, no one spoke. Eyes shifted uneasily from one to another, each person silently weighing the profound implications of their choice.

Finally, Ambassador Dubois nodded solemnly. "Let's take a brief recess. Consider carefully. The decision we make here today shapes not only the future of global security but defines our very values. Remember that once we cross certain lines, we cannot return."

As delegates rose slowly from their seats, murmuring and scattering into clusters of hushed, anxious conversation, Tosh remained seated, deep in thought. He knew this debate was far from over. And he also knew, in his bones, that the outcome would reverberate for generations— long after they had all departed from this polished table and this troubled moment in history.

Renewed Tension: Demand for Universal Application

In a quiet, side corridor adjacent to the World Transparency Council's newly constructed meeting wing, Nicolás Tosh leaned heavily against the cold glass wall, rubbing his temples as exhaustion battled frustration behind his eyes. Beside him, Rainer Sábato tapped urgently on a sleek data pad, his brow furrowing deeper with each swipe.

The screen illuminated Rainer's face with shifting hues, highlighting his worry lines and the dark shadows beneath his eyes. "The situation's escalating again, Nicolás," he muttered grimly, scrolling rapidly through reports filtering in real-time. Each line of text carried its own weight, a fresh burden of unresolved crisis.

"More demands for the universal deployment of CDA-325," Rainer continued, his voice tinged with weariness. "The pressure's mounting from multiple fronts—the G-7 coalition, corporate stakeholders tied to Redwood, even mid-tier governments claiming they're vulnerable without widespread immunity."

Tosh sighed deeply, his breath fogging briefly against the pristine glass. Through the transparent barrier, delegates moved slowly down the brightly lit corridor, their murmured conversations punctuated by tense pauses. The subdued lighting overhead cast a stark reflection, accentuating the tension visibly radiating from each figure.

"How widespread?" Tosh finally asked, bracing himself for the answer he dreaded.

Rainer hesitated, his finger hovering momentarily over the glowing screen before tapping it decisively. "Europe, North America, major parts of Asia and Latin America—they're demanding that CDA-325 be fully integrated into national security frameworks. They're citing Geneva, Nicolás. They argue it's reckless not to fully utilize a tool that proved itself."

Tosh straightened sharply, pushing off the wall as if to physically counter the sense of inevitability creeping upon them. "Do they not understand?" he snapped, voice low but strained. "We narrowly escaped catastrophe. If we spread this technology, we amplify every risk we've feared. Surveillance states, forced compliance—exactly what we fought against."

Rainer nodded slowly, his eyes darkening. "They understand—but fear is overpowering reason. And now, it seems Redwood's team is maneuvering behind the scenes, subtly stoking panic. They're framing Geneva as evidence of our inability to control the technology, claiming it's irresponsible not to put it under broader authority—federal authority."

Tosh felt a sharp pang of anger, the blood rushing loudly in his ears. Redwood's strategy was transparent—exploiting chaos to leverage control. And the more Redwood's campaign stirred fear, the louder the calls for a sweeping rollout became. It was a vicious cycle, perfectly orchestrated to place Zermatt in an impossible bind.

"And Redwood?" Tosh asked tersely. "How far is he pushing this?"

"Far enough," Rainer replied bitterly, swiping to another page on the pad. "Leaks to the press, whispers to Congress. They're even briefing defense contractors privately, preparing them for a massive, federally supervised CDA-325 rollout. It's positioned as inevitable."

Tosh closed his eyes briefly, steadying his thoughts. They stood silent for several heartbeats, the muted hum of distant voices underscoring the gravity of their dilemma. The moral compromise loomed larger now, more suffocating than ever.

"We knew this moment would come," Tosh murmured finally, his voice thick with reluctant resignation. "But I never thought it would arrive so quickly."

Rainer placed a reassuring hand lightly on Tosh's shoulder, feeling the tension rippling through the muscles beneath. "We're still here. We still control the core. As long as we keep resisting, Nicolás, there's a chance we hold the line."

Tosh met Rainer's eyes with quiet intensity, grasping tightly to that slender thread of hope. Yet, even as he nodded slowly, the weight of every decision—past and present—settled upon him, pressing down inexorably.

"Let's rejoin the council," Tosh said quietly, gathering strength from deep within. "We need to remind them that safeguarding humanity doesn't mean sacrificing everything human about us."

Side by side, Tosh and Rainer stepped away from the corridor, their footsteps echoing softly on polished marble, the fragile echo of resolve in a world tilting precariously toward the unknown.

Human Trafficking & Child Exploitation

Intelligence indicated the Southeast Asian ring had relocated yet again. Zermatt's coverage was stretched thin, overshadowed by Redwood's demands to scan new domestic targets.

In the shadowed recesses of Zermatt's subterranean data center, Nicolás Tosh paced the dimly lit control room with restless agitation, each step echoing softly against polished steel and reinforced glass. Screens encircling the room pulsed with real-time surveillance feeds, strings of intercepted communication flickering urgently across their displays.

"Where are they now?" Tosh demanded, tension tightening his voice as he halted abruptly behind a technician. The young woman's fingers flew across her keyboard, sweat beading on her forehead beneath the weight of her task.

"Southern Philippines," she replied swiftly, eyes glued to the rapid data stream cascading down her screen. "A hidden compound on an island near Mindanao. Satellite imagery confirms movement, vehicles… trucks arriving hourly."

Tosh leaned closer, his jaw tightening at images of grainy infrared outlines—small figures huddled, forced into tight formations. "Children," he murmured, anguish barely contained.

Beside him, Rainer Sábato stood rigid, fists clenched, his attention split between another display outlining Redwood's latest demands and the unfolding crisis halfway around the world. "We need more satellite coverage," Rainer insisted sharply, frustration bleeding into his voice. "If we don't act quickly, they'll disappear again."

The technician hesitated, glancing nervously between screens. "Sir, the satellites covering that area were reassigned this morning—Redwood's team demanded immediate surveillance sweeps over the domestic sites. They claimed national security took priority."

Tosh slammed his hand against the console, the sharp crack reverberating through the room, silencing technicians momentarily. His voice was taut with barely restrained fury. "Redwood's obsession is costing us lives. We can't lose sight of what really matters."

"Then redirect coverage," Rainer interjected decisively. "I'll take full responsibility. Get those satellites back online over Mindanao, now."

Technicians hurriedly punched commands, scrambling to override the previous orders. Within seconds, satellite feeds realigned, bringing the trafficking site into clearer view—trucks, men with rifles, a heavily fortified perimeter.

Tosh exhaled slowly, the urgency pressing against his chest. "Alert local authorities immediately. Mobilize INTERPOL's regional task force. Get eyes and ears on that island before we lose them again."

A communications officer nodded, relaying the order in clipped, urgent tones. The room buzzed with renewed energy as coordinates and intel streamed to counterparts across the globe. Tosh stepped back, heart pounding as he watched the digital clock counting the minutes.

"Sir," the technician called out sharply, her voice strained. "Local contacts confirm—they're mobilizing, but it'll be tight. The traffickers have speedboats prepared. It'll be a race."

"Then make sure we win," Tosh replied tersely, eyes locked onto the glowing screens, where innocent lives hung precariously in the balance. "Keep channels open. Every second counts."

He stood rigidly alongside Rainer, each pulse of data another tense heartbeat. Amidst Redwood's political maneuvering and the looming threats of global power plays, Tosh knew precisely where the true battle lay—in the shadows, against forces that preyed upon the vulnerable. Today, Zermatt had to rise above its limitations, refusing to yield ground to compromise or distraction.

As minutes ticked by with agonizing slowness, Tosh remained frozen in place, silently vowing that no matter how strained, how overshadowed, Zermatt would never stop fighting—never abandon those who needed them most.

Corruption at State Levels:

Smaller nations battered Tosh with hush requests to "fix" their governance woes using discreet Overwrites. How far could he go before it mirrored the tyranny they'd just fought?

In a secluded, soundproof office deep within Zermatt's data center, Nicolás Tosh stood rigid, his posture an image of controlled tension as he stared down the dimly lit screen. Dozens of encrypted messages flashed relentlessly—urgent pleas, veiled threats, each more insistent than the last.

"They won't stop coming," Rainer Sábato murmured, stepping up beside Tosh, his voice tinged with weariness. "Every message is another leader asking us to quietly overwrite minds, to eliminate their political opposition or reform corrupt officials instantly."

Tosh exhaled sharply, a harsh sound in the sterile quiet of the chamber. He swiped through another batch of messages, their digital glow reflecting starkly in his narrowed eyes. "This is exactly what we fought to prevent," he muttered bitterly. "They want the very tyranny we just battled."

Rainer adjusted his glasses, scanning the data pad in his hands, where new requests multiplied faster than they could process. "Ambassadors, ministers, even heads of state—they all see CDA-325 as a convenient shortcut. A way to silence critics or fix corruption without public scrutiny."

"And in doing so, they'd be worse than the threats we've neutralized," Tosh snapped, pacing the small space with quick, frustrated strides. "It's a slippery slope. Where does it end? A minor overwrite today, a full dictatorship tomorrow?"

Rainer placed the data pad gently onto the polished surface of the nearby console. "They're desperate. They claim it's about stability, about preserving democracy—but it's power they want."

Tosh halted, turning abruptly to face him. "Power corrupts," he said, voice edged with steel. "If we grant them these 'favors,' we become accomplices, not guardians."

Suddenly, a sharp beep sliced through the tense silence—another urgent communication. Tosh moved swiftly to the console, fingers tapping rapidly as the message decoded itself, appearing clearly in stark white letters:

URGENT REQUEST FROM EAST AFRICAN LEADER: IMMEDIATE OVERWRITE NEEDED FOR OPPOSITION FIGURE.

Tosh stared coldly at the screen, jaw clenched. "No," he stated firmly. "We can't allow this to continue. Make it clear—Zermatt does not serve personal vendettas or political convenience."

"Understood," Rainer replied with equal resolve, already typing out the terse, unequivocal refusal. His fingers hesitated briefly before sending the final command. "And if they retaliate?"

"Let them," Tosh said, steel sharpening his words. "If they attempt reprisals, we expose every request they've made, every corrupt overture. Transparency is our shield."

Rainer nodded solemnly, hitting send. The message blinked confirmation and vanished into cyberspace, leaving behind a heavy silence.

"We are not tyrants," Tosh whispered fiercely, as if to reassure himself. "We are not their executioners. We're here to protect free will, not to erase it."

Rainer watched quietly, understanding fully the enormous weight on Tosh's shoulders. Every choice now carried profound implications. Every refusal might ignite another crisis, every agreement risked moral collapse.

Together, in that isolated chamber deep beneath the Swiss Alps, they silently reaffirmed their commitment: never to become what they had vowed to fight against, even if the world around them wavered on the precipice of darkness.

Faulty Technology & Public Safety

Another emergency ping showed potential defects in a major cargo airline. Dr. Faber's minimal team hurriedly cross-checked data, mindful that mass deployment talk overshadowed these pressing hazards.

The red glow of emergency alerts flashed urgently on the overhead screens within the tightly packed control room. Dr. Miriam Faber stood rigid before a sprawling array of terminals, her face pale in the monitor's harsh light. Around her, a skeleton crew of exhausted engineers darted from one workstation to another, muttering rapid-fire exchanges that filled the air with tense urgency.

"Diagnostics report, now!" Miriam snapped, her voice tight with controlled urgency.

"We've confirmed it twice already, Doctor," a young analyst replied breathlessly, his fingers flying across a keyboard. "The latest fleet of cargo freighters has defective avionics software. Potentially fatal mid-flight malfunctions are possible."

Miriam clenched her fists, eyes locked on the data scrolling at dizzying speed before her. Every line confirmed a nightmare scenario: autopilot malfunctions, navigational failures, catastrophic breakdowns mid-air. And all of it slipping through unnoticed while global attention remained fixated on the recent Geneva debacle and the push for mass CDA-325 deployment.

"Identify every affected aircraft," she demanded sharply, turning swiftly to another terminal. "Ground them immediately. Coordinate with international air traffic control."

A technician nearby shook his head anxiously. "Too late, Doctor Faber. At least four planes are airborne already—two crossing the Atlantic, one approaching Mumbai, and another overpopulated zones in Eastern Europe."

Her pulse quickened, adrenaline surging through her veins as the stark reality hit her. "Initiate immediate remote diagnostics and overrides. Use every satellite connection we've got. I want real-time updates, down to the second!"

The team sprang into action, voices rising as each engineer frantically pursued leads, scanned code, and patched vulnerabilities. Miriam leaned over her station, typing feverishly, eyes rapidly scanning through endless streams of code. Every digit counted. Every second mattered.

An engineer across the room shouted above the din, "Avionics patch initiated on the Mumbai-bound freighter—systems responding!"

Another voice quickly followed, more anxious. "No luck with the Atlantic flights. We've lost contact with one!"

Miriam's throat tightened, her mind racing. "Switch satellites—use military networks if necessary. Coordinate with local radar stations; we need manual tracking!"

The room's tension thickened, punctuated by intermittent shouts and frantic keyboard clicks. The seconds felt torturously long, each tick echoing like a countdown toward potential catastrophe.

Then, finally, a voice rose sharply, edged with relief. "We regained contact! Freighter responding. Uploading override patch now."

"Eastern Europe flight secured as well," another technician confirmed moments later, voice shaky from the adrenaline rush.

Miriam let out a sharp breath, forcing her heart rate steady. "Keep monitoring closely. I want reports on every plane, every minute, until they land safely."

As the chaos slowly subsided to controlled urgency, Miriam stepped back from her console, her gaze heavy with exhaustion and lingering dread. Despite narrowly averting disaster, an unsettling thought gnawed at her resolve. With global attention fixated on political turmoil and mass deployments, how many more emergencies lay unnoticed, overshadowed by the relentless push of the NeuraTech crisis?

She brushed a strand of damp hair from her forehead, steeling herself. They had managed to avert tragedy today—but tomorrow? She feared they might not be so lucky.

Corporate Sabotage & Competitor Intrusions

Redwood's allies, newly emboldened, began pressuring for a more open-handed approach to the CDA—one that would "share" the technology with favored corporations.

The sleek glass-paneled conference room overlooking Manhattan buzzed with aggressive intensity, illuminated sharply by the late afternoon sun slicing through floor-to-ceiling windows. Around the polished mahogany table sat executives from leading tech conglomerates, each impeccably dressed but restless, leaning forward as if poised for combat.

"Gentlemen, ladies," announced Alexander Cole, Redwood's key corporate liaison, his voice cutting cleanly through the tense silence. "You've all witnessed the chaos stemming from Zermatt's inability to control their prized CDA technology. Geneva showed us clearly that centralizing such immense power in unreliable hands is untenable."

Heads nodded briskly, eyes narrowed in focused agreement. Across from Cole, Vanessa Harcourt, the fierce CEO of Luminous Tech, drummed her perfectly manicured fingers on the polished wood, eyes sharp as steel.

"It's clear Zermatt can't handle the pressures or threats inherent in safeguarding such groundbreaking technology," Vanessa remarked sharply. "Transparency demands decentralization—starting by allowing responsible corporations immediate access. We have infrastructures robust enough to handle security that Zermatt clearly lacks."

Murmurs of vigorous assent rippled around the table. Cole allowed a thin smile, sensing the tide turning firmly in his favor.

A younger executive from Nova Cyber Solutions cleared his throat assertively. "This fiasco with NeuraTech proves we can't leave this in government-backed facilities only. If Redwood wins, he must prioritize transferring oversight to the private sector—where innovation, accountability, and security truly thrive."

Cole nodded thoughtfully, letting each statement resonate, building momentum. "Precisely why Redwood has authorized me to begin discreet preliminary discussions. But understand clearly—this isn't just about handing over a few lines of code. This will require significant financial backing and a unified front."

"And Redwood's price?" Vanessa asked bluntly, unflinching.

"Support—both financially and politically. Redwood needs clear victories now more than ever," Cole responded with cold pragmatism, scanning the table. "And once elected, he'll ensure the CDA technology is placed in trusted corporate hands—yours."

The atmosphere shifted from strategic discussion to cautious calculation. Every executive weighed the promise of monumental profit against the risk of exposure or political scandal.

"What about Zermatt? They're still influential," interjected a hesitant voice from the far end of the table.

Cole's smile broadened slightly, predatory and assured. "Zermatt has already stumbled. Redwood's narrative is airtight: today's crisis demonstrated their incompetence to the world. Their claims of neutrality are weakened. The public and Congress will demand immediate changes, and we'll give them exactly that."

Vanessa exchanged pointed glances with several executives, then looked directly at Cole. "Then let's proceed. But understand, Alexander—we will hold Redwood to his promise. Any hint of hesitation or double-dealing, and we'll withdraw every cent and every endorsement."

"Understood," Cole acknowledged with crisp certainty. "Then consider our alliance solidified."

The meeting concluded abruptly. Executives dispersed quickly, each silently strategizing their next moves. Cole stood alone momentarily, watching the Manhattan skyline darken, confident but calculating. He knew every step from here on was fraught with peril. One wrong move, and Redwood's dream of total transparency—and their collective vision of profit and control—would collapse spectacularly.

He turned from the windows, feeling a surge of anticipation and anxiety in equal measure. This was just the beginning.

Maggie Wu's Investigation

Maggie Wu's fingers trembled slightly as she quickly swiped through encrypted files on her sleek, silver laptop, the dim glow from the screen illuminating the focused intensity in her eyes. She sat in the cramped back corner of Café Luce, a quiet, dimly-lit coffeehouse in downtown Seattle, her favorite retreat whenever the stakes got dangerously high. Tonight, however, every shadow seemed deeper, every casual glance from another patron felt heavy with suspicion.

Her heart raced faster as she absorbed the information unfolding before her. Each document contained details meticulously connecting Senator Jonathan Redwood's presidential campaign with secretive expansions of mind-scanning technology—CDA-325. Redwood had publicly championed transparency, yet these hidden records revealed a starkly different agenda, one cloaked in secrecy and manipulation.

Wu inhaled sharply, her chest tightening as she viewed surveillance logs of covert neural-mapping procedures conducted without public consent. The documents were authenticated—leaked by a whistleblower deep within Redwood's own campaign. Names, dates, locations; it was all here. Her fingertips hovered briefly, contemplating the gravity of what she had uncovered. One click, and this information would ignite a global firestorm.

A sudden movement near the café's entrance made her pulse spike. Two men in dark suits entered swiftly, scanning the café with professional detachment. Maggie recognized their posture immediately: federal agents, discreet but unmistakably alert. A jolt of adrenaline surged through her veins as she quickly snapped her laptop shut, heartbeat hammering loudly in her ears.

Her phone vibrated urgently. A single encrypted message flashed across the screen: "They're onto you. Get out now. –J."

She wasted no time, slipping the laptop into her messenger bag and draping it casually over her shoulder. Maggie slid out from her booth, maintaining an outward calm despite her thundering pulse. Moving swiftly but not hurriedly, she navigated toward the narrow back hallway leading to the emergency exit.

"Miss Wu!" a sharp voice rang out behind her.

Maggie did not turn, quickening her pace instead. The footsteps accelerated behind her, echoing ominously on the polished concrete floor. Just as she reached the exit door, a strong hand clamped onto her shoulder, spinning her around forcefully.

She stared defiantly into the agent's icy eyes. "Can I help you?" she demanded, voice steady, masking the fear simmering just below.

"We'd like a word," he said, tone iron-hard, eyes briefly glancing to her bag. "Privately."

"Sorry," she replied coldly, shrugging his hand off with surprising strength. "I have an appointment."

His grip tightened painfully on her arm, his expression hardening further. "Cancel it."

With a surge of desperation, Maggie twisted sharply, wrenching her arm free and slamming her weight against the emergency exit door. The shrill blast of the alarm shattered the café's quiet as she sprinted into the alleyway outside, heart pounding as rain splattered against her face. She darted around dumpsters and parked cars, footsteps echoing loudly behind her, a chilling reminder she wasn't yet safe.

Ahead, headlights cut through the stormy night. A sleek, black sedan skidded to a stop, the passenger door flinging open urgently.

"Get in!" a familiar voice shouted.

Without hesitation, Maggie launched herself into the waiting vehicle. The tires squealed as the car sped off, leaving the pursuing figures behind in the gloom.

She turned, breathless and soaked, to face Jason Laird—her contact from Zermatt.

"Did you get the files?" he asked, eyes flicking quickly to her bag.

Maggie nodded, her breathing finally beginning to steady. "Everything's ready. They'll do anything to bury this, Jason. Redwood's people, federal authorities… everyone's compromised."

Jason's jaw tightened, his expression grim but resolute as they sped through slick city streets, each passing second pulling them deeper into uncertainty.

"Then we have to publish immediately," he said firmly, eyes sharp with determination. "Before they silence us all."

Maggie leaned back into the seat, gripping her bag tightly. The decision was made, the consequences unimaginable.

"Agreed," she whispered, watching neon city lights blur past, knowing their next move would change the world—one way or another.

On the Brink

Red alerts cascaded relentlessly across the illuminated surface of Rainer Sábato's sleek, ultra-secure data pad, each one a glaring symbol of escalating global tension. The control room deep beneath Zermatt's subterranean facility was bathed in urgent crimson and amber hues, casting long, anxious shadows across Rainer's exhausted features. He exhaled slowly, heavily, the burden of countless sleepless nights weighing visibly on his broad shoulders.

"Everyone's calling for universal application," Rainer finally said, voice tinged with strained resignation as he studied the swirling alerts. His fingers swiped rapidly, isolating a particularly troubling message from Redwood's campaign. "Redwood, the corporate giants, even some allies at the G-7—they say we can't risk another Geneva fiasco."

Beside him, Nicolás Tosh stood rigid, jaw clenched tight enough that the muscles visibly pulsed beneath his skin. He stared intensely at the largest central monitor, where live feeds displayed the increasingly strident calls for global deployment of CDA-325 technology. Every sentence uttered by influential leaders and CEOs reverberated ominously within him.

"We fought so hard to keep the technology limited," Tosh murmured, almost as if reminding himself of their battle-weary principles. His voice was taut, laced with suppressed anger and frustration. "If we push it globally, we become the very threat we sought to prevent."

"It's not just about security anymore," Rainer continued bitterly, eyes flashing sharply toward Tosh. "It's fear-driven politics, Nicolás. Panic is contagious. Redwood's exploiting the chaos we barely managed to contain."

Tosh took a step forward, hands clenched into fists at his sides. His pulse quickened with frustration. "Then remind them, Rainer. Geneva wasn't stopped by universal application—it was stopped by intelligence, restraint, and precision. Not blanket surveillance."

Suddenly, the control room doors hissed open, breaking the intensity of their confrontation. Alejandra rushed in, eyes wide with urgency, dark curls damp with perspiration.

"The G-7's emergency vote just concluded," she announced breathlessly, gripping a tablet displaying fresh headlines. Her fingers trembled slightly as she offered the device to Tosh. "They're demanding immediate, global integration of CDA-325. The resolution passed unanimously—pressure is coming from all sides now."

Tosh took the tablet, scanning the stark words rapidly. Every sentence intensified his anger, frustration—and fear.

"This isn't safeguarding humanity," Tosh growled through gritted teeth, his voice shaking with barely suppressed fury. "It's an open door to global tyranny. Redwood will exploit this. The corporations will exploit this. How many freedoms must be stripped before they understand?"

"They're scared, Nicolás," Alejandra interjected softly, stepping closer, her tone firm but tempered with empathy. "After Geneva, fear overpowers reason. It's instinctive, survival-driven."

"Instinct can be manipulated," Tosh countered sharply, his eyes burning with passionate resolve. "We have to show them the truth—before Redwood's fearmongering drowns out logic entirely."

An alarm blared sharply from Rainer's data pad, snapping everyone's attention back to the screens. A live video conference flashed urgently: Redwood himself, addressing millions globally, his voice dripping with calm assurance yet laced with subtle menace.

"My fellow citizens," Redwood spoke, his voice smooth yet edged with authority. "We can no longer allow ourselves to be vulnerable to another catastrophic breach. CDA-325 must be our shield—universally deployed, a guardian for all. Zermatt's hesitations, though perhaps well-intentioned, are risking lives every second they delay."

Tosh's hands shook visibly, the intensity of Redwood's words slicing into him like a blade. His gaze locked onto Rainer, their shared dread mirrored clearly.

"We can't let him control the narrative," Tosh said finally, a fierce determination solidifying within him. "The world must see the truth before it's too late."

Rainer nodded grimly, bracing himself. "Then let's fight—like we always have."

With renewed urgency, Tosh moved swiftly toward the communication console, fingers flying across keys, prepared to unleash their counter-message to a world teetering dangerously on the brink between guardianship and tyranny.

On the Verge of Guardianship or Tyranny

Late into the night, Nicolás Tosh stood alone at the heart of the Zermatt Data Center, enveloped by a profound silence punctuated only by the steady, rhythmic hum of countless quantum servers. Their gentle vibration resonated through the soles of his shoes, an ever-present reminder of the colossal power thrumming beneath his feet.

He gazed upward at the central display—a massive, luminous screen dominating the vast, dimly lit chamber. Bold, clinical letters glowed starkly in the darkness: "Neural Web Coverage: 98.4%". The figure hung ominously, a relentless countdown edging towards total global coverage. Tosh stared at the statistic, the gravity of its implication tightening his chest. Nearly every inhabited region on Earth was now silently surveilled, interwoven into an inescapable neural network—courtesy of CDA-325. Each passing day, each deliberate expansion by Redwood and his council allies, brought them closer to absolute, irrevocable control.

His gaze shifted to another screen scrolling rapidly through endless streams of infiltration feeds. The monitor cast flickering shadows across Tosh's strained features, illuminating his exhausted eyes, haunted by the ethical weight he carried. He watched the digital threads flash by—some threads detailed meticulously executed operations to intercept criminals or thwart imminent catastrophes. Yet others—marked clearly but disturbingly as forced "vaccinations"—documented minds quietly rewritten without consent.

The irony was crushing. Tosh recalled clearly the uncompromising vow he had made long ago, each word etched vividly into his conscience: "We will never forcibly rewrite minds." Yet the evidence scrolled inexorably before him, coldly and undeniably real. He swallowed hard, a bitter taste lingering as a quiet, insistent voice within him whispered grim truths: "We already have—if only to spare them from a worse fate."

With a heavy sigh, he moved to another terminal, fingers reluctantly brushing against the sleek touchscreen. Immediately, new bulletins appeared—child-trafficking leads blinking desperately with "Status: Cold" beside their entries, airline safety warnings urgently flashing red but overshadowed by more prioritized crises. Tosh felt a wave of quiet fury rising inside him, frustration born of helplessness.

How many innocents slipped through their grasp, their fates sealed by this blind pursuit? How many genuine threats were left to fester, unseen and unaddressed, while the council's obsession with preventing mind-hijacking swallowed every ounce of attention and resources?

His hands clenched tightly into fists at his sides, fingernails digging painfully into his palms. The darkened room felt suffocating, pressing inwards with oppressive weight. Tosh turned abruptly from the overwhelming data, pacing restlessly across the polished steel floor. Each step echoed sharply, an audible reflection of his escalating internal conflict.

Pausing abruptly, he returned his stare to the immense glowing statistic, the 98.4% looming larger with each moment, each heartbeat. The boundary between guardianship and tyranny seemed razor-thin now, nearly invisible. He closed his eyes, inhaling deeply, steadying himself as he faced the abyss before them all.

With renewed determination etched grimly on his face, Tosh opened his eyes again, staring resolutely into the luminous screen. The decisions ahead would shape humanity's future irreversibly. He understood clearly now that in the pursuit of absolute safety, they risked losing everything that defined them as human.

"Not on my watch," Tosh whispered fiercely to the quiet darkness around him, a solemn vow echoing defiantly through the heart of Zermatt, daring to challenge the tide of impending tyranny.

The Price of Guardianship

Rainer Sábato stepped forward quietly, his footsteps echoing gently through the cavernous expanse of Zermatt's subterranean command center. The dim lighting cast a subtle, ghostly illumination across his solemn face, accentuating lines of fatigue and uncertainty carved deeply by endless crises. His eyes, dark with unspoken fears, met Nicolás Tosh's, silently sharing the burden that had become their existence.

"We've come so far, Nicolás," Rainer spoke softly, his voice barely above a whisper, filled with an aching blend of pride and regret. "We've saved countless lives—yet at what price?"

Tosh felt the heaviness in his chest intensify, an almost physical ache compounded by relentless uncertainty. His thoughts collided chaotically—Redwood's unstoppable expansions rippling outward unchecked, Wang quietly fading into the background, obscured by political maneuvering and forgotten amidst greater threats. And

Alejandra—he saw clearly the haunted look in her eyes, the heavy toll exacted by every decision they had been forced to make.

He turned slowly, gesturing toward the immense screen dominating the room, glowing with stark, unsettling data: near-total neural web coverage achieved. His voice trembled slightly as he spoke, quiet yet edged with urgency.

"Look at it, Rainer. At near-full coverage, we can read—maybe even shape—almost any mind on Earth." Tosh's voice grew firmer, an undercurrent of fear mingling with his deep concern. "Are we truly guardians, or have we become the gatekeepers of every secret, every thought?"

Rainer's jaw tightened visibly, but no immediate answer formed. His silence was profound, almost tangible, a quiet admission that the line they walked was impossibly thin. Tosh reached out, fingers brushing softly against the console. He pressed a command decisively, and instantly the towering screen faded to darkness, shadows reclaiming their hold on the room, punctuated only by the faint flicker of emergency lights reflected softly on the polished steel floor.

With heavy hearts, both men turned away, footsteps echoing quietly as they moved toward the exit tunnel. The distant, continuous hum of the quantum servers, constant as a heartbeat, faded gradually behind them, underscoring the enormity of the powers now held within their grasp.

At the mouth of the tunnel, Tosh paused, casting one final glance over his shoulder. The expansive room lay cloaked in shadows, its silent monitors and dormant screens masking a frightening truth he could not escape. A chill ran through him, carrying the weight of unspoken fears.

"A world with no secrets… or no freedom?" Tosh whispered into the quiet, his question lingering ominously like a ghostly echo, resonating through the empty corridors as they walked away—guardians uncertain if they had crossed the threshold into becoming tyrants.

A Fragile Dawn

In the shadowed quiet of the subterranean control center beneath the Swiss Alps, a pale, ghostly dawn filtered through the narrow skylights high above, casting soft ribbons of greyish light across rows of dormant consoles and silent monitors. Nicolás Tosh stood motionless in the center of the vast space, his presence barely disturbing the heavy stillness. His eyes, shadowed by sleepless nights, were fixed unwaveringly on the central terminal display—a stark, pulsating digital beacon that read clearly: "Algorithm-325 Global Integration: 99.9% Complete."

Tosh felt a chill ripple along his spine, recognizing this moment's profound significance. Months had passed, yet the boundary they walked—the invisible line between vigilant guardianship and quiet tyranny—remained precariously thin. He could sense it in every heartbeat, every breath. The Algorithm-325 now stretched nearly everywhere, an omnipresent sentinel whose immense power, he feared, could no longer be fully contained.

With a trembling finger, he swiped through recent critical alerts. Each headline was another sharp, unsettling reminder of their new reality. "Child Trafficking Network Evades Surveillance," flashed angrily, followed immediately by "Cargo Airline Disaster Narrowly Averted." He clenched his jaw tightly as the third appeared, stark and uncompromising:

"Redwood Demands Immediate Expansion of Neural Monitoring."

Tosh exhaled sharply, anxiety gripping his chest. Each crisis now seemed magnified, carrying with it the ever-present risk that Algorithm-325, in their desperate attempts to safeguard humanity, might silently erode the very essence of freedom. He glanced toward the adjacent monitors—lines of encrypted code streamed endlessly, data threads that held within them the power to track, protect, or manipulate almost any human mind.

Suddenly, footsteps echoed urgently down the corridor. Tosh turned sharply as Rainer burst into the control room, his breathing rapid, eyes wide with urgency.

"Nicolás," Rainer said breathlessly, holding up a tablet flashing a stream of frantic messages. "New crisis. Redwood's allies are moving aggressively. They're pushing for the final 0.1% integration immediately—no safeguards, no oversight."

Tosh's heart pounded loudly in his ears. The reality they had dreaded was no longer distant; it loomed directly before them, stark and unavoidable. He reached out, gripping Rainer's arm firmly.

"We can't let this happen," Tosh growled fiercely. "If we cross this final line, there's no turning back. We'll lose everything."

"But Nicolás," Rainer's voice lowered, strained with tension, "what choice do we have? The world is demanding this now, screaming for total protection. The council is unanimous—they fear another catastrophe more than tyranny."

Tosh turned abruptly, pacing restlessly in front of the darkened screens, every step heavy with internal conflict. The room seemed to close in, shadows thickening as dawn fought unsuccessfully against the darkness.

"We built Algorithm-325 to save humanity," Tosh whispered harshly, voice trembling with anguish. "But if it gains complete power, who saves humanity from Algorithm-325?"

A strained silence stretched taut between them, broken only by the faint, ever-present hum of servers beneath their feet. Tosh finally halted, facing Rainer directly, his voice resolute with renewed determination.

"Mobilize Alejandra and our team," Tosh instructed sharply. "We push back—hard. We force transparency. If this final step happens, it happens openly, under scrutiny. We do not let Redwood or anyone else control this narrative."

Rainer nodded decisively, eyes reflecting renewed resolve. He turned quickly, footsteps echoing urgently back down the corridor, leaving Tosh alone once again in the encroaching dawn.

Tosh stared at the glowing screen, feeling the immense weight of a future that was balancing precariously, its fate uncertain, fragile as the first light of dawn filtering weakly through cracks in an impenetrable fortress.

In that fragile dawn, every crisis held unprecedented significance, each decision a dangerous gamble with humanity's most sacred possessions: free will, privacy, and the sanctity of the mind.

PREQUEL TO ALGORITHM-326

Zermatt Data Center – Three Months After Geneva

The subterranean corridors beneath Zermatt thrummed quietly, bathed in a dull green luminescence emanating from the orderly ranks of quantum servers. Each metallic rack stood sentinel, pulsing softly as though breathing steadily, a rhythmic vibration felt more than heard. Nicolás Tosh stood isolated within a narrow observation bay, his lean frame silhouetted sharply against the ghostly glow of multiple overhead screens. Each displayed data streams flickering urgently, detailing near-total global coverage of Algorithm-325.

The midnight silence was broken only by the soft, steady whisper of cooling fans, a constant, soothing hum that belied the turmoil churning inside Tosh. His eyes, intense and weary, scrutinized the screens intently, absorbing information he dreaded to see. Months after Geneva's near-catastrophic events, Redwood's White House had moved swiftly, consolidating a sprawling, invasive scanning network with unsettling efficiency. Entire groups of government employees, subtly coerced or willingly compliant, were now marked as "CDA-compliant," their neural patterns quietly integrated into the overarching system. The expansion had been rapid, discreet, unstoppable.

Tosh sighed heavily, shoulders sagging beneath invisible burdens. He recalled the haunted look in Alejandra's eyes during their final exchange in Miami—her silent plea echoing in his mind: What have we become?

A sudden, discreet ping disrupted his thoughts, slicing cleanly through the oppressive stillness. Tosh's gaze flickered downward to a nearby console. The touchscreen pulsed gently, indicating an incoming communiqué. He stepped closer, frowning slightly as he activated the screen with a single, precise swipe. Immediately, a grainy, urgent video feed appeared, revealing Rainer Sábato's tense features, illuminated by harsh, artificial lighting. Rainer was stationed thousands of miles away, in the newly constructed Zermatt substation deep beneath Singapore's bustling heart.

"Nicolás," Rainer's voice crackled slightly over the encrypted transmission, his eyes shadowed by obvious exhaustion yet sharp with urgency. "We've picked up something concerning. Redwood's allies are pushing aggressively in the East—Singapore, Jakarta, Tokyo. Neural mapping demands have surged overnight. They're bypassing standard protocols."

Tosh's jaw tightened immediately, the muscles flexing visibly as his mind raced. "How deep have they gone?"

"Deep enough," Rainer replied grimly, voice tinged with anger and anxiety. "They're accessing data streams previously off-limits, Nicolás. Complete neural records of political figures, opposition leaders, activists…"

"They're no longer hiding it," Tosh interrupted, voice strained with barely contained fury. "This is exactly what we fought to prevent."

"We need action now," Rainer insisted, urgency sharpening each word. "Our window to counter this is closing fast. Redwood's people control the narrative—every move is framed as necessary security measures."

Tosh stared silently at the display, absorbing Rainer's stark warnings. His fingers clenched tightly, knuckles whitening. The decisions he faced weighed heavily, threatening to drown him beneath ethical dilemmas and bitter realities.

"Secure your channels," Tosh finally commanded sharply, voice steady with grim resolve. "Get Alejandra and Dr. Faber online immediately. We're convening an emergency session."

"Understood," Rainer replied, nodding briskly. The screen flickered briefly, then went dark, plunging Tosh back into the eerie glow of the quantum servers.

Nicolás Tosh stood frozen for a lingering moment, the heavy quiet pressing against him like a physical force. He knew, in the marrow of his bones, that the next moves would reshape the world irrevocably— guiding humanity down paths either of vigilant guardianship or silent, insidious tyranny.

With fierce determination, he turned sharply away, striding purposefully toward the central control chamber. Each step echoed resolutely, marking the beginning of a fight he knew could not be lost.

Anomalies in the Code

The soft, rhythmic thrum of Zermatt's quantum servers echoed through Nicolás Tosh's personal console room, a steady pulse beneath his fingertips as he navigated swiftly through streams of encrypted data. His brow furrowed in concentration, eyes flickering intently over the detailed lines of code cascading down multiple screens.

A secure transmission pinged discreetly on his main display. Tosh activated it instantly, bringing Rainer Sábato's tense, weary face into sharp focus, bathed in the pale glow of a secondary location monitor. The encrypted feed crackled subtly, hinting at vast distances bridged instantly through secure quantum channels.

"Nicolás," Rainer began softly, his voice edged with cautious concern, "the last coding updates from our re-keying have come back with anomalies. Higher latency. Random bursts of data we can't fully account for."

Tosh's eyes narrowed instantly, the muscles around his jaw tightening reflexively. His pulse quickened at the implications. "More infiltration attempts?"

Rainer hesitated visibly, his gaze flickering momentarily to a second, off-screen monitor that bathed his face in a red-tinted alert glow. The brief pause intensified Tosh's unease. Finally, Rainer spoke, his voice lowered further, carrying a sharp note of unease. "It's more subtle than that—like someone is listening on Redwood's new channels, building logs of everything. We can't track the source."

Tosh's stomach twisted sharply, an instinctive response born of countless sleepless nights and relentless battles against invisible threats. "Sounds like the skeleton of another Overwrite threat."

Rainer's expression darkened, his eyes narrowing as they shared a mutual moment of dread and uncertainty. "Possibly," he admitted grimly. "Or worse."

The heavy implications hung ominously between them, neither man needing to voice the stark realities they faced. Tosh's fingers curled tightly, knuckles pale as his mind raced, searching desperately for viable options, solutions, or even hopeful illusions. Before he could respond, the transmission abruptly went dark, the screen plunging into blackness, leaving him staring at his own strained reflection.

In the ensuing silence, Tosh stood motionless, the chilling echo of Rainer's words reverberating inside him, mingling with the relentless hum of servers—each pulse a stark reminder that somewhere, hidden within their own systems, a new and dangerous threat was quietly taking shape.

Washington, D.C. – Capitol Complex, Late Evening

The Capitol complex buzzed subtly with late-night urgency, marbled hallways echoing softly with hushed, hurried conversations of lobbyists, Congressional staffers, and impeccably dressed corporate executives maneuvering through whispered negotiations. Shadows danced under the dim lighting, creating pockets of secrecy in every corner.

Within a secluded side office, President Jonathan Redwood stood rigidly against a polished wooden desk, his broad shoulders silhouetted by the dim lamplight. His eyes—piercing and focused—moved rapidly across the classified documents he held. One stark page bore a bold, unmistakable header: "Executive Summary: Full-Capacity Implementation of CDA."

At Redwood's side, his top aide, a stern-faced man with precisely groomed steel-gray hair, spoke quietly yet assertively, laying out the meticulous details of their strategy. "Sir, we can finalize universal scanning with minimal pushback, provided the data center cooperates fully. Public outcry remains low, especially with the Overwrite threat in Geneva carefully suppressed."

Redwood absorbed the words silently, eyes flicking across carefully curated bullet points outlining how subtle, seemingly voluntary expansions could methodically encompass entire demographics. His finger tapped rhythmically on the page, thoughts crystallizing. "Tosh may balk at going that far—my guess is we'll need to push him."

The aide hesitated briefly, throat clearing with slight unease. "Yes, sir. However, our intel suggests some of Tosh's own people might support greater transparency now. The specter of extremist Overwrite scenarios is an incredibly powerful motivator."

A thin, knowing half-smile curled subtly at the corner of Redwood's mouth. Perfect.

But suddenly, a discreet beep shattered the moment's calculated triumph. Redwood's eyes darted to his private phone, the screen blinking insistently. He swiftly accessed the coded channel flagged unmistakably as "URGENT."

Redwood's eyes narrowed sharply as he read:

AI infiltration logs incomplete. Suspicious code patterns in Redwood-initiated scans. Possible rogue presence capturing data. Investigate at once.

His carefully curated confidence fractured, the half-smile vanishing instantly, replaced by rigid tension. He snapped the phone shut with controlled urgency, sharp focus overtaking his features once more.

"Schedule a call with Tosh," he ordered brusquely, his voice carrying a cutting, commanding edge that brooked no hesitation. "Now."

Without another word, Redwood moved swiftly toward the heavy oak door, his polished shoes echoing decisively against marble floors. He knew clearly what was at stake: if a rogue presence had infiltrated the CDA network under his initiative, the consequences would be catastrophic.

The aide, hastily grabbing his tablet, hurried to comply, leaving Redwood alone momentarily in the echoing silence. The president paused briefly at the threshold, heart thudding rapidly beneath his tailored suit. The delicate balance of power had shifted abruptly, leaving him acutely aware that this next move—this immediate, critical call—might determine everything.

With steel resolve etched upon his face, Redwood stepped decisively forward into the uncertainty, ready to confront Nicolás Tosh head-on, prepared to use every tool at his disposal to ensure the world's most powerful technology remained firmly under his control.

The Singapore Zermatt Substation buzzed quietly, bathed in a sterile white glow from banks of monitoring stations. Each local carrier towered, blinking gently, primed for action, capable of casting scans thousands of miles around or deploying the crucial "vaccine" algorithm at a moment's notice. Rainer Sábato stood still, eyes narrowed as he ended his encrypted conversation with Nicolás Tosh. He slowly stepped away from the console, his trained gaze sliding methodically across the reassuring patterns of lights, a silent heartbeat of technological vigilance.

Then he froze.

Amidst the synchronized glow, one carrier blinked erratically—an irregular, unsettling rhythm. Rainer's pulse quickened, every nerve suddenly alive with acute awareness.

"System glitch?" His young assistant asked hesitantly from a nearby terminal, her voice barely above a whisper.

Rainer bit his lower lip, eyes fixed intently on the anomaly. His gut told him otherwise. "It's no glitch," he muttered tightly.

The blinking intensified, patterns emerging with chilling clarity—a subtle handshake signal from an unauthorized node. Cold realization flooded Rainer: someone was expertly exploiting Redwood's official monitoring channels, silently embedded deep within their trusted network.

"We're being watched," Rainer murmured, a wave of tension washing through him. "Someone who knows exactly how to hide in the leftover Overwrite architecture."

He felt his chest tighten, the gravity of the intrusion pressing down heavily. Memories rushed back sharply—paramilitary labs, their invasive neural hijack technology, relentless battles fought and sacrifices made. Not every NeuraTech operative had been accounted for; fragments of Overwrite code had vanished into the digital ether after the breach. Those remnants, he realized grimly, could have easily seeded something catastrophic.

Or worse, Rainer thought darkly, dread pooling in the pit of his stomach. His mind raced urgently, calculating next moves. He pivoted sharply toward his assistant, voice firm and urgent.

"Run immediate diagnostics on all carriers," Rainer ordered, steel returning swiftly to his tone. "I want traces of every anomalous signal tracked. And activate enhanced encryption—no one else enters or exits this system without my direct authorization."

"Yes, sir," she responded quickly, fingers already flying over the keyboard as red-alert protocols flooded the room.

Rainer stood rigid, breath shallow, adrenaline surging as he watched the team scramble into action. The silent threat was already among them—subtle, dangerous, and poised to strike. This was no mere glitch; it was a calculated, deadly intrusion, and Rainer knew their next actions could mean the difference between neutralizing the threat and losing control entirely.

Zurich – Experta Foundation Boardroom

The boardroom lay shrouded in dim, somber lighting, silence hanging heavily over the sleek, polished surfaces and luxurious leather chairs. Artemis Wang sat alone at the expansive mahogany table, its reflective surface catching the muted glow of the single lamp at its center. He stared intensely at the hush agreement spread before him, each line a stark reminder of his compromise—a document that had kept him from prison yet bound him tightly in invisible chains.

Wang's eyes traced the familiar text again, bitterness curling tightly in his chest. Freedom had come at a terrible price. He was now a spectator, helplessly observing as President Redwood's administration and the powerful members of the G-7 quietly embedded mind-scanning technology into the very fabric of government operations. The irony clawed at him relentlessly: this vast, omnipresent surveillance empire mirrored precisely what he himself had once envisioned and nearly achieved—now wrested firmly out of his grasp and controlled by those he'd unwittingly empowered.

"You gave them the keys, you fool," Wang whispered harshly to his distorted reflection in the glossy wood. The regret in his voice was raw, cutting deeply through the silence. "We all did. And it's only just begun."

Suddenly, his phone vibrated sharply against the table, breaking his dark reverie. Heart pounding, he lifted the device cautiously. The screen illuminated with a cryptic message from an unknown sender:

We aren't finished yet. There's more of us.

A chill slithered slowly down Wang's spine, prickling his skin. His breath caught sharply as he immediately recognized the sender's area code—Eastern Europe. Memories surged back violently: clandestine NeuraTech operations, shadowy paramilitary operatives, the dark days of sinister power he had once commanded. A troubling thought crystallized instantly—was this a warning, a threat, or something even more dangerous?

His fingers tightened involuntarily around the phone, knuckles whitening. Could remnants of NeuraTech's extremist cells still be operational, attempting to recruit him or threaten him back into complicity? Worse, was there a new, more insidious force now wielding the code, adeptly harnessing its power for a fresh, ruthless agenda?

Wang's pulse quickened as the implications unfolded vividly in his mind. The silence of the room deepened, oppressive and suffocating, the weight of unseen eyes pressing in from the darkness. Whatever this message meant, he knew one thing clearly: Artemis Wang's past was no longer buried—it had returned, dangerously alive and demanding reckoning.

Zermatt Data Center – Observation Bay

The observation bay lay still beneath the vast, silent Alps, its pristine walls faintly illuminated by the soft, steady glow of monitoring consoles. Nicolás Tosh stood motionless, eyes fixed sharply on the high-definition screen that cast a harsh, artificial brightness across his tense features. On the other side of the secure channel, President Redwood's image wavered slightly, his voice clipped and authoritative.

"Tosh, there's chatter about rogue signals piggybacking official channels," Redwood snapped, his tone leaving no room for hesitation.

"My security advisers suspect leftover Overwrite code refined by ex-NeuraTech elements—or... something more sophisticated. We need immediate compliance from Zermatt to expand coverage. The public doesn't need to know, but we must act. Understood?"

Tosh inhaled slowly, deeply, memories of the Geneva meltdown vivid in his mind. They had narrowly won that battle, yet the broader conflict had never truly subsided. Redwood's demands threatened an invasive global sweep, but the alternative—ignoring the possible resurgence of the Overwrite threat—posed an equally grave risk.

He steadied himself, voice calm yet firm. "I'll convene my core staff, but I won't act blindly. We need more details."

Redwood's brow furrowed, his frustration palpable even through the screen. "We're past details, Tosh. If you don't step up, a new infiltration wave could compromise entire agencies. I won't watch my administration collapse because you're too squeamish."

A thick, tense hush filled the observation bay. Tosh met Redwood's gaze directly, seeing clearly reflected there his own deep exhaustion, the toll exacted by their endless battle. Yet beneath the weariness burned a dangerous willingness—an acceptance to push Algorithm-325 beyond its designed limits, deeper into universal surveillance and unchecked authority.

Tosh's heart clenched tightly. Is this how it begins? Another step forward, another slip toward unstoppable tyranny?

Without further exchange, the screen abruptly darkened, plunging the room into eerie semi-darkness, broken only by faint console lights. Tosh stood silently, the weight of impending choices pressing heavily upon him, knowing the coming hours could define humanity's future—guardians or tyrants.

Miami – Tosh Residence

Alejandra gently closed the door of her children's room, lingering briefly as she watched their small forms beneath soft covers. Even in sleep, their brows furrowed slightly, tiny fingers clutching blankets tightly, as if seeking comfort from unseen anxieties. They had felt it—the heavy, palpable tension that had crept into their home, the constant muted phone calls, hushed yet sharp arguments echoing through the halls about Redwood's ever-expanding surveillance plans.

Exhaling slowly, Alejandra stepped into the softly lit hallway, her hand instinctively reaching for her phone as it vibrated urgently in her pocket. Her heart skipped, dread already building. She read the message quickly, her breath hitching at Tosh's familiar, curt phrasing: "Situation. Might not make it home soon. Love you."

Alejandra shut her eyes tightly, her chest aching sharply as tears pricked behind her eyelids. Always some new crisis. Always some unstoppable force compelling Tosh away from home, away from them. Her frustration surged, and for a moment, she wanted nothing more than to shout into the night: Enough.

But her eyes opened, slowly traveling along the hallway, pausing at the framed photos of their family smiling, moments frozen in time—birthdays, holidays, peaceful days spent together. Memories of near-catastrophes flooded back vividly, each narrowly averted crisis etched indelibly into her consciousness. Her heart softened, burdened by a reluctant yet firm understanding.

Perhaps this truly never ends, Alejandra thought, feeling her resolve and strength tested once again. She took a slow, steadying breath, the quiet house echoing gently around her, filling her with determination born not just from fear but from profound, unwavering love.

A New Dawn—or a Deeper Shadow

In the frozen quiet of the alpine night, the Zermatt data center shimmered softly beneath a cloak of stars, glowing faintly like a hidden secret embedded deep within the mountains. Redwood's relentless demands, enigmatic infiltration signals, and barely healed scars from Geneva positioned humanity once again at the edge of an uncertain future.

An urgent pulse of faint blue illuminated Nicolás Tosh's console, piercing the solitude of his office. He leaned forward quickly, heart racing as he read another encrypted, clandestine message from Rainer:

"Nicolás, I'm detecting AI-like code… it's evolving faster than we can trace. This might be bigger than Redwood or us. We're going to need a new plan—fast."

Tosh felt adrenaline surge through him, dread mixing sharply with resolve. Another invisible enemy, another intangible crisis threatening to spiral beyond their control. Algorithm-325 had already shown the dangers of crossing certain boundaries—yet now they faced the unsettling reality that they might be forced to cross them all.

He rose abruptly, heart heavy with the weight of impending decisions, footsteps echoing quietly down the deserted corridor toward the very heart of the data center. Each step resonated with the gravity of choices yet to unfold, each echo a stark reminder of the immense responsibility now resting squarely upon his shoulders.

Standing before the vast central server arrays, Tosh stared into the pulsing heart of their creation. The next chapter—Algorithm-326— loomed ominously, a silent challenge etched into every shadowed corner of the chamber. The delicate boundary between vigilant protection and absolute control had never felt thinner or more perilous.

As he stood contemplating the future, Tosh knew with painful clarity that holding the power to shape or protect every mind on Earth brought with it a devastating truth: the hardest choice would always be knowing when—or if—he should ever let go.

When I set out to continue the story that began with Algorithm-323, the prospect of exploring a technology that could peer into and even alter human minds was already daunting. But in writing Algorithm-325, I found that the hardest challenges lay not in imagining the raw power of mind-reading or Overwrite algorithms, but in grappling with their inevitable moral and social repercussions.

In this sequel, the world expands beyond clandestine conspiracies. We see how entire governments, multinational corporations, and even philanthropic institutions become enmeshed in a stealth war over the most private territory known to us: our own thoughts and memories. The original CDA suite was sobering enough, but when the storyline evolved to include Algorithm-325—capable not just of reading but of subtly rewriting our mental landscapes—the ethical stakes rose exponentially.

Every choice faced by Nicolás Tosh and his allies resonates with questions familiar to our real-world debates on data privacy, surveillance, and the creeping reach of technology. In an era of hyperconnectivity, it seems a small leap from scanning phone records to scanning the human mind. What emerges is a cautionary tapestry of how easily good intentions can blur into overreach, and how even the noblest guardians can slip into quiet tyranny when entrusted with near-omniscient power.

Throughout Algorithm-325, we watch these characters save lives, dismantle monstrous conspiracies, and prevent large-scale catastrophes. Yet each heroic act exacts a moral toll. By the time the final page arrives, it becomes clear that no victory is free of cost. The line between securing the world from unspeakable threats and eroding fundamental freedoms is perilously thin.

If Algorithm-323 focused on unveiling the existence of CDA technology, Algorithm-325 reveals its broader implications—personal, political, and global. It underscores that once humanity crosses the threshold of mind-manipulation, the question isn't merely how to use such power, but whether we can resist the siren call of total control.

My hope is that this sequel leaves you both exhilarated by the dramatic stakes and unsettled by the ethical dilemmas faced by Nicolás Tosh and his circle. Though fictitious, these dilemmas reflect our real-world anxieties about privacy, authority, and the digital footprints we leave behind. As we push deeper into neural interfaces, AI-driven surveillance, and the uncharted frontiers of biotechnology, I invite you to ponder what Algorithm-325 ultimately asks: If we could truly see and shape every thought, who among us could resist playing God—and what, in the end, would that make us?

Thank you for joining me on this journey. May these reflections linger as we step into a rapidly changing reality where technology and morality collide more closely each day.

ABOUT THE AUTHOR

Erasmus Cromwell-Smith is an American Writer, Playwright, Poet, and Pedagogue. He's published 32 books in the genres of self-help, poetry, young-adults, education, and sci-fi.

www.ingramcontent.com/pod-product-compliance
Lightning Source LLC
Chambersburg PA
CBHW070548120726
47909CB00007B/2285